ALL OF YOU
EVERY SINGLE ONE

ALSO BY BEATRICE HITCHMAN

Petite Mort

ALL OF YOU
EVERY SINGLE ONE

A NOVEL

BEATRICE HITCHMAN

The Overlook Press, New York

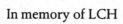

In memory of LCH

Prologue

THE LAKE IS FREEZING. The words—gelid, boreal, glacial—don't do it justice. Chunks of the whole break away, float, and sink. Black oiliness, the consistency of nightmares; impossible to see where you should put your feet.

Snow is falling, silent and determined. The beach is quickly smothered—the pebbles, the upturned boat, and the reeds become mere gray shapes. The lawn, sloping upward to the house, glitters.

The occupants are in the deep sleep of the very cold. They knew the storm was coming, but the body does not always understand what it's told the first time. The blood retreats in such circumstances to the inner organs; fingers curl into soft palms; the hair forms a nest around the neck and shoulders.

The nursery is different. In this room, the fire burns all night—it's hard enough to get a three-week-old to sleep without the added complication of the cold. The baby is awake, waving her fists in vague figures of eight, staring up at the woman bending over the crib, who makes a shushing sound, and though the child is too small to understand, or to make out more than the blurred outline of a face, she closes her eyes.

An ember from the fire lands on the rug. The woman stares at it as it flares and dies. She picks up the haversack, in which are packed cloth diapers, blankets, some stale bread that won't be missed, and fifty Kronen stolen from Herr K.'s wallet. The baby is gathered up in a bundle of warmth and cloth. She turns to the door, opens and listens: the rasp of the butler's snoring. She spares a thought for him—he has always been kind to her—then walks down the corridor and hesitates at the top of the stairs. The child smacks her lips in the darkness as she creeps on.

In the downstairs hallway, she puts the baby, very gently, onto the carpet runner and goes to accomplish the business of covering her tracks. On her return, she unhooks her coat from the coatrack next to the front door. It is even colder on this level, heat rising, as it will; she can feel her fingers stiffening already. She lifts the coat and shrugs it on.

An oil lamp has been wavering, unnoticed, along the corridor from the back of the house: gold corona, craggy shadows. A man's face, bruised with sleep. His fingers, where they hold the lamp base, are a throbbing, sea-anemone pink.

"I heard a noise," he says.

He must already know something is wrong, but he has always been slow to cross into the waking world. He raises one fist to grind it into his eye—trying to appear charming and childlike, even now—and with the other he puts the lamp on the hall table. The halo moves, showing him what's on the floor: the blind-mouse eyes and pale round face, bundled in bonnet and blankets. The bag.

"Where are you taking her?" he asks. The beginnings of a sneer. "Out for a walk?"

She snatches up the first lamp and brings it around in a wide arc; it connects with his temple. The clunk of bone sinking tectonically into itself: if she's lucky, a compound depressed fracture of the left parietal bone. He folds to the floor like a cheap prima donna, and she picks up his daughter and moves to the door. Oil has spilled on the carpet and the lamp is extinguished. There is no blood that she can see. The door creaks as it opens but it is too late to worry about that. She steps out into the suffocating quiet of the snowstorm.

In fairy tales, such things happen at midnight. In fact, it is half past two in the morning, in a home belonging to the prominent Bauer family—the engineering Bauers—in the small community of Podersdorf on the shores of the Neusiedlersee, Austria's largest lake. It is 1913, and somebody in this house is stealing a baby.

1910

—

Eve

VIENNA—INTO WHICH EVE PERRET steps, crying frightened tears—is the greatest city in the Western Hemisphere. This is known for sure by its one and a half million inhabitants. Art and music flourish; actors are gods, discussed in hushed tones in every coffeehouse. Is it true that Fanny Erdrich will reprise the Queen of the Night? The boy-poet Stefan Zweig, who'll survive the Great War only to end his own life in a suicide pact with his wife, struts along the Ringstrasse with his latest collection warming his breast pocket. Meanwhile, Maestro Leon is said to be consulting Herr Doktor Freud for an illness in which he believes his human feet to have been replaced by the feet of birds.

Even at this late hour, a mile to the west, Adolf Loos is at work on the new Modern House on the Michaelerplatz. The foreman calls him over: shards of glass and fragments of twine have surfaced among the new foundations. Loos unpeels his scarf from around his face and remembers the rumor about the Habsburgs' greenhouses being buried nearby. With fingers clumsy from the cold, he makes an annotation on the civic plans—a flourish of the pencil—here in the greatest city, new discoveries are made hourly and recorded for future generations. And there's this, too: the foreman holds up a Roman coin. The dirt has been rubbed off, and by the gaslight it shines gold: *Vindobona* is written around the ring. You see? Layers upon layers of lives, because Vienna is not just the best, but the oldest: people have flocked here since glaciers smoothed the peaks of the High Tyrol.

The giant amusement park, the Prater, is lit up. Because Vienna is cosmopolitan, a replica Somali village is being erected for the general edification, complete with real Somalis. There is a problem with the structure of the pen; opening will be delayed until next Tuesday. The Somalis, watching, wearing three pairs of gloves each, are unmoved. They are lodging with a Frau Pichler, who serves them only vegetable consommé because someone told her they cannot digest meat.

Omens abound. Mahler's Symphony in E-Minor reprises, triumphantly, but its hurrying chromatics are held to signal disaster. Migraine attacks afflict all women within a five-mile radius. The conductor falls from a stepladder. When he dies, he has a bell installed in his coffin, as is the fashion: a precaution against being buried alive. Students make a vigil at the great man's graveside in the Zentralfriedhof, just in case.

But Eve Perret knows none of this. She's shakily lighting a cigarette, and standing in the shadows of some municipal building. Needles of freezing rain fall on the delicate skin of her parting. She is furious, heartbroken. Worse: she knows she has only herself to blame.

They arrived at half past five that same evening. The train swept, triumphant, into the Hauptbahnhof, and as it drew to a halt, Julia Lindqvist looked at Eve and said: "Shall we?"

Eve dared to look at Julia's face, really for the first time since the beginning of their journey. Julia, who has chosen Eve; who has left her husband behind. Julia, who escaped through the orchard gate that morning, hurried to the train; who has been too bright to observe, except when, between Annecy and Geneva, with the blank white mountains on either side, she fell asleep. For those fifteen minutes, when her beauty was slackened out of its perfection, Eve had looked.

Now, Eve finds she can only squeak a "Yes." She gets up. Her hand hovers at the small of Julia's back. How is Julia so confident, moving down the train corridor, stepping out onto the platform? Her eyes are so merry: all seems like a game to her. And perhaps, Eve will think later, this is where it went wrong, or began to: the idea that it could really be just a game.

Julia is snapping her fingers rapidly. "A cab, we need a cab." She holds herself, arms crossed against the cold, and scans for the station exit. Eve scans too, and is aware of her own puppyishness, her lack of savoir faire. Julia has traveled. (But has she traveled? How far? In their short acquaintance, there has not been time to ask all the pertinent questions.) She knows about cabs, carriages, whether to tip hotel porters, how to move through a crowd. This is the farthest Eve has ever been from Annecy; the farthest she has ever been from home. Nevertheless, she spots the exit first, and points.

"Ah," says Julia. She is briskly practical: a last sweep of the platform. "At least we weren't followed."

Eve, who sees Julia's husband in every male face in the station, nods. It seems miraculous. He is a man of reach and vanity, and even though they had a few hours' start, she does not trust he won't somehow have arrived ahead of them.

Eve helps Julia up into the taxicab, then aids the driver in lifting their suitcases onto the roof. This is new, too: his searching gaze, looking for the swell of her breasts, which isn't there, looking for the bulge at her crotch, which isn't there. She is a puzzle, in her suit and hat, and in her muteness. At home—but Annecy is no longer her home—everyone knows her. They brought casseroles when her mother was dying. She is not remarked upon. The cabman's gaze says *Not my business* and *I must know* at the same time.

The cab smells of male sweat, boot polish. It is the first time they have been alone in an enclosed space with a stretch of some uninterrupted minutes before them. Eve chooses to sit on the opposite banquette. The cab starts to move and rock; Julia laughs and holds out a hand and says, "No, here," and Eve jumps up and sits beside her. The contact of Julia's hip and shoulder is intoxicating. Eve wants to slide her hand under Julia's skirt and into the crease of Julia's thigh, but to do so would, perhaps, breach some unspoken rule; it is better to try to be calm.

The carriage moves. The pulse point in Julia's throat is jumping. She turns her head into the crook of Eve's neck; takes Eve's arm and slings it around her shoulders. Outside, the city looms and recedes, a dazzle of almost-snow and flickering shadow, and none of it matters, because Eve holds her—shy, protective—in this position, for the first time.

Julia

—

THEY MET THREE MONTHS PRIOR, in the house in Annecy that Per, Julia's husband, had rented for the summer. Per was indoors, working on the third act of his commission for the Dramaten. High hot weather: the house, all through the afternoon, had been full of a secret giggly energy that seemed to shut Julia out. As she went downstairs at the appointed hour, she heard Per, in his study, laughing at one of his own jokes.

She told the cook to bring tea out to the orchard when the tailor arrived—no sense wasting the sun—and swept past her through the kitchen, only just remembering the old suit Per had left out to be copied. Out through the long grass. The green hummed around her, drowsy with late pollen.

A pair of slender shoulders, seated, facing away from her, at the outdoors table; a brilliantined bob, newly shaved hair on the nape of the neck. Of course nobody told her the tailor was already here. Of course the tailor was early. Julia smiled a wide, practical, bitter smile, walked around the table and introduced herself.

The hand that took hers was small. Eve's timid eyes, barely flickering over Julia's face. The snap of the buckles on Eve's case, so that it was open on her knees; she was, surprisingly, not shy, but all business, hiding in the unspooling of measuring tapes and the finding

9

and testing of pencil lead. Holding up Per's old suit and squinting at the seams.

Julia knew a woman like this, once, in Stockholm, who played cards with the men. But she had thought, somehow, they were all elderly. If one followed (and she did) the arguments of Mr. Darwin, such creatures were anti-evolutionary, a race about to die in the face of the age of logic. They were not in their middle twenties and handsome as noon. She resolved to be professional, and not let the bright curiosity of her face give anything away.

"What are you doing?" she asked.

"Copying your husband's measurements. Will he want the same material?"

A bitter joke hovered: *Who knows what my husband wants?* "Yes," she said.

She listened to the scritch of the pencil in Eve's notebook; she watched the lick of a forefinger to turn the pages back and forth.

"And how long have you owned your outfitter?"

Eve looked up from under her eyebrows. A pause before speaking. "I don't own it." Another pause. "It's my father's business."

Blood from a stone, Julia thought, for the benefit of her invisible audience.

Another excruciating pause. "I took it on when my father started to lose his sight," Eve said. The notebook was closed and pushed into the briefcase. "Shall we say a week till the first fitting?"

"A blind tailor," Julia said. "Is he? Completely?"

Eve frowned at the outline of the mountainside, above the house; frowned so hard that Julia thought: *She is going to cry.* She saw, fascinated, that this person contained a lifetime of hopes and fears, just like anyone else. She rushed on: "My husband will be so pleased with what you're going to make him. And the wives?"

"The wives?"

"They don't mind? Their husbands visiting a lady tailor?"

Bits of white dandelion clock drifted in the air. "I'm not sure I count as a lady."

Julia laughed, dazzled. The last of the instruments were packed away. Eve folded the suit with a quick loop of the hands and then there was no reason for her to linger.

She stood, and Julia did, too, and Eve's hand was once again in Julia's.

Julia brushed her thumb over the palm; held on a fraction too long. *Is this a person I can do as I please with?* But it wasn't that; not at all. Her own face, she could feel, was a lonely mask.

"Till next week," Eve said, disengaging. She turned away through the long grass. At the gate, she lifted and dropped the latch with precision, making a joke of it. A half-wave; the edge of a smile.

Julia paced the rooms all afternoon and into the evening. She thought about Eve, and how she pretended to be unassuming, and not to have power, and was in fact flooded with it.

They kissed for the first time three weeks later, electrically, in a corridor of the house, with the maids changing sheets in a room nearby; Julia's memory is entwined with the lift and settle of white fabric, the sound of footsteps approaching, and the way Eve kept her eyes closed. Since then, they have been private on only two occasions. Once, alone for five minutes in the orchard, crouched in the shadow of the apple tree, but overlooked by the house. Once in the back room of Eve's shop, for seven minutes, while the errand boy was out. On both occasions, they have held back, from lack of time, but also for another reason. Eve wiped her mouth and said miserably, "Let's wait," and Julia had agreed. There was something to postpone, something she felt comfortable putting off. Because wait for what? Julia, consumed by curiosity, passion, understanding this thing about herself for the first time in her twenty-six years, has no idea how to touch another woman in that way.

Eve

———

THE CARRIAGE RATTLES TO A HALT. Eve's underclothes are silky between her legs; her suit is too tight around her body. Just an arm around her in the back of a cab, a thing that most couples might disdain: but the effect on her has been immense. Julia is still, too; then she sits upright, spiders a palm on Eve's chest. Her pupils are dark and drowsy; the pressure of her hand is soft on Eve's tender flesh. It seems that matters might progress here, in the cab; it seems for a moment this is the only way (spectators be damned), but the steps are being unfolded, and the cabman's face is in the window, florid, peering in.

Unrivaled views of the Stephansdom, the hotelier wrote to Eve; *greatest comfort*. She has spent half her savings on this one week's refuge. The hotel sign has a letter missing. Its windows are cloudy and dark, and geraniums stand on either side of the door, brown leaves lining the top of the soil. They stand on the sidewalk—Julia pays the cabman, who unloads their cases, draws away with one last curious look—and Julia pulls off her gloves, finger by finger, looking around with anthropological interest. "Well," she says. "Well, well."

Eve watches Julia, watching. A man brushes past, elbows flying, and makes her, Eve, jump. He looks nothing like Julia's husband, but there was something in his impatience, the unsteadiness of his gait.

She turns to Julia, mute, startled, and Julia says: "I know." She takes a breath in, and smiles. "I know."

She enters first, hips swaying through the double doors and into the reception, where a small boy is waiting behind the desk.

"Booking in the name of Perret and Lindqvist," Julia says. "We wired ahead."

The boy takes the offered papers, reads them carefully, then asks, round-eyed: "One room or two? For the *geehrte Dame, und* . . ." The sentence falls away as he looks at Eve.

Julia says: "Two." Says it airily, as though it is obvious.

This has been discussed: the need for propriety. Still, it hurts. The boy pushes two sets of keys across the desk and withdraws his fingers before he touches Julia's hand.

"Will you require a breakfast tray?"

"Oh," Julia says. She looks at Eve: suddenly daring, sly. "I shouldn't think so. No," and Eve forgets about the two rooms.

There are small, peephole windows on the way up the stairs; each frames a mauve sky, across which sleet is falling. The chill comes in, pooling around them as they climb. Eve focuses on the quick flurry of Julia's boots ahead of her. The corridor, when it comes, has a burgundy carpet runner—threadbare—and scuffed boards to either side.

Eve follows Julia to the end, where two doors are opposite each other. Julia flips the key fobs in either hand.

"This is the one with the best view, I think," she says, and steps toward the left. She slots the key and turns it. "Coming?"

In all of Eve's night-thoughts, this has not occurred to her: that Julia would go first into the room, cross to the shutters, and open them wide. That she would say, in a voice quivering with hope, "Yes, this is very satisfactory"; then, with a smart practical movement, snap open the locks on her valise and begin to unpack.

What has Eve pictured? She has thought of lifting Julia over the threshold. She thought they'd tumble into the room, straight onto the bed; she hadn't thought the bed would have a frayed orange coverlet, silky-looking disc-shaped stains on the old chenille. The next image is of Julia's mouth, stretched open; the rhythmic thud of the headboard. She has not imagined Julia looping clothes around her hands to fold them; shaking out Eve's tweed jacket and hanging it in the wardrobe in the corner.

"We'll go tomorrow and see the apartment that Grete recommended," Julia says. "But we might as well get settled, even if it's just for tonight."

She turns, blinks, frowning at something. She is outlined in the white of the streetlight through the window: Julia Lindqvist, with her slightly too pointed chin, her courtesan's laugh. Now is the time for Eve to be a man: to take Julia uncomplicatedly in her arms. To take what she wants. (But what does she want?) Perhaps, indeed, this assertiveness is what Julia is waiting for.

Julia turns, hands on hips. "Are you hungry? We haven't eaten. We could go out to a restaurant. I could eat something. Could you?"

Eve sees—and it is glorious—that Julia is nervous, perhaps even as afraid as Eve. Julia rubs her hand on her neck, massaging the nape. "Or there is the Café Schwarzenberg—I've always wanted to go—or we could just take a stroll, Grete says that's the thing to do here about this time of evening—"

Julia looks as though she may cry from fright: it's this that makes Eve cross the room, on an impulse to soothe. The *one-step-two-step-three* across the room, which seemed impossible ten seconds before, passes, and Julia is in her arms. Eve's hands slide around her back, and Julia's forehead is pushed into her shoulder.

Julia laughs. "So ridiculous," she says. "He's not here, is he? He can't be here."

Eve has stiffened at the mention of Per. She kisses the top of Julia's head, thoughtful, and the blood rushes through her. "And ridiculous," Julia says with a sigh, "to be shy of you—"

This is familiar, from the corridor in the house at Annecy: the way Julia's teeth feel under her tongue, the heat of her mouth. Eve holds on to Julia's waist, careful not to move her hands, at first, until Julia places them herself, smoothing them onto her buttocks. The motion is practiced, and this gives Eve pause, but is also exciting. Eve opens her eyes to see Julia pressed against her, feels Julia's heartbeat knocking at her own chest through the fabric of her blouse.

"Please," Julia says.

Eve thinks, *She is thinking we may only have a short time.*

Eve grips Julia's forearms and walks her backward across the room; lays her on the bed. Eve feels whole, with Julia spread out on the coverlet: that look of pleading submission. The impulse to take and take makes her gentle, and she puts a finger to the curve of Julia's chin.

"Come on," Julia says. She sits up and pushes Eve's jacket off her shoulders. "Come on." She reaches for Eve's waist with a frown of concentration. Eve realizes, joyfully, that she is looking for a belt.

In Eve's life, there is one thing she has consistently desired: to have a woman tug at her belt with want in her eyes. The fantasy came to her at age twelve. But she has never gotten further than this, in her imagination: the belt has never been tugged from its loops and dropped to the ground. What should happen next is unclear. The image is the thing: a sense of completeness. Not just the frustrating ticklish rub of fabric against her, the slick wetness and slipperiness and hardness between her legs.

Julia snakes the belt free and flings it aside. She fumbles with the buttons on Eve's trousers. Eve cradles Julia's head. Julia's hands work to shimmy the material down. Eve reaches for a strand of Julia's hair, twists it around one finger; on a drugged and blissful impulse—because what could be better than fixing this long-awaited image?—she looks over to the now-dark window.

She sees her own brutal ugliness. The white cotton workman's shirt rolled up to the elbows. Her cheeks, shamefully red. Her hips jutting forward, begging for someone to touch, to kiss: what? Julia, beautiful, forced into this. The worst thing is the lock of Julia's hair, taken as if playfully; no, the worst thing is the look of sheer goblin-greed. And Julia's face: playing along. Just as she would have done with—

She pushes Julia away. Julia's eyes widen; but Eve sees relief, too—she's sure of it.

"What?" Julia says, wiping her mouth. "What did I do?"

Eve has retreated two paces. She stands at the foot of the bed. Her trousers caught, ridiculous, around her knees.

"You don't have to," she says. Even to herself, she is a spoiled child.

Julia blinks. Snakes of damp hair at her temples. But she is lovely. The vision shifts, hovers, and Eve sees that perhaps she has got it wrong.

"Come here," Julia sighs. She levers herself up from her elbows, crosses to where Eve is and puts her hands on Eve's shoulders. "All right," she says. "It's all right."

Eve stands poised for flight. Julia's hands continue to smooth her shoulders, working their way down. She breathes out. Julia begins to unbutton her shirt, working at the mother-of-pearl discs. It feels like being taken care of: a protective promise.

The buttons slip free and the halves of Eve's shirt separate. "It's only us here," Julia murmurs. "It will only ever be us." The blood is gathering again, pulsing concentric circles inside her. Julia pushes the shirt off Eve's shoulders and the last confusing minute has been erased.

Julia's face fixes. She looks down; stares at Eve's chest.

"I never thought of it," she says. "I don't know what I thought."

She puts a fascinated fingertip up to the bandages binding Eve's chest, and—this is the worst thing—laughs, short and incredulous. Her hands move over the fraying fabric, over Eve's breasts; she tugs experimentally on the loosening material and it is like being with a doctor, like those cold childhood examinations in drafty rooms.

Julia lets the hands drop. The bandages snake to the floor. Her eyes are tired. "Oh, no—" she says. "Sweetheart, it's safe—" But Eve is gathering her shirt and shoes, her abandoned jacket, and running away.

Sheets of half-rain, half-snow; the sky above is black but the streets glitter with light, and everyone seems to have a purpose: a long drift of spectators toward the Opera House. Eve runs from one street corner to the next, head down, until she finds a doorway to shelter in. There she stands, trying to take a big breath, unable to get enough air.

When Eve was eighteen, she thought she'd met the person she'd leave her village for. The wife of a local worthy, already in her forties, stout but curious. There had been kisses. Eve had plotted a kind of marriage ceremony; imagined tears of joy in her father's eyes, her

ALL OF YOU EVERY SINGLE ONE

brothers standing, confused but stalwart, by her side. When Eve's hands had crept below the waist, the woman had pushed her away. *Whatever were you thinking?* The darkness fell for months. And then the boredom of the years; all the while the safety, the appalling sameness, until that day in the orchard. Julia's long pianist's fingers and way of clutching ironically at her heart when you said something funny or moving.

A man in a homburg looms into view, asking for something. It takes a few seconds to understand him; he mimes putting something to his lips. Eve fishes for her matches and cigarettes. The man says *danke* and moves away, just a glimpse of nose and mouth in the flick of the match, the inevitable upturn of the eyebrows when he sees she is a woman. Her unbound breasts hang against her ribs, their weight unfamiliar.

Two days after their encounter in the shop, two weeks after their first kiss. A note from Julia arrived. *Meet me at Roche de l'Aiglon. Please come now.* Eve, leaving her shop on some flimsy excuse; ascending the stone steps to the lookout point: Lac d'Annecy two hundred feet below. A party of Swiss hikers standing by the viewing platform, their boots crusted with dried mud. Julia, in her gray dress, in the attitude of one who has been waiting a long time; rising to meet her and saying in a low voice: "I can't, anymore, with him. I have tried. I am afraid it must be you."

The sun winking from behind the clouds. Eve, careful: "What do you mean?" Julia: "I mean I can only . . ." She licks her lips, looks away. "With you. My cousin, Grete, wrote to me about Vienna. I'm fairly fluent. I mean, I have a reasonable competence. Is it far enough? Do you think he will follow us there?"

Eve tries to remember how it felt: that sharp swoop of joy that someone was choosing her, finally. The frantic hope on Julia's face. "I can understand some German," she'd said. "I can learn," and watched as Julia started to cry, covering her mouth with her hand, big sobs of relief. But now she hears something different in the remembered words: Julia running away from Per, not running toward her.

She could take the morning train home. She could explain to her father that it had been a mistake; resume the running of the tailor's shop. The gossip would die down. Her life—dull, but rarely desperate—could simply be picked up, and unspool comfortably into middle age. She would never run away again, but she would never feel so lonely again, nor so ashamed.

She thinks of the thin strip of tongue that appeared between Julia's teeth at the sight of the hotel room; the *we-must-make-the-best-of-it* folding of the clothes. When has Julia, of the catlike smile, ever shown a great unexpected kindness?

The Stephansdom clock rings eleven o'clock; there is a shake of livery as the horses are put to bed. At the Modern House, Adolf Loos is packing up his things, blowing on his fingers and stamping his feet; the foreman extinguishes the lights, and places the gold Vindobona sestertius in his wallet. Maestro Leon sits on the edge of his bed, staring at his toes, which grow more webbed every day. In the Zentralfriedhof, the vigilant students are jerked awake by the tinkle of the bell beside the great man's tomb, and stare at each other; they have been waiting for just such a thing, wanting it, but now it comes to it, they hope it was just the wind.

It is past midnight when Eve comes back to the hotel. The small boy has long ago vanished from the reception desk and the lobby is empty.

The door of the room they chose is unlocked, unlit, and Julia is a huddled form in the bed. Eve knows intuitively that she is staring out at where the window-shape would be, where a crack in the shutters lets in a faint shimmer.

Eve undresses; folds her shirt; places her boots by the door. She has no hope, in the dark, of finding the key to the room opposite; there is no armchair in which she can curl up.

She pulls the coverlet back as gently as possible, slides in, and draws it over them again. She lies on her back. The reflection of early snow dances, shaken lace, on the ceiling. A long pale shape on the top of the dresser comes clear—her chest bindings, folded into tidiness, safely stored away.

Julia's hand steals across the mattress: the fingers locking tight with Eve's. They are quiet for a minute or more.

"Does it hurt?" she asks.

"More at first. It's been years."

"How long?"

"Since I was thirteen."

The click of Julia's palate as she swallows. The mattress shifts as she turns toward Eve. "You know you don't have to do it for me. You can be yourself—"

Eve says: "It's for me. It is me."

"But if it hurts you—"

Silence. Julia says: "I don't know very much, do I? There's a lot I don't know." The sound is smothered by her hand, half over her mouth.

Then say sorry, Eve thinks. *Say sorry for hurting me.*

"I am trying to understand."

Eve tests her own depth of feeling. It is not enough, not nearly enough, to try to understand.

"We should sleep now," she says, pulling her hand away, turning onto her other side. In the morning, she tells herself, she will go back to the station; she will take the first train.

She is surprised when she wakes up, and the room is gray with early light; surprised to have slept at all, and for a moment she does not know where she is. Panic, sadness, heat, shame. Sadness again, as she remembers the flight into the evening; the doorway where she sheltered like a criminal.

Julia is lying on her back, one arm flung above her head. She is naked, the covers having been pushed down the bed during the night. Her legs are parted, one knee bent, lying like the Tarot of the hanged man. A shock, to see her naked for the first time while she is asleep. Eve looks at the wiry hair, the shape of Julia's stomach and breasts: all the forbidden things.

Julia moves her head toward Eve; her eyelids twitch, and her breathing deepens; the eyelids move again, and now she is awake. She focuses on Eve.

They watch each other. Julia is shuttered and wary.

"Are you going to leave?" she asks.

There is quiet in the hotel, in the corridor; no thundering footsteps, no angry pursuit.

Eve says: "I don't know."

Winter light inches into the room. Julia reaches for Eve's hand and places it over her sex, runs it down past the tuft of hair and into the cleft, where the skin is already slick and ready. She settles her thighs further apart; the tip of her chin points to the ceiling, as she says, "Ah"; keeps holding Eve's hand, moving it up and down.

Eve watches Julia's face change, her frown deepen, clear, and deepen again; a snatched breath when Eve's hand slips; the sigh as the rhythm is resumed. Julia opens her eyes wide and stares at the ceiling. Her grip on Eve's fingers makes the skin whiten; everything is still for a moment, then she snarls; her body jumps as if an electric shock has gone through it.

She pushes Eve's fingers inside her; winces, then settles. Eve is not sure whether she is allowed to move, so she holds still. From outside the room, they can hear the city waking: trams hissing on the Ringstrasse and the clack of shutters opening. Julia's pulse is strong inside her; she sighs, as if confirming some long-suspected answer. "Come here," she says, pulling at Eve's hips. "I don't care what you are. Come here."

Julia

———

JULIA AND EVE LEAVE THE HOTEL at one o'clock in the afternoon, two days after their arrival. They have sent a letter to a Frau Berndt, who was Cousin Grete's landlady. They are expected.

They have barely slept, and food seems now to be a theory. The clouds have rolled back and revealed to Julia this glorious truth: she has a lover, perhaps for the first time in her life, because the men (what men?) no longer count. She looks sideways at Eve as they walk. Eve's overcoat, collar, and cuffs are immaculate; the suit is in beautiful taste, a houndstooth check and a cream shirt underneath; her gloves a second skin. *Look*, she wants to say to the people around, *look at her*. She blushes at her own good luck, remembering the steady push and slip of Eve's fingers.

They walk through the Innere Stadt. The city is tall and sleek around them, the cobbles still silky from last night's snow. She has missed this so much—the haberdashers and florists, theaters and beggars, street jugglers and apartment blocks, bakeries and expensive restaurants. The cold is nothing compared to Sweden, but enough to make her feel at home. She beams, reaches for Eve's hand: *Don't you love it?*

Eve draws her fingers away. "People may look . . ." she says.

Julia laughs, incredulous; but Eve's face is agonized, pleading, so she makes her own expression carefully blank. She brushes Eve's palm with her fingertips, and retreats. "Very well," she says. "But sometime—sometime soon—I want everyone we pass in the street to know who we are."

They cross the Ferdinandsbrücke, and so enter Leopoldstadt. The suburb of beautiful irony: named after its creator, Emperor Leopold the Indecisive, who in 1670 ordered the Jews out of the city. Sighing, they moved the minimum distance outside the walls, and called the settlement by his name. The jokes are what you'd expect, old and so vicious and weak as to be not worth repeating, and the graffiti that appears on the walls of the synagogue is no wittier. So: there is a Committee for Washing Off Remarks, but also several committees for fun. The Cabaret of Unearthly Delights meets in a club off the Taborstrasse, where bearded ladies strum zithers until late; Pusillanimous Shlom and his Traveling Entertainments are liable to pop up in any unsuspecting person's salon. The Sabbath is sacred, of course, and as the sun lowers to the horizon on Fridays, Leopoldstadt closes its shutters and remembers its dead.

"It is cosmopolitan," Julia hears herself say, though what she really means is *shabby* and *frightening*. They are in a cobbled, triangular market square; the air smells of salt-beef and sweet bread baking. The buildings here are not as clean as the Innere Stadt. There is the sense of people watching from doorways and corners. "Is it not? Charming." A row of ribcages dangle in the butcher's window. Crumpled paper lifts and settles in gutters running with sooty water.

She unfolds Grete's note, with its hand-drawn map, and holds it out in front of her. Her hand trembles slightly. "I think—" she says, peering at a street sign. Herminengasse, Nickelgasse . . . Why does everything end with -*gasse*? Do they not have any other kinds of street? At the end of the road, there is a stone archway, and beyond that, a courtyard. A four-story building rises on three sides. "Yes. Here."

Eve trots beside her, head down, and Julia feels a loss. She was used to giving plenty of direction with Per, but always hiding it behind other things, lest he take offense: *Should we not perhaps rather . . . ? What if we were to . . . instead?* Now, she must take the lead.

◆

In the center of the courtyard, a woman in widow's black is sweeping in long, harried strokes. She looks about sixty. When she straightens, Julia sees that she is barely five foot tall. An ivory cameo sits at her throat. Seeing them approach, her hand flies to it.

Julia fixes on her brightest smile and extends her hand. "Frau Berndt, I presume?"

Frau Berndt's voice is tight and quavery. "You are Julia Lindqvist," she says. Her palm is dry and cool, and Julia thinks: *Am I? A Lindqvist? That name will have to go.*

Frau Berndt is looking past Julia, at Eve. The look travels over Eve, and back; away, and back, fascinated, then away again. She dusts her hands on her apron. "Follow me."

Eve looks at Julia, and the apology in it, the soft acceptance that this is how things are, could break your heart.

Frau Berndt goes first across the courtyard and into a small, dusty hallway; her tiny shoulders bobbing, she talks as they climb. Frau Berndt herself has lived in Vienna for many years; is practically a native. Her husband, Thomas-Berndt-may-his-memory-be-a-blessing, was of the Floridsdorf Berndt Family Cakes and Fancies Konditorei; when he died, she bought the apartment block as a going concern. One must keep occupied. She provides a great service to the local community by offering housing to artists and persons of promise and interest.

Up and all the way up. Frau Berndt opens the door to an attic apartment. There are graying floorboards and peeling plaster walls. One window looks over the courtyard; the other shows the dark-green fringe of the woods in the distance. There is an adjoining kitchen with a spotted ceramic sink, a stove in the corner. In the main room: two straight-backed chairs, a spindly table, and, through a fringed curtain in an adjoining room, a double bed.

Julia steps in. She crosses to the window; averts her gaze from the mold lining the frame. Behind her, she can feel Eve: a vague, hovering presence. "Is that the Wald one can glimpse on the horizon?"

"Your German is very good," Frau Berndt says. She sounds resentful. "How did you learn?"

"At school. My father was a diplomat. We traveled." Julia peers at the distant treetops, and longs for the pines of Söderbysjön on a late spring evening. "I plan to seek work as an interpreter, possibly at the Swedish Embassy."

"Grete's letter mentioned an unusual circumstance . . ."

Julia turns from the window to find Frau Berndt still by the doorway, her hands smoothing the front of her apron. She looks, compulsively, at Eve, who stands staring at her own shoes in the corner of the room.

Frau Berndt says: "I don't want trouble here. For the good of the community."

Julia takes a breath in; tamps down her fury (they are not *criminals!*). Father always said: *Honesty may be best, but sometimes you need persuasion.* "I may also give piano lessons. I trained at the Stockholm Conservatoire. And Madame Perret is a tailor, very fine, and hopes to find employment in a gentleman's outfitter."

She runs through the possibilities. They could stay at the hotel for two more weeks, apply for an apartment, perhaps via some personal announcements in the *Allgemeine*. They could pose as sisters—

"There will be no trouble," she says. "I can promise you that."

A spiral of pigeons rises from a nearby roof.

Frau Berndt says: "The price is one hundred Kronen per week, or three hundred and seventy-five per month."

Julia says: "We can pay you a month's rent in advance." It is all the money she has in the world. "The apartment comes with the furnishings?"

Frau Berndt turns her gaze on Eve, uncannily bright. "Oh yes, *alles* included. *Alles frei.*"

At the hotel, Julia packs and Eve paces. "Did you explain about Per?" she asks. "What to say if anyone comes?" She has not followed all the German—only the part about the money, because numbers are the first thing anyone learns. She turns a face white with worry to Julia. "It's too expensive. How will we manage?"

Julia puts her hands on Eve's forearms. "He won't come. We will get work. It will all be all right."

They leave the next morning, dragging their suitcases through the slushy snow, not wanting to spend money on a cab. By the time they arrive, their hands are stiff and aching with cold.

Frau Berndt is in the courtyard, dusting frost from the leaves of her plants. Julia fumbles in her coat pocket for the envelope with their rent. *What a thing*, she thinks—she who used to take carriages everywhere, to the opera, and sit alongside Per in her black velvet dress with the gold filigree— She can't feel her fingers. The envelope slips, and is caught by Frau Berndt, who in turn produces a key and drops it into Julia's cupped hand.

"*Willkommen*," she says, leaning on her broom, watching them. Eve is blushing, and murmurs, "*Danke*." Julia tries to smile. She is not given to seeing herself from the outside, but for this one moment, the vision is clear: stooping in the thin remnants of snow, grimacing, the hem of her skirt heavy with freezing water.

They trudge upstairs, dragging their cases. Wind whistles through a cracked pane in the kitchen window; the apartment is only a little warmer than outside. "We shall have to get something for that," Julia says, and crosses to the stove, where someone—Frau Berndt, presumably—has stoked up a sooty glow. There is a little coal in the bucket, but not more than an evening's worth. On the table there is a heel of bread and a dish of butter, an end of cheese.

Eve puts their suitcases in the bedroom, then comes to sit on one of the spindly chairs. Julia stands in the kitchen. She opens the cupboards one by one hoping to find—what?—but they are dusty and bare. She is vaguely surprised; someone should have anticipated their arrival; someone should have made proper arrangements.

In the afternoon, they walk out of the city and up to the villages: to Unterdöbling, then on to Josefsdorf, with its deep medieval doorways, the smell of burned sugar and bonfires. The cobbled streets wind through the foothills of the Wald; there are taverns, boarded up now for winter.

"When the weather is finer, we will come here, and lift a glass with the working men!" Julia says, with a conviction she doesn't feel. "We'll walk in the woods and you'll rescue me from footpads."

Eve's black overcoat is pulled around her, the collar turned up; she leans into a breeze. She is pale and handsome, and Julia fixes the image in her mind, of her shy smile, scuffing leaves on the dirt track. A priest with a lean appearance, with Per's flyaway hair, elongates himself around a corner, startling them. *How long must I suffer?* Julia wonders. *How long until he stops appearing everywhere?* And then answers her own question: haunting is the price of escape.

They walk back through the darkening city. In the courtyard, the concierge's lodge is lit; as they pass, the door flies open and opera—something modern and atonal—blares out of the gramophone. Frau Berndt is there, dressed for a party: still in black, but with a spot of rouge on either cheek. "Come in!" she cries, beckoning wildly. "Someone I want you to meet!"

The lodge smells of boiled potatoes and the sharpness of cognac. "A little schnapps! A tradition!" Frau Berndt says, bustling to the tiny kitchenette, uncorking a bottle. The small room is full of furniture: a horsehair sofa, two ceramic bookends in the shape of donkeys, a stained-glass lamp. In an easy chair by the tiny window sits a man. He is in his early thirties, wears a green velvet jacket; one leg is crossed over the other at the knee, and his foot jiggles; on his bearded, handsome face, an expression of lively hostility.

"Rolf, my tenant from the apartment across the courtyard," Frau Berndt says fondly, and then, as if to a child: "Rolf, say hello. These are the Misses Lindqvist and Perret."

"Hello," Rolf says. He makes it sound amusing. He pushes his forelock out of his eyes with one elegant fingertip; looks at her— *There is nothing*, Julia thinks, she who is used to some reaction, to being admired—and then at Eve. His glance moves from her ankles up to her face, and here, too, he remains blank, but there's a caution to it; an interest. "Hello," he says again.

"Rolf is an impresario," Frau Berndt says. "He works in the theater."

"How interesting," Julia says. "Which one?"

"Here and there," Rolf says. He smiles, suddenly. In the before-times, Julia thinks, she might have found him attractive. It is strange to feel nothing. She watches him curiously. He meets the challenge, looking at her, very level; just the bouncing of his foot giving him away. The look says: *Who are you to disturb my comfort?* She holds his stare until he lifts the corner of his mouth, showing his teeth.

Eve

—

THE FIRST TAILOR'S SHOP in the directory is owned by a frightened-looking woman of about thirty, who peers through the glass door at Eve, and flips the sign over. The second is unctuously sorry: there are no vacancies at present; has the—the gentleman—considered the cloth factory in Atzgersdorf? They are always recruiting, all sorts of people. . . .The third, fourth, and fifth stare, and say a simple *no.*

She saw a painting once, in a church near Lyon, on a walking holiday with her father: a saint shot all over with arrows, his face agonistically turned to his pursuers, gore dripping from his chest. She allows herself this image, this self-pity, as she walks home, and the associated sense of purity of purpose. Though she feels flayed by the stares of strangers, she will do this for Julia: turn her face to the bright pain for as long as it takes.

Toward the end of the week, the cold intensifies. Snow piles up on the skylight, so that they wake into a landscape of gray, phantomatic shadows. Julia has written to three contacts in the Embassy, suggested by Grete, where she has an introduction; no use contacting theater folk, she says, Per will have poisoned their minds. That is the phrase she uses: *poisoned them against us.* She has taken to tearing at the skin around her fingernails with her teeth. Each morning she goes to inquire about post with Frau Berndt, and there is none. Eve watches the little dumbshow from the window, as Julia smiles brightly, shrugs, mimes vague disappointment, diffidence.

Late one Tuesday morning, a rap on the door. They have slept in, because of the cold: it is warmer in bed than anywhere else. They untangle, stare at each other. Julia, wrapped in the rose-colored blanket, goes to listen. "It's me," says a voice. "Wait," Eve says, but Julia has opened the door to Rolf, who stands, resplendent, impatient. He ignores Julia, her semi-nakedness; he points through the doorway, to the bedroom, directly between Eve's eyes. "I hear you are in want of a job."

Eve and Julia confer, hurriedly. Julia is purse-lipped and disapproving, but they are also both excited. "I suppose you'd better go," she says, and Eve kisses her.

He waits for her in the courtyard, hands plunged in pockets, breath pluming. He walks fast, outlining the plan. He has an old friend—a school friend, as it happens—someone he has known for a long time, a tailor, who is good and generous; occasionally Rolf helps on the shop floor, unless something comes up. They will propose Eve as a surrogate, a substitute; thus Rolf will be freed from his obligations and can take up other opportunities that may present themselves. Eve doesn't dare ask: *What opportunities?* She thought he was in the theater, but must have misunderstood.

They turn south, toward the Innere Stadt. He matches his pace with hers. It is a relief to be with someone who doesn't look at her as though she is a zoo animal; she tries, in her stumbling way, to say as much. He looks at her, narrow and amused. "You're from a small place? A village? You like reading? Magazines, papers?" She nods. "You must like theater? Music?" She nods.

"I had a lover in that apartment up there"—he inclines his eyebrow skyward, toward a handsome block on the edge of the Danube—"and another up there. Murder on the thighs." He mimes jogging across the bridge, hiding from unseen, speculative eyes.

The word *lover* is masculine.

He sees her flush. "Yes," he smirks. "I, too, am a creature."

They walk on. She does not know what to ask first; is pink with the pleasure of recognition. Does he feel happy, every day, she wants to know. Does he feel safe? How did he first know himself? How do people treat him? Is there a way to know each other? Must he be careful? How can he be with a man in bed? Does everyone just invent, when it comes to sex, what they like? The scientists say it is the next turn of the evolutionary wheel. And the poets? Has he told his family? She has heard that Mozart had a boyfriend; that Schubert's *Schöne Müllerin* was a *Müller*. Is there anyone he currently loves?

"Have you been together a while?" he asks. His face glitters ungenerously at the thought of Julia. She hesitates. It is an enormous thing, just to name it. Tells him about the orchard; about the meetings in the shop, that time late at night when Julia came to stand outside her apartment with a look of nameless pleading. Then finds she is unable to stop, although he sometimes has to supply the right word.

"A *husband*," Rolf says. "Two a penny. Could you, if it came to it? Knock him out?" He studies her fists.

She feels he has not understood. "He may try to win her back. He may find us."

"Well, then, you shall have to just—" He shadow-boxes. "With your honorable hands."

She is suddenly worried about being disloyal. Julia disliked Rolf, called him *intolerably rude*, and what if he isn't reliable? They have crossed half the city: the Rathausplatz is minty, wintry green; their feet crunch on frost.

He spins around to face her, letting her see just how he looks: handsome, like someone who has grown up outdoors; crow's feet at the corners of his merry eyes.

"How is it?" He shades his forehead against the sliced autumn light. "Being with a woman?"

"I only know Julia."

"Really?" he says. "*Really?*"

She is flustered that he thinks there could have been others. "It was a small place."

He turns to stare down at her. "I have often wondered what it would be like."

He looks at her mouth and up again. His smile has not changed. He turns back so they are both facing forward, and whistles a little tune. So elegant a pass, she almost misses it.

Nothing is said for a further few seconds; she is trying to think what she can possibly say—*Thank you, but I only want her*—and as she realizes there is nothing *to* say, he clutches her arm, and the grip is comradely. She blushes as she realizes that his advance, and her clumsy rejection of it, matters not a jot. It is just something he wanted out of the way, as a kind of challenge to himself.

"We're here," he says. They are outside a tailor's shop; the torso of a female body, wearing a plum velvet high-collared dress, sits in the window.

Rolf goes in first. *Grüss Gott. Grüss Gott.* He kisses the shop-keeper, a thin man in pince-nez, on each cheek. The smell of cold cloth makes Eve long for home. The shop is the same as hers but the details are different; bolts of corduroy for dirndls, the sheen of moleskin for waistcoats, not in fashion in France. She is drawn to a row of neckties, reaches up to pinch the fabric between finger and thumb. Rolf chatters in German, explaining; walking his fingers coyly over the polished desk as he makes his pitch.

The shopkeeper turns toward her. She braces for the scouring glance at her hips, at where her breasts should show. She feels the color rising. "*Sehr gut,*" she says, indicating the cravats: a pathetic attempt at deflection. The shopkeeper tilts his head, assessing. But instead of lingering on her figure, his gaze goes, sharp and profes-sional, to her collar, cuffs, to the polish of her town shoes; takes in the sheen of her hair, the invisible stitching at her ankle. It occurs to her, with another flush, that he, too, is *like them.* Maybe he has been one of Rolf's lovers.

"You speak German?" he says.

"*Ein bisschen.*"

He nods. Can she fill in, three days a week, in the back room, with the mending? Mending? (He mimes a rapid cross-stitch.) If things go well, she can help on the shop floor. He rubs his eyes like a child; jerks his chin to where Rolf stands. "You cannot be less reli-able than this fellow."

Rolf laughs, sudden and booming. "You love me," he says to the shopkeeper. "I add interest to your life."

The details settled, they walk back toward Leopoldstadt. Rolf whistles into the afternoon—the sun has already begun to look anemic, lowering toward the horizon. He talks about the theater. He wants to have a little troupe of his own one day, when he has enough money saved. All beautiful, of course, all men. He winks. "It will be something." She has to hurry to keep up. A woman in furs, her breath like a steam engine, tuts, and dives off the sidewalk to avoid him; he turns and snaps his fingers after her. Eve is astonished. She tries to think of something warm to say. "You are—" she says.

"I know," he says, "too much. You'll learn to be too much, too." Then, gently, "I think it might help."

Eve runs up the stairs. Julia is scouring the inside of the stove with a rag; she is making a terrible fist of cleaning it.

She looks up with the frozen expression that's come to replace hope, and then with hope. "Yes?" she says. "A job? It worked?"

The job is no longer what Eve wants to communicate. "He is *like us*. Rolf. He loves men. He told me so. He is so *brazen*. He doesn't care what people think. There may be others, here, perhaps in Leopoldstadt. Anyone could be! Anyone we pass on the street!" It occurs to her for the very first time that all the staring, everyone looking at her, might not just be animosity. Some of it could be desire. She might, in time, learn to strut. She pushes the thought away: it's too new. "The tailor, I think, is like us too. That's why he is letting me work there. I'll be in the back room, and the pay is two hundred Kronen per month, only mending at first, but if I excel—"

Julia's hands have gone to her cheeks. "Two hundred? But the rent alone is three hundred and seventy-five. Didn't you think to negotiate? What good is Rolf being *like us* if he can't help?"

Eve stares at her. "But he has helped. I have work. I will find something else, too. Julia . . . we are not alone!" The conversation has gone wrong, somewhere upstream: a fish flipping, its cold eye appearing amidst the foam. They still have not found anything for the windowpane in the kitchen: the wind slips through into the room. "Have you heard anything from the Embassy?"

She has meant to keep her tone light, to encourage, but as she says it, she knows that is only half true. She is suddenly furious. She wants to ask: *And where is your portion of the rent going to come from?* It hangs in the air anyway. Julia gapes. For a moment, she looks ugly, entirely different.

"I'm going to bed," she says. "I have a headache."

And her parting shot: "I'm glad he is *like us*. I'm glad you've found a friend."

Julia

———

JULIA STANDS OUTSIDE THE SWEDISH EMBASSY in the Liechten-steinstrasse. Under her arm is a leather portfolio full of translation examples: a little Goethe, and some of Per's plays, to English and to German.

The Swedish flag, hoisted at the front of the building, snaps in the wind. She walks down the few steps to the entrance, and is let into the building by a man in uniform; his glance is deferential. She lifts her chin; the hem of her skirt needs mending, and the overcoat could use a clean, but she has done her best. The Swedish—*Won't you sit here? Are you expected? No? As it happens there is an opening. The Ambassador is engaged, but Undersecretary Holm will see you presently*—does not come easily. The man smiles: "So you're rusty. It happens to us all after a while."

He seats her in a small office with a stove in the corner. There are almond biscuits that taste of her childhood; a pot of coffee is brought. She eats two biscuits and pockets the rest for later, and thinks of Eve. Her stricken face, last night. Their first argument. For Julia, an old hand at marriage, this is to be expected; but for Eve, it must have seemed a tragedy. She'd come tapping on the bedroom door, slipped inside. Julia, lying on the bed, still thrumming with anger: "I want to be alone." Then finding herself saying, in one of those sudden swoops of contrition she remembers from married love: "I will go to the Embassy tomorrow. I will ask them, even if I'm not invited." It had felt so good to curl up in Eve's arms, to blot herself out against the strength of her shoulders. "I promise I will try." For once, it is sunny: mid-afternoon light, streaming crisp through the window, making the skeletal trees of the Lichtentalerpark stand out like a stage set. She turns her face up to its warmth.

The undersecretary, when he comes, is young—barely out of his twenties—and wears a smart gray flannel suit. His hair is pale red, flyaway; he looks distracted.

She is aware of her own expression: eager to please, as she hops to her feet and is guided into his office. He looks at her from under his eyebrows. "Frau Lindqvist?" he says in Swedish, moving around the papers on the top of his desk. His eyes are sleepy; it is just after lunch; the faint smell of red wine follows him. "The clerk said you are a new arrival. I hope it is not trouble that brings you here? That our fair city is agreeable?"

She starts to say the expected things: how pleasant, how welcoming. He listens, and he is looking at her coat, at the stains on the lapel from snow and rain, but picks up his pen and makes a note of some sort, then signs, with a flourish, another piece of paper. "Apologies," he says. "I am dreadfully sorry. *Tempus fugit.* Always so much to attend to. How can I help?"

She opens her portfolio. She is appalled to see that her fingers are shaking. She slides her exemplars onto his desk. They seem childish, handwritten, next to the stack of typed paper across from him. "I am a translator. English, German, some French. I would be obliged to have some little occupation, while we are in the city. Literary or business. I am indifferent."

He pulls the Goethe toward him and studies it; shakes the paper, and looks at her over the top. "Lindqvist," he says. "I could swear I've seen you somewhere. Do I know the name? What does your husband do?"

"I don't think you will know it," she says. "My cousin Grete is an actress. My father was in the Diplomatic Service."

He slaps his palm on the blotter. "Julia!" he says. "I knew it was you. Gustaf Holm. Yes? We were at Conservatoire parties, all those years ago. I had more hair, then, of course"—he ruffles his tonsure—"and I studied the fiddle to your piano, but don't you remember?"

She is aghast. She has no memory of him at all. "Of course!" she says, and she can tell he does not quite believe her. She imagines what she will tell Eve later, and hears her say, in her mind: *Poor man! I bet he was in love with you.* "Gustaf," she repeats, and struck by sudden inspiration: "Did we play a duet for the Prix Stenhammer? When we were seventeen?"

She has invented it, although it could be true—it could have been him, that slight gingerish boy, nervous around her—but he says: "I believe so! I believe we did." He leans back in his chair, claps his hands; looks at her again. He is thinking—she is sure of it—that she is thinner. That she has aged.

"I will try to do something for you, then. Anything for an old friend."

She gushes her thanks, and looks down at the desk, at her portfolio, meaningfully. He puts his fingers together. "But it can't be as a translator, unfortunately. We are inundated. Everyone keen to get out of Stockholm; to come somewhere warm." He wraps his arms around himself, mimes shivering. "How long are you staying? I honestly recommend you don't bother with an occupation. Go to the opera! Fanny Erdrich! *Die Zauberflöte!* The new Somali exhibit! The Christmas markets, when they come. What did you say your husband was posted here for?"

Two things happen. The first: she remembers him. He was a small, scurrying boy, and the error is his: they have known each other for far longer than he thinks. She remembers him at five, six years old, frightened to talk to anyone, perched on a stool at a children's party; his shabby suit and starched white collar, on the verge of tears of loneliness. They never played a duet at seventeen, but she recalls him at nineteen, holding a champagne flute at some soirée or other, talking earnestly to Frieda Karlsson, a chesty blonde; his interest in her, his avidity, painfully on display. She has the vague impression that Frieda, too, rejected him, turned laughing to Julia, with a shrug.

The second thing to happen is that she is in imminent danger of crying. She inhales sharply through her nose, folds her hands, looks to the window. No good. A betraying tear spills from the corner of her left eye.

"Goodness," says Gustaf Holm, "goodness. If ... I had no idea it was that serious."

He must have known, she thinks viciously, from the moment she walked in. What woman comes alone to a stranger's office, begging for work, in a second-best coat and unpolished shoes? "I find myself—" she begins. "Straitened circumstances—" Something has happened to her breathing; she can't get to the top of the scale, as it were.

Gustaf says helplessly, "Has your husband— No, I don't need details. Is there not some relative you can ask for assistance? Your father?"

She shakes her head.

"We can offer, of course, emergency repatriation costs, in the event you find yourself without lodgings and in urgent need," he says. He looks at her narrowly. Suspicion is blooming.

She shakes her head. "I don't want to go back to Sweden! I just need a little income—"

He draws a straight line on his blotter: A to B. "Or, *in extremis*, our domestic manager, here at the Embassy, is always in want of help. But I cannot imagine that is the kind of work you had in mind. Or that things are truly that bad."

He is peering at her closely now, trying to puzzle it out. He is trying to be kind and she cannot bear it. She gathers her portfolio, her coat, and stands. "Things are very far from being that bad. I will speak to my husband. Thank you. Goodbye."

On the way home, she enumerates her losses with a kind of dull astonishment. *My pianoforte. My enamel box with the porcupine quill hidden inside. My garden at the summer-house in Gothenburg: the alliums like ruffle-headed children, the ornamental mosses, the blackcurrants winking from the bird-nets.* These are not nothing. She will no longer be received in the artistic houses of Western Europe—

Frau Berndt, in the courtyard, says: "Rolf is looking for you—" But she ignores her, with a wave of the hand; she cannot speak.

All the way up the stairs, she tries to be calm. Eve meets her at the door; follows her inside the apartment. Julia knows, as she is pulling off her gloves, how her voice sounds: shrill, indignant. "He offered me cleaning work. Of course I said it was out of the question. Will you put the kettle on for coffee, please? It's been a hell of a day."

Eve sits on the dining-room chair. "You turned it down?"

Julia pulls at her boots. The laces won't come undone. The leather is too tight across the bridge of her foot: a dull throb. "I am a translator," she says, "and a musician."

Eve settles forward in her seat, her hands laced. Her expression gentle. "We are still short one hundred and seventy-five Kronen for rent, and that's assuming we eat air."

Julia says: "It's not the same for you—"

"Why isn't it?" Eve is carefully blank.

"Because you are. . . . Don't make me say it."

From the courtyard, they can hear Rolf's voice—his booming laugh—as he says something to Frau Berndt; her flattered giggle in response.

Eve sits back. "Because I am not a lady." She rubs her palms over her face. *Are we here again, so soon?*

"No! Because you have not given things up like I have." *My ivory hairbrush; my silk gloves . . .*

They stare at each other. Eve says, "Then go back to your fine things. Nobody is stopping you."

Julia sniffs. "It was humiliating. The way he looked at me."

"I feel like that every day."

A knock at the door. They look, startled. They have not heard anyone on the stairs. The door opens, and it's Rolf, beaming, with a knowing look that suggests he has overheard. "Hello, lovebirds," he says. "We're going out."

"Not now," Eve says, pleading, but he snaps his fingers.

"Yes now. I will brook no argument. And"—this last with kindness—"I promise it will help."

They walk out past a surprised Frau Berndt. "Will you be very late?" she asks, and Rolf booms: "Extremely!"

He grips Julia's elbow. "Don't worry. Not far now."

"This is ridiculous," she says, "we can't go to a restaurant. Don't you know there's no money?"

He doesn't look at her; he looks behind, instead, at Eve, who is scuffing her feet, walking three paces behind. "The drinks are on

Uncle Rolf. Oh, did you have other plans? To drive each other mad talking about being poor all night?" He is merry, uncompromising.

On the streets of Leopoldstadt, people are hurrying; always hurrying. The butcher's boy smiles softly as he passes by, wheeling his barrow; the sun glints over the tops of the roofs and vanishes, leaving the street puddled with blue shadow.

A side street she has not encountered; an ordinary residential block; five steps, leading down to a basement level surrounded by iron railings. Eve catches up with them. "What is this place?"

Rolf, still holding Julia's forearm, walks down the stairs ahead of them. "It's a present," he says, and knocks at the door.

It is this: a large room, low-ceilinged, filled with cigarette smoke. A bar runs along the far wall. There are perhaps fifty people dancing; a band in the corner—cello and accordion—plays a slow waltz. Rolf leads them through the press of bodies. One man, his color high with rouge, says, "Excuse *me*," and turns back to his dance-partner, another man. Another kisses Rolf on both cheeks; some words are exchanged; a hand at the small of the back, a smirk. Eve reaches for Julia's hand, and Julia clutches it in return.

They reach the bar. Julia looks at Eve: her eyes are enormous. She leans in and whispers: "Everyone here is—" She points to Julia's chest, and then her own. Mouths the word: *Homosexual.* Rolf lifts a finger and is served three small shot glasses full of clear, viscous liquid. Eve tips hers down her throat. She is blushing. Julia looks at hers and puts it down on the bar.

Heat creeps up her spine. One has heard of such bars, of course. How could Rolf think this was a place for them? It is all men, isn't it? Besides, it is dirty, and smelly: sweat and warm beer and everything is cheap. But she sees, following Eve's gaze, that it isn't all men. There is a group of three women sitting back from a table in the far corner. Their hands are thrust in their pockets, their hair cropped close to the skull. They look lazy, confident. One of them looks at Julia and Eve, away, and back again; leans in toward her comrades. Laughter runs around the little group.

Rolf dips his head close to theirs. "Go and talk to them," he says.

"Not yet," Eve says, eyeing Julia.

Rolf shrugs. *Please yourselves.* He looks hungrily around the dance floor over the top of his drink.

A table is freed up, as the occupants rise to their feet; a woman, like Julia but with gray hair, a Roman nose, is pulled up by her companion, laughing, and onto the dance floor. They entwine, begin a slow sway. One puts her chin on the shoulder of the other and closes her eyes.

Rolf, Julia, and Eve move into the vacated seats. The music speeds up; someone has castanets, someone else a triangle. The dancers form a circle around a young man. Rolf lights a cigarette, squints, lifts his hands over his head to clap in time. "Oh, really—" Julia says, and holds her hand instinctively over Eve's eyes, as the young man flings his shirt to the side, where it's caught by someone, and pressed to his nose.

The women in the corner are speculative; one is nominated, and dispatched, to their table. It reminds Julia of a debutante ball; she thinks, flustered, *All a fuss over nothing.* She readies her brisk retort: *Thank you, I'm spoken for*—when they get home, they will laugh about this, she and Eve, and agree never to follow Rolf anywhere again—but the woman is directing herself elsewhere. Julia realizes, with shock, that the woman has come to court Eve, not her. Indeed, she magics a cigar from her breast pocket, presses it into Eve's hand, motions to the table, where the other women are studiously turned away.

Eve looks at Julia: *Can I go?* Julia nods. The heat is making her hair wisp around her face, the sweat pool in the dip between her breasts. Eve gets to her feet, clumsily crosses the dance floor. A round of introductions—shaken hands—a smile—Eve leaning in to hear better. The beloved anxiety of her face, as she tries to follow the German, in the noise—a shy smile—Eve has never, Julia thinks, seen anyone else like her before, with short hair and a suit. Recognition floods her, as she considers what this must be like. Eve must have thought she was alone in all the world.

Rolf, who has been watching Julia closely, leans away, spreading his arms over the adjacent chair backs. *What?* she mouths. She is still startled by the sudden epiphany, and guilty. He shakes his head. Leans close. "You are lucky."

She looks at him. How dare he say this? When he must know the money problem? And the problem of Per, and how Eve is looked at? When she can barely begin to reckon with the losses—

He says: "Yes, you are. You have a place to live, and you have a fire, and food."

Can he be so naïve? "We don't have coal, or money—"

"You can borrow from me. So the rent will be a little late! So what? You can come here when you feel sad."

The effrontery! What he is proposing is utterly childish. He looks at the dance floor, at the waltzers holding each other close, and then over at the far table. Eve is listening to one of the other women tell an expansive anecdote; blushing, laughing. "And you have her. If you want her. Do you? Want her? Because if you don't, you know what you must do."

He inhales thinly, looks at her through narrowed eyes. Smoke trails upward from the cigarette end: a question mark.

"I do want her," Julia says.

He raps the tabletop, decisive. "Drink?" he says.

She hesitates. She wants, more than anything, right now, a glass of chilled Mosel Sekt with a dash of elderflower. But such a drink is too expensive. She points instead to his half-tumbler of home-distilled digestif. "One like that, please."

He gets up, smoothing his waistcoat over his belly, and steps toward the bar. She sees how he is admired, by a young man with curly blond hair, on the way across the dance floor; she sees how he notices, but pretends not to notice; how he preens discreetly. The smoke in the room is lit red by the fringed velvet lamps on each table. Yes, it smells of stale alcohol, but also of sawdust and cloves and human bodies. Julia thinks: *Perhaps it could have been different for me. If I'd found my way somewhere like this.* Because it isn't true there were no signs. That schoolteacher, when she was fifteen, with the clever smile, that frankness of posture. . . . You arrive where you are and you don't know how. And now, in a basement, of all places—all the while, Eve was out there somewhere, and now is sitting just twelve feet away, and now she's looking back. One of the women is telling her Julia is beautiful—the sideways glance is sly and obvious—and Eve is nodding, shyly, unable to believe her luck.

Julia beckons to her; Eve's face brightens. She all but points to herself. *Me? Yes, you.* Eve turns to her new friends and, with a wave, leaves the table, comes back to Julia.

Julia half-rises, plants a kiss on Eve's lips. From the women at the next-door table, a wolf whistle, a burst of applause. She says: "I will go back tomorrow and ask about the cleaning job. We will find a way." Eve buries her head in Julia's neck.

The confused impression of more liqueur; at some point, red wine, which burns the back of the throat. Rolf's greedy face, lining up more glasses. The music speeds up, slows down. Faces loom in and out of the darkness; Eve is shouting *goodbye* to their new friends, who live only two streets away, just above the chandler's on Tabor-strasse. . . . Then the bite of cold air, the ringing silence of the street; their footsteps, sharp and uneven on the cobbles.

The lodge light is on. Through the window, Frau Berndt can be seen asleep in her armchair, draped in a black shawl, her hair done in rags. The gramophone hisses, and resolves into song: Fanny Erdrich, taking a run at the high notes of O *Zittre Nicht.*

They stand for a moment, looking up, breathing in the metallic smell of winter air. Away toward the Innere Stadt, the city light blooms, turning the sky coppery-mauve.

1911

—

Eve

———

THEIR FRIENDS HAVE ARRIVED, damp and gasping from the cold. The bed is piled with coats; in the salon, Frau Berndt hovers, ready to escort the guests to the buffet. *A little tipple? Perhaps some cold cuts?* She and Julia have spent weeks planning the menu, and the guest list, which is mostly composed of Frau Berndt's ever-growing list of tenants. Frau Berndt has been surprisingly choosy about whom to admit to Julia and Eve's arrival anniversary party: *Not her; not him, the backs of his hands are too hairy, like a murderer's. How would you know? Let's say I've lived a life.*

Now the murderer (Gunther) and his wife (Heidi), whom they have invited anyway, who live in the downstairs flat, are arriving. Julia leans in for a kiss on either cheek, and as she does so she looks pointedly at Gunther's hands, and catches Frau Berndt's eye in an extravagant wink.

In that way that sometimes happens, it seems the party may fail before it's gotten started. Everyone is standing around with plates, appearing to enjoy themselves, but nobody is talking. Ephraim, the melancholic musician from the first floor, has fallen out with Maria, his girlfriend, who works the corner of Schiffamtsgasse. A pair of students are staring at Maria and her glance back is sarcastic: *If you want it, just ask.* Eve would like to have a quiet conversation with Julia and find out what to do, but she also wants to stand here in the corner, where nobody will see her. Besides, if the party fails, she won't have to make the speech. "Will you say something to them?" Julia'd said, wide-eyed, when Eve had suggested it, in a fit of *galanterie*. "Will you really speak in front of a crowd?"

Heavy steps on the stair, the door is flung open and Rolf is there: a miracle in a sheepskin coat. "Who goes there?" he booms, and then: "I do." He flings open his arms for Julia, whom he holds pressed against his beard. He holds up Julia's wrist, and lets it drop. "What are you feeding her?" he asks Eve. "She's a twig."

Frau Berndt is animated tonight; denying, to anyone who will listen, her favorite familiar story that her husband, Thomas Berndt, was a spy. "He was not, of course," she says, winking broadly. There is talk from the guests of the ghost of the Empress Maria Theresa walking by the Danube; the third time she has been seen this year. Ephraim, who has been edging toward his violin, snaps open the case with a defiant air.

Seeing this, Rolf moans: "Oh God, not the bloody fiddle." He pushes Eve into the kitchen. They stand sandwiched between the oven and the crockery cupboard. Rolf takes a cigar from his waistcoat.

"Don't ask me where I got it," he says, which means *ask*. He shakes out the match and a cloud of blue smoke envelops his head. "He says he'll take me to Italy this summer." He squints out of the window. "He has a house on the Lido."

By the time she has learned their names, Rolf's gentlemen are old news. Some of them come from the cellar bar and some from somewhere else, unspecified. The theater plans have not yet come good and he is vague when asked about them. He never seems to hold any casual job for more than a couple of weeks, keeps odd hours, but always seems to have nice things. "Imagine," he is saying, "me in a bathing suit. We shall have to take our regime more seriously." He flexes one arm, admiring the bicep that jumps beneath his shirt. She smiles, remembering their morning sessions, calisthenics in the Augarten, that summer; Julia coming to watch and laugh at them, sitting comfortably in the shade.

She lights one of her own cigarettes, blows out smoke, and when it clears, she finds him watching her. "Nothing?" he asks.

She shrugs. They have speculated that the anniversary of the elopement would bring something from Per Lindqvist: some effort at first contact; some creeping billet-doux. Every day this week, Frau Berndt has brought the post to them, noting the absence of any strange envelopes, whispering: "Well done."

"That's good, then, isn't it?" Rolf says. "And so? Julia is well?"

It is a gesture, from him, this swerve away from the fascinating story of his own life, but he has put his finger on the tender spot. She is too preoccupied, anyway, tonight, by the fear of public speaking. "Will you listen to the speech?"

She begins, pathetically, to unfold the paper from her back pocket. She has been working on it in the evenings, and in the breaks in the back room of the tailor's, for three weeks. "I've tried to get it all in, about how grateful we are for being made so welcome. I've tried to mention everyone by name."

He sucks in a stippling breath of cigar; sighs it out. "Go on," he says.

The violin music has reached a frenzy—it is easier to start Ephraim than to stop him—and she hears Julia clapping for everyone to be quiet. Silence falls in the salon and she feels ridiculous for hiding. It is worse to have to make an entrance.

Rolf pushes her forward through the kitchen doorway. She is met by expectant faces: Frau Berndt lets out a tiny *hoorah* and waves her glass. Julia, twinkling with loving, cruel amusement, crosses her arms and lifts her chin. Heidi and Gunther, standing together, vaguely bovine; Maria, leaning on the salon wall, sleepy eyes half shut. Their friends from the cellar bar, Simone and Hanna, enlaced toward the back. The room is full of their dear ones. Some further gesture is required. She gets up on an empty chair and stands with her arms raised like a conductor.

"My dear friends," she croaks. "Comrades." *Comrades* is a wrong note. They are none of them what you'd call political; only trying to get by. Maria leans on Ephraim's shoulder. Arms are crossed in loving forbearance.

"My friends, words cannot express—there is no end to our gratitude, Julia and me, for your welcome this past year." The native speakers in the room nod encouragingly. "You have made us feel so special." Is *special* the right word? Hushed laughter. Special, *ungewöhnlich*, also means strange, doesn't it?

The dreaded betraying blush creeps up her neck. "You have made us feel loved." Now she sounds insincere. "Though we are incomers, we hope in time to become like you, and to return with interest the enormous kindness you have shown us." She thanks them all by name: Gunther for putting their shelves together, Rolf for the job at the tailor's shop. It is taking too long; she thinks that everyone is looking, in the old way, like when they first arrived. Tears of frustration grow in the back of her throat. Julia's face is a loving appeal: *Keep going.* "I would ask you to raise your glasses—"

She hasn't got a glass. A concerned murmur breaks out as she hurriedly reaches down, for a champagne flute on the table, wobbles on the chair. Gunther comes to her rescue, holding up his big murderous hand.

Gunther looks at Heidi, and says, "Before the toast, we have a small announcement of our own." Heidi dimples, a look of fat satisfaction on her face. "We wanted to tell you tonight, all of you here assembled. We are having a child."

It has been a marriage. One morning, Julia empties their cutlery out of the window in a shimmering, deadly waterfall. Julia cries, often, over the cleaning job—*My hands are turning into claws!*—and then cries again when something comes up in the secretarial pool, and her hands hurt all over again from the typing. Julia's sister writes, more than once; then, because Julia's replies are unsatisfactory, her mother. Julia flattens the sheets of paper on the table to read it. Her lips part, as if in expectation, but what comes out is agonized. *You are no longer my daughter.* They expected more diplomacy from the Ambassador's wife. It is a loss.

A day, nine months after their arrival, three months before the party. It is high hot summer, a Sunday in August, and they go for a walk in the Prater. Foamy lime trees lining the avenues, cinnamon smell blown in from the arcades.

The gossip in the apartment block is Frau Berndt, who is in one of her moods. She has retreated into the concierge's lodge and stayed there for two weeks, speaking to nobody. Music comes from the radio inside, the notes rising and falling frenetically, but the shutters stay closed. Meanwhile, outside the walls of the apartment block, tuberculosis, the Viennese disease, hangs on street corners. "Is the world becoming terrible?" Julia asks, as they walk. They pass the African exhibit, where the Somalis lounge in the shade, playing cards. It has been so popular that the Somalis have been invited to stay, their pay doubled, and superior lodgings found in a modern block near the Rathaus; some of them have accepted the offer. Then into the long grass of the meadow. Poppies nod around Julia's skirt, and Eve lifts her legs like a wading bird. They laugh at each other. The world cannot be terrible.

But someone, nearby, is crying—somewhere close to the ground. The grass stems part and a head appears, bobbing toward them. Red hair, like Julia's, and skin that's pink from the sun. The child holds its arms out and runs, wailing, toward Julia. It clutches her around the knees and buries its face in her skirt.

Julia stoops and pries the little girl's hands loose, then holds them in hers. "Are you lost? Where is your mother?"

The child looks around. Julia shushes and soothes, picks the girl up and places her on her hip.

Eve hangs back, shy. The girl's wails rise over the meadow. Julia turns to Eve and there are tears in her eyes. One hand cups the back of the girl's neck.

A woman is running across the grass toward them; breasts jiggling under her dress, skirts held high. Her face red and fearful.

The first thing she says is: "She's always running away."

"Of course," Julia says. "I have nephews myself." She places the girl back on her feet. The child runs without hesitation to her mother. The woman smiles, her gratitude now icy—she has spotted Eve. She takes the child's hand and shakes it, once, in anger. A warning about strangers will surely follow. Together, they move off, without a backward glance.

"What a thing," Julia says, smiling brightly. And, on the way back to the apartment: "What a peculiar thing."

Rolf breaks the silence with a storm of applause. "Bravo," he shouts. "Lovely news." Maria places two careful congratulatory kisses on Heidi's cheeks. Frau Berndt lifts a bottle of schnapps skyward. "All shall have prizes!" she says.

The clapping for Gunther and Heidi's announcement goes on and on. Eve climbs down from the chair, is aware of Rolf's big hands moving; the way he draws all the glances in the room toward him. "Splendid," he says, "wonderful!" He lifts his glass in a toast. *To new lives!*

The news makes the room giddy. Perhaps the world of the baby will be bright, different? Perhaps the mayor, who is handsome but vicious, will be more favorable in his policies toward Leopoldstadt? Gunther shakes hands with everyone—"Thank you, thank you"— and laughs uneasily when Rolf says, not really joking: "You're stuck now. You realize?"

Eve cannot look at Julia; she moves through the party in a dream, congratulating, smiling blankly, sheltering near Rolf where she can. Half an hour later, Gunther escorts Heidi to the door—"An early night for us"—his hand on her waist, newly protective. Heidi waves like a celebrity as she leaves.

Now they are gone, the mood alters: introspective, universal. Frau Berndt changes the record on the gramophone to something mournful; Maria sways in Ephraim's arms, and the students excuse themselves. Rolf says loudly, "Shall I help you tidy?" And one by one, the remaining guests pick up their coats and tiptoe away.

The four of them wash up in thoughtful silence. Frau Berndt finishes drying the dessert spoons and places them in the drawer, then puts her palms on Julia's shoulders. "*Courage, mon brave.* It was a marvelous party."

Rolf folds Eve and Julia in his arms separately, then together. He drops a kiss on each of their heads. "People to see," he says, "places to go."

Eve watches Julia move about the kitchen, parceling up leftover food, humming, artificially bright. *What is the shape of this problem?* Eve would like to ask, but doesn't dare.

Twenty thousand rotations of the Ferris Wheel in the Prater. Adolf Hitler, who every day now sells his watercolors on the streets, decides against applying to art school a third time: in a year, he'll dodge the draft and go to Berlin, head full of ideas. Ephraim and Maria separate; she puts his cardboard suitcase in the courtyard and he sits on the steps of her apartment, hands laced together, contemplating it as it melts in the spring showers.

It is not until a Saturday in April, when the tulips are nosing through the lawns of the Augarten. They are sitting on folding chairs in the courtyard, taking the final sun of the afternoon.

They have been silent for some minutes. Julia tips her chair back; squints up at the sky, and then looks at Eve in a way that's rueful and an invitation, so that Eve knows it's time.

"Was there any thought of children with Per?" she asks, as gently as she can.

Julia's face is pale pink, tilted upward in the crisp sunshine. "No interest," she says. "I was glad."

"Was he perhaps too old?"

Julia laughs. "My love," she says, in mild reproof. The chair legs tip and click against the cobbles. Through the open door to the concierge's lodge, Frau Berndt can be heard humming. The afternoon feels delicate, ready to tear. Eve tries to imagine what it would be like: a small thing chirruping in the back room. She tries to imagine someone with Julia's hair and her eyes and hands; the horizontal line that appears when she wrinkles her nose in pleasure. It is too beguiling a prospect to touch all at once with her mind. Julia's face is determined, shut off; her eyes fixed on something in the distance that Eve cannot see.

They talk about other things. A mistake in the German that Eve made with a client, which led to an unfortunate incident with buttons. Eve's boss at the outfitter, who has become snappish and exacting; Eve suspects some unhappy love affair. Julia attended the leaving party of Gustaf Holm, the undersecretary, last Friday: his palm moist in hers, refusing to meet her eye as he said goodbye. They don't talk about money. The air gets cool and the sky is streaked with orange, and Frau Berndt shuffles out of the lodge with blankets, glasses, and a mottled silver tray on which sits the inevitable bottle. She pours them each a measure and sits down to join them. Silently they decide this must remain private between them, and so they sit without mentioning it, drinking.

Heidi waddles in with her shopping basket on her arm. She is not really big enough yet to have such a rolling gait, but she puffs and puts her hand on her stomach as she moves toward them. She accepts Eve's seat without saying thank you; settles onto it with a groan. "I'll just rest here a moment," she says.

"Tired?" inquires Frau Berndt.

"It is tiring," Heidi admits. She has a voice like a little girl's. "You look tired, too," Heidi says to Julia. "All the color has gone from your face. But then, you work so hard."

She means to be kind—or doesn't. She thinks Julia flirts with Gunther. Julia doesn't, although Gunther sometimes looks at Julia in a way that makes everyone blush. Julia looks at her fingers. Typing is no better than cleaning, she always says: thirty hours a week in the secretarial pool takes its toll. "At least when I start playing the piano again, my hands will be strong."

"There is no calling like motherhood, is there?" Heidi says. She brushes her stomach with her palm, up and down, and Eve sees that Julia is watching the movement closely.

Frau Berndt tops up their glasses. She pours each measure very carefully. Heidi sighs again and says that Gunther will want his supper on the table. She levers herself up from the chair, kisses them each on either cheek—a treacherous little peck—and vanishes into the apartment block.

Eve looks at Frau Berndt; if she weren't there, Eve would put an arm around Julia, but it is too late anyway: tongue between her teeth, Julia hisses at Heidi's retreating back.

Frau Berndt says: "Oh, my dear—" and looks distressed. Eve holds Julia tight for a moment, hoping Heidi is not looking back, or out of her window, then escorts Julia upstairs. Julia pauses at the halfway point, palm to the side of the stairwell, to start breathing in and out in enormous waves. Eve worries that Heidi will hear them, and come asking, and hurries Julia to the top.

In the apartment, Julia begins to cook, or rather, to lift and slam down pots and pans onto the tables and cupboards of the kitchen. She seizes a bag of potatoes and a knife and starts to peel, viciously, then makes a deep cut in the side of her thumb. The potato is abandoned, a bloody mess.

Even when she has been very angry before—when Eve and Rolf went to the cellar bar and stayed out all night and reappeared, still drunk, a full day later—even when Eve, full of rage at some imagined infraction, refused to eat her birthday cake—Julia has always felt within reach.

Julia says: "Perhaps I can't have them anyway. It was never something I wanted." She's striding around the apartment. Her thumb bleeds onto her sleeve. She opens the kitchen cupboard and fetches a strip of bandage to wind around the injury.

"Is there not some way by which—" Eve is thinking of the evolutionary theories of Unger and Mendel. How plants are said to reproduce by grafting. She has been trying to become educated; by looking at the journals in the library on Zirkusgasse. There have been pamphlets, slid toward her by the elderly librarian, across the desk in the reading room: some by Herr Doktor Freud, on the topic of what the subconscious may achieve that the conscious mind may not. Some of the theories are extraordinary to her: they talk of magic, totem, taboo, hypnotism, and of children, their secret lives and dreams. Some things are possible, surely, that they are simply not aware of. "But a way that is perhaps kept secret? By the powerful? To prevent us?"

"A world birthed just by women," Julia says, and sighs. "Not in our time, my love."

There is a moment of thinking about this. Then she crosses the room, her face defiant, and reaches for Eve's belt, uses it to pull them into each other's orbit; Eve feels the familiar rush of blood, the tingle, the swelling between her legs; Julia knows how much she likes this, how much it gratifies. Her hands work the buckle and the belt snakes loose onto the floor; she slips to her knees in front of Eve. Her gaze lowers and focuses.

"If you want to make a baby, that's not the way to do it," Eve says, as Julia begins to shuck her trousers down. They have had this joke, sometimes, wistful, when Eve is fucking Julia: *If I was a man, you'd be pregnant with twins. No! Triplets!* They start the complicated dance of lifting her feet, one by one, to remove the trousers from around her ankles—Julia likes to push her toward the bed, lay her on her back, and there spread her legs, to say "You are beautiful" and other blandishments, wicked and merry.

Julia pauses for a moment. "I don't care," she says, and Eve believes her.

For Julia's birthday—she will be twenty-eight—they invite Rolf and Frau Berndt to Mitzi's on Taborstrasse. Frau Berndt appears in a disastrous hat: tall, of black silk, with a matching ostrich feather. "Too much?" she asks, and they don't have the heart to tell her it is, definitely, too much.

The restaurant is full of people they have come to know, or have, at least, a nodding acquaintance with. Young Silber, the butcher's boy, who has been paranoid for several years, sits muttering in a corner, breaking his bread into pieces. He gives no sign of having seen them. Elderly widowers dine on pikeperch and goulash and wipe their mustaches with dignity. Mitzi herself stares at them from over the top of her legendary chest, and shows them to a table specially decorated with flowers.

Flowers, a great indulgence: Julia leans forward to smell them, examines the bright globular petals of the irises and tulips. The centerpiece is made of tiny bright stars, edelweiss, native to Austria and Sweden. Eve, who has paid for the display, stands behind her chair, unable to take her eyes off Julia and her tender, probing fingers. *Thank you*, Julia mouths.

Also unable to take his eyes off her is Rolf. "You look wonderful," he purrs. He is leaning on his palm like a lover. "If I were a man, I'd ravish you here and now, on this table, right in the middle of the florals."

It is an old joke, how he pretends to flirt. Everyone laughs, but always for Eve, that catch in the throat, the secret fear—even though she knows he says these blandishments to anyone and everyone, that it is just part of his friendship with them. She tries to smile as widely as the others, to show that she finds it as funny as Rolf. Always that terror, of having Julia on short-term loan. "No, really, truly," says Rolf, hand flattened to his breast, showing the whites of his eyes to prove his sincerity. "You—you two—make me wish for things I cannot have."

They over-order—latkes and schnitzel and champagne. Eve watches Julia, who puts her palms to her cheeks, then the backs of her hands, in protest at their sudden alcoholic warmth. Mitzi hovers, ready to clear; they ignore her, but when Frau Berndt and Rolf threaten a rendition of *O du mein Österreich*, they creep out of the restaurant and back through the deserted Taborstrasse. Mitzi flips the CLOSED sign onto the glass door behind them. Outside Heidi and Gunther's apartment they part, in a parody of whispers and stealth. Frau Berndt has tears in her eyes; Rolf murmurs, "Goodnight, sweet ladies, goodnight," and then it is just the two of them.

Julia dumps the armfuls of flowers on the table and takes Eve's arms for an impromptu waltz. She hums a wavering tune, in the darkness of the apartment, and then presses her lips to Eve's collarbone.

The kiss has the pressure of desperation rather than desire; it is a willed blotting-out. Julia's arms tighten around Eve's chest and Eve feels as if she will drown, so she pulls away and says: "What about if we asked Rolf."

It hasn't been on her mind until tonight, and the thought is repulsive, of course, but she must say it. She doesn't mean it, but wants it said, so they can move past it. It is a generous thing to do, and may help them break through whatever this impasse between them is.

Julia's pupils are large. "Asked him what?" Their hands are gripped together. They lumber from foot to foot in a slow dance.

"For the baby," Eve says.

"Because of what he said, at supper? Because he said he would ravish me?" Julia blinks. "Darling, he couldn't. It's just his joke. You know that." Julia squeezes their fingers together. She kisses Eve's forehead and turns away. "What an idea."

It is natural, Eve thinks, to be jealously protective. As her name suggests, Julia is beautiful like summer; Eve has never quite gotten over the sense of her own good fortune, that Julia should have noticed her. Most of the time, she manages to hold on, to stop the poison before it leaches out. She had an insight, once: it is Julia she is jealous *of*; her merry carefree way through the world. Julia is the object of admiring stares, whereas still, on occasion, Eve notices the hostile looks of women on the street toward her dress and person, and minds them very much. But sometimes, the rage and suspicion fill her, an inky cloud, darkening her vision at the edges.

She is tearful before her mind can understand where, exactly, they have gone wrong. She follows Julia into the bedroom, where Julia is pulling her dress over her head in a long shrug. Eve gets undressed, full of unwelcome thoughts, and they lie down together under the coverlet.

Then it comes to her. She asks: "Would you go with him, for that reason?"

A rustle as Julia flips up onto her elbow. "What?"

"You didn't say you couldn't do it. You said *he* couldn't."

Julia sits up. She is staring straight at the wall. "Was it a trap? Then why did you ask me?"

"No," Eve says. It is just that the thought of Julia with a man, any man, is too much to bear—

"I would never betray you like that," Julia says. "Never." She lies down, reaches for Eve, and puts her temple in the crook of her collarbone. Her thumb begins a slow sweep of Eve's belly. One minute later, the thumb stops; the flutter of her lashes as she closes her eyes.

Rolf

—

ROLF GRUBER IS THIRTY-FOUR YEARS OLD; in his prime. He leaves Mitzi's, the sad cares of others, and after a brief stop in his apartment to collect his hat and cane, walks out into the night. He crosses the Donaukanal, and as he goes, he thinks, of the city at night, in springtime: *You are mine.* These are his people: the beggars lounging on the banks of the canal; the pickpockets and swindlers who come out in the dark, and furtively meet his eye. Yet he is also perfectly able to pass; he dusts off his white gloves, adjusts his hat. When he slips in among the finery and feathers of the opera-going crowd, as he does almost every evening about this time, they will have no idea he is not one of them.

When he reaches the Opera House, the doors are still closed. From inside, the penultimate aria of *Jenůfa* rising on the air. He takes his usual position on the right-hand end of the steps. Billy is here again, standing at the left-hand end, a cheap cigarette waving on the air. As usual, they pretend not to have noticed each other.

Tonight, there is only one man, slipping out of the auditorium early. He emerges onto the steps, patting his pockets in a panto-mime of loss. He might as well be saying, *My wallet! Can somebody help me find my wallet?* He has a stomach on him; not easy to get a fix on the face, the age—not that it really matters. . . . In a few quick steps, Billy is next to him. "Lost something, sir?" The eyes are good: wide, innocent, the concerned hand on the man's forearm, but Rolf could have told him the approach is too quick. Billy is wearing too much rouge.

The man straightens. He sneaks a quick look to his left, at Rolf, who stands with his shoulders back, trying not to look expectant.

"No thanks," the man says. Billy drops away into the shadows of the colonnade with a shrug.

The man is hesitating, peering, trying to get a better look at Rolf. Leave it one moment: a moment longer, and Rolf begins the slow saunter toward him.

The man is paunchy, white under the lights; older, by some years. Rolf moves close, places a firm grip on his shoulder. "You look tired, comrade. What about a drink somewhere?"

The man's face creases in relief. "I know a place," Rolf says, and puts a hand on the small of his back, turning him about toward the alley that leads behind the theater.

In the alleyway, the man turns blank, frightened eyes up to Rolf, and Rolf holds him capably, and kisses him, to take the edge off. The man returns the kiss, holding on to Rolf's lapels like a girl. In a few seconds, the hands creep up to the top of Rolf's head, smoothing his hair, the sudden assertive pressure downward. Rolf sinks to his knees.

From above, gasping sounds. If the man could speak, he would be saying things like *my wife never* and *my whole life I.* His fingertips massage Rolf's scalp.

When the business is accomplished, the man sagging against the wall, Rolf straightens, delivers a smacking kiss on the lips—he likes them to taste themselves—and holds out an unambiguous hand. The missing wallet appears from under the man's dinner jacket and the man licks his forefinger and counts out fifty Kronen, which is the going rate. Rolf considers asking for more, but with a light generosity of soul—the poor man is clearly suffering—he accepts them.

The man disappears back out into the street, and after a moment, Rolf follows. The whole has been so well-timed—the man's climax coinciding with Jenůfa's farewell to Laca, the high notes spiralling arctically. Ostrich feathers, satin, and silk spill out onto the square in front of the Opera House: Rolf watches the man meet his wife in the crowd, miming having found his wallet after all, expressing regret at missing the finale. The wife looks at him with a kind of sad, knowing sorrow, and they move away.

The thought comes to Rolf of Eve and Julia, earlier: the way they'd seemed tied to each other invisibly as they sat opposite each other in the restaurant. How Eve had seemed to hang on his words, but even as she'd nodded and listened, her gaze kept flickering toward Julia.

As he is thinking these things, he sees a man step out into the light on the colonnade, and immediately recognizes him, although this cannot be true because he has never seen him before. The man is no older than thirty, short and stocky, and Rolf can see that he, too, is pretending to belong. He misses handsomeness by a hair's breadth; so that Rolf isn't sure whether he is, or isn't, handsome, and spends a few seconds considering it. Something spoiled about the mouth, as though he's been nursed too long. His suit is good and fits him closely. The son of some cavalryman, but the way he looks about him, as though the crowd is the enemy—he doesn't know much about opera, not by a long shot.

By his side, a woman of about thirty years, beautiful in a cheap sort of way, whose arms are linked with a thin-faced girl—too old to be his daughter, surely, with hair so blonde it seems gray under the lamplight. An older gent and his wife bring up the rear: he rotund, she mouse-like, huffing and puffing with impatience. They make an odd party. The man grins at something the older gent has said; smiles too widely, revealing a row of sharp white teeth, but underneath that, Rolf can see his nerves and unhappiness. The thin-faced girl fidgets. The paterfamilias laughs too, gratified, lifts his hand for a cab.

Rolf has stepped forward before he can think it through. The urge to reveal himself to this little family has carried him onward. He walks up to them, says, "Allow me," puts his fingers in his mouth and issues a piercing whistle—his party piece. There's the smart clop of hooves as a cab draws around in answer.

The paterfamilias is offended, of course, at the intrusion; the older woman clucks, but the man, whom he has already begun to think of as *his*, laughs in surprise and, Rolf thinks, admiration. "*Damen und Herren*," Rolf says, stepping out of the way with a sweeping bow, allowing himself to look at the man for a moment longer. "See you again," he says meaningfully, tipping his hat, as he retreats. It is a joke, and also deadly serious: a lure trailed in the water for the days to come.

Ada

—

IT HAPPENS FOR THE FIRST TIME the day after her sixteenth birthday. She and her family—the Bauers—are on the shore of the Neusiedlersee, for a picnic, which everyone will later agree was a poor idea in the first place.

They have walked down from the house, which is half a kilometer above the beach, set in the beginning of the treeline. The picnic things—boiled eggs and cold schnitzel and potato salad—are laid out on a rug, but it is uncomfortable. A flurry of wind blows over the lake; the pebbles dig into them from beneath. Mother pours coffee from the flask, saying, "Isn't this a treat?" in a bright society tone, but it is not a warm day, and besides, they are tired from the night before, arriving back late from the city, the opera.

Everyone is there: Father, Mother, Cousin Emil, Cousin Emil's wife, Isabella. Emil and Isabella are staying another night before going back to their apartment in Vienna. The housemaid hovers to one side, shivering, hoping to be dispatched back to the house, ready to serve their food if they ask her.

"Sixteen! I can hardly believe it!" Mother says, for the hundredth time that weekend, shaking her head. "My great girl. Can you believe it, Emil? Your cousin, almost an adult. She's the same age as you were when you came to live with us! She was just a little thing, a little slip of a thing. And now look—she's almost as tall as you are."

"Not *too* tall," says Isabella, reaching out a protective hand to smooth Ada's hair. "She won't shame any gentleman callers. Will you, darling?" She is sitting close enough to link her arm with Ada. Ada turns in gratitude to look at her. It is always a pleasure to have the opportunity to look, with justification, at Isabella's lively, mischievous face. "And you already have the hair of a grown-up, don't you?" Isabella says. She means the color, which is silver-blonde: they joke that it makes her look like an old lady.

"It is a great age," Emil says, sententious. He is, as always, partly turned toward Herr Bauer, Ada's father; directs all his remarks that way. He has worked in Father's company for almost eight years now, since being apprenticed at eighteen. "After lunch, shall we look again at the plans for the railway?"

This sets Father off. He points out where the new Graz line will go; follows the imaginary fretwork with a forefinger around the edge of the lake, and away into the vanishing blue. Mother huddles her shawl around her, and tries to listen; Emil nods, very serious, as if his only wish is to hear more about the railway. Isabella nibbles on a boiled egg, and winks merrily at Ada: this sends a bolt of pure pleasure to Ada's groin, and she looks away. If she could, she would spend her whole birthday just with Isabella; they would go away, to some mountain hut, with a crackling fire, and they'd lie together, entwined in blankets, and eat curds and rustic bread and berries picked from the bushes. What would happen then is a startling blank; she can never get any further than their legs entangling, than a drowsy serious look coming over Isabella's face, before she turns her mind away to other things. Still, there is the promised trip to the Zoological Gardens to look forward to, tomorrow. Isabella has said it will be just the two of them, that they will go and admire the leopard prowling in his den . . .

Father drones on. "I may count on your help, with the specifics, the hire of labor, and so forth?" He is looking at Emil very seriously from under his eyebrows. Emil flushes with pleasure; all but presses a hand to his breast in gratitude. Isabella rolls her eyes. *He idolizes your father,* she says to Ada sometimes, *it's almost embarrassing. I suppose it's gratitude for taking him in after his own father—you know . . .*

Now Isabella says: "Wilhelm, it is terribly interesting, all this, but I wonder if we might change the subject. It's Ada's birthday, after all, and I doubt she wants to hear any more about the bridge, or whatever it is . . ."

She is so bright and twinkling that it is impossible to resist her. If anyone else were to speak to Father like this, they would get a sharp retort; be banned from the house, practically, for their *insufferable impertinence*. But ever since she came, laughing, into their garden—hanging on Emil's arm, one day in summer—she has bewitched them all. None of them can say no to her. Father blusters for a moment, looks stunned, then softens. He reaches for a piece of schnitzel and anoints it with lemon juice. "Of course," he says. "What would you like to talk about, Ada?"

Emil has turned his cold gaze on her. He is furious, she knows, at the interruption; somehow blaming her for it, though it was Isabella's suggestion. He is always seeking some angle for advancement. If not the bridge, he will want to talk about the summer home he hopes to build, next to their own, here on the lake shore; the apartment near the Hofburg he and Isabella have their eye on.

"I don't mind," she says, and is then inspired: "The opera?"

"The opera," Father accedes. He reaches for a grape, sucks it into his mouth, spits the pip. "I thought the soprano struggled for security in the upper register."

Isabella bursts out: "But that final aria—how can you say such a thing? Wilhelm, you are a philistine. It made me cry, didn't it, Ada?"

Ada will remember that moment for as long as she lives, she thinks: Isabella, leaning forward in her seat, her expression rapt; smelling of warm perfume, lily of the valley, as they listened to the crowning duet. The way she'd swiped tears from the corners of her eyes; stood to applaud, dragging Ada to her feet, too. Afterward, linking her arm with Ada, leaving the Opera House: "That—that is true love they were singing about. Make a note." That warm squeeze of the elbow, as they'd walked out into the night together.

"Sentiment," Emil says. He sounds uneasy. He looks out at the lake again. "I might take the coracle out."

The family's rowing boat can be seen, upturned at the edge of the reedbeds: its hull like a smooth chestnut carapace. In summer, Emil sometimes goes all the way to Podersdorf, talks to the fishermen, wheedles some of their catch, returns triumphant with quicksilver hanging from each hand.

"Oh! That *man*," says Mother, clapping her hands in sudden remembrance. "That strange person, who hailed us a cab. Where did he come from? Did anybody know him?"

Father shakes his head, and tuts. "Were we supposed to tip him?" Mother wonders. "Is it some new thing? I thought for a moment he knew you; that he was a friend of yours, Emil. Are you sure he wasn't some connection from the firm? Someone from when you were in lodgings?"

Emil shakes his head. "Never seen him before in my life."

"How strange," she says.

"Actually, I will go out on the lake." He stands, decisive.

"Oh, no, Emil, it's too cold," Isabella says. She has dropped Ada's hand. "And we said we'd get the five o'clock train—"

"Aren't you staying tonight?" Ada asks. She has had the evening all mapped out in her mind: Isabella and she will sit on the couch in the salon, and Isabella will stroke her hair, and they will read a magazine together: Isabella's face close to hers, poring over the fashions, in which Ada will have no interest. "What about the zoo, tomorrow?"

Mother, too, looks confused at the change of plan. "I thought we'd have a nice supper together, and there's Ada's cake—we didn't get to it yesterday—"

"A quick trip out to take the air," Emil says. "I won't go far. Maybe Ada could come with me. Ada, come."

Ada opens her mouth and closes it again—later, she will think, this was when it began, when the noise she hoped to make was not the one that came out. "But the leopard—" she says. Humiliating tears have come to her eyes and started to fall. She lowers her head, hoping to hide it from them, but of course it doesn't work.

Isabella looks agonized. "I know, dear one, but some other time? The zoo isn't going anywhere. We'll go together, later in the summer?"

"Oh, Ada," says her father, in the tone of voice that means: *Why must you always be upset by every little thing?*

She sits, with her mother clucking, Isabella gripping her hand, Emil standing over her, and she cries in earnest, in front of them all, and is ashamed. "I wanted to see the leopard," she says.

She is aware of the maid, shifting uncomfortably in the background. Her mother murmurs that it has been too much excitement, that Ada has always been delicate; they should never have gotten her home so late. "Emil is offering to take you out on the water, now, Ada, why don't you go with him? A treat? You barely get to see him as it is. It will be refreshing."

"Yes, come with me, Ada," Emil says. He walks away from her, toward the boat.

"No," she says, and her mother makes a little ruffled sound of shock.

"We won't go far. Just to the first inlet and then back." He runs a thumb over his chin.

"Ada," says her father, stern, "why not go with Emil?"

"I won't." The sound is a croak.

Father again: "I don't see why you're being so difficult."

There is nothing for it but to go. She wants to cry, *Don't take me away from Isabella, from you all.*

She goes to stand—she wants to kick one of the huge beach pebbles at Emil's face—and her left foot gives way. She slips back onto her rear. They look at her, astonished, as she tries to stand again. Now her left arm is tingling, too. She makes a strangled sound, surprise, dismay, and looks back at them: the semicircle of faces, all turned her way. She cannot move. The sky gets white, the air too thin, and she falls.

She is put to bed and stays there. After three days, the movement returns to her left side; she can flex and open her fingers, reach for the water glass, turn the lamp on and off.

Her mother comes to sit with her, to encourage her, but still she cannot speak. When she tries to, it is as though her throat simply closes and nothing comes. It is opined that perhaps there, on the beach, after her *attack*, she caught cold, and that it is simply a sore throat. But in a week there is no progress. She resorts to an exercise book and pencil. *I am trying. I can't. It doesn't work.*

"What can be behind this?" Father asks. "Is it because you didn't get your own way? Because Isabella refused to take you to the zoo?" He stands in the doorway, fists on hips. "Be honest, Ada. Are you pretending?"

She scribbles: *No.*

Beyond the bedroom door, she hears hushed conferences. Isabella arrives from Vienna. She bends over the bed and places the back of her hand on Ada's forehead. "My poor little kitten." Then: "I know a good man for this sort of thing, in the city," she murmurs, as much to Ada's parents as to Ada.

When she says the name, Ada's father recoils. "But yes, Wilhelm," Isabella says. "She needs help. I have heard of this kind of thing happening before. It is called aphonia. Poor poppet. It is a health problem like any other."

Ada's mother says she is sure she has no idea about modern medicine; Ada stares out of the attic window at the fishermen's boats bobbing on the lake, and so it is decided.

Rolf

——

THE OPERA HOUSE, AGAIN. Over the weeks, he has seen Billy's watchfulness flare, and the boy has started to preen, misinterpreting Rolf's constant presence as interest in his own waif-like person. More rouge, ever more spotless white gloves, meaningful glances. Rolf ignores him. To justify his presence, he turns the occasional trick, but he does so well before the end of the performance. He is always there, waiting, on the steps, when the doors open and the crowd appears. The runs and trills of *Der Rosenkavalier, Maria Stuarda, Eros Vainqueur* sing to him and only to him.

These last few nights of waiting he has felt like confiding in someone. He has wanted to talk to Eve and Julia, to say: *I saw a man, and he is different to the other men,* except that both of them have been distracted. He knows their trouble, but in his airy practical way, he wants to shake them both: *You cannot have a child together! It is physically impossible! But I, I need you now. Look at me!*

In the way of such things, the man appears like a stage trick—hey presto! One moment you don't see him, then you do, and it seems inevitable that he would appear, and that it would be this precise evening, with the lindens around the square in front of the Opera House starting to froth with white blossom. When it happens, Rolf is striding out of the alley, and there the young man is, on the steps before the rest of the issuing crowd and without the hangers-on from last time. He is smoking furiously.

Rolf pulls himself up, still pocketing the Kronen, while his gentleman from just now scurries back inside. He allows himself a moment to look, and ask himself the questions that Eve and Julia would have asked, had he confided in them: *Why him? Why is this one special?* Is it that he is handsome, in the way that a spoiled child is handsome? Is it that he looks as though he has walked through some great trial, and come out laughing? Rolf cannot tell. He walks forward, to where the man stands, and says, "Hello, again. Can I trouble you for a light?"

The man turns toward him with a startled glance. For a moment, he seems to have forgotten. Then, clouding knowledge. He flicks a match. "You're welcome," he says incongruously.

Behind them, the shuffle of feet, laughter; the crowd start to pour out onto the steps. They look at each other, and move a few feet to the right, out of the main flow. There is a gold wedding band on the man's finger. Rolf says, pointing to his own heart: "That last aria always pierces me here."

"Yes," the man says.

"Some say it's entirely too modern. But I think, *Salomé*—a tale as old as time . . ." Rolf affects nonchalance: they are just two people in conversation after a shared artistic experience. He makes sure his face is in the light, to its best advantage; he has always been told he has a strong, aristocratic nose. "Not with your chaperones tonight?"

The man's long lashes flutter. He isn't sure whether or not to be offended. Then the sharp bark of a laugh. "Not tonight," he says. "Frau Bauer has a headache."

"And your wife?"

The man blinks. "She has a headache too."

It is so obviously a lie that Rolf grins; almost laughs in his face. "So you're alone," he says. He almost proposes they use the alley straightaway, but something stops him: fear on the man's face. He is younger than Rolf first thought: twenty-five at the outside. "They are the engineering Bauers," he says, "Herr Bauer is my employer."

Rolf pretends to search his memory. "Oh, *those* Bauers. And you are a Bauer?"

The man smiles, looks down. "I am a Kellner. Emil. Emil Kellner." He says his own name as if testing it for the first time. The hand holding his cigarette seems to tremble, or it may be a trick of the light.

Around them, the crowd swells, calls to each other; there is the jingle of bells as fiacres draw around. Rolf taps out his own cigarette. "Well. Here's what I propose." He produces his card. "It's clear you are a lover of the greatest art form in the world. You work in the Innere Stadt? How about a drink, say tomorrow afternoon? Around six? I know a place on the Michaelerplatz where we can talk in private."

He puts a hand on Emil's forearm. Emil says yes, it should be possible. He pockets the card, frowning, perhaps knowing he has been the victim of some kind of unorthodoxy, and that he has walked into it willingly. "I have to get back now," he says.

"See you tomorrow," Rolf says smoothly, and Emil says, again, "Yes." He pats the pocket with Rolf's card in, and walks away; turns once as if to say something else, but decides against it.

Just another trick, Rolf thinks to himself, *money in my pocket*, as he walks home.

When Rolf walks into the Michaelerplatz the next day, he sees Emil already sitting outside the Café Chrome. It wouldn't be Rolf's choice: it is flashy, touristic. Emil's hands are folded in his lap and he looks expectant, penitent, and wicked. Rolf is sure, then, that he knows what he is about; he has done this before, picked up men; maybe often.

But when Rolf sits, he sees that Emil is also agitated, and so he revises his opinion. Emil orders coffee, then corrects himself: he will have red wine. He keeps wiping his upper lip with a nervous pinching gesture of the left hand.

"I'm glad you came," Rolf says. Sometimes honesty is best.

Emil squints into the late sun. "I'm glad I came too," he says, sounding surprised at the words.

It would be too soon to take him somewhere now. Rolf asks questions about the opera, about politics, but Emil gives one-word answers, so he asks again about the Bauers. "Such a great man," Emil says, fidgeting with his wineglass. "My mother is Frau Bauer's sister. They took me in when I was sixteen. I have become something of an intimate in the family."

He is curious, with questions of his own. Where does Rolf live? What is his occupation? *Danzig, theater agent.* He never tells anyone that he lives in Leopoldstadt. And where is he from, originally? He, Emil, comes from a small village near Salzburg; not a very original place. He was glad to come here, to the city, under the auspices of his uncle, of course.

"I am an outsider," Rolf says, and smiles. He has no intention of saying more. His life before Vienna seems to have happened to someone else.

At six o'clock they graduate to Kir Royale. The crowd around them has started to thin out—too late for an aperitif, too early for supper; the waiter hovers, bored, by the café entrance. Judging it is the correct time, Rolf begins to speak of local history. It's said that the city walls were financed with the ransom money for King Richard the Lionheart, of England. Richard was found by Blondel, the faithful minstrel, who toured Europe singing under castle windows until one day he heard the song echoing back. "Some have said it was a love song they wrote together," he says.

Silence. Emil's eyes have turned dark; he fiddles with his napkin. He says: "I'd heard that too."

Rolf gets up and pushes his chair back and after a moment, Emil follows.

As they leave the Michaelerplatz, Rolf keeps glancing to his left, to see Emil is fixed on a horizon that seems unclear. The mechanical movement of their legs is nicely distracting, and the fact that they do not have to look at each other helps.

The evening is bright, high, and hazy; the days have begun to lengthen, and there are thin streaks of cloud across a Poussin sky. Everywhere, clerks and lawyers and businessmen and musicians and waiters with their ties loosened around their necks are making their way home to loved ones and families. At the next corner, where the entrance to the Rathauspark is, Rolf casually turns left. The iron gates rear up, still open. Emil stops and clears his throat. He is about to say something like, *I can't.* Some sap is rising up in him.

"We're just walking," Rolf says. His own voice sounds surprised. Emil hesitates, then steps toward Rolf, through the gate.

They jam their hands in their pockets and affect a long-legged stride. Emil is looking all over, evidently fearful of being recognized. He can almost hear the excuses being made: *This is Rolf, a friend of my employer. This is Rolf, an acquaintance from my school days.*

69

Rolf listens to the tap of their feet on the gravel, the shifting of the cloth of their waistcoats and trousers, the cries of children on a tour of the menagerie half a kilometer away.

They are approaching the thickets. It is still light, so there will be risk. Emil clears his throat, and Rolf slows his steps.

They have both stopped. "Well," Rolf says, with a smile, "I'm going in here." He walks nonchalantly toward the clutch of trees and bushes, where the undergrowth starts. He walks slowly, and for a long moment he feels Emil waiting behind him. He is patient, counting his steps: *One, two.* . . . Then he hears the crunch of feet on dry grass behind him.

Rolf pushes aside the branches at head height. He doesn't mind the twigs breaking across his calves. Behind him he can hear Emil's faltering footsteps.

Twenty slow seconds later, they are out of sight of the world, in a small space enclosed by bushes at head height. Above, the branches of lime trees extend, sticky with sap. The sound of the wind high in the tops, funneled down into the space, and a damp carpet of trampled grass beneath their feet.

Emil's face: he stands in the spotlight, the midpoint between being appalled and helplessly amused. He lifts his hands, whether in surrender or defense is unclear, and Rolf draws close, pulling at his lapels, pressing his lips to Emil's.

Emil lets out a little noise of surrender deep in the throat that makes Rolf dig his fingers into his upper arms. Then Emil stiffens, and begins to resist, and the noises edge into discomfort, alarm. "I have not—" he says.

"Haven't you?" Rolf asks. He is not sure whether this is true; sometimes the gentlemen like to protest their innocence too much before the act, as a last-ditch attempt at morality. He kisses Emil's face, his eyebrows; holds Emil capably, reaches for his fly and undoes it. "Like this?" he whispers, feeling the stiff silky warmth in the palm of his hand and hearing the low moan that comes with it. Emil slumps forward. Then his hands fly to Rolf's shoulders; he grasps the collar of Rolf's jacket, making the material uncomfortable around his throat.

Rolf strokes him. Emil's eyelashes flutter like a girl's: a frown of concentration appears. His palms press down on Rolf; his legs tremble, and he chokes out a series of escalating cries. A flurry of wind lifts his hair. Then that hallucinatory second: a glint of late sun in their eyes. Emil looks directly at Rolf, his mouth half-open, searching. His body jack-knifes.

Rolf is deft with a handkerchief; Emil leans against him, heavy-lidded. His weight is blocky with muscle. Then he appears to remember himself. He buttons up, stands back.

Golden light in the tiny space. Emil runs his fingers through his fringe. Rolf looks at the outline of Emil's wallet, held snugly in his jacket pocket. When they came into the park, when they came walking down the *Allees*, looking like older and much younger brother, like who knows what, when he led this boy here, he had it in his mind to charge a hundred Kronen—

"Can I see you again?" Emil asks. Rolf goes to answer. He frames the usual response—a flat *no* or a more courteous *I don't think so*— but instead finds himself thinking, *I can always charge double next time*, and saying: "Why not?" Emil smiles; a smirk, really. He catches at Rolf's hand, brings the forefinger to his lips to kiss.

Ada

————

IT'S ISABELLA WHO TAKES HER to Freud's; insists, to Ada's father—
"It needs a woman"—with that sideways half-sweep of the eyes
that says, *And you know your wife won't help.* It's Isabella who reaches
up for the buzzer by the front door of the clinic; who stands back
brightly and smiles, narrowing her eyes in thought. They wait in
silence, looking at each other. The sun seems bright on the cobbles,
on the recently rain-washed houses, on the line of Isabella's neck
and shoulders.

The door opens, and the doctor himself is there. He tells them
to come in. His secretary is away. He leads them away down a passage, and because Isabella is first and the passage is dark, Ada can't
see anything except his wiry back, the stoop of his shoulders.

They go up two flights of stairs and reach a waiting room and he
goes behind the desk and says: "Miss Ada Bauer! And . . ." Isabella
leans forward to make sure he has her name right. She underlines
the word hesitantly with her finger—companion.

The doctor stands watching, smiling as Ada stoops to write her
own name. He polishes his spectacles on his waistcoat. "Now you
come through here, that's right," he says.

Ada looks at Isabella, then back at the doctor, and he holds the
door open wider.

"The ferryman only admits one passenger," he says. The door
closes on Isabella mouthing, *I'll wait here,* and, *Don't worry.*

•

Inside the room are various *objets*. An Egyptian bust of a woman, nostrils flared; a homunculus made of clay. "You may wish to lie upon the couch," the doctor says, though it isn't yet midday.

Ada tests its dense, feathery compactness. The doctor is saying something about her voice. "Muteness? States of paralysis, according to your father? Down one side of the body only? Don't fear. It is never a case of not having anything to say. It is always a case of having a great deal to say. We will have, you and I, conversation." He cracks his knuckles.

A sheaf of paper and a pencil flop onto the couch. He is writing on his own little stack of notepaper, legs crossed at the knee, looking primly down. "Where should we begin?"

She is seven; holding a dandelion clock; bored, puffing to get the silk strands to disseminate, vaguely cross because they won't. The first time she sees Emil, he is with a woman who looks like her mother: thin, standing a few steps behind him. Her own mother, who must have been with her, rushes forward. "Ada, this is your aunt. My sister. Aunt Hilda. Say hello."

It already feels like a question she won't be allowed to ask: where have they come from? Why doesn't she know them already? The woman, Aunt Hilda, is wearing a gray dress like a maid's, and no gloves. "And this is your cousin Emil." A blur of pink features, and his eyes, a very dark brown, and he stoops to take her hand in his, and kisses it. His face is symmetrical—there is nothing wrong with it, as such—but he is sweating, which she finds disgusting, and, though he is very close, he won't meet her eyes. Her mother claps her hands together as if something has been settled that was in question: "What a gentleman! Delightful! You will be friends with your cousin, Ada, won't you?" She remembers how he runs his finger across his upper lip to remove the sweat.

"Ada, Emil is spending the summer with us, and then he will go to a young man's boarding house in Vienna and, in due course, start work in Father's firm. Won't that be fun?"

She is not sure what part of this she is supposed to find fun. It is well known in the village that she has no siblings, and when strangers ask, she says firmly, "No, and I have no wish for one, nasty business," and it makes the adults laugh, and there is always relief in the room. They go inside, and she is invited to show them the drawing room and second drawing room—"Here are Father's instruments"—guests are always told to admire his enormous brass set square and slide rule—"and more books, and Mother's embroidery chair." Hilda and Emil nod politely, some undercurrent running beneath their silence, and nobody comes to take them away. She realizes, with dawning irritation, that the guests will be staying to lunch. She likes it when it's just the three of them, her and Father and Mother, and when Father asks her about her day. Now she won't get to tell him how next door's dog broke into the garden, how she helped the maid with the laundry and the maid said she was such a clever little thing, and see him wag his finger and say, "You know we pay them for a reason. You are my great girl. You are a lady."

At lunch, Emil stares at the silver knives and forks until someone else starts eating, and this, too, is strange, because he looks hungry to her: hungry and thin, like his mother. Aunt Hilda chatters, and Ada dislikes her, because she is what Father calls *a bore*, like the Mayor of Neusiedl, with his *racehorse obsession*. It's all about train timetables and what a good boy Emil is and how far advanced in his studies and how pleased he will be to get to know his family better. She supposes the distance has been the reason; she cannot think why they fell out of touch so completely, when in truth they were in her thoughts every day! It really is so good of them—*so good*—after. . . . And here she trails off and dabs the corners of her eyes with her handkerchief and Ada sees, with further disgust, that she is crying. She looks at Father, who cannot abide a weepy woman, and at the table.

Her mother reaches across and places her hand over Hilda's. "It's not your fault," Ada's mother says, darting little glances at Father, who is bright red, drumming his fingers on the tabletop.

All he says, with a sigh, is: "We did try to warn you before you married him—" But her mother says—and Ada draws in a breath, because she never raises her voice to Father—"Wilhelm, we all wish the situation was other than it was, but is it helpful, now, to keep on saying he was no good? We were all fooled. He was a soldier, wasn't he? And for many years, he seemed perfectly respectable . . ."

She turns to look at Emil, making some kind of decision. "I am sorry, dear. We shouldn't, perhaps, discuss this in front of the boy—"

"It's perfectly all right." Until now he has barely spoken. His voice is low and pleasant; it would be useful to sound like that, Ada thinks; one could persuade an adult of anything.

Who *are* these people? He goes on eating placidly, appearing not to listen as they discuss the mysterious someone, a Captain in the Hussars, whom they evidently do not like. Just the fine tremor of his hand gives away that anything is wrong at all.

That afternoon, when she is supposed to be having her nap, she looks out of the window and sees Emil and Aunt Hilda standing by the gate. Or rather, Emil is standing still, while Hilda droops from him; hangs around his neck, like Ada used to with Mother, when she was little. The window is open and so she can hear Hilda's wailing from here. Ada says, out loud, in the relative cool of the room: "Making a spectacle of herself." Emil's hands are hopeless by his sides, his face expressionless. Mother stands a few feet back, watching, and eventually, when the whole ghastly business has gone on far too long, she steps forward. "Come now, you'll miss your train. Come. Let him go." She pries Hilda's arms from around Emil's neck—he reaches up to massage his throat with his long fingers—and escorts her to the carriage waiting just by the gatepost.

Emil lives with them for the rest of the summer. He keeps out of Ada's way, and spends his days studying or swimming in the lake. At first, Father and Emil do not take to each other, to Ada's secret delight. "Too like that bloody man," she catches him muttering to Mother, when he thinks he is not overheard. Mother does not protest too much. Ada sees it in Emil: his consternation. He is always trying to get a private word with Father, to take him for walks, or to tempt him with an *article of interest in the* Allgemeine *on the topic of the Wannsee Bridge.*

But there comes a day, toward the end of August, when Emil bursts into hot tears at some offhand remark of Father's; she feels for him, because he is sixteen, and to cry would be shameful even at her age. "You do not want me here," he rages. "You think I am like my father—rotten, disgusting!" To her surprise, Father folds him in his arms. "I do not think that. I do not think you are no good." Later that afternoon, Emil is invited on the walk she usually goes on with Father alone, down to the beach. "Ada, don't pout. Emil is our guest, and our family." They skim stones, stones that are too big for Ada to fit in her hand, and Emil quickly achieves the maximum number of skips she and Father have ever managed, which is seven. The flat pebble arcs away, spritzing the surface of the water, vanishing, and he grins and shades his eyes to watch. On the way back to the house, he and Father walk together, and Father points out a hawk, hovering over the forest; he places his palm between Emil's shoulder blades as they stare. The hawk shoots down and pierces the treeline, impossibly sleek and fast.

He leaves for the Internat, the boarding home for young boys, in Vienna one day in early autumn. Father hands him an envelope; he folds it into his waistcoat with a deferent nod, and Mother kisses him on either cheek. "Be good. Be clever. Show those city boys what you're made of."

He writes; twice, sometimes three times a week. Father reads the letters over the dining table, frowning at the handwriting, which he says is still very juvenile. The paper is cheap and greasy and Ada sees many crossings-out and splurges of ink. Emil writes that the other *young men* are all *good sorts* and that it is *good to get to know a few different fellows.* He has one especial friend, Peter, and otherwise is something of a friend to all; not all the young men have the benefit of such generous families willing them on. When he does return, he spreads his arms and walks forward into Mother's. He is broader of shoulder and clearer of eye; he looks at Ada and says, "Hello, little duck," and Mother smiles. Ada remains stony. "Give your big cousin a kiss hello," Mother says, prodding her forward. She stands on tiptoes and brushes his chin with her lips. The bristles are spiny like an urchin; he turns his cheek so that his cheekbone bumps hers.

◆

Emil is on one of his man-walks with Father, where they disappear into the forest for hours on end, their hands laced behind their
backs, talking about God-knows-what. She creeps into his room
and goes through his things. There is money—considerable money,
to her, a wallet full of Kronen, the bills much handled and burst-
ing out of the leather wallet, like so many green tongues; a card-
backed photograph of a man in cavalry uniform, against a painted
mountain backdrop. She lifts it out. The eyes are the giveaway: that
hunted, pleading, austere look; the way the man holds his silver
sword to attention, and manages to make it look not a part of him
at all. She puts the photograph of Emil's father aside and upends
the haversack but not much else falls out: an ivory-handled pocket-
knife, a dog-eared pack of cards in a faded cardboard container.
The knave of clubs slips to the floor and grins up at her.

   She returns to the wallet. There are fistfuls of notes; it is jingling
with cash. This cannot, surely, be right. When they went to the out-
door swimming baths, she was permitted shavings of strawberry-
flavored ice in a paper cone, and to ask the vendor for the item
herself, trotting across the cobbles. She remembers how the pink
liquid snaked down her hand. That was just a couple of Kronen.
There must be hundreds here, and hasn't Father said, *Poor Emil, but
we must keep him on a tight financial leash until we see how he turns out?*
Where has he got so much money from? Isn't he supposed to be
her pauper cousin? She stares at the knave of clubs, and kicks him
under the bed.

After she has told him, after she has slipped into Father's study and
explained, and he has listened and taken the wallet and counted
the notes himself, she feels sick, like the brackish water around
the reedbeds. She wants urgently to be with her mother, and runs
to the salon. "This is a nice surprise, darling, but wouldn't you
rather play outside?" It is not too late in the year, though the pine
needles have begun their slow, settling descent. She shakes her
head and buries her face in her mother's stomach. She is gently
pried away: her mother has gone pink, as she always does when
Ada *rushes at her*, and she reaches for her book with an absent,
confused air.

Ada hears the door to Father's study open. Emil's voice says, "You wanted to see me?" And the door closes quietly. She perches on the edge of the sofa and says: "You'd love me, wouldn't you, you and Father? However bad I was? Not like Emil, where his mother sent him away?"

Mother puts the book down—it is one of those romances of which Father disapproves—and looks at her. The gaze is milky, unfocused. "Ada. What a question. It was different. Hilda was sad. And there was no money. That is why. It's not the same. At all."

Ada expects the rumble of her father's temper, the undulation of raised voices. She hears instead low, reasoned argument. Cold settles in her stomach. She needs the toilet. The voices hum and drone, and she sits. The first fire is in the grate, and the wood is green, spitting. It is a sharp white day outside; some hours of light left. She could run to the forest, lose herself there. She pictures herself found after some days, shrouded in a blanket; her mother's tears.

Father comes and it is terrible. He seems tired, instead of angry. "Ada," he says. He hangs on the doorframe. Emil, she senses, is just behind him. Mother looks up, quick and frowning. "Ada, Emil has something to say to you, and you, I expect, to him."

So they are going to do the telling-off in front of everybody. Sure enough, there he is, sliding through and into the room. He comes across and sits on the ottoman and laces his hands between his knees. He says: "I know it must be difficult for you, having been an only child for so long, and as an only child myself, I can sympathize. I, too, never liked having to share."

He smiles as if at a private joke. Father has crossed his arms. Mother says, "Wilhelm, what's this about?"

Emil says, in his good, honeyed voice: "I know you are jealous and that is understandable. I know you were only trying to protect your father by looking through my things. Perhaps you think I am unreliable. The money is not stolen. It is not gambled for. I am keeping it for a friend, for Peter, who is at the Internat, only temporarily. I think I mentioned him in my letters."

"You mentioned him a lot." She is courageous in misery, miserable in her courage.

Her mother says: "For shame, Ada."

Emil blinks. "We must try to be friends, Ada, you and I. I will prove to you that I can be a brother to you, if you let me."

He is very close. He will chuck her under the chin and she will hit him. She looks him in the eye, knowing what is expected. The room hesitates, hovers. "I am sorry," she says. There is no feeling behind the words and she knows it and he does too.

Her father lets his breath out. "That's settled. No more, please. Emil, you have behaved handsomely. I apologize, too, on behalf of our daughter."

Emil turns his gaze on Father. "It was a misunderstanding. May I take Ada to the lake? Perhaps a boating trip? That is what brothers do, isn't it?" He looks at her now, fully and frankly, without warmth: "There are still a couple of hours of daylight left."

He fetches her coat himself, lays it gently around her shoulders. She had it for her birthday; her birthday coat. The green velvet collar rubs her neck.

He walks ahead of her on the path down through the garden, over the road and onto the beach, his arms crossed. He says nothing and nor does she. She thinks that she could run back to the house at any moment she chooses; plead a headache; be gathered in her mother's arms; at least until they are out of sight of the house. But there would be a scolding: the thin line of Father's lips. So she wastes time, wondering, and then they have dipped down onto the beach, and they are both slipping on the pebbles.

At this time of year, the reeds in the shallow water are starting to rot; their stalks lie flat and brown, and give off a smell of failure. They make the tugging-free of the little boat awkward; he is not quite a man, not yet, his waist is narrow and for a moment it seems he cannot manage it. Then she sees that he is strong enough, after all: he flips the boat over and pushes it, scraping and groaning, toward the water.

"Get in," he says, his face turned away from her. He leaps over the bow. He lifts the oars from the base of the boat and slips them into the locks; sits.

She could run. But she moves forward. Her feet and ankles become wet. She clambers over and into the boat; lifts her skirt out of the inch of slopping, scummy water. Hasn't Mother always said that boating is for gentlemen? She sits opposite him, on the passenger bench.

"You are what? Eight?" he says. He draws the oars in big broad strokes, toward and away. The water funnels around them. Strips of cloud lie on the horizon, over toward Podersdorf; a couple of boats over toward the village; the glint of a fishing line. The light is flat and angular.

She sinks her chin into the velvet of her collar. "Who is Peter?" she asks. "The one in your letters, that you write about endlessly. Why would you be keeping money for him?"

His nostrils flare, which is how she knows her instinct was correct. There is something there: what it might be she doesn't know. "A boy," he says. "Nobody. You wouldn't understand." He looks out at the lake and shakes his head, as if for one of his invisible audiences: the temerity of her question.

"How did you get the money? What really happened with your father? What did he die of?"

There is nothing new about his expression of cold dislike. He says: "He died in battle."

"Liar. They found him, dead, in a house of ill repute. Worse than a usual one." She isn't sure what this means, but remembers her mother's phrase. It seems a bad enough thing to say, here, to wound him, to let him know she knows. "Gambling is when you play cards with bad people, when you're in with the wrong crowd. Is that how you got the money?"

He shakes his head. "You know what happened to me when I was eight?"

How could she know? The oars dip and spin. A slender arrow of geese ascends from the surface of the lake, two hundred feet away. The inch of water in the bottom of the boat has become two, or three. "I didn't have Mummy and Daddy to adore me. I didn't have smocking and dirndls and patent-leather shoes. I didn't have apple sauce when I was ill. Everything you want, you get. How is that? *And* you're a girl."

He leans on the oars. The boat starts to drift in a semicircle. They are in their own eddy. His fingers are long and thin. Her piano tutor would kill for her to have those hands; she can barely make an octave.

"And you're a girl," he says again.

She knows from what her parents have said about other families, other little girls, that they grow up to marry gentlemen, who
can maintain them and take on the business at the right time. "I
wouldn't marry you in a thousand years," she says. She feels her
smallness, her loneliness, in the slick wind whipping her hair around
her cheeks, bringing the scent of pine needles from the shore.

"Stand in the gunwale," he says. "The front of the boat. The tip.
Get up and stand there, and close your eyes."

She can see he is quite serious. He locks the oars in place, leans
forward on his knees, hunkering down.

"I won't," she says, at the same time as he says, "You must. Little
children must be shown their place." He snatches for her, grabs
her arm and hauls her to her feet. The boat rocks crazily. He lifts
her, his feet spread apart—it is easy, so obviously easy that she goes
limp and allows herself to be carried—and deposits her in the front,
where the prow makes a V, where one could lose one's balance. She
almost pitches forward and he holds her by the back of the coat.
"Stay," he says. "Stand still."

She is poised as if for flight, her arms spread wide, balancing. The
water is deep and green and glassy. There is nothing: no drifting
weed beneath the surface, not the winking of fish.

He lets go of her. He is behind her. The boat sways.

"Look at the water. Look at yourself." Her own reflection swims,
ghastly: the whiteness of her extended fingertips. Beyond that, the
lace of the clouds. "Say this: *I deserve this. I deserve it.* If you ever
misbehave again, I will hurt you, and it will be worse than this, and
you'll never see it coming. Say it. *I am a bad girl.*"

She mouths the words. "Again. Louder."

"I am a bad girl."

"Louder."

She shouts it. Tears in her eyes. The sound rings out across the
water.

She hears him sit, and pick up the oars. "You can get down now,"
he says. His tone is friendly. "Let's get home before it rains."

"Darling, how was it?" Isabella follows Ada through the street to
the cab. She catches at Ada's hand before Ada can mount the steps.

"Are you cured?" Ada shakes her off, but gently, and gets into the back of the carriage, where she lets her head loll against the inside wall and closes her eyes, hoping that Isabella's curious gaze will slide away.

Once home, she runs out of the cab and up the stairs so fast she almost doesn't hear her father saying to Isabella: "Well?" In a tone that means: *Why isn't she speaking already?*

Later, her mother and father come up and sit with her. Her mother holds her hand, and her father sits on the other side of the bed (unheard of) and they look at her for a long time. Isabella is there too, in the doorway, with one hand on the doorpost.

"What did the doctor say?" her father asks. He fixes her with a frowning gaze, as if the question, and the lack of an instant answer, were somehow her fault. He reaches for her hand (also unheard of: he is playing the father for Isabella's benefit) and taps the back of it briefly.

"Was he very pleasant?" her mother asks, her voice quavering. "Did he tell you about some of his other patients, in your situation?"

Ada plays with the edge of the quilt. She is so tired. She wants everyone to go.

With an air of heavy disappointment, her father gets to his feet. "We'll leave you to rest," he says. Her mother follows—"Sleep well, darling"—though it's only four o'clock in the afternoon, and the business of the day will go on uninterrupted for hours. The bustle of it, tantalizingly out of reach.

And then there is just her and Isabella, Isabella standing in her odd lounging position in the doorway and Ada feeling very young, with the blankets held high around her.

Isabella crosses to the bed. She makes a business of smoothing the already-smooth coverlet; lifting a strand of Ada's hair. "I think you were very brave today," she says.

Ada squeezes her eyes to stop the tears coming out. Isabella has lifted her hand to her mouth and is kissing it, and resting it against her palm. Her eyes are closed, her chin turned down toward Ada's wrist.

The thing Ada has so longed for seems as if it might be possible. She plays out her hopes silently, leaping ahead five seconds: imagines Isabella opening her eyes, only halfway, and with a drowsy look leaning in and pressing her lips to—but instead, Isabella keeps her hand captured for a moment, then places it back on the coverlet. On her face is guilt. "I am sorry I can't make it better for you." Ada nods; takes back Isabella's hand and holds it, shy but firm.

In the small hours, she wakes and finds Emil sitting on the edge of the bed, looking into the darkness in the corners of the room. Seeing she's awake, he fixes his gaze on her—the whites of his eyes, thin rinds, are visible—and sends her a simple message. *If you tell the doctor about me, I'll know.* Then he stumbles out of the room.

Julia

——

THERE WAS NO PRECISE MOMENT of longing for a child. The desire has been growing in her with the stealthy patience of a wave approaching the shore. That time in the Prater, with the lost little girl, with Eve was a crystallization—how sweet it had been, to see Eve bend toward the child with an expression of such concern—but the truth is there have been many shocks, different in nature. Sometimes, it's been possible to see it only in negative: when Heidi told them she was pregnant, for example; the sharp pain of it. Sometimes, it blooms out of the darkness: the sensation of chubby fingers in hers. Sometimes it's just a hollowness. *There should be something there*, she thinks, often, on waking from yet another dream, touching her stomach with the flat of her palm: a promise.

She finishes work around three o'clock that Friday. Lately, with the warmer weather, she has taken to walking the long route instead of going straight home; the chance to buy flowers, if there's a little money at the end of the week, or to browse for Frau Berndt's birthday present. The city is lit with spring's generous clarity. If she is alongside the river, she can imagine the glassy inlets and rippling waves of Stockholm Harbor.

She takes care to watch everything as she passes: the gaggle of students, turning to look her way; the outline of the piano teacher's face on the second floor of the music school, her hands waving as she conducts an invisible student; the tubercular cough of a waiter, leaning aside from the table to splutter into his hand. It is useful to notice everything, because it stops her from thinking too much. Useful, too, to be in motion: the swift brush-brush of her skirts against her legs.

She walks down to the Ringstrasse, across—she is narrowly missed by a whistling tram—and into the old city. She likes to walk the smart streets around the Stephansdom, where the rich people live. Her dress is careful gray and she would, she imagines, be taken for a servant by any observer; but she moves with her shoulders back, imagining the Louis XIV chairs, the vast mirrors.

At home, with the saucepan boiling for coffee, Julia examines the post. The stamps are both Swedish. The handwriting on the first envelope is bold and angular and belongs to Cousin Grete. The second is thin and faded, the lines of her address rising slightly toward the right-hand side. It takes her a second—more than a second. Later, she will be relieved, that he has slipped so completely out of her existence that his handwriting was not obvious.

A thing she has never told Eve: that he saw her go. She was at the top of the stairs with her suitcases, and he at the bottom; Eve waiting in the orchard. One of his hands was on the newel post—he had been about to come upstairs.

There was no need to state the obvious: or was there? He was poised, upward looking. The blue discs of his irises, the famous flyaway hair.

"I'm going," she said. It sounded like a line from something. She began down the stairs, and each step got dizzier and harder, until he was very close.

He turned his head to follow her progress to the door.

"I'm leaving," she said. *He thinks I'm coming back*, she thought. Perhaps not this year, but next year, or the year after.

Fascinated, she stepped closer to him again. "Will you grieve?" she asked. "Of course not. You'll write a play about it."

She left under the auspices of her own cruelty. The rest of the business of the house went on: through the open window, the leaves in the trees sounded like cards being shuffled.

He has written an elegant letter, the subtext to which is, as always, that words come easily; that this is his enormous fortune and it makes him invulnerable, all-powerful.

She reads three lines, puts the letter down, goes to pour the coffee, spills coffee on her skirt, curses, works on the stain for five minutes before she picks it up again. *Julia*—the temerity of the informal address—*it seems you have chosen the greatest city in the world to be your home. Your mother was prevailed upon to share your address, thinking no great harm could come of my writing after such a time apart.* (Julia hisses.) *I myself have moved to Gothenburg, where my latest work is premiering before a full tour of the Low Countries and beyond. The work is the work and yet on some days it seems we make progress.*

In one passage he describes the snow outside his house in the mountains—violet in hue at dawn and dusk, glittering like a mad thing. He confesses to envying her the cosmopolitan nature of the city. *The boldness of your gesture makes me question myself. Have I simply stayed with what is safe? I have your pianoforte here—I shipped it back with me from France—and occasionally think I hear you playing in the next room.*

In the final paragraph, he speaks about the moment of writing. *It is midnight and I am, surely, the last one awake. I am unsure of the reason for this letter if not to ask one question, Julia: are you happy?*

Rolf

—

ONE OF THOSE EVENINGS, where everything is made strange by the warm and hovering air; the plants in pots either side of the door are waxy and silent, watchful. Rolf ducks into the inner doorway and puts the key that Emil gave him into the lock.

The door opens without creaking—there is gleaming parquet, the shutters are bright white, outlining the late-afternoon sun. To make things feel more natural, he stands as if he owned the apartment—pretending to be a rich engineering contact of Emil's, staying overnight to do some deal.

The books on the shelf in the bedroom are boringly touristic—slim volumes on the pleasures of Vienna for the business traveler. There are no hairs in the washstand, only one wineglass under the sink, and the coverlet is not rumpled. There are no portraits or pictures. Nothing down the back of the chest of drawers. He makes fish-faces at his uncertain self in the mirror.

Leaving the shutters open, he goes back into the salon and there he dances, slips on the glossiness of the floor. He runs his finger along the mantelpiece; sits in the green velvet horsehair chair. He is forced to admit that the apartment is very fine.

Emil arrives at quarter past seven, carrying bags of shopping. "You found it without any trouble," he says, earnest, brushing the hair out of his eyes. He lifts a bottle of red out of a bag with a flourish; adjusts it on the table. The light makes it bloody.

They are both thinking, probably, of two days ago, in the Rathauspark again; Emil had turned his face to the tree trunk and braced. Rolf, gentle, reaching for the vial in his inner pocket. "Have you done this, before?" "No, but I want to now." He'd turned back: coquettish, pale. "I don't want to hurt you," Rolf said, out of nowhere; still half cross at finding himself here again. The bushes tickled his ankles. *Too old for this.* As if he'd heard it, the boy, after his cries had built into moans, after he'd come without touching himself, his whole body shaking: "I have an apartment. The Bauers do. Let me take care of you." Bright red smeared on his buttocks, trailing down his thighs. "Did it hurt?" Rolf had asked, surprised to find he wanted to know the answer. "Hurt?" Emil had said, blinking, puzzled. "Yes." It seemed not to have occurred to him that it should have been painless.

Emil has brought warm food from a *traiteur*: delicate little things that make Rolf want to laugh. Emil fidgets, casting nervous glances around the apartment. "It belongs—" he says, and Rolf waves a hand.

"I know—to Herr Bauer. Tell me more. About you."

It is an old trick; never fails with the shyer clients. His mental tally has gone up: he is owed, by his reckoning, three hundred Kronen.

Emil says: "I am not interesting. Tell me about you."

He has put down his knife and fork; very well brought up, he is, sandy eyelashes fluttering as he checks the position of the cutlery. He pours more wine; leans forward in a position of rapt attention.

Rolf laughs. If this is part of the game, then he can play. It might be fun to tell him a few things. "I grew up in the mountains. The Tyrol," he says, and waggles his eyebrows. "Goats were my only company, along with my mother and sisters. That enough for you? It was despicably boring, a small village. There really is nothing to say." He laughs, wanting to change the subject.

"More," Emil says. "What then? Why did you leave?"

"Who wouldn't? There was nobody like me there. There was *no opera*." He is trying to make Emil smile, too. As he says it, he recalls the feeling: the loneliness in the pit of the stomach. His sister's shocked face, when she caught him wearing one of her scarves, when he was just a little boy. "I left as soon as I could and I've never been back. When I see a postcard of a mountain in a news kiosk, I feel sick."

Emil cuts a sliver of meat. "No lovers?" he says.

Rolf snorts at the idea. "Whom would I have loved? The village priest?"

The knife screeches on Emil's plate; he looks out from under his eyebrows. "Did you? Do I require to be jealous?"

He's like a woman, Rolf thinks, wildly flattered, melting. *He has learned this from somewhere; has learned to flirt and finesse a situation. But then,* he thinks, *he's married—in some ways he knows more about this—this having of dinner and staying the night—more than me.*

Emil takes the plates into the kitchen. It is the first time Rolf has admitted to himself that he won't ask for any money; that it is too late for this to be considered a material exchange. His leg jiggles on its own under the table. Emil pauses, shy, in the doorway. "Coffee now, or later?"

The bed is vast, dark wood, like something from the Belvedere; the sheets look expensive. Rolf turns, capable, reaching for Emil, but Emil bats his hands away.

He stands back from Rolf; takes off his jacket and waistcoat. Unbuttons his shirt. All the time keeping his gaze steady. They are eye to eye. Rolf sits on the edge of the bed. The shirt is shrugged off. "I want you to see me—" Emil says. "Just me—"

"My dear boy"—the words come unbidden. The torso emerges; flat planes from exercise, the skin littered with freckles. A vest, lifted overhead; shoes kicked off, the smart shoes that Rolf admires, of daring tan leather, the soles still lined with mud from the park. The trousers slide down his hips.

He is not showing off. It is a statement of fact. An image, from the height of some imagined summer: this boy, running toward Rolf, in the shallows of a lake, water in his eyes. This person and no other. Now he advances on Rolf, who leans away at first; the image is too heavy and too bright, and he feels an urge to push Emil away, to be out on the streets, among people. Emil shushes him, and Rolf lets himself be held, manipulated; rubbed and stroked, whispered to. In the privacy of his mind, the clink of coins, but distant. "Let me take care of you," Emil says again. Rolf says, "Yes."

Emil puts his hands in between Rolf's thighs and pushes them apart; settles on his stomach on top of Rolf: "Will you let me?"

Rolf laughs, uncertain—it is not his practice to be submissive to another man. He usually works with just his mouth; the occasional older gentleman wants to be serviced, in a hotel or in the thickets of the park; there, and in his private life, he makes sure to be on top. He cannot remember the last time anyone asked him for this—five years ago? Seven? It was not so much that it was painful; but he remembers not feeling like himself, lying spreadeagled on his front. There was no elegance; no control.

"Let me try," Emil says. "If you can?" He is frowning down at Rolf tenderly; his body is tense with restraint, his teeth set; the picture of frustrated desire. *I can give him this favor*, Rolf thinks. It is like a spell: Emil looks, with the evening light slatted through the shutters, as though he's made of porcelain and gold. "I will have to turn over," he says, "my hips—" Emil makes a sound like a growl, and watches him turn onto his stomach.

Later—much later—he confesses: "I was going to ask you for money, that first time. And again tonight."

Emil is lying next to him, on his back; leans over to play with a wisp of Rolf's springy hair. "I know," he says, and settles his head on Rolf's shoulder.

Ada

———

ADA HARDLY SEES EMIL for several weeks. He keeps to her father's study, where they pore over maps of the new railway. One day, she passes him in the downstairs corridor and he is standing at the window looking out, his Adam's apple jumping in his throat, and he does not seem to see her at all.

She becomes something to discuss in polite company. He and Isabella are there most nights at these summer supper parties in the house by the lake: she, twirling the stem of her wineglass, all teeth and eyes; he, holding his knife and fork, but really gripping the silver. Herr Bauer will say: "Our Ada is undergoing a course of psychoanalysis, you see, for her voice." Inquiring murmurs from the guests; questions about the doctor. "Herr Doktor Freud," he'll respond, and there are more polite, imprecise sounds, because Freud is a known genius, is definitely expensive, but also a Jew.

"And is it helping, dear?" one middle-aged lady asks, leaning into the table with an expression of sympathy. "Oh, but—" She has confused herself. "Is it an improper question? Can she not speak at all?" She looks around at the other guests and blushes and laughs. Then asks the question again, of Ada, who sees Emil watching her as she shakes her head.

After the fourth session, Isabella stops offering to accompany Ada. "It gives me the creeps," she confides to that night's supper party, "all those totems in the waiting room." A theatrical shudder, and she looks at Ada from under her eyelids. "But you are brave, my girl, aren't you? You can go alone?"

In fact, her voice started to come back after the first session. It is not yet reliable, but when she is alone in her room, she can make entire sentences before her throat gives out; and sometimes, with Freud, she is entirely fluent. For the time being, however, she prefers, in the lake house, to remain ignored.

So she goes to the next appointment alone. At the door to the doctor's offices, she is met by the secretary, and shown into the waiting room. None of this is unusual. There is another woman leaving at the same time, through the main door, her face red and tear-streaked; a small, pop-eyed dog under one arm.

"Ada Bauer," is all he says in welcome: with a smile, as though her name gives him some special pleasure. He holds out an arm at right angles and beckons: *Come, come.* She lies on the couch and assumes the position of a crusader effigy. He moves to the chair behind her; there's a gust of cigar smoke, and the swish of him crossing his stick-insect legs; the rustle of chin-bristles under a stroking thumb. "We do not need pencil and paper for you today, do we?" he says. She shakes her head.

"And now you will resume your telling." He always sounds eager. His voice is far younger when he is analyzing her than when they are in the brief bursts of conversation after every meeting, the hellos and goodbyes.

She tells him about her fourteenth birthday, two years prior; a Sunday in April, the weather already warm and drowsy feeling. The lake is busy with pleasure-boats and families from Vienna. Emil has been absent for more than a month, and is expected at teatime to bring gifts.

"It will be so nice to see him," sighs her mother. "You'll like it, won't you, Ada? I wonder what he'll bring you from the city."

She nods. It is easy to be vague and polite, to try to make her feelings fit what others think they ought to be.

They arrange to have coffee and cake on the lawn. From her mother, her own set of dressmaker's scissors—"Careful, the blades are very sharp"—despite her total absence of interest in dressmaking. From her father, a book about von Kempelen's Turk, the legendary chess-playing automaton—"All a farce, a trick, you see!" He opens the pages to show her an illustrated plate of the machine: its staring papier-mâché face.

Emil, arriving. He is twenty-three and at some point has moved into a smooth, uncomplicated handsomeness; the kind that Ada is keenly aware she will never possess, for her chin is too sharp and her eyes too hooded. He is tanned from weeks supervising the extension of the Amstetten line; he is laughing, his sleeves are rolled up, his jacket slung over his shoulder, and he is carrying a box from a Konditorei.

A woman is with him—Mother clucks, for this was not foreseen—and the woman has a face that's sharp like Ada's, bright blackcurrant eyes that dart everywhere, and she is laughing. The sharpness *makes* her beautiful, Ada thinks. The woman walks close to Emil, steps forward and says, "I do hope you'll forgive this dreadful intrusion, I am Isabella, Emil has spoken of you so warmly, and of Ada, I couldn't wait any longer to meet you all, here, we have brought you this cake—"

Emil flips the cardboard box open like a magician to reveal a magnificent *Schwarzwälder Kirschtorte*; cherries nestle amidst the clouds of cream. Ada feels her parents stiffen. It is unprecedented in its rudeness. How dare he bring a woman here?

Isabella is saying, "Herr Bauer, Emil has told me all about the operations of your business, these marvelous new bridges. I am awestruck; my own late father was the third son of an offshoot of the Mayer-Meinhofs, a clergyman, of course, and would say that he wished he'd had the courage to make something, to *build*. He'd say that was the Austrian zeal, really, not to be hidebound by the past but to *progress*. But I'm gabbling." She looks around, laughs. "I'm nervous, I suppose. I suppose that's natural. In any case, at least, we brought cake."

Everyone finds themselves smiling. Isabella's shows her teeth; she looks around at them, one by one, asks, "May I sit by the birthday girl? Hello, Ada." She squeezes Ada's hand and takes the chair next to her. "I've heard so many good things." Her palms are warm and damp, and she smells of roses, petrol, cigarette smoke, and the city.

•

It is confusing, because when Emil visits now, so does Isabella, and that is something Ada looks forward to very much. Everything is confusing. One day Ada flings her textbook across the room, startling her mother, and bursts into tears. Another day, there are red spots on her underwear and she thinks she is the victim of some secret internal injury, all the worse because painless. She washes her things in the laundry, privately, until the maid catches her and they have a quiet word; the maid blushing, saying, "You are a woman now, and you'll have to be careful." In what way she is to be careful is not specified.

A Saturday in winter: the evening long and bluish. She is in the garden, on one of what Mother calls her "solo walks," when Emil arrives, unannounced. He sweeps up the lawn, carrying his old haversack, past her without a word. This in itself is rather commonplace. What is different is his face, which looks old, haggard. The phrase comes to her uninvited: *Sorry for your trouble. Whatever it is.* To feel sympathy for him is new. But he is already past her and into the house, explaining: "I had to get out of the city. To feel the country. I hope that's all right."

Her first thought—awful even to consider—is that Isabella has left him. Nothing has been specified, nothing said aloud, but it is clear there is an *understanding*. Mother and Father share not-so-secret looks. They are looking forward to an *announcement*; this much was said to the Mayor of Neusiedl, in between his tedious equine anecdotes. "We might venture to be so bold as to have certain expectations." Father has long since looked up the Mayer-Meinhofs, traced the family line to Innsbruck and the great pine and beech plantations of the Steiermark. *That will be useful, in due course.* He is imagining cutting down the forests and using the wood for planks. And this is the first question that, following Emil indoors, she hears her mother ask: "Is Isabella here?"

"No," he says, "she's with her brothers, for her niece's christening." He walks up the stairs and they hear the door of his bedroom slam.

He does not come out for tea, or for supper. They worry, as a collective activity, passing the sauces between them, humming with nerves. The story about Isabella's absence was surely too detailed to be a mere story? Mother arranges for a tray to be sent upstairs and put outside his door, and says, "I do hope the poor lamb isn't suffering too much."

They retire for coffee and little vanilla cakes, and Father, who cannot leave an idea alone, snaps open the paper to the Engagements and Announcements column. A harrumph of surprise. "Peter Hietzing—wasn't that the name of Emil's friend at the Internat? Weren't they in cahoots? I recall he went into import-export and left for the Black Sea? Marrying a Rothschild, no less. Wonder if he and Emil kept in touch?"

A cautious silence settles. Ada remembers slack, silky water around her ankles; Emil's nostrils flared in alarm. *Who is Peter?*

The day they have expected comes two weeks later. Emil and Isabella arrive together from the station at midday on Saturday. Isabella is all clasping hands and dazzling smiles as she receives their congratulations on their engagement. Ada's mother calls for champagne, despite the early hour. "Thank you, thank you." Emil stands back, grinning, white faced, while Father claps him on the back. "You have secured yourself a real pearl there, Emil. A real pearl. God give long life and happiness to you both."

It happens for the first time in *that way* a month later, in the deathly days after Christmas.

The festivities have been, largely, a success: Isabella has visited every day and exclaimed over her presents, and made an enormous fuss over the white silk scarf Ada bought her. "Little duck," she says, smoothing Ada's fringe. "You always know what I like." But the day after, Isabella and Emil vanish into his room and she emerges half an hour later, stalking like a leopard up and down the corridors, and announces she will go back to the city early; immediately, if Wilhelm wouldn't mind ordering the carriage? Emil follows her down the stairs and stands, helpless and white, hands drooping by his side.

"What about our walk?" Ada asks, and Isabella turns, looks over her shoulder, says tonelessly: "Next time."

She leaves in a flurry of stole and heavy overcoat; just the smart tap of her feet on the flagstones of the hall.

"I will take you for a walk," Emil says.

It has been many years since the incident in the boat; she barely remembers. Does she suspect what is about to happen? Not exactly; not the shape of it, or the confusing afterimage, which will send her running to the bath, to scrub and soap and scrub again. She is wary, as they walk, wary of the way he picks up his feet and puts them down very precisely, as though much depends on their placement. And she knows, instinctively, not to speak or ask questions.

They go along the road a little way, downhill toward the station, and then Emil appears to reach a decision: they turn up the bank and in under the trees. The sounds of the wind, and the light pattering rain that began to fall as soon as they left the house, recede.

He walks fast, in a straight line, hands in pockets. "We won't be long," he says, to himself. "Just taking the air."

He asks some vague questions then, and this is strange, because he never asks her anything, nor she him. *What will she wear to his wedding? Does she think her father will give Isabella away, her own father being deceased?* He frowns to himself, when she says *not sure*, to both.

They reach a clearing. His white, strained face. He stops walking.

"Will she come back? Isabella?" Ada asks. She cannot bear it if the answer is *no*. "Sorry for your trouble." It sounds stilted and formal.

He looks away, pinches his lips together. She sees the whites of his eyes. "She wants certain things, even before we are married," he says. "I am happy to oblige where possible but I—" He runs a hand through his hair; the palm settles on the nape of his neck and rubs there, and he looks speculatively at her. "If I could practice—"

He moves quickly. The last, dreadful thought before he is upon her is that he really has bloomed into handsomeness, something quite special; she can see, objectively, why Isabella likes him. He pushes her to the ground—she feels the slip of pine needles under her back, the pebbles digging into her spine.

"Nobody must know," he says. One hand wriggles under her skirt; the other shucks his trousers to his knees. She has no idea what he is trying to do. Does he want to kill her?

"I'm sorry," she shouts. "I'm sorry, sorry about Peter—"

He has put his hand on some tender flesh, which she did not

know was there; it tingles, then shrinks from him. She tries to get free. He pinches and grasps. "This is nothing to do with him, nothing do to with Peter." A part of him is revealed, through the open fly of his trousers: a flaccid pink thing, the drooping stamen of some giant orchid. He is swearing and crying.

"What are you doing?" she screams.

"Hush, hush," he says.

A further squirming of his fingers around her groin and he retreats. His weight is lifted. He folds himself away and walks to the edge of the clearing. Tears on his face. He says: "I wanted to do it, at first, with Isabella. Now I can't. It is surely a question of practice."

She can still feel his phantom weight as she sits. She massages her lower back. "I am not my father's son," Emil says, and walks away. "You won't speak of this to anyone. I am not like him." The whole episode has taken less than fifteen minutes. She has no way to describe what has happened to her, even if there were anybody she could tell.

The scratching of Freud's pencil stops. She imagines his eyes very piercing behind his spectacles. "And then?"

"And then we went back to the house. He pretended it hadn't happened. We went on. I found a book of my father's, later, which had some descriptions. I understood what he was trying to do."

"And was this the only occasion on which such an advance was made?"

She swallows. Tells him it was not. That there had been other attempts, other fumblings, every few months, none of them what he'd call *successful.* The last time, he'd casually slapped her, and thrown money on the bed, contemptuous. And she supposes that at her birthday, when all this muteness started, there was the disappointment of the canceled trip to the Zoological Gardens, and also the threat of the boat trip with Emil, and she could not say no, and so perhaps her body said it for her—

"What did you feel when Herr Kellner attempted such intimate relations with you?" the doctor says. "What were your feelings? Were you perhaps intrigued?"

"No."

"There is no shame in the enjoyment of a sexual advance, and he is not a first-degree relative. You have described him as a young man of seductive appearance?"

There is no way to talk to him of the dubiousness of Emil's face. She can't speak, again, and the glottal sounds she makes as she tries to form words allow the doctor to start one of his sequences of talking aloud. The slate-colored smoke from his cigar wanders.

"I had a dream once," he begins. It is always a dream, with him. "It was the week after my father died. A railway station. I was on the platform, and I was running, almost missed the train, which was going to some insignificant outpost of the Empire. As I stepped up into the carriage, what did I see but a signpost, and the signpost, which I knew was directed at me alone, read: *You are requested to close the eyes.*

"I had been late for my father's funeral, you see, earlier that week. I must have felt that I deserved reproach. I should perhaps have placed coins on the eyes of the dead person. Perhaps I was happy that he was no longer alive. In the waters of the subconscious there swim many fish, my Ada, large and small, fanged and not-so-fanged. It is impossible to know what one has caught at first glance." *His dreams*, she thinks: a child could see through them.

The next morning, at breakfast, a telegram arrives for her father. Ada watches as he frowns at it and announces that he must go into the city that morning for a meeting. He tears the telegram up and hands the pieces absently to the waiting servant.

The Kellners are in Lobau until the evening—they have gone to bathe in the springs there, in Vienna's inland jungle—and Ada spends the day reading in the downstairs salon, while her mother crochets. Mother insists on lighting the fire, even though it's late spring; she shivers, and sits close, staring at the coals as if there is some meaning to be had.

"You are happy, aren't you?" she asks Ada, at two o'clock. "The doctor is helping?"

Ada looks at her face, at the sad-clown droop of her mouth, and nods that she is; he is.

"They can really do anything nowadays," her mother says. Then she turns her head to the side of her armchair and falls asleep, her wool in her lap, and hands resting slack on top.

Ada walks down to the beach. The smell of pine resin is everywhere and somewhere a daytime owl flutes to itself, but a drifting gray rain is coming down from the plains.

She does not have to wait long. She turns to see her father crunching down the beach toward her. His feet slip on the large pebbles, as though he's walking a tightrope.

He comes to a stop next to her. His face is florid, and there is a coiled energy to him. "I have been to see Herr Doktor Freud this morning."

He says: "He contacted me because you had made certain statements, you had said certain things, about Emil."

She looks at him, sidelong, at the webbed skin hanging in folds from his neck.

"He believes you are genuine. I believe you are saying such things to damage Emil, because you are jealous of his place in our family. You have always been jealous. I must advise you to stop. Herr Doktor Freud says that you may have felt some neglect, that I have in some way been derelict—have behaved not as a father should."

His blue eyes, which everyone says she has inherited, are fixed on the fishermen in the distance, hauling in their nets. "Imagine what would happen if you were to persist. Emil would have to stop our acquaintance. Isabella could not come here anymore."

She considers it.

"I understand," she says, bright and casual.

So you can speak? He shakes his head a little, dazed. This, of all things; that she might casually reveal it to him here, that she is cured, and has perhaps been for some time. He says: "I doubt it. I won't dignify this by discussing it with Emil. I will spare you that embarrassment."

He looks at her: narrow and incredulous; then starts to make his long stumbling way back up the beach.

Julia

—

ONE NIGHT IN MID-MAY, the rising cry on the air they have all
been waiting for. Hurrying footsteps, the clank of a bucket, the hiss
and spit of the kettle. Frau Berndt rushes from the lodge with towels; Rolf, rubbing his eyes, is told to pace the courtyard with Gunther, while Eve is sent for the doctor.

They are so awake that they are convinced the whole of
Leopoldstadt is awake with them. The doctor walks with firm steps
in under the archway and enters Heidi and Gunther's quarters; he
pauses to shake Gunther's hand—he doesn't linger, and they consider this a good omen. He carries a black case in which are surely
kept many cruel but specific instruments whose names they will
not know.

Julia takes up a position in the window seat, overlooking the
courtyard, with a cup of coffee. Eve has joined the men in their
pacing; Julia looks down on her head, her hair ruffled from sleep,
her pale hands laced behind her back, her earnest face, and feels
a vivid, sickened pain. The hunter's moon begins its descent and
leaves in its wake a glow, like the aurora borealis over Stockholm.
She prays, for the first time in ten years, fingers locked together,
that all the bad thoughts she has had about Heidi should not infect
the child. That her selfishness should not now, not ever, be inflicted
on others.

Somewhere, a horse whinnies, in pleasure or alarm. There are no signs to be discerned in the flurry of bats returning to roost, or the first smell of old blood as the butcher's opens its door. The terracotta tiles on the rooftops turn gray, then shade into their usual color; Julia feels, in her stomach, an enormous wrench—and the next moment, along with a startled shout of encouragement, there is the sound of a baby crying.

Heidi is a sweaty Madonna, her hair in tendrils, like some trailing plant, over her forehead. The room smells animal. "You can stay five minutes, no more," the doctor says, as he packs away his tools. "Hello," Gunther says, in a dazed, society tone. Frau Berndt is in a corner of the room, wringing out a sponge. The water runs slick and red into the porcelain bowl.

"Julia, you came to see us," Heidi says. She parts the blankets to reveal an infant locked to her breast. It is the pink of a burn, scrawny where it should be plump. Its eyes are puffy, as though it, too, has not slept, and when they open they fix on Julia and waver away as if she isn't there. Only the mouth is doing the recognizable work of sucking and pulling.

"You should sleep," Gunther says. "She should sleep."

"Of course." Julia steps away from the bed and leaves Heidi settling against the pillow, the baby still nursing, exposing the white of her throat as she shuts her eyes.

The collective house-life is reorganized. Gunther leaves for work in the mornings haggard from lack of sleep. Frau Berndt takes up crocheting; a row of pale yellow mittens appears, and then a pale green hat made for an elf. Rolf is glimpsed holding the baby in the courtyard one day with a confused expression. "I think he looks like me," he announces, and promptly hands it back.

Julia gets a summer cold; a sneezing fit that takes her one evening, suddenly—"Goodness," all wide ironic eyes and handkerchiefs-a-flourish—and does not go. Two days later she feels so ill and weak that she stays in bed. "It's so strange, but I can barely lift them," she says, staring at her arms, then at Eve, who tells her to rest. She will deliver a note to the Embassy to let them know Julia won't come in.

The illness extends to a week. Julia lies in bed, barely able to rest, with a high temperature, turning in the sheets every other minute. The nights are disordered, too. She often cries out, in Swedish; little shouts of desolation of the soul.

Three days later, with Eve sitting on the edge of the bed, suggesting that a doctor's visit might be in order, Julia gets up. "It isn't the influenza, or the cholera," she says crossly. She wanders about the apartment on wobbly legs, saying, "I can manage," and Frau Berndt brings her liver noodle soup. Julia eyes the soup. "I'll be well now," she tells Eve firmly, with a shudder and a smile.

The day that the baby is three weeks old, Heidi invites Julia to join them for a walk. Gunther has bought, at no small expense, a magnificent secondhand perambulator. Julia walks down to the courtyard and waits, hand resting on the back of one of Frau Berndt's chairs. She meets Heidi and the baby—invisible in layers of blankets, even in the June sun—and they perambulate, Heidi gripping the rail, toward the Augarten.

It is very bright because she has not been outside for some days. There's the feverishness that comes from it being almost the end of term—shrieks from the school on Malzgasse—and when they pass the head teacher, Herr Doktor Hasper, on his way home for lunch, he smiles broadly at them, then stops, and asks after the new arrival. "A little boy?" he asks, peering into the pram. "Gunther, like his father?" He nods—faintly tolerant, these goyish naming traditions!—and then he discusses the summer to come. He and Frau Hasper, not themselves blessed with the gift of children, will go up to the hills on a walking holiday. He paints a picture: wild vines along the track, heavy with fat purple grapes; picnics with melting cheese and toast. Taverns where Frau Hasper, after a few glasses, can be prevailed upon to sing the virtues of their country. He presses a palm to his breast—"A privilege to meet young Gunther"—and goes on his way. For the first few steps, he doesn't turn his back on them, just retreats, smiling.

Julia and Heidi walk on for a few meters. "Now there is a man who knows how to talk," Heidi says. "He's educated. Like you."

Julia looks at her. Heidi sounds unhappy; there's no mistaking her tone. It has never occurred to Julia that she has had anything to worry about, with her perfectly attentive husband. But then,

Heidi is pale, from lack of sleep. "Wouldn't it be something? To take a holiday?" she says. All the while her knuckles are fixed on the rail of the pram; young Gunther's face is turned to the side in sleep.

Julia says: "Perhaps you will. When the baby's older. You could take a hut near a lake, couldn't you?"

Heidi says flatly: "Gunther has debts. And besides, he wouldn't want to."

They walk a little further. Julia feels dazed by revelation. When she has pictured the interior of Heidi and Gunther's apartments, it has been simplicity she's seen; perhaps Gunther rubbing the soles of Heidi's feet with a sponge soaked in lavender water. They met when they were thirteen, Heidi says, but he still holds the door open for her every time.

"I just wonder sometimes what it would be like, to be married to a talker," Heidi says. It's a light tone, but they have known each other long enough—albeit in a glancing way—for Julia to say, "Hmm," and not to try to fill the silence. When nothing comes, she says: "It isn't all it's supposed to be—" and Heidi turns, and says: "But it's something, isn't it? You and Eve talk about everything together, don't you?"

"I'm not so sure about that," Julia says, thinking of Eve's sudden flights into reticence; her obstinate refusal to discuss the really huge things.

Heidi says, mulish: "You have your job, and your papers, I've seen you reading, and you go to the theater—" She puts a clutch of fingers up to her lips and says: "I'm sorry. Forgive me. I've been very jealous." A few paces more. "I thought I would want to hide my baby from you, to keep him secret and mine, and now I find that after all this time..."

"Yes," Julia says, "we are friends."

When they come to the Obere Augartenstrasse, with its rattling traffic, Heidi seizes Julia's wrist and holds them both back until it's safe to cross.

Rolf

———

BY THE ENTRANCE TO THE SILBERGASSE, in the Old City, there's a tobacconist and wine merchant. Rolf hesitates, and asks for help choosing an expensive wine to go with the lamb chops he has bought. The proprietor scans the shelves and picks something, holds it up to squint at the label. One of the other clients turns his head to see what is chosen. The proprietor names a price that is far in excess of anything Rolf would usually buy, but he waves his hand to say yes; the client turns back to his cigarette, and the proprietor betrays no emotion and takes Rolf's money. "*Grüss Gott. Grüss Gott.*"

Rolf lets himself into the apartment just as the Stephansdom bell strikes the half-hour. He imagines Emil stepping off the tram, his steps turning toward the Kärntnerstrasse, the slope of his shoulders, the fine wool grain of his coat. Now he will be at the corner, near the Eckhaus; all the time, he will be thinking of Rolf.

At around ten to seven, Rolf goes to the window, rattles up the sash, and leans out to look. Nobody in the street below; just the hurry of dark suits passing at the end of the road, where it meets the square. A blur catches his eye; he looks up and across, to find an old lady standing at the window opposite. They are close enough that he can see her crow's feet. Her wrists, as they emerge from her black sleeves, are stick thin.

He pulls the shutters closed to block her out. He will have to close them anyway, when Emil arrives, and if Emil inquires why he's shutting the light out he can say he's cold. He closes his eyes and sits in the chair with his palms on his knees, and sends his mind out searching. There has been a tram crash, and there are bodies. It is the fourth time they have met at the apartment, the fourth successive Friday, and each time he has suffered similar thoughts. But no: the sky outside is fragrant with pollen from the hills; Emil has been delayed buying wine, or a book. He will step into the apartment lightly, holding a brown paper parcel. *I thought this might be something you'd like.*

The sound of light, rapid footsteps. Rolf sits, charmed, in a haze, because Emil is hurrying; the door opens and he's stepping through. In his hands, a bottle wrapped in green paper. They laugh at the fact that they have both brought wine.

Once Emil has gone into the bedroom to wash, Rolf pushes the tray with the chops under the grill, and boils water for the vegetables. Frau Berndt was only too happy to share a recipe that made the late Herr Berndt smile.

Emil stands for a moment in the kitchen doorway, looking at Rolf, who is wiping the dust from two of the plates; uncertainty on his face.

They have said that they can either tell each other such things or be crushed under them. Emil blurts out: "We had chops at our wedding dinner." So that Rolf can finish polishing the plates with a speculative swooping motion and a smile and say: "Were they any good?" and Emil can smile and say: "Frankly, no."

They sit in the salon with the wine. The shutters block out most of the street noise, but not the slap of the horses' hooves, the great distant hurry of people. It is all still new and strange—so Rolf, arching an eyebrow, asks Emil about his day. They both laugh, and then Emil relents, and starts to mutter about plans for a new bridge. He reverses his knife and fork, with an apology—a boyhood habit he has never grown out of, he says—and Rolf glows with the secret knowledge.

"And you?"

Rolf beams. "Another day at the office," he says. "You know." He has told Emil that he works as a theater agent; he has made up an entire inventory of imagined colleagues.

"And your friends? Julia and the other one? The strange one?" Rolf has been truthful about Julia and Eve. He has described Eve's dress habits, and the idea of a curiosity has stuck in Emil's head, although he cannot remember her name. Rolf finds himself laughing along with Emil about Eve's suits and mannerisms. It feels like betrayal, but also self-preservation: Emil is not ready to be confronted by too much strangeness.

When the meat from the chops is sucked from the bone and the potatoes and broth and bread and spinach are finished, Rolf takes the plates to the kitchen and stands for a moment, struck by the idea that Emil will leave while he is gone. When he returns to the salon with the second bottle of wine, Emil is studying the bookshelves. The lamps are still on, low, and the awkwardness is back in the room.

When Emil turns, his face is dreadful. Rolf cries out: "What's wrong?" Puts the bottle down, steps forward, and folds Emil into his embrace.

Emil moans into his shoulder that he is a monster. Not the person everyone thinks he is. That he could lose everything if anyone knew. The log in the fireplace falls lower, and Rolf tells him that they all have these thoughts: it is because of how they were raised. That the way the world sees them is wrong. There is nothing wrong with this.

They go into the bedroom. Rolf lays him on the bed and tries to calm him—this is what it must be like, he thinks, with a frightened child—and eventually Emil settles, sitting with his back braced against the headboard, his legs lolling. He seems to be in a state of glazed indifference, bordering on aggression, watching Rolf from beneath lowered lids. Rolf bends to unbuckle Emil's trousers and open his fly, and draws Emil into his mouth. It usually works when Emil is in a pet about something.

Emil puts the back of his hand across his eyes and swears. He makes sounds that grow in pitch and intensity. Rolf thinks of the woman at the window across the street; the fine wrinkles of the skin around her neck.

Emil throbs as though he's going to come but instead, he pushes Rolf's head away. He reaches for Rolf, pulls him onto the bed, pushes him onto his stomach; spits. He is frantic. Rolf grits his teeth; in his stomach, a coil of unwelcome surprise. "Not today," he says.

Emil grunts. He is still pressing and pushing. Rolf struggles, then subsides. A minute of trying; it is too painful. Rolf half-turns. Perhaps Emil has not understood. "I said it's no good—"

Emil's face is hectic; his teeth are bared. He slaps Rolf, light, experimental, then again with more force; groans. After a little more effort, movement is possible. Rolf collapses, riveted, feeling the sting of Emil's palm on his face.

Emil rolls off and lies spreadeagled, little aftershocks pulsing down his body. Rolf feels cold and shivery. He presses his thumbs into his eyelids until he sees shapes. When he can work out what he wants to say, he says: "That hurt."

Just sometimes, that old blank look on Emil's face: he could be the stranger on the Opera House steps. "I thought you'd like it," he says indifferently. Then his expression changes. He rolls toward Rolf. His face is too close. "I'm sorry. Oh God, I'm so sorry. Should I have been gentle? You should have told me what you wanted."

"You didn't give me time," Rolf says.

Emil is crestfallen. "Sometimes, women like it—"

"Telling me that helps?" Rolf allows himself a moment of anger, where usually he is tentative. "Am I your wife?"

Emil takes Rolf's fingertips and kisses them. He murmurs his sorriness, his shame. *I am but a poor sinner. Ever, yours.* Eventually, Rolf softens.

When the Stephansdom strikes eight in the morning, they wake. Emil pales with panic. He swings his legs out of bed and sits, confused.

"I have to go to lunch with the Bauers. With Isabella," he says. He picks up his shoes; straightens his shirt, and tries to smooth his hair.

Rolf says: "I wish I could come with you."

In the split second before Emil turns, Rolf wonders whether he has made a mistake; whether Emil will flare up. But he says, very tired: "So do I." And then he does leave—and without making another appointment, not yet—but it doesn't matter, because Rolf will hug these words to himself until they meet again. And the name of her, this information, serpentine and falsely elegant: *Isabella.*

Julia

——

SUN LIKE A STRUCK GONG. People leave the city on trains, in carriages, or any other way they can. In the back room of Eve's shop,
where the silk cravats are rigorously run up and down the sew-
ing machines, three men faint of heatstroke, and when they wake,
their first thought is: *I'll never live this down*. On the occasion of Gunther's three months in the world, Julia tells herself she will buy him
a bonnet of some sort to protect him from the heat. She checks
with Heidi, who is flustered and tearful—"Would you, Julia? You're
an angel"—tells Eve that she will be some hours, and sets off for the
boutiques of the Kärntnerstrasse.

Julia is twenty-eight years old. A pulled muscle in her right calf
seems to be permanent now; she finds herself squinting at signs
that are more than ten meters distant, although when Eve teases
her, she will say she doesn't need glasses. Her contemporaries in
Sweden—those mannequin beauties—have made long marriages,
some of them brilliant; the *Stockholms-Tidningen*, which she reads in
the Embassy lobby, always has some snippet. And here she is, living in a dusty attic; walking into the center of Vienna, with sweat
snaking down between her shoulder blades.

The main shopping district is meltingly hot and full of people in
their weekend clothes. A woman holds her fingers to her mouth in
delight outside a jeweler's window; her fiancé two steps behind.

Outside M. Neumann's, Julia pauses to look at the sheer white glass windows, radiating sun; shades her eyes and picks out a wooden toy duck on wheels. In the store, it's warm and drowsy, and in the mothball-smelling shadows, the shop assistants move like ghosts. On a shelf in the toy department she finds the duck, tests its wheels, which whir smoothly, and has it gift-wrapped; at the till, remembering her original errand, she takes a cream cotton bonnet from a nearby stand and that, too, is carefully encased in tissue paper. "A lovely piece," the shop assistant murmurs, and the sound is deadened by the felty, stifling air.

Outside the store, parcel under her arm, Julia hesitates. She looks up to the sky for a sign, but there is nothing: the birds are asleep under the rafters in the midday sun. Thinking that luck is simply a question of choosing a direction, she turns south toward the theater district.

It is true, isn't it, that at any stage she could turn back toward Leopoldstadt, and home? She drifts on through the Heldenplatz and across the Ringstrasse, past the lunchtime crowds picnicking on acid-green grass, until she stands outside the Volkstheater.

He has done well to get his play here, she thinks, translated into German and performed in the very heart of Austrian national art. But here is her reflected image, staring her down: a banner above the colonnaded entrance. The poster reads: "THE PEAR ORCHARD: A PLAY IN THREE ACTS by Per Lindqvist. Opens 7 September." Underneath the text is a watercolor: a wash of green leaves, and a woman with her face turned maliciously away, red hair tumbling down her back.

She'd pushed the envelope and its contents into the bottom of the chest of drawers. There could be no hidden meaning to decipher, nothing to be gained from rereading. That same evening, though, when Eve had gone, wrench in hand, to fix Frau Berndt's stovepipe, she retrieved the letter. The words induced no effect other than a vague irritation at the overfamiliarity of his tone and, reassured, she took the letter and envelope to the fire and burned them.

Three weeks later, another letter arrived. She took it from Frau Berndt quickly, before there could be discussion about this new correspondent; this time, she opened it on her way up the stairs, intending to skim-read and tear it up straightaway.

I write furiously. All around are the young wolves waiting to snatch glory from me. And still I find I discard almost everything. I am coming to the limit of my powers. I fear I have nothing to say, apart from this latest work on the topic of your leaving (you did tell me I should write a play about it).

I have no expectation that we will establish a correspondence. I know I gave you good reason to flee. What is it, then, that I desire? For it not to have been meaningless.

The next letter was more troubled still. He had written one way across the page and then back the other at right angles, so that Julia had to squint to read it. She took it to the Augarten with her, and held it up to the light, except that this obscured whichever line of text she was trying to understand; with a scornful sound, she was forced to sit on a bench and lower the paper onto her lap.

I remember what I was like as a young man. When we met.

She remembered, too. He'd been thirty-seven the first time she'd seen him: Struwwelpeter hair, thin as a rail. Limbs full of lanky electricity. He'd picked at the food, at the supper where they were introduced, and barely looked at her all evening, and there was a hush over the room. She couldn't imagine him ever being older than he was that night.

Now I come to the twilight part and find the things I have cared about have not been the things that matter. I look at my play and feel that it is wanting but there is no special sadness. It simply is bad, but commissioned, bought and paid for, and so the show must go on, and then I'll have the money. It, and I, will come to Vienna in September. Pretending is living, you once told me.

She tore up his letter and sprinkled the pieces on the wind. At home, she scribbled a short note: *Please don't write to me anymore. I am well, and happy. Wishing you success with your play,* and underlined her signature three times.

Now here she is, standing outside the Volkstheater, with the August hush on the streets. The sound of wood being sawn from somewhere backstage, and a man is whistling. In the café adjoining the building, someone who looks like an actor stretches his legs out before him, crossed at the ankle, and shades his eyes as he looks at

Julia. It makes her think that Per might already be here, sitting in the dark of the auditorium with one finger laid along his upper lip. On an empty, dusty stage, someone who looks like Julia, perhaps in a red wig, is being told to start or restart a speech.

As she walks rapidly away, she rehearses. Frau Berndt takes the artistic journals and will be sure to see Per's name, and the news of the opening of the play. She will mention it, perhaps in passing, with a sideways look, afraid of finding out that Julia already knew. Julia will shake her head, with a slight frown. *Is that so?* she will say to Frau Berndt. *Coming to Vienna?* A smile, broad and disarming: *I had no idea.*

Ada

—

"YOU'LL COME BACK," THE DOCTOR says, when Ada tells him her analysis is finished. He leans in over the couch, wags his finger under her nose: "You are not cured."

Not unless you know the cure for love, she thinks, and walks out of his office.

It is a relief to leave the baking city behind. At home, she finds her mother sitting in her usual armchair, staring into the empty grate. "Did you have a nice time?" she asks. She has forgotten where Ada has been. "Did you buy any nice things?"

Ada says that she did, and that she has already given the parcels to the maid. "Isabella is here," her mother says. "Upstairs. Emil has left on business. You must have passed him at the station!"

Ada walks up the stairs; keeps one hand on the glossy chestnut banister, snaking its way up alongside her. She knocks at the door of her father's study, and hears him clear his throat and say come in.

Isabella, in a peacock-blue dress with short sleeves, leans over her father's blotter, pointing something out. Her father looks up as Ada comes to stand before them. "Good. You're here. Whichever way the columns add up, we cannot make them right."

He looks at her from underneath his eyebrows and beckons her forward. She is known to be good with calculations—he has taken to saying this to family and friends. Since their conversation on the beach, he has sometimes dropped little scraps of comfort or praise like this, and at mealtimes he often watches her, shaking the wine in his glass from side to side a little. When she looks at him, he looks away, embarrassed.

She bends over their errors, which are childish and multiple. A wave of hair is escaping down the side of Isabella's neck toward her collarbone; and her shoulders are red from the heat of the room. "Here," Ada says, placing a fingertip on the first place the column of numbers wobbles astray, "and here." Her father and Isabella crane inward.

"Of course," Isabella says. "You are clever." She straightens, puts her hands on her hips and blinks at Ada. "We have been here for an hour, haven't we?"

Her father grunts, and his pen scratches the paper as he makes the changes. Isabella stretches her arms above her head, then turns to Ada, all brilliant smiles. "Shall we go for a walk?"

Ada's mother insists they ought to take a picnic but Isabella waves her concern away. "We'll be back long before dark." She waits, still smiling, twirling her sunhat in her hands, in the dark hallway for Ada, and then they step out into a light so bright as to seem artificial.

There are shrieks of pleasure from the direction of the beach: someone being dunked, gasping, and splashing free with a shout of triumph. The sounds fade as they move back into the trees behind the house. Isabella's skirts swish and rustle. She seems set on some destination that she won't share with Ada. It is, as always, impossible to look directly at her without feeling some danger, just as one should not stare at the sun.

"Tell me about the doctor," Isabella says. She is a few steps ahead, and she trails her hand against the rough bark of a tree trunk. "Is he uncovering fabulous truths?"

"He told me about his dreams."

"And did you tell him about yours?"

With a rush of bravery: "I told him about you."

Isabella spins around. The scent of hot pine needles underfoot. "You told him that I was fabulously intelligent and your most especial friend?" She laughs, but there is something beneath the laugh; some desire to know. When Ada says nothing more, Isabella laughs again. "I'm teasing," she says, "of course I am. It's sweet of you to mention me. And my husband, did you talk about him, too? It seems your voice is quite recovered?"

Ada looks at her feet, plodding over the soil of the forest path. The shoes are the same ones she was wearing that day on the lake shore, for her sixteenth birthday picnic. Now they are crusted with red dust. "I didn't talk about him so much because I prefer you."

Isabella laughs. This time there's real pleasure. "I am much better. Everybody says."

They must be a mile out from the house. Isabella cuts ahead, in little zigzagging runs, circling back to point out something among the trees ahead. A squirrel sits on a branch, deadened by the heat, but vanishes, spiraling up the trunk. They skirt past clearings because of the thick pools of white light beating down on them.

"Are we going to walk to Podersdorf?" Ada asks. "What's it like to be married?"

"Just a little further. Now there's a question." Isabella stands to look up and down a fork in the path, then selects a route, and walks with energy and purpose. "Some people say it is a conversation that goes on for your whole life."

"And is it like that with Emil?"

"I never said the conversation idea was true. If it were true, then I would be married to you, wouldn't I?" She laughs. "You know all my secrets."

The path has narrowed to a scrubby thicket. They push through, and Isabella says: "Here is what I wanted to show you."

The trees open out into the blinding brightness of a clearing, and when her eyes adjust, Ada sees a row of tiny crosses. Six of them: made of wood standing not more than a foot from the ground.

"I found it while I was wandering about in the spring," Isabella says. "I don't think anyone else knows it is here. Dogs, or cats, I should think, from the size. Oh, did you think they were babies? Well, it's possible." Isabella chews her lower lip. "Ones that weren't right. It's so curious, isn't it? It can be our secret."

She moves to leave the clearing; pauses. One hand goes to a tree trunk; the other, momentarily, to the side of her ribcage, to press some invisible wound.

"What is it?" Ada asks, and Isabella says: "Nothing. A stitch. It's nothing."

They hold hands for part of the way back, loosely, casually: Isabella leads Ada through the thicket, keeping back the branches from snapping in her face. They are on the right path back toward the house, but still a mile or more to go. Ada is giddy with the smell of the pine resin and the pulse of the blood in Isabella's hand; she wants to brush the inside of her wrist with her thumb.

"No," says Isabella, "to your second question, what is marriage like, I do not think that anyone can say what it is like for all people, just what it is like for them. There is an assumption of choosing this person"—Isabella squeezes her hand—"and then of constructing something. You see? Marriage is like a house, and it takes many years. Like your mother and father."

"I'm not sure that house is solid."

"Ada, how can you say that? Your father is devoted to your mother's comfort. Besides, the house isn't finished until it's finished."

She disengages her hand to wipe it on the front of her dress, and doesn't pick up Ada's again. "Emil is going to build me a house," she says, "next to yours, when your father finalizes his promotion. Then we'll be neighbors!"

Ada imagines her own face: damp and florid, like her father's when he is angry. Her armpits are soaked. She stumbles onward, a couple of paces behind Isabella, who talks about what kind of house will be built, its relation to the Bauers', and how the gardens will intersect with a little green gate, the precise shade of which Isabella has already picked out.

The boundary wall appears ahead. Ada's head droops with the heat as they cover the last fifty yards; Isabella is proud as a queen.

At the gate in the wall, they stop. Isabella runs her fingers over the smooth wooden top and says: "I hope that when you marry you will find a small proportion of the happiness I have found with Emil. He is a fine person, so sensitive, and he means everything to me."

She hovers, eyes wide with something like fright. Her gaze runs over Ada's chest and exposed collarbone; the light changes, from sharp white heat to late-afternoon treacle.

"Your house is solid?" Ada says.

"I believe it is."

Ada thinks that if she leans forward just a little, she could kiss Isabella. She imagines the quick wonder on Isabella's face; the clouding of doubt, then the clearing away.

From the back door of the house, the sound of shuffling footsteps. Ada's mother is there, shading her eyes. "Are you going to stand there forever?" she cries.

Rolf

—

WHILE JULIA IS HESITATING outside the Volkstheater, Rolf and Emil are lying in bed at the apartment near the Stephansdom. Barred sun comes through the shutters. Emil turns, protective, onto his side, wraps his arm around Rolf, and puts his lips to the nape of Rolf's neck.

They have met in the apartment every Friday night for five weeks: the same dinner, the same evening spent with wine in the salon, the same night. It is not in their gift to each other to linger in the morning. Emil will lay his forearm over his eyes and say nothing for a long time, and then get out of bed and put on his clothes. A kiss, and he's gone, back to his marriage.

Today, Rolf is aware of a shifting, squirming behind him. Sometimes this is a prelude. But the slow tick of his thumb on Rolf's belly suggests something else.

"Shall we go to Lobau today?" he says, into Rolf's neck.

Rolf's hand has tightened over Emil's in instinctive joy, and he releases it slowly. "To the bathing spot? Where the kingfishers are?" he says. Julia and Eve were talking about this very place with Frau Berndt the other day: it's to the east, it's meant to be like a jungle—spread-out rivers and streams and vegetation—where one can get lost from the city. He imagines himself returning to Leopoldstadt, and someone remarking on how well he looks: "Oh, we went for a bathe," he'll say. He is uncertain whether or not he should probe further. He does not want to ask about Isabella and find that she is unavailable today. He does not want to know whether this is a sudden decision on Emil's part. He hopes it may have been on Emil's mind for a while.

He tests various responses out in his mind. A lazy, considered *I suppose we could*, or *I can make time for a quick trip*. What he wants is to turn to Emil and take his face between both palms and kiss him. He pictures Emil's face, surprise shading into alarm, and so when he says yes to the plan, it is in the form of practicalities. He asks about a picnic—which Emil gives due consideration to and then says he isn't hungry—and the tram journey. "The world and his wife will be there," Rolf says, "so I suppose we might as well go too." They lie there for a moment, together, dazed with the possibility; then get up.

Getting off the boat, Emil almost panics. They have been the only two men traveling together from the Innere Stadt, and it's true that there was a leering boy opposite them, whose gaze wandered from Emil's feet to his hair: the sense of being discovered, by some means unknown to them, to be a couple. Emil is too new to all of this: he can't meet the unfriendly stare like Rolf can, with a level, challenging gaze of his own, nor can he throw his jacket over his shoulder with a fey action and shrug off the encounter. So now here is Emil, trapped on the platform, unsure where to turn, possibly on the verge of tears.

"This way, I think," Rolf says. All it takes is to pick a route: they can go anywhere they like, into the green undergrowth, on or off the paths. There is a family ahead of them: grandmother, husband and wife, servants, perambulator, three children of assorted sizes, heading in a determined direction. Rolf guides Emil and they follow, somewhat shyly, behind.

The path leads between beech, birch, and alder, and then into a swampy patch fringed by baobabs—"My shoes," Emil complains, picking his feet up in disgust. There is a smell of rotten fruit and stagnant water, and for a moment it seems Emil regrets coming. Then, exclamations of joy from the family ahead, and they come out onto the bank of a sunny, rushing stretch of gray river, some fifty feet across. The grassy slopes on either side are sprinkled with lounging men, women, and children.

They spread their towels, and Emil stands, in his bathing trunks, squinting at the water and shading his eyes. "Coming?" he asks, and before Rolf can answer, he has started to sprint toward the edge. He runs straight in and duck-dives under; then reappears, bobbing and gasping, shaking the water out of his eyes. He waves, childlike, triumphant.

Rolf returns the wave. It is exquisite and painful: so like what he imagined it would be. And he has seen something that perhaps Emil hasn't: a young man standing at the edge of the trees on the other side, leaning against a tree trunk, apparently just waiting. Another man emerges from the trees further up the bank, barefoot and wearing only his bathing costume, flushed and nervous looking. There are the usual old queens, too, parading by the edge of the water, sucking in their guts. One is wearing makeup. Around them all, families play, oblivious to the secret scene being played out.

Billy is there, of course, unfolded onto a thin gray towel some meters away. He lifts a lazy hand to wave and then gets to his feet and picks his way over to talk to Rolf.

"Hello," he says, his gaze wavering hungrily over the other clientele. He stands so that his shadow falls on Rolf's face. "Here with your beau." It isn't a question. He is watching Emil now, who has adopted a matronly breaststroke, puffing the air in and out of his cheeks.

"You?" asks Rolf.

"Walter will be looking for me," Billy says, with a vague wave of the hand toward an elderly gentleman who is making his way back from the concessions stand with two cones of shaved ice and a searching expression.

Rolf nods. Professional appreciation. Walter must be over sixty but he has a straight back and a flat stomach: an ex-soldier. Some of the military pensions can be very good, and if he's titled, that's another thing entirely. *One must think of one's security* is Billy's favorite maxim.

"He's lost me," Billy says, looking toward Walter with vicious satisfaction, as Walter swivels from the waist, this way and that, making it a physiological exercise. Then, back at Rolf, with narrowed eyes. "And your one?" He lifts his thumbnail to his mouth and starts to chew at the corner. "We don't see you around anymore."

Rolf says: "We don't get out much." He is full of savage happiness.

Billy eyes him. All the usual questions, he will have answered for himself: they are connoisseurs, the two of them, and the male form holds no mysteries. In Emil's hair, cut to a fashionable length, Billy will have diagnosed social standing; in his posture, a strict upbringing. Rolf can see Billy making assessments. He wants Billy to do the calculations and see that it adds up to more than just wealth: it adds up to some kind of future.

"We have plans," he says; murmurs it really, so that only Billy can hear—both because Billy is, he is realizing in this moment, an ally, and because he is frightened to say it out loud. "There's life outside Vienna, you know."

Billy sighs. The sigh is an acknowledgment, perhaps, that all the years of tricking outside the Opera House were a personal competition after all; that Rolf has won. "Walter keeps suggesting we go to Salzburg," he says. "But I think I'd miss the people."

"Maybe," Rolf says. He wants Billy to go away. He wants to revel in this new fresh feeling that he will ask Emil, today, to make a solid plan.

"Be good, or careful," says Billy, sprinkling his fingers in a wave. He moves away. Walter has spotted him, and is moving toward them with a look of smiling relief, the cones leaking a trickle of water down his wrists and onto his bare feet.

Rolf watches Emil sink into the glassy water, bobbing speculatively so that only his eyes are visible, like an alligator's, above the surface. Around him, other men are gathered at a discreet distance; one of them dives under, and resurfaces a few feet from Emil, explosively showing off, brushing the streaming water from his hair. Emil stands up, looks back toward the shore, like a lost child, and Rolf's heart squeezes—Emil waves and starts toward him, the water dragging on his thighs.

"Shall I get us something to drink?" Rolf asks, when Emil has sat down again, cross-legged on the towel. He is blushing all over from the cold of the water, and the heat of the day. Emil says, "No, stay with me," and now he blushes from embarrassment, but he also takes Rolf's hand into his lap. He threads the fingers through his own, and lets his head hang down.

"Who was that man?" he asks.

"A colleague," Rolf says.

Emil blinks. "Not a friend?" He means, *Not a lover?* He is mutinous, staring down at their interlaced hands.

It's Rolf's turn to blink. How can Emil be jealous, when every week he leaves Rolf alone and goes home to his wife?

"I know I shouldn't ask," Emil says, miserable.

"You are a cipher," Rolf says. "You think I'm out at all hours, seducing other men?" He hesitates on the edge of saying: *You're the only boy for me.* He is thinking of the times Emil has cried in his arms at night and called himself a monster. Rolf knows it is because he thinks he should not love other men; he is so full of shame. Rolf has been assiduous in calming him; he has smoothed the worry away night by night, held his shoulders and told him nothing is his fault. The psychoanalysts have said it is natural, even seen in the animal kingdom. (This had made Emil swipe his tears away, and say: "Chimpanzees? Really?") Now it seems Emil is not so new to the erotic imagination, after all; he can think of Rolf with a baroque series of male romances, and torture himself that way. "You amaze me," Rolf says. "Really."

Emil brings his knees up under his chin. He puts his forehead onto his kneecaps, hiding his face.

Then he says: "What's the worst thing you have done to another person?" It comes out muffled.

Rolf thinks. There are many options to choose from. "I stole a thousand Kronen from a shop I worked in and said I'd been held up at gunpoint."

Emil smiles; peeks sideways at him. "That's not so bad."

Rolf thinks about his mother, who writes spidery cards at Christmas and Easter, asking for him to come home; banishes the thought. "I suppose I have hurt people. Family. I suppose somewhere, someone misses me."

Emil acknowledges this with a wince. "What's the worst thing you could forgive someone for?" he asks.

"You mean, like murder?" Rolf is careful not to say adultery.

"Not quite that bad," Emil says.

Rolf takes a deep breath in. "I think I could forgive you a small murder." He makes a gesture like a fisherman showing off a minnow: *About so big.*

Emil looks up. "You forgive me a lot already."

Another deep breath. "I don't think I will have to forgive you everything forever. Will I?"

To freeze this moment: light on the water. He says: "People do live like us. They find ways. With a little money and discretion."

He daren't look at Emil's face. A family, pink from the sun, is waddling down to the water's edge, dipping their toes in and screaming; a child clutches its mother around the thighs and presses a tearful face to her stomach. "We might have to leave the city. It could be managed. We could go to Salzburg, for instance." There is more that he could tell Emil—that he would make any sacrifice, hold and rock Emil through his night-terrors; he could plead, *You like our evenings at the apartment, don't you? What if it could always be like that?* But an old instinct prevents him. Emil must come to this as an equal or not at all. Neither of them have spoken about love and this is for the best, because to run away together, if it works, will take a lot more than just that. What was it Julia says, flicking Eve with a dishcloth, talking about how they got through their early days in Vienna? *Love is the least of it.*

"A small murder," Emil says. He turns his head toward Rolf; puts his cheek on his knee. His eyes are quite dark, like a different person's. "You'd forgive me that, and anything up to that?"

Rolf nods. He is helpless and knows he is helpless. "It's not a challenge," he says. "But if it came to it—yes."

Julia

—

A WEEK AFTER ROLF has returned triumphant and mysterious to the apartment block, shaking his wet hair, young Gunther opens his eyes and sees Julia for the first time. She is bending over his crib, adjusting his blankets, and the quality of his gaze changes. Where before he has been unfocused, now he looks straight at her and fixes her with a beady stare. She moves, cautiously, to left and right, and he follows her movement with his eyes.

They look at each other for some moments. She leans in close, and whispers: "I will always be on your side." He yawns in her face, turns his head away.

Two weeks later, Heidi comes running up to the apartment at eleven o'clock in the morning. Julia is alone, having finished an interpreting contract the day before, and Eve is at work. Heidi knocks briefly—just the rasp of her knuckles on wood—and enters. Her face is red and she is out of breath. "Could you take him for a few hours?" she says, and bursts into tears.

Julia snaps the magazine she's been reading shut. "Of course."

Heidi says, "He won't go to sleep. I can't tell Gunther. He thinks I'm doing it wrong." She wipes her eyes with her apron corner. "Maybe I am. How can you tell? Frau Berndt says to give him Inländer Rum but I don't like to do it too often." Frau B., it's true, often lurks in the courtyard with a bottle of clear liquid and a tea-spoon. The image makes them both laugh; enough for Heidi to recover her equilibrium—she moves her feet further apart, steady-ing, and sniffs and says: "Would you mind? You could take him to the Augarten, or—" Tears threaten again.

"Or somewhere," Julia says. "I understand."

"Yes," Heidi says. "Anywhere, really." She grips Julia's hand for a moment and releases it.

An hour later, Julia is pushing the pram through the park. Gunther has fallen asleep, and in his slack-jawed perfection he looks like his father. At times, by turns, he looks like all of them—sometimes even Rolf, because Rolf has been the most determined at teaching him to smile in his own image.

The pram's wheels squeak on the path. She has no particular plan, other than to find some shady spot to sit. There are benches along the central avenue of lime trees, across which she's seen other mothers and nursemaids spread themselves.

She passes a crocodile of schoolchildren, those damned to extra summer classes, solemn with their pencils and workbooks, paused in the act of identifying different types of leaves; their teacher stands at the front, comforting one small boy who holds a horse-chestnut with a worried expression. In the middle of the alley there's a bench, and sitting on the bench is a large woman dressed in black, also with a pram, which she is pushing back and forth. Julia asks if she may sit and the woman looks up and smiles, absently, as if the question has come from someone far away.

Julia sits and, for a minute or two, they don't speak. They watch the schoolchildren stoop, pick up things from the lawn, and go run-ning to their teacher to show them off. Both jog their respective pram forward and backward idly. "How old?" the woman asks, with a nod at Gunther.

"Almost four months," Julia says, and then realizes she is sup-posed to ask: "Yours?"

"Six," the woman says, and it's a sigh, long, exhaled through the nose. She doesn't ask any more questions, and nor does Julia. It's peaceful there, with the sun dappling through the lime leaves, and the children's careful stooping study. "Father ran off at four months," the woman says conversationally. The rocking back and forth of the pram gets a little harder.

"I'm sorry," Julia says.

"Oh, not like that. He's a soldier. He's gone out on maneuvers in Prussia. Wasn't sad to go, though. Yours?"

This is new to Julia, this instant camaraderie. It is odd and touching, and perhaps that is why she says: "He's a tailor. He hates leaving for work, actually. It's another side to him that I hadn't seen."

The woman glances sidelong at her. In her inspiration, Julia realizes, she has broken some fundamental rule of female companionship. "We are both very tired, though," she says.

The woman relaxes. "Of course the servant is no good with her." She jiggles the pram aggressively again, and the baby squeaks in protest. "We couldn't get a decent nursemaid. She just coos over her and doesn't discipline."

"It must be difficult," she says.

"Do you ever think your child is just bad?" the woman asks, to the air in front of her face. She has said it humorously, with a desperate laugh at the edge of her voice. "I think sometimes, in the middle of the night, when it's just us, that she's doing it all on purpose."

Julia would like to gather Gunther up and put her hands over his ears. "I don't know," she says.

"Maybe one day I'll just leave her in the park and someone else will take her. Do you ever think anything like that?"

Julia looks at the woman properly for the first time. Her face, which is well nourished and attractive—the kind of face Julia might in other circumstances turn on the street to see more of—is droopy with tiredness, and there's a hard and bitter set to her eyes.

"No, of course not," the woman says, to herself. "It's just me." The jogging of the pram becomes too hard, and the baby starts to cry: squawks of upset that sound oddly like the mother's complaints. "Not again. Be quiet!" She rocks the pram so hard that it catches on a pebble and wobbles, and almost tips to the side: Julia puts a hand out to right it, and the woman is already apologizing.

Julia operates on instinct. She leans into the woman's pram and sees the child's huge blue eyes staring back up at her. "She's beautiful," she tells the woman. "Your daughter. Perhaps a change of staff? An overnight nurse, to help you get more sleep?"

The woman's eyes fill with tears. She covers her face with her hands, then removes them. "Yes," she says. "Yes." She takes the pram's handle, gets to her feet, dusting the green pollen from her skirt. "Thank you." She meets Julia's eyes fleetingly. "Good luck." And she wheels the pram away down the avenue, back straight.

Julia sits, thoughtful. She looks in on Gunther, who has slept through the commotion: lips pursed and cheeks full, like Raphael's cherubs; she worries he will burn, and so she gets to her feet and walks the pram along the avenue, in the opposite direction taken by the woman. She feels the need to wash the clinging residue of the woman's unhappiness away—small chance of rain—and the only thing to do is to walk fast. At the Porcelain Manufactory, there is a fountain and a clock: she stands in the spray of the fountain for half a minute, watching Gunther wrinkle his nose at the contact of the water. The clock says one o'clock. Heidi will perhaps just be lying down, after hanging out the washing and organizing the chaos of the apartment: it would be a shame to go back too soon.

Without really deciding, she lets her feet take her out of the northeast exit. The streets are glaring bright and the heat seems to have taken away the usual smells: horse manure has been baked hard into the cobbles, and even the dust smells pure. She clings to the wall where it's shady, so that Gunther won't get burned, and keeps walking.

By the time she reaches the Prater, the sun has passed its high point and become fuzzy, like a child's drawing: the shadows are longer and she is thirsty—Gunther, too, is smacking his lips, even though he is intermittently asleep. The smells here are more vivid: she skirts a crowd of tourists, and even their smart clothes can't disguise the onion scent of hours-old sweat. She casts about, and buys a cup of lemonade from a stall. "Not long now," she says to Gunther. "There, there." He stares up at her with a look of bleary-eyed trust.

Women turn to look into the pram, and this is new: the way they soften around the eyes when they see the baby. One or two ask how old he is, and reach out to push their fingers into the curl of his fist. She would like more of them to stop, and she never corrects the error of thinking that she is the mother.

She has as her destination the swimming pond in the south-east corner, near the Kaiserallee. Gunther will like to see the children splashing, and there will be others to talk to: maybe she can even hold him with his toes dangling in the water. She walks, and walks—the lemonade is finished and she ignores the pulse at her temple. A clutch of young boys in their dark smocks skip down the path toward her and part like water around a rock.

Finally the pond comes into view—the happy shrieks and splashing sounds lead her to it—and she pushes the pram off the grass and sits, tired, next to the shallow end. Gunther is asleep, and has pushed his blanket down take around his knees. She smiles widely at two women who are sitting on a picnic blanket a few feet away, and starts to fan herself with the flattened cardboard lemonade cup.

She will just sit for a while, and observe. There are children everywhere. White knees and pink shoulders, elbows flying as they run in and out of the water. Women shade their eyes and shout instructions, and fuss over the toweling-off process. A man passes in and out of the rows of picnickers, selling pretzels and small bottles of cider. Julia shakes her head and smiles at him, and he smiles back, broad and sudden, and she feels the warmth of it in her stomach.

She doesn't know how long she has sat there, or that she has closed her eyes, except that someone is touching her shoulder. "Excuse me," the woman says—it is one of her picnicking neighbors—"but your baby—" Julia sits. "Thank you," she says. "Sorry." She checks on Gunther. When he sees her, he cries harder. The top of his head is hot and pulsing. "Give him some water," the other woman advises, and passes her a cup. "Just a few drops in the corner of the mouth."

Julia takes the water and dribbles it in: he chokes and cries harder, then shuts his eyes and turns his head to the side. All seems well. "How long was I asleep for?" she asks the woman, who laughs, a little shakily. "It's five o'clock," she says. She puts a hand on Julia's forearm and pats it, twice, short bursts. "Time to get out of the sun." It's kind, but hard, too.

"It's our day out together," she explains. "I'm helping out a neighbor."

The woman smiles again, vague and troubled, and moves back to her own group. Julia's back is stiff. The water has taken on a shimmering quality: the ripples catch the late-afternoon sun, and most of the families have packed up, leaving a layer of detritus behind. She is angry, unreasonably so, though with whom, she could not say. She pushes the pram fast, rattling its wheels over the sides of the path. In the patches of shade under the trees, the air is quite cool.

It takes an hour to get to the northwestern edge of the park, and her feet are stinging; her shoes filled with summery grit. Gunther, in the pram, is still asleep. The evening crowd have begun to filter into the park: wide-eyed boys and girls; the air is sugary and salty. These people do not make way as the mothers did, but jostle the pram carelessly, and don't notice the baby.

She is very tired but there are no trams, and anyway, it will be impossible to get the pram into a carriage. There is nothing for it but to walk. She is still angry, and her anger has a bruised, defensive quality, though if you asked her, she would tell you that she has nothing to apologize for.

She reaches the Taborstrasse, near home, as the Silbers' boy is rattling down the shutters on the butcher's—seven o'clock. He grunts a greeting, and she tries to smile as she hurries past, but she is worried that it might turn into something else.

They are visible from the end of the street: clustered under the archway. Eve, seeing Julia, clutches Frau Berndt's elbow, who shouts for Heidi, and Heidi comes sprinting out. When she reaches Julia, she scoops up Gunther—looks at his face, runs back with the baby in her arms toward the concierge's lodge. Frau Berndt turns to follow.

Julia reaches the archway and stops. Eve stands in front of her, very white in the face. "Are you all right?" she asks.

"Yes, why? I suppose I am back later than expected—"

"She was terrified," Eve says, "Heidi. You were only supposed to take him for an hour or two. We had no idea where you had gone."

"We didn't specify a time," Julia says. They are being very unfair. "We have had a lovely day. I took him to the Prater."

Eve takes a breath in. "Do you understand what you've done?" she asks, and Julia spits: "Nothing's happened. I'm back a little late. I'll apologize to Heidi. She asked me to look after him." *They are all meddlers*, she thinks, *with no understanding.*

Through the open door of the lodge, she sees Heidi has laid Gunther on the sofa: she is dripping milk from a bottle into his mouth. Frau Berndt lays a flannel on his forehead. She turns to look at Julia. "Go," she says.

Halfway up the stairs, the air around Julia seems to fold at weird angles. Eve catches her, putting warm arms around her waist and murmuring to her as you might soothe a startled animal.

In the apartment, Julia sits in a hip-bath and Eve sponges cool water over her head. She is sunburned: a vivid pink on her shoulders and face down to her collarbone, and the touch of the water stings. She welcomes it: penance. Eve's face makes her cry more: it is stern, understanding, deeply worried.

"I don't know," she says, when Eve asks her, very gently, what happened. A tiny splinter of her still believes it was a misunderstanding—Heidi never said what time she should be back. After a few minutes, she manages to say: "It was good to be with the baby," and Eve folds her into her arms. Her shirtsleeves are soaking but she presses Julia closer.

Frau Berndt's knock, and as usual, she enters without waiting for a response. She stands, hovering, in the doorway.

She says, "I have made Heidi and the child some soup."

"It was a bad mistake," Julia says.

"Heidi is angry. The baby is all right." Frau Berndt turns to go. She looks as though she wants to say, *No harm done*, but she cannot manage.

Rolf often sits with her in the afternoons. He senses that she can't cope with too much thinking, so he gossips: the Baron von Ephrussi passed on last week and at his deathbed were four women, only one of whom was his wife. A captain in the artillery has been deposed because he is having a liaison with a seventeen-year-old hussar. His eyes twinkle and he clenches her hand a little too tight. "Sorry. But it's hopeful, is it not? For our kind to be in the papers, even for a wicked reason."

The hints he has dropped have been enough for her to form a picture. Herr K. is handsome, Herr K. is kind; he is gentle and shy. She daren't ask whether Herr K. is married; she assumes from

Rolf's silence that he is. Whenever the subject threatens to stray too close—whenever it moves toward coupledom—Rolf's gaze becomes fleeting, rushing to all corners of the room.

One day she says: "I can't picture you domesticated. I thought you'd go on forever, happy with your own company." *And your big toothsome laugh*, she thinks, and feels a pang of future loss.

Rolf says: "And you? Are you different? Are you getting better?"

"Some days," she says. "And then I hear the baby and I'm so ashamed."

He blinks. "But the child is blooming. Like a weed." He thinks of the baby-snatching as a mildly eccentric moment, something to be laughed over.

"Am I bad?" she whispers.

He puts his head on one side. "I hope so. Just the right kind."

In the evenings, Julia feels better. She gets up around five o'clock and manages to dress before Eve gets home. One evening, feeling brave, she goes downstairs and knocks at the doorway of Frau Berndt's lodge.

They sit in the courtyard and drink schnapps—"Good for the soul," Frau Berndt says, keeping a watchful eye on Julia's glass—and when Eve comes home, her look of relief at seeing Julia awake and up is delightful. Heidi's apartment is silent; the door stays closed. "Give her time," Frau Berndt says, pressing her veined and wrinkly hand over Julia's.

Julia manages to cook, more often than not, though it's Eve who brings home food, and they sit in front of the stove. The tail end of August has cooled considerably; brown beech leaves whirl on the wind outside. A new kind of shyness has descended. In the silence, Eve holds her hand, and wipes the tears when they come.

One day Julia braves the outdoors. She feels nervous and sick as she reaches the archway of the courtyard; it is almost certain that Frau Berndt's eyes are on her from behind the curtained windows of the lodge.

She walks as far as the butcher's, with some idea of buying food for a Friday-night supper, and inviting Heidi and Gunther as a peace offering. When she arrives, there is a queue outside, a hot smell of innards and a stream of watery blood running from the doorway into the gutter, and she has to turn away. She walks back toward home; each step is an anticipated moment of relief.

As she nears the archway, Frau Berndt emerges from the lodge. She takes Julia's elbow. "Not too far the first time out of doors, hey? You and Eve can eat with me tonight. Here is your post. And here is your soup."

She hands over a flask of warm liquid and some envelopes. As Julia passes Heidi's door, it opens a sliver: Heidi's sharp white face peers out, with the round moon of Gunther's head below. She looks at Julia for a moment, then closes the door with a downcast, apologetic look.

Julia goes up to the apartment, pours the soup into a bowl, and lays the envelopes on the table. She knows she must not open Per's letter and yet she cannot help it. She tells herself she is angry and must know what it contains, the better to write and tell him never to contact her again. She tears at it, tears the enclosed sheet of notepaper almost in half, but can nevertheless read the contents.

I know you asked me not to write. Nevertheless, I thought you might like to see how you have been written about. I enclose two tickets to the premiere of THE PEAR ORCHARD. *Should you wish to meet to discuss any aspects of its composition, I would be pleased to receive you at the theater on any day prior to the opening on 7th September, between midday and two. I remain, &c. Per Lindqvist.*

That evening, they go to Frau Berndt's. Rolf is there, too; they light candles; he makes a play of placing them at flattering angles so that he will look younger. Eve laughs at his jokes. For Julia, the food, for the first time in three weeks, has some flavor.

"You look better," Frau Berndt says when they are sitting with a digestif in her salon area. Eve turns her head, expectant, to see Julia's response.

"I am going to try to apologize formally to Heidi tomorrow." There is a ruffle of acceptance in the room.

That night, she slides over in the bed and puts her lips up to Eve's. Eve, surprised, lets her. "Aren't you too melancholy?" she asks, and Julia whispers: "Not tonight."

◆

Julia spends as much time alone as she can. She declines offers of a longer walk accompanied by Frau Berndt, and she sends Rolf away when he comes to sit with her—she is up and about, you see, so much better already. On 6 September, she makes a special supper for Eve, and afterward, pulls her over to the bed and kneels at her feet. She has a vision of herself from above, of how her own eyes must look, drowsy and large-pupiled, as she bends to her work. Her mind is whirring, made of hundreds of ceaselessly mobile parts; this will make it still—it has to. She takes Eve's hand and forces it to cup the nape of her neck.

The next morning she kisses Eve goodbye as always and then she sits in her favorite chair for an hour. She is thinking about what Stockholm would look like—frost on the sidewalks of Drottning-gatan after dark—the students hurrying to their first classes at the Conservatoire.

At eleven o'clock she gets to her feet, puts on her overcoat and steps up to the mirror. She has made no special effort with her appearance, these past weeks; now she corrects some of the smeared kohl under her eyelashes.

She has almost reached the archway when Frau Berndt comes scurrying out of the lodge. "Where are you going?" she asks.

"Shopping."

Frau Berndt smooths her palms on her apron. "You have forgotten your bag."

"Just to the Kärntnerstrasse for some small bits."

"You are going to the theater."

"What theater?"

Frau Berndt cries out: "To see him. You're going to meet Per Lindqvist."

The light in the courtyard takes on a slant; it seems the windows and doors are half-open, listening, in the tremulous early-autumn heat. "You have been opening my post," Julia says. The fine tremble of her hands, so blissfully absent for the past week, starts up again. Frau Berndt stands very still. "Meddling," Julia says. "Mixing yourself in things that don't concern you."

"You concern me. I've been so worried—"

Frau Berndt, unsticking and resticking the envelopes of her private correspondence. "You had no right," Julia says.

"As your landlady—"

"Lonely person," Julia says. "Viper." It comes to her then that Frau Berndt has been on Heidi's side all the time, not Julia's. She has been whispering bad things to Heidi, painting Julia in a dreadful light, taking her part on the matter of the baby.

Frau Berndt draws herself to her full height. "There is no great sadness that can't be shared away. And I know a bad mistake when I see one."

"Goodbye," Julia says. As she passes under the archway, she hears Frau Berndt say, "I am not lonely," and begin to cry.

A memory, from two months after they moved in, when Frau B. had just begun to be a friend; when they knew little about each other. In the depths of the winter, on her day off, Julia, taking a string bag to the Tandelmarktgasse, pointing out cheap cuts with fingerless gloves. The cobbles were covered with glassy frost.

She'd walked toward home, and passing Mitzi's, glanced in at the fuggy windows. Frau B., in her best hat, sitting opposite a young man; laughing, rising from the table. Julia, cold inside and out, stopped on the sidewalk opposite. *The streets are slippery*, she told herself; *I will lend an arm.*

The young man dusted his hands on his thigh; he and Frau B. vanished, presumably to the till, and then appeared in the doorway. Julia lifted a hand in greeting, but Frau B. was looking narrowly at the gentleman. She could see him now: a good suit, those drooping walrus-mustaches that make men look sad, not disguising his extreme thinness; towering over Frau B.

A lover? Not impossible. Julia lowered her hand. Frau B. was fussing with the carpet bag she carried everywhere, drawing out her wallet, counting out notes. She shook her head as she spelled out the numbers; a sheaf of green and a few coins dropped into the man's hand. She closed the man's hand over the money and patted it; the wallet returned to the bag, and then the moment of parting. Too far away to hear the individual words, but Julia imagined briskness: *Till next time. Goodbye. Goodbye.* The young man patted his breast pocket in thanks, and moved away; his face preoccupied, as though his mind was already on the next thing.

Julia decided to make the best of it. She waved frantically. Frau B. crossed the street to join her, picking her way across the cobbles. Silence as they turned toward home. Frau B.'s lips were pursed, her gaze fixed straight ahead. "Steak?" she asked, and Julia proffered the blood-streaked paper bag. "Good. One should keep one's man well fed."

Julia kept quiet. She could always ask Rolf later: *Frau B. has a paramour?* She imagined him waving it away—*We must all get by somehow.*

Her feet skated from under her; the shopping bag flew up in a perfect arc, and she fell. Frau B.'s fingers gripped her forearms, help-ing her up. "My son," she said. "My smallest boy."

"I didn't know you had children."

"Three. Well, two, now. One died. This one, my youngest, my most troubled, is always in want of something. He likes wine, and smoking, and has no sense of finance. Not like his father. That is why I give him money." She sniffs. "Often quite considerable sums. In between times . . ." She sprinkles her fingers to indicate he is not seen.

Julia turned away to pick up her bag. She had bruised her knee; bent to rub it.

They walked on. The silence seemed calm enough to ask: "And that is . . . not an inconvenience? That he comes to see you for money?"

Frau B. turned an astonished face to her. "You mean, not for love?" She is shocked. "But money and love are not always differ-ent things. It doesn't mean that. Not at all."

Ada

———

IN THE DAYS AFTER THE WALK in the woods, Ada cannot catch Isabella on her own. Everywhere Ada is, Isabella is not—fleeing down the stairs and out of the house, waving in passing, on endless errands to the city. The advantage is that Emil, too, is absent; often in the city, working on one of her father's accounts. Ada's mother sighs: "What a shame he cannot have more of a holiday," and resumes her long watch at the empty grate.

One day, with the sun glaring down at the house and making bright white pools on the carpets, Ada's father summons her to his study. She enters to find him behind his desk, head in his hands in concentration, staring at a purchase ledger. When he looks up, he says, "Ah," and "Hello," as though she were a surprise, or a stranger.

He asks after her voice. "You seem better," he says, as if the information pains him. He tips his chair back. "I have been thinking about the future." He leans forward and draws a careful circle on his blotter with the tip of a finger. "There is a school near Innsbruck for young women. The headmistress reports that one of their recent graduates went to the University and may one day become a lady physician. There is a waiting list, references to be gathered, but she could admit you as early as next spring." He drums on the blotter. "If you liked."

She is silent. She is looking at his face and trying to understand the gesture.

"I could see you becoming a doctor. Couldn't you? Helping others?"

She discerns that he is truly trying to be kind. He shakes his head, as if it surprises him, too. "Say something," he says. "Or don't. Consider it. What would be the disadvantage? You aren't happy here."

She has a sudden urge to run to him, as she used to when she was tiny; to be wrapped up in his pine-and-tobacco smell and have the breath squeezed half out of her.

"Or do you not want to go away? Even if it means something good in your future?"

He has his palms on his cheeks, leans on the desk with his elbows, as if she were a difficult but soluble problem. His eyes look very blue in the fierce light. The distant sound of someone shouting, out on the lake, in excitement or despair.

She says: "If I were to go away, I would have to stop my acquaintance with Isabella. We could not be together here anymore."

He blinks. Then nods, slowly; tired. He sighs. "Give it some thought, about the school. Nothing stays the same forever. Go on now. Go outside. Enjoy your youth."

When Ada returns to the house after her walk, the servants are bringing the washing in from the lawn under the first spots of rain. It is a Friday and the Kellners are supposed to dine there that evening. She breathes in the linen smells and the last of the quiet, and then the door is opening, and Isabella stands with her hands on her hips in the doorway. "We've just arrived." She comes forward and clasps Ada's shoulders. "Those cheeks," she says. "The wind has given you roses."

She plucks at the skin just below Ada's cheekbones: sweet pain. "What do you say to one last turn around the garden? I think it's the last warm day, don't you? Let's go around to the stables."

Ada will be expected at four o'clock, for coffee and cakes with her mother. "Don't worry about that," Isabella says, confidential. "Come on—let's stretch our legs." She slips her arm through the triangle of Ada's. "Did you have a nice day?" she asks, pressing her body to Ada's side, as they turn the side of the house.

"I did," Ada says.

"Good." Isabella is looking levelly ahead, and frowning. Ada relaxes: she is in one of her elsewhere moods. She will come back in a swoop and a smile, in just a few minutes. She will ask about the treatment, and Ada will be able to say that it is complete.

"Shall we go to look at Doby?" Ada names Isabella's favorite horse, the one Ada thinks of as theirs because they always feed him together. Ada prefers the older ponies, droopy and threadbare.

"Perhaps," Isabella says. Then she digs gently into Ada's ribs. "Or should we go into the woods a little way, instead?"

Ada allows herself to be steered. They pass into the woods; their feet crackle on brush and twigs. Looking up, the trees rise around them, like the long under-teeth of a pike.

"My father has suggested a boarding school for the spring," Ada says.

"Oh, the medical one from the newspaper?" Isabella turns, delighted. "So modern! You are clever enough, I'm sure."

"I declined. It would not do for me to be very far from here."

Something is wrong in Isabella's face: a fierce blazing concentration. Ada feels the slip of their arms moving together. The air is taking a hot tinge around them, a scent of metal and lilies. Or perhaps—Ada dare not hope—perhaps it is a very right thing. Isabella might say: *After our talk the other day. I know I shouldn't feel as I do about you, but I can no longer pretend—*

"I have a question for you," Isabella says, stopping. She takes both of Ada's hands in hers. "How would you like to be a godparent? Or a kind of aunt." She reaches for Ada's cheek and brushes a strand of hair behind her ear, and while she is petting Ada she says: "I haven't told your father yet. We—Emil and I—wanted you to be the first to know."

There is a howl rising, somewhere: the wind in the trees. Isabella tries to brush a speck of dirt from Ada's shoulder. Ada seizes her hand and grips the fingers, squeezing them together.

"You're hurting me," Isabella says.

"You said I was special."

Isabella's eyes widen. "You are. That's why we are telling you first—"

"We went for that walk and you held my hand all the way home."

"I don't know what you mean."

Ada drops her hand. "You have been doing it for years. Being near me when you could. Stroking my hair. Calling me *darling*. You made me think you loved me."

Appalled, appalling silence. "Is that really what you think?" Isabella says. "Ada, I had no idea you were so. So ill."

She holds the fingers of the hand Ada has discarded. They stare at each other. "I didn't know," Isabella says. "I had no idea. I won't tell anyone, of course. Emil, or your father—"

"I'm not just someone's secret. And you knew. You did know."

Isabella has whitened. "How could I guess something so—" She clicks her tongue and looks away, still nursing the fingers of her right hand. "Ada, I have always been on your side, I have always tried to help."

"You never did anything that wasn't for you," Ada says, and Isabella turns and walks away.

Father sweeps Isabella up into his arms when he hears the news; lights the first fire of autumn in celebration. The evening passes— Ada sees her mother's watchful eyes on her during supper. She imagines that there will be a conference, of a kind, between her father, mother and Emil, remarking on her quiet behavior. *Ada does not like disruption. Give her time.*

After the supper is over, the adults stand in the salon. Emil has a glass of brandy with her father. He circles the liquid slowly; leans in to listen to Herr Bauer's advice. If it's a boy, teach him to swim early. For a girl, not too much freedom: don't let them run rings around you. Apple sauce with rum at bedtime. Gradually, the evening dies along with the fire; the adults make their excuses and go to bed. Ada sits alone, watching the last log fade into a crinkled gray.

When the house is quiet, she picks up one of the oil lamps from the window, goes out of the side door, and crosses the path to the woodshed. She finds the wood ax lodged in the block, next to the neatly stacked logs, and levers it out with a seesawing motion.

She doesn't meet anyone on the way to the beach. The pebbles grate under her feet; she turns toward the dunes, where the tall reeds are. She finds the boat, a smooth upturned shape, and carefully sets the lamp down on the sand. She lifts the ax over her head. There is a splintery crack, and another, and another. The boat is dying; a hole appears in its side, blacker than the dark around it, until there is more hole than wood. She leaves the jagged pieces where they lie on the sand and sets out toward the house.

Rolf

—

ROLF LETS HIMSELF INTO THE APARTMENT, waving to the old lady in the window opposite—they have become almost-friends, or at least not almost-enemies—and hulks his groceries upstairs.

He peels twirls of lemon rind for the syllabub; decants white wine into two glasses. He has brought guidebooks to Salzburg— foaming waterfalls and dark pine forests—and a local newspaper with advertisements for jobs. There are several opportunities for trade agents and he is not above factory work if it comes to it. The cost of living, they say, is not prohibitive.

He lights the fire—an indulgence, but it's not his fuel—and has a nip of brandy. Emil is expected at six: Rolf pictures him hurrying through the fine autumn rain, pressing his hat to his head. He will have, as he always has, that expression of nervous urgency; and when he sees Rolf watching from the upper window, his face will split into an enormous smile.

The day before, Rolf went to see Julia in the afternoon with a clutch of asters from the main bunch he'll bring Emil, and found her sitting at her table, writing a letter. When he came in, she covered it with her hand, like a schoolchild hiding homework from prying eyes, and then saw what she was doing, and laughed at herself. "You're better," he said. She replied: "I am." He felt a pang: he has liked the fact that she has had some trouble that he can help with. He has formed a new picture of himself: leaping up the stairs, arms full of flowers for a convalescent friend.

They sat at her table, drank tea, and gossiped. Tears only threatened once, when the subject strayed too close to Heidi. "I can't think what came over me," Julia said and Rolf, in his new persona, reached out for her hand.

"You were unhappy," he said. "And now you're better."

As he left, turning theatrically as he always did in the doorway, it occurred to him that there might not be very many afternoons like this to come, not that many evenings either, if he and Emil are to move away.

"Would you miss me?" he said, and Julia blinked.

"When?" she said. "Do you mean will I miss you? But when is there a chance to miss you? We see you every day, thank the Lord." She came to him and clutched his hand in her fingers and put the other hand up to his cheek. "Thank God for you, Rolf. What a question."

It was odd, then, that she was on the verge of tears, too. If he hadn't known better, he would have thought they were somehow taking leave of each other. But he'd put it from his mind, and it's only now, shaking the brandy in the glass, his feet warmed by the fire, that he thinks: *It was like a parting of lovers after a final quarrel.* He shivers—someone walking over his grave—and looks at the clock to find the time has gone faster than expected: it's ten past six.

Rolf's thoughts fly to a tram crash, the trampling of a horse, or a robbery. He gets up from the chair and walks to the window. The old woman opposite is not there; instead, there's an adolescent boy, stretched lankily in the armchair where she often sits.

Rolf paces the salon; picks up the books and smooths their covers, one by one. There's a smell of smoke from the kitchen; the roast duck is burning; he flaps ineffectually with a cloth, and opens the window facing into the interior courtyard. Supper will be ruined. Of all the nights to be delayed. For once, he may not crumble immediately, when Emil puts his hands up to his face and says, *I'm so sorry, I didn't mean to frighten you.* He may be cold, say something like: *Will you behave like this when we're in Salzburg?* It will be good for Emil, that spoiled summer child, just for once, to meet resistance.

He continues the imaginary conversation as he watches the lemon fool droop into itself. He pictures Emil first sulky, then penitent, saying how sorry he is; that he would never cause intentional hurt. He imagines the silkiness of Emil's cock in his hand and the warmth of his breath on Rolf's neck. Best of all, he imagines Emil picking up the guide to Salzburg, and flipping through the pages: his gaze coming to rest on one of the shepherd's huts, strewn about with edelweiss like a new constellation.

At ten to ten, the door opens, and Emil falls through. He comes straight to Rolf, and there is the musty scent of dried sweat and the sweetness of stale hops. He loops his arms around Rolf's neck and begins to try to kiss him—he pushes his hips aggressively into Rolf's, trying to back him against the wall.

"Sorry," he says, "sorry, sorry, sorry, sorry, sorry—" With each repetition, the word gets blurrier. Rolf tries to push the smear of his lips away, but Emil keeps pushing his mouth back onto Rolf's. Finally, he stands back, glittery-eyed.

"Don't you want me anymore?" he says.

He tries to turn Rolf around, to bend him over the arm of a chair. He does this by twisting Rolf's arm behind his back. Rolf kicks out, on instinct, and it connects with Emil's calf. Emil howls and spins away; sits down sharply, then springs back and seizes Rolf by the fork of the trousers.

"What is wrong with you?" Rolf shouts. He lifts himself up on tiptoes, to stop Emil from hurting him. Emil lets go, but tries to kiss him again and ends up whispering something in Rolf's ear that he thinks he can't have heard.

He takes Emil's wrists. "What?"

Emil says, as clearly as he can: "Isabella's pregnant." He rubs his face. "Five months. Due in December."

Rolf has to ask several more times. The answer is the same. "Why were you still sleeping with her?" he asks. "When did you find out?"

Emil has slumped into a chair. He picks up the Salzburg guide and drops it again. "She's my wife." A two-day stubble glints on his chin when he rubs it. "It's regrettable," he says.

"Regrettable?" Rolf lets the word sit on his tongue. It makes sense, of course, that Emil would still have had intercourse with Isabella. He might even have done it to avoid suspicion, which in a way, would be doing it for Rolf's sake.

"Are there any avenues?"

Emil looks up. "Avenues?"

Rolf licks his lower lip: a quick furtive swoop of the tongue. "From what you have said, she isn't the motherly type."

Emil laughs. "Oh, she's not. At least, not until they're a little older. She doesn't seem to mind them then." A brooding silence. "But it's what we do. People like us. And I might want them." He says this last thing slyly. "Children."

Cold panic. "You've never said." As if this was something he could give Emil, in any case: a child. He says: "Plenty of men choose to live their life apart from their family, for many different reasons. You could still play a part in their upbringing. We could say you had been transferred to Salzburg for your work."

From somewhere, floating music: a waltz being played on the piano in another apartment in the block. "No, you haven't understood at all," Emil says. He stands up. He seems to have simply thrown off the effects of the alcohol. "It is sad, it is regrettable, but this—whatever this is—is going to have to end."

Rolf feels his mouth slacken. *Whatever this is.* "Why? Nothing needs to change—"

"As I've said, I feel very sad about it," Emil says.

Rolf cannot see any emotion at all. "Come in and sit. Eat something. I know you love me." He crosses to Emil; puts his palms to Emil's chest. "It can be good, with us."

Emil has recoiled at the word *love*. He says—his voice cold, clear as a bell—"This is me telling you I don't want you. Can't you understand?"

"You feel responsibility toward the . . . toward the child and that's understandable. You are a fine person. You want to make me hate you, so it's easier on me, because you feel you have to leave. But can you be sure the child is even yours?"

Emil looks to the side, and in the lamplight, Rolf sees—or thinks he sees, which is enough—that his eyes are liquid and tearful. "You're wrong," he says.

Rolf picks up the Salzburg book and throws it at Emil's chest. It slips off and falls to the floor. "You are a good man," he says, "I know you are," but Emil has already opened the door.

Rolf clears the plates and cutlery back into the cupboard and puts the cork back in the wine. It seems important that everything is meticulously clean. He turns out the lamps in the salon and arranges the guidebook titles in a neat pile, and then goes to bed.

He sleeps suddenly and early and for one blissful half-second the next morning, he has no idea where he is or why he is there. Then he remembers. Does it help to cry out loud? He tries it: a stagey moan from his own mouth that sounds like someone else. He is out of practice and barely any tears come.

Very carefully, he collects his belongings and steps out. It is almost midday: everything is too bright and full of shopping crowds, and he walks mechanically toward the river. He has one thought, which is to find Julia and tell her what has happened. He realizes halfway home that he still has the apartment key in his pocket and that he probably forgot to lock the door behind him. *Let them be robbed.*

He walks down the Taborstrasse and under the archway. Frau Berndt is not in the courtyard: the curtains of her lodge windows hang still, but he has the odd feeling she is at home. He doesn't consider knocking on her door: it's Julia he wants; Julia can make sense of this, hold his hands and help him—*But, darling, it's just a lovers' tiff—he'll come back when he's calmer.* She will explain to him about the longing for a child; how it is a livable grief—look at her, she is almost better! Eve, later, can offer cigarettes and firm friendship.

He runs up the stairs to Julia and Eve's. As he nears the door, he is aware of a growing sound, low and repetitive. He stops on the little landing outside. There is a shushing sound inside the room—Julia's skirt; he realizes she must have come home just before him and not had time to change into her housecoat—and then the thud of someone, suddenly, kneeling.

"I didn't go in," Julia's voice says, behind the door. "I never would have gone in. I just wanted to see what it would feel like. I knew as soon as I got there that I didn't want to see him, that the worst thing I could think of was for him to come walking out."

"Why? Why did you go in the first place?"

Silence.

Eve again: "What were you hoping would happen?"

Silence.

"Oh God. You'd sleep with him to get a child? And then what? What would you have told me, if it had worked?"

"I don't know. I didn't think."

"You *always* think."

There is a crash, like a chair being tipped over, and a longer silence.

"You would have made up some story, and I would have believed it, because I'm stupid, aren't I?"

"I've been so unhappy. But it was the wrong answer to the wrong problem. I see that now—"

"Why can't you let it go?"

"I said it before, I didn't know, until I met you—"

"Why can't you be more like Frau Berndt? She's had suffering in her life. Or Rolf? He has nobody, nobody at all."

Rolf steps back from the door. It is a cold, clean cut. The blood rushes to his cheeks and recedes. He feels sick.

"You have me. You have always had me."

Julia: "I'm sorry, I'm so sorry, please don't go—"

The door flies open and Eve stands there. Her complexion, usually so smooth, is covered in angry blotches. Behind her, crouched on the floor by an overturned chair, is Julia. Her skirts are wide around her body. She looks up and sees him; sees immediately that he has been listening. "Oh, Rolf—" she says, and it isn't clear whether she is pitying him or asking for pity for herself.

Eve takes his arm and pulls him away, shutting the door behind her. "Don't you dare. You were my friend first," she says, and drags him with her down the stairs.

She talks and cries, sitting on the divan-bed in his studio, and he brings her cocoa and says nothing about Emil. His face has frozen into place as he nods and listens. It seems that Julia's ex-husband has been in town with his latest play, and that Julia arranged to meet him, but that she never kept the rendezvous. Eve's eyes are red and her voice is hoarse from the torment, and all Rolf can think is: *But she never kept the rendezvous. She came back to you.*

He suggests this, gently, and Eve's head whips up: she stares at him. "But she went," she insists, and then goes quiet, wiping her eyes with her sleeve. "It was all secrecy and lies. Why didn't she come to me?"

Rolf tries to think. He can't understand Julia's specific pain. Emil's face occupies his mind: last night, it had been so cold; at the hot springs, so alive. (*Just a small murder.*) "Only desperate people try desperate things. It doesn't mean she doesn't love you."

"It might," Eve says.

"Don't be childish."

She says: "If I were childish, a child, she might love me—"

He takes her by the shoulders. She recoils: it's true that she has never seen this Rolf, full of the fire of conviction. "She came back of her own accord. Now you go back and take care of her. Because that is what you promised you would do."

Eve looks up at him. "What if she lies again?"

"You're lucky to have what you have."

She climbs down off the divan and puts on her shoes, which she had kicked off in a rage on entering; shrugs on her coat. "Wish me luck."

She looks for a moment as though she will ask whether he is all right. She is conscientious even when she is in pain and she must realize from the ecstatic mask that has covered his face that something is terribly wrong. "I'm fine," he says, before she can phrase the question, and he knows he must never tell her—never tell anyone—what happened with Emil last night. Nobody has ever left him before; he is always the one to leave. Besides, the contretemps, Emil's premature departure, will not prove to be permanent. Like Eve, like Julia, all he has to do is a little bit of work.

Ada

—

LATE AFTERNOON, LATE SEPTEMBER. The seasons change faster outside the city. The grass is a crème-de-menthe green—yet to be the white spike-tips of winter. When Isabella and Emil arrive, Ada is in the hall to greet them. Isabella is wearing her best clothes and a full, false smile, and carrying her stomach before her, with that triumphant waddle. Emil fusses around her, his eyes darting everywhere.

He leans in and kisses Ada on each cheek, the traditional greeting, but his lips only ghost her cheeks, and his hands dance just shy of her shoulders. When he draws away he is already looking everywhere but at her.

Ada is wearing a dress that, for once, doesn't hide her.

"Won't you come in and have some drinks," she says.

Isabella says: "Haven't you grown up?" Her eyes are twinkling. She lays her hand on Ada's forearm. "Quite the hostess."

They sit in the salon—Emil helps Isabella into a low armchair. Ada's mother, a quivering bird, glances at Ada. Ada's father nods approval below bushy eyebrows at the butler, handing around little snacks. Isabella is a bright glittering queen. She folds her hands over her stomach.

They each take a small glass of sherry and discuss arrangements. It has been decided that Isabella will see out her confinement at the lake house, away from the smog of the city. Ada's father will hire a staff of new nursemaids and a doctor will be on retainer in the village. Everyone says the baby will be a boy because of how far forward the bump is carried. Isabella, hands waving, tells a story about shopping in the Holstenplatz. After a while, the story takes on a more and more exaggerated style; the threads interweave. She leans in confidentially to deliver the punchline and they all hang on her words and pretend not to notice that it makes no sense. Laughter and applause. Emil clasps his arm around Isabella's shoulder proudly, and looks around; showing off a clever child.

All is jollity. Ada's father puts his hand on Emil's shoulder as they go in to supper. Isabella glides; she exclaims, as she always does, on the beauty of this room: the glossy table, the showy silver cutlery. The dark panes of the French doors.

"Always so envious of your garden," Isabella says, allowing the butler to flourish a napkin over her extended belly. She smiles around—somehow her smile floats over Ada and away without settling.

It is impossible not to look at her, and they all do. She tells stories; Emil laughs at everything she says. Ada's father holds his ribs comically. Isabella displays all her white teeth. During the main course, emboldened, Emil tilts his chair on its two back legs, lays his arm along the back of Isabella's chair and tells a story of his own. He wants Ada's father's approval, casts nervous glances toward him. Ada's father sweeps a careful forefinger back and forth along the edge of the table, listening, watching the faint pink reflection of his own hand. As the story goes on, Ada allows her eyes to rest on Isabella's hands, on the precise way she cuts her meat and the way it vanishes into her mouth. Isabella looks up and catches her at it. And turns red. She looks Ada directly in the eye as she swabs her mouth with the napkin.

A flash, a blur, behind Isabella's chair, out in the garden— someone moving past the window. Ada shouts out in alarm. "What is it?" her mother squeaks. Isabella half-turns to follow Ada's gaze.

"What, Ada?" Her father, irritation already clouding his face.

"I saw something," Ada says. "Outside. Something moving."

A pause. "Perhaps a late bird?" Emil suggests. He gets to his feet and crosses to the window, makes a show of peering out. "Nothing there now."

"It wasn't a bird," Ada says.

"Well, what? A visitor? Don't be ridiculous, Ada, nobody comes out here."

The mood has turned cross. Ada's father starts to mop the last of his sauce with his bread, in swift, angry movements. "You are alarming Isabella," he says. "You are drawing the attention toward yourself, as usual." He shakes his head.

It is a nothing, a bagatelle, to apologize, so Ada does it swiftly and mechanically—"I am sorry for causing you a fright"—and returns to her inner world for the rest of the evening. She is sure of what she saw: a white, strained, staring face.

The second apparition is early in the evening of the following day. It has been one of those days in which the threatened rain has not yet come. Ada gets up to turn on the lamp by the salon window, looks out. Gunmetal sky darkens a fraction, and the maid Regine springs from the back door and sprints for the washing. Her skirts flutter, showing her ankle; drops fling themselves on Ada's window like a handful of pebbles.

Ada watches Regine tug the white linen from the line. It is close enough that she can see the pink of her fingers reaching up for the wooden pegs. Beyond Regine, there is the tree, its branches spreading finger-like and low; and beyond that the yew hedge that borders the back garden, before the woods. Just inside the gate is a hovering specter of a person: a tall man in a gray suit, face unclear, standing very still.

He is so clearly not supposed to be there that it takes a moment to register that he is real, and that he may have been watching for some time, may even have seen Ada come to the window. Regine cannot have seen him, or she would squawk in alarm and run inside. Ada watches her, the pegs captured between her lips, pulling her way along the line of sheets; but she has no reaction, even though she is facing in the right direction, and the person is in her line of sight.

Would a ghost not have some object in view? While she is considering the matter, he (it?) starts to take long slow steps toward the house. It is as if he cannot see Regine.

Some commotion at the door; the housemaid appears, standing on the patio, shielding her forehead with one palm, shouting to Regine. Regine is smiling with relief, walking to the patio, and together they are manhandling the damp cloth inside and in the time it has taken to observe this, the man has vanished.

Ada might ask her mother about the man. She plays the scene out in her mind: *Would you not like to go back and see the Herr Doktor? I am sure arrangements could be made.*

The next afternoon, she is waiting, watching for him in the seat in the salon window. Isabella is there, one hand on her stomach as she sits reading by the fire. Its merry crackle sounds like the bad kind of gossip.

Ada watches the changes that herald the oncoming night. From four o'clock the light hardens off and diminishes and the colors of the yew hedge and the lawn and winter roses begin to turn gray. "Aren't you reading, darling?" Isabella asks. "Shall we play a game?" Ada shakes her head without looking at her and feels Isabella's mild reproach, and the little shiver of her shoulders that means: *Suit yourself.*

Perhaps it is Isabella who has brought him, because there he is, creeping around the yew hedge; an architect pacing out a measure. The fire spits, a log turns, and Ada watches him. He must have done a lap of the garden; now he goes to stand by the yew gate with one hand resting on it, staring straight ahead. He makes no sign of coming close to the house.

It is almost a minute before she realizes he is looking at her, or at least into the room. She can see him more clearly now: gray suit, white shirt, white face, reddish beard. He has an extraordinary gift of standing still but she is sure he is a person. And she is sure, from the way he stands, that he is waiting for something: then she understands that he wants Isabella.

Rolf

———

AFTER EVE HAS LEFT, to go back to her safe and happy home, Rolf sits for a long while. He sleeps, until the evening, when Eve knocks.

He opens the door and she says, smiling: "I think it's all going to be all right." She looks tearstained but relieved. She doesn't ask to come in. "And you?" she says. "Are you?"

He tells her he is glad that the quarrel is over. It is marvelously easy to fool her: the casual flap of the hand as he says he is fine, rarely better, and will they have a drink in the lodge that evening, or is the argument between Julia and Frau B. still too raw? Eve shrugs—they can try—and so half an hour later he finds himself sandwiched between them on Frau B.'s ottoman. Julia looks thin but determined, and when she moves she takes care, as if each gesture is planned remotely. Frau B. is taciturn at first and then reaches forward to slap Julia's wrist; finally she bursts into tears and says, "You gave an old woman such a fright," and she and Julia sit hugging each other on the sofa for a long time. He feels embarrassed for them, and also the void of his own loss opening in his stomach, even as he grins and grins and smiles and smiles. Frau B. sings old Bohemian songs and he knows his performance is so perfect that nobody will even think to ask.

•

Time passes uncertainly for him. A week, then another, as if he is moving underwater. He leaves the apartment as little as he can without arousing suspicion. When he bumps into Eve or Julia or Frau B. he exchanges the day's news and excuses himself as swiftly as possible.

One Monday he arrives at a decision. He leaves his studio, waving cheerfully to Frau B., and walks into the Innere Stadt. He arrives at the Bauer business flat at quarter to ten and ascends the stairs. The old woman opposite is not there, and neither is the young lad.

As soon as he is inside, rushing from room to room, he recognizes that the feeling wasn't dread: it was hope. He had hoped, perhaps, that Emil would be curled up in the bed, or sitting in the armchair waiting for him to come.

He cannot fathom it, that he isn't there. He sniffs the pillows, smells the cushions, but there is no scent of Emil to comfort him. So he goes to the corner table, where a guest register is kept in a drawer, and copies down the address he finds embossed in the leather folder. He doesn't allow himself to flip to the last page, where he had written HERR UND HERR KELLNER, for a joke.

He arrives at the Stiegengasse at around eleven. He follows the road until he comes to the blank gray building whose address he had written down. Holding up a finger, he scans the brass plates by the main door until he finds it: *Bauer & Cie.—Konstruktion. Geschäfts-führer: W. Bauer.*

Across the street and two doors down, a small café is setting out tables on the sidewalk for the lunchtime rush. He asks for a table outside and orders goulash, which he leaves untouched.

He tells himself he is not watching the doorway, and then he admits that he is watching the doorway, but only so that he can see how Emil looks: if he's tired or unhappy. The waiter offers him a selection of newspapers, and then hovers, hopeful of a repeat purchase; Rolf orders two coffees, the second with whiskey, and when he asks for the time, having read everything and retained nothing, it is quarter past four. His rear is numb from the wrought-iron chair and the waiter is staring. "I'm waiting for a friend," he says. "Another coffee. No—a wine. Red." The waiter lifts an eyebrow— *Some friend*—tucks his tray under his arm, and turns inside.

The purity of the skin of Emil's back; not a single mole until you reach the lowest vertebra. Wasn't it strange, that night at the opera, that they should have seen each other there, for the first time, out of all the possibilities in the city? The Julia-of-the-mind wags her finger: *You made it so by wishing.* She's wrong. At quarter past five, Emil steps out of the doorway of the building opposite. He has the same gray coat on. He is in company with another man, and Rolf's heart rate builds until he sees that it is Herr Bauer. There is something slavish in Emil's concentration on his every word.

Rolf puts money under his dish and rises from the table with no sense of what he will say, but a feeling of loving confidence; Herr Bauer turns and, evidently thinking that Emil has a friend waiting, pats him on the shoulder—"See you in Neusiedl." He walks away, and Emil turns.

"I won't talk to you," he says. He holds up a palm; he doesn't move toward Rolf, who is forced to walk to him instead. "I won't talk to you about this." He is looking over Rolf's shoulder, at the waiter and the other diners; one woman has lifted her napkin to her mouth and is staring wide-eyed at them over the top.

Rolf comes to within three steps, and Emil turns on his heel and starts to walk in the same direction that Herr Bauer went. "How are you?" Rolf asks, falling into step. The thing is to be casual, to re-establish a friendly feeling.

"Fine," Emil says. "Leave me alone."

"You left suddenly the other night."

Emil turns a face that's cloudy with horror. "I left *you.* What are you doing? I don't want to speak to you. Stop following me."

"We could just talk," Rolf proposes. The first time they talked, they ended up in the park, in the glory of the green-gold surrender amongst the bushes.

"You could have embarrassed me in front of Herr Bauer," Emil says. A horse-and-cab is approaching down the street; the driver's whip is lifted. Emil raises his right hand and the cabbie shouts, "Whoa."

Rolf says: "I'd protect you from everything. Don't you see?"

"Why won't you just leave me the fuck alone?" Emil hisses. The taxi slows to a stop and he hops up on the running board and shouts at the cabman to *go now.* He is swept away down the street, clinging to the side of the carriage.

•

Rolf waits in the same café the next day, from half past two till six o'clock. He does not see Emil at all; he must not have come into the office. At half past six, Herr Bauer steps out, and turns the key in the lock—the last to leave.

Rolf puts some money under his empty coffee cup and walks after him. At the tram stop, he lounges against a corner of the wooden shelter. He follows Herr Bauer all the way to the Haupt-bahnhof and out onto the platform and, without buying a ticket, he boards the same train as him, toward the Neusiedlersee.

The train rattles on, and Rolf sits opposite Herr Bauer. He is amazed that he isn't recognized: he has been—they have both been—so close to Emil, it seems extraordinary that Herr Bauer doesn't know him. But nothing happens: Herr Bauer cracks open the newspaper, and his face disappears from view. At one point, when night falls, he lowers the news to stare, frowning, over the top of the headlines at the flicker of pine-tree silhouettes, but otherwise, it is as though Rolf does not exist at all.

At the station in Neusiedl, Herr Bauer swings himself up into a waiting carriage, and Rolf is left on the dusty road, helpless. He hesitates, then goes to the newspaper kiosk, and shows the elderly man waiting patiently behind the counter his wallet. "I found this on the train. It says it belongs to a Herr Bauer. Was that him, who just left? Can you direct me to his house?"

To his right, the vast faint shimmer of the Neusiedlersee; pinprick lights from the night-fishermen's boats bob in the distance. On his left, the shoulder of the forest, coming close to the road. This is unlit, and he stumbles over his own feet more than once; then sees, as he climbs, two lamps lit either side of white gateposts, just as the newspaperman said. The hair on his forearms prickles under his shirt and jacket; he hugs himself to warm up. The last train for Vienna is in two hours; he will just go up the drive a little way and see what the house looks like; see what kind of place Emil is spending so much time in.

He stands at the gatepost. If anyone asks, he will say he is lost. The house is fifty yards away. A maid is lighting the lamps on either side of the door, so that the scene is suddenly illuminated in color; her uniform turns from gray to blue.

He waits for an indeterminate time: long enough for the birds to stop singing and for it to be completely dark. The lights in the house turn on and off as the inhabitants move from window to window, but the shutters are being closed all over; he cranes and strains his eyes but cannot see Emil, at this distance, so the only thing to do is to move closer.

As he walks up toward the house, a light goes on in the right-hand downstairs window: a glossy table, candles, a butler standing by a sideboard. Five empty chairs. Behind the glass, a faint hum of sound—and a group of people walk into the dining room and take their seats.

It is like watching a play. Emil is there, taking the seat with his back to the window; next to him is a woman, maneuvering herself into the chair next to him. She is pregnant, and Rolf cannot see her face.

He moves closer. If he keeps out of the circle of the light he won't be seen. He stops at the edge of the yellow oblong. Opposite him, in the only seat facing the window, is a girl, scrawny-necked and with her hair scraped back.

This must be Ada, the daughter of the family, whom Emil dismissed with a wave of the hand: *She's like a puppy-dog around my wife.* Is it the same person he saw with Emil at the opera, that first time? That person was smaller, and more hunched.

He moves closer still. From here, he could almost stroke the back of Emil's neck. She widens her eyes; a muffled sound of alarm. She is looking directly at him.

He lets the oncoming night swallow him until he can't see his feet fall on the road, and he doesn't stop until he sees the station lights come into view. *Never do it again,* he repeats to himself with the rhythm of the train. *Never again.*

The next day he sleeps late, and when he wakes up his head quickly fills with plans, and lying in the fusty semi-dark, he narrows down the options until he is left with just one. The sun pours through his windows when he opens the shutters, so he takes his pencil and paper to the courtyard.

◆

Heidi and Julia are sitting on Frau Berndt's chairs in the oblong of sunlight in the courtyard just north of the archway. Heidi has young Gunther in her arms—he is clamoring to be held upright—and she and Julia are talking quietly. "Rolf," Julia says, with pleasure, when he approaches, the third chair hooked under one forefinger. She looks tired but peaceful. "Catching up on some correspondence?"

"I owe my mother a letter," he lies. He feels better, in the company of these women. Young Gunther crams his fist into his mouth, stares at him, and makes an inarticulate sound: a baby's hello. Julia and Heidi smile, and turn back to their conversation.

He notices, even as he starts to write to Emil—long, looping phrases of love and commitment—that Heidi, for once, is doing more listening than talking. She has her head on one side, eyes narrowed, and Julia is speaking of the past. She talks about Per Lindqvist; about her younger self; her longings and opportunities, and Heidi listens to it all. At a certain point, she passes Gunther over to Julia without a word, and Julia buries her face in the back of the baby's neck.

You will be giving up a great deal, I know that, in leaving your family, Rolf writes, his hand chasing over the page, *but I promise you the risk is worth it.*

"Lucky Rolf's mother," Julia says, watching the pages multiply. She sits cheek to cheek with Gunther, holding him up to the light. Rolf thinks: *She knows,* but then he realizes she can't possibly know; she is far too dazed with her own pain. He will explain the whole situation to them, the whole misunderstanding, one of these days.

He goes twice more to the house at Neusiedl, intending to deliver his letter, and twice he fails. The first time is just after he's written the letter; in the evening again. A maid is bringing in the washing, and so he cannot get into the house—he plans to leave the envelope somewhere on a table or desk—and reluctantly he turns for home.

The second time, he is more daring. He visits in the early afternoon, when Emil and Herr Bauer will probably be at work; he walks with quick, precise steps—*I am but a weary rambler who has lost his path*—around the inside perimeter of the garden and stops at the yew gate to look at the house.

Two shapes are visible behind a ground-floor window. The girl, Ada, is sitting in the window seat, but it's the person behind that makes him hiss out his breath and stand, airless. He is forced to admit, as he tries to make sense of every single feature through the swirling glass, that it's a good face. The mouth spiteful, the eyebrows arched. A person who would eat the world whole. She is sitting, one hand resting on top of her bump, focused on some interior scene. He watches for a minute or so longer, until he has everything memorized.

On Friday he sits in his room and drinks a bottle of wine and thinks about the summer and the hot springs, about Emil's face turned toward him on the green grass; when Frau Berndt comes knocking, asking for a favor in her fluting voice, he pretends not to be home. He slips out at quarter past three in the afternoon, walking quickly past the lodge, and thinks he sees the corner of a curtain twitch disapprovingly, the purse of Frau Berndt's mouth in the gloom.

He takes the five o'clock train to Neusiedl—neither Herr Bauer nor Emil is on it—then the familiar path up the road. It is almost seven o'clock by the time he arrives at the house: as he rounds the gateposts, he sees that the downstairs windows are all lit up. On the right-hand side, the dining room: servants move around in the reddish lamplight, laying cutlery and rearranging candlesticks and dishes, their faces fixed. On the left-hand side, in the living room, a drinks party of some kind is in progress. Figures stand with glasses in hand: marionettes in a puppet show. Isabella is there: wineglass held to her lips.

He moves closer. Her face comes into focus more sharply. She is listening to something the bald man standing opposite is saying: her face is clear and responsive; she nods occasionally, and smiles. He can see how having such a person listen to you in this way might be enough to keep you trapped; one might come to rely on her advice.

Another few steps, and a change of plan has settled: he won't just leave the envelope on a table somewhere; he'll hand-deliver it. He wants Isabella to see his face.

He is two steps away from the door when it opens and someone slips out. The pale girl. He tries to move past her but her hand snaps around his wrist. "You're the ghost," she says.

◆

Two days later, they sit opposite each other in the Café Chrome in the Michaelerplatz. The venue was his suggestion: he may be able to catch some apparition of the time spent here with Emil. It may help to explain to her his feelings.

They covered the specifics while her hand was still on his wrist, there in Neusiedl—*Who are you here for? Him? Her? A letter? Why not give it to me? Why are you here really?* She surprised him by asking: "Are you his lover?" He'd laughed in delight—that she should be so perceptive, that she should understand what it meant—and said he was, before he could be afraid to be honest, and she'd said: "I remember you. From the Opera House. You called us a cab. We should meet. Not here."

He assumes she wants money. She could blackmail him by threatening the police. She is wearing what he can only assume is her "town" outfit, although it's still monstrously drab: dark dress, dark coat, that odd silver hair pinned up like a spinster. She sits very still as she listens to him. He explains, or tries to, what brought him to their house, though now it seems, even to him, like an outlandishly reckless gesture. "I just wanted to see him," he says, rubbing his face, "I suppose." He tells her how long they were together; the promises that were made. He has some idea of playing on her adolescent romantic fantasy, but in truth, she is very easy to talk to: the blankness of her face is like an invitation. "You are his cousin? Ada Bauer? The one with the speech problems?"

She nods. "All quite better now," she says. Then she is silent again. He thinks that if she were going to ask for something from him, she would have done so by now.

"Can you arrange for him to meet me?" he asks. "You could talk to him." At the same time, he thinks how piteous this is, to be asking for help from a girl of—what? "How old are you?"

"Sixteen."

He is surprised. She seems older. "Don't go to the police," he says. "Please don't tell them I was trespassing. I can give you money—"

She shakes her head. "I don't want money . . ." She pauses. "I want to be heard. And then, when you've heard, you will listen to a proposition."

She tells him about the day Emil came to their house, when she was seven. How he became part of the family. The boat trip; her terrors. The letters to Peter, his boarding-school friend. And then— Isabella, arriving one day, changing things. Her voice softens; her whole body. He immediately recognizes, though she looks down at her lap, what's between her and this Isabella. *You're like me*, he thinks. At least that explains how she knew he was Emil's.

"You love her." He shades his eyes, looks at her; laughs.

She looks past him, frowning; up at the sky. "I'm not sure anymore," she says.

He knows denial when he sees it. "All right," he says. "Fine. You don't love her. Can you arrange for me to see Emil?"

She tells him more. About the day in the woodland clearing, where he pushed her to the ground and tried to force himself on her, but could not manage it. About the fumbling efforts, whenever he felt like trying again; the long history of being enemies; about his cruelty. "You look like my father," she says. "Whom he idolizes."

This is absurd. Apart from the fact they both have beards; they are both confident men, slightly older. And to hurt this child-woman. Why would he? Impossible. "Impossible!" he says. She is lying, for attention. This is something young girls do, or so he's heard. "He's a good man. He feels ashamed, and does not see a way out of his current predicament. With the baby, I mean."

She blinks slowly. "Did he ever try to hurt you? I mean, physically?"

He recoils. He is thinking of the times in the apartment, when Emil said *yes* to Rolf's *no*: the quick, bitter slap to the cheek. At the time, he'd thought he hadn't minded; he'd put it down to a case of nerves; ascribed it to Emil's great desire for him, which would not be repressed, and ignored the lingering sick feelings. What had been the alternative? To say no, and lose him? He thinks of Emil's tears: *I'm a monster*, his need to be shushed and reassured; and at Lobau, the swimming spot, asking to be forgiven; and of his coldness, when they separated. *As I've said, I feel very sad about it.*

She says: "Emil is built to cause suffering. He takes some of you and if he likes it, he comes back for the rest. He doesn't feel things like normal people."

Rolf says, and it sounds like a child's voice to himself: "Does he love Isabella?"

She shrugs. "Does it matter?"

They sit for a long time in quiet. Rolf shades his eyes and looks into the sun and pretends the light is making his eyes water, that he's not crying. He remembers how it was when he first came to Vienna. He'd hitched a lift into the city on someone else's coach, rolled along the Ringstrasse, terrified of the tall buildings. The work at the Opera House, shocking at first, filled what he needed, and gave him money. The tall buildings became necessary; soon they were like his friends. Best of all, he was free. *I was always free*, he thinks, *until I met him.*

"You said you had a proposition," he says.

She smooths her hands on her skirt. "Have you considered the child?"

He laughs. *Only every other minute.* She says: "Have you thought what it might mean for Emil Kellner to have a baby? What he might do to it? Think about what I've just told you. How he was with me."

Moments fly past in rapid calculation. He is still unwilling to believe. He watches her: she won't meet his eye. "What are you saying?" he says. "What are you asking?"

She is a pale filament; looked at too closely, she might fly away. "I think we can help each other."

Julia

———

JULIA RETURNS TO HER JOB at the Embassy at the end of October. Financially, there is no other choice for them, even though they both know it's too early. She has lost twenty pounds; her cheekbones stand out. "Am I gorgeous?" she asks Eve, with a bitter laugh, as she gets ready to go. On the first day, Frau Berndt accompanies her, and comes into town to walk her home again. This continues for a week, until one morning, Julia says she can go alone.

It is a day of rushing weather and showers that hurl rain against the windows of the building. "Grim," says one of her colleagues, without looking up from her typewriter; she hits the carriage return for emphasis. Julia has forgotten her umbrella; the sky outside gets dark at two o'clock, and she suddenly wants to be at home very much. She has misunderstood the vague panic that rises from her gut and threatens to choke her, its ebb and flow. She makes her excuses to the other secretaries—a stomachache, a quick apologetic smile—and leaves, hurrying for the tram stop on the corner.

All the way home, her hands shake, whether in her lap or clutching the guardrail, wherever she tries to put them. Frau Berndt, who has been reading up on neurosis, has explained that it is just another facet of her hysterical problem, and that it should go in time, if she keeps talking. There is no money to see a proper analyst, and so there is not much she has not told Frau Berndt, in tears or not in tears, perched on the sofa in the little lodge.

She quickens her step as she turns into the Taborstrasse. On the way into the courtyard, she stops outside Frau Berndt's to knock. Eve won't be home for hours, and she doesn't want to be alone. As usual, she raps on the door and then turns the handle without waiting. It doesn't budge.

Footsteps from inside, moving toward the door. There is the clunk of a key turning; instead of Frau B., Eve's frightened eyes looking out, her long white fingers curled around the edge of the frame. "We didn't expect you back so early," she says.

"I didn't have an umbrella," Julia says, uselessly. "Why's the door locked? Can't I come in?"

Eve holds the door open; pecks her on the cheek as she passes. Inside the tiny living room, there's Frau Berndt, sitting on the edge of the horsehair sofa, and Rolf, cramped as he always is, folded almost double. Both look startled.

"I was going to come and collect you," Frau B. says, rising to her feet. "Poor thing. You're soaked."

"I'm fine—just a little rain." They look at her, blank, inquiring, vaguely irritated. "Have you been talking about me?" Then she sees, from Rolf's flushed face, that they have been arguing.

He is leaning over the drinks table, as if to cover a piece of newspaper with his elbow; she sees the edge of the *Neues Volksblatt*. Seeing her looking, he lifts it, flips it over, rolls it and stuffs it into his inside pocket. "Job-hunting?" she asks, and he nods.

"Has something happened?" she says to them all. She feels ridiculous.

"Nothing at all," Rolf says.

"Sit," says Frau Berndt. Someone knocks at the door—Heidi's voice calls "Only us"—and she comes in, with Young Gunther asleep in her arms. "What's this all about?" she says, as she walks over to the chairs.

"Shall we go home?" Eve turns to Julia. Her face is pleading. She takes Julia's elbow, in a grip that's a trifle too strong, and steers her toward the door.

In their apartment, Julia rounds on her. "What was it?" She has found a possible answer, too cruel to be real. She sits on one of their dining chairs. "I have been much better. I feel I can be better still. If you are going to get doctors—if you are going to have them take me somewhere—"

Eve takes her hands. "Nothing like that." She is white faced. "Just one of Rolf's crazy schemes."

"Is it money again? I don't mind if you want to lend him some." She would do anything to keep the safe warm feeling between them.

"Not money."

"Then what?" Julia asks unhappily. "Why won't you tell me?"

Eve says: "Trust me. It doesn't matter."

"I don't understand," Julia says. "You're frightening me. It would be better if I knew."

"It wouldn't." However much Julia wheedles, she will not say another word.

The next week, Julia brings home a bonus—a tip from a diplomat who's taken a shine to her—and suggests a group supper at Mitzi's. It will be a chance to prove her wellness: to sit in company and not excuse herself once; to stay put, instead of staring with vast dark eyes at her own reflection in the bathroom mirror. Eve, sitting behind the newspaper in her armchair, looks over the top of it at her. "Can't it just be you and me?"

"I thought you'd like to see everyone. Rolf is hardly ever home."

Eve crosses the room and clutches her by the waist: every inch the gallant. Her look is turned down at the corners; she's focusing on a spot by Julia's feet. "Whatever happened to romance?" She pushes a kiss, slightly too hard, into the angle of Julia's collarbone.

"Well, nothing happened to it. Wouldn't you like to see our friends?"

"I want to see you more."

They leave for the restaurant, slightly cross with each other, Julia stalking two paces ahead. Frau Berndt tugs aside the curtains to the lodge and gives them a wave as they pass. Julia waves back. *See you later*, she mouths, and Frau Berndt vanishes from the window and appears in the doorway a second later. "I wanted to say goodbye for a few weeks," she says.

Julia frowns. "Goodbye?"

"My cousin cannot manage with her gout. I have said I will help her move into her son's house."

Julia says: "We'll miss you." In the two years they've lived there, Frau Berndt has never been away for more than a couple of days in the summer, to the medicinal waters at Zeefeld; a bird-watching expedition to Linz.

They order the best of everything—Julia insists on it, with a rising quality of desperation. She presses veal stew on Eve, and a bottle of Sekt, presented with a flourish by Mitzi herself. They discuss an opening at the tailor's—the manager has left suddenly—it would be perfect for Eve to take his place, and more money. The problem: there is another assistant who is technically first in line for a promotion. He would consider it disloyal if Eve were to make herself available for the job. "Let's stop talking about it," Eve says, stabbing at her meal with a fork.

Julia feels smooth and in control, just like the old days. She makes jokes about the Swedish ambassador's cat, an evil-tempered Burmese that accompanies him to official functions. Eve says nothing, so she talks instead about Young Gunther, who has recently begun to crawl, and was found exiting the courtyard and heading down the Taborstrasse. Dessert comes: *Sachertorte* with cream, and Eve sighs and separates the icing from the crumb.

Julia puts down her fork. "What?" she says. "What is it?" She stares at Eve. "I am tired of guessing."

"I promise I'll tell you, but not yet," Eve whispers.

Phantom pains yet to come loom large in Julia's mind. Eve may be ill and hiding it from her: last week, in a fit of paranoia, she studied every part of Eve's body while she slept, and found not a single blemish. Perhaps some young thing has caught Eve's eye at the tailor's shop. It isn't out of the question; and now, it seems the only thing that makes sense. After all, isn't that how they met? "Let's go, then." She pays the bill, throat tight, says goodnight to Mitzi, and they step out into the street.

Frost is scattered like icing sugar on the cobbles. For a few paces they walk in silence. Eve slips, flails, and Julia catches her and rights her.

"I've saved you. Now you have to grant me just one wish."

Eve looks wild; her hair in tufts, her breath in clouds from the cold. "What?" she says, though she must know what is coming.

"Why are you behaving as though the world is on your shoulders? I am better, aren't I?" As she says it, Julia knows this is not quite true, and that Eve knows it, too. She is better, but not herself, not yet. She laughs, shaky: "I am beginning to think you have a paramour." She stops dead. "Do you have someone? Someone that's not me?" Pressure builds up behind her eyes.

"Of course not."

Eve has stopped, too. Julia looks at her face for reassurance. "There couldn't be anyone else. That's the problem."

Julia laughs. They start to walk again. "Why is that a problem?"

Silence again. It has begun to snow, in complete silence, a whirling of tiny flakes. They pause just before the archway.

Eve says: "If you had a choice. To do something that might make one person unhappy but another person very happy? If it was morally justified?"

"Is this about taking the first assistant's place? Why shouldn't you have it? I'm certain you are the better seamstress."

Eve holds herself, wrapped in her own arms. Julia kisses her cold lips; retreats, assessing, and says: "Depends. *Cui bono?* For you—of course—I'd do anything at all."

Ada

———

JUST AS SHE IS CALM in everyday life, Isabella is calm about the baby. In November, a new nursemaid is hired from the city, but she has nothing to do, and spends her days in the living room, knitting hats and boots and tiny clothes. Doctors pass through the house and make pronouncements: Isabella waves them away, confident. Of course the child is in position. Of course it will be a boy. She often has Emil sit with her, his palm on her belly, a dutiful expression on his face as the creature moves behind its membrane of skin. "There," she will say to him, fiercely joyful: "Did you feel that?"

One morning, with the ground outside toughened by frost, Ada goes to her father's study. She knocks and enters to find him adding up a wavering column of figures. He doesn't look up.

"I have been thinking about the future," she says, and he refocuses, from desk to her face. Expectant but cautious: "Yes?"

"I think the boarding school is a fine idea."

He puts down his pen. It rolls onto the floor and he ignores it. "Are you sure?"

He is frowning; the pads of his fingertips have ink on them, and he moves them distractedly. "You don't have to go this academic year," he says. He sounds almost wistful. "You might like to start your study of the *corpus physicus* here at home. I have some of your grandfather's textbooks somewhere—"

166

"I should go this year," she says. She looks around the room: any-where but at him. It is large, and square, with big bright windows, and filled with things he has collected on his walks and travels: pipestems found on the paths in the forest, spent shell casings, a porcupine quill. "I want to go."

He sits back, locks his hands behind his head. "If you're sure," he says. And then: "I had hoped you might get to know the baby."

She wants to tell him everything: to perch on his knee and play with the brass letter opener, as she did when she was small, when she was still a child to him. "I can't."

He gets to his feet and crosses to the bookshelf by the window. He bends away from her, searching for a book, so that his face is hidden, and clears his throat. "I will miss you," he says.

The first truly cold night, Ada is woken by a murmuring from the next room. Two people are talking—one calm, one agitated. She gets out of bed, pads over to the door, and peers outside. Looking down the corridor, she sees her mother is doing the same: lamp held high, her frightened face visible in the crack of her bedroom door. The voices are louder. A door opens and closes: someone in the hallway downstairs is saying, "Yes, go now, quickly."

The next morning, the house is quiet. It has snowed heavily for the first time, leaving a deadening coating on the ground, and there is no sound from outside. Emil sits in the living room, lips pursed, his hands on his knees. "Try not to worry," Ada's mother advises, and he nods. Footsteps scurry back and forth in the upstairs corridor: the doctor's, then the nursemaid's. Sometimes a door opens and closes and Isabella can be heard, making hissing, grunting sounds. Herr Bauer locks himself in his study and asks for trays to be sent up at lunch and supper.

There is no precisely identifiable point when the baby comes: only that toward six o'clock, with the fire crackling in the grate, the doctor comes downstairs, washing his hands on a wet towel, and invites Emil up. He does not reappear before supper, so Ada and her mother dine alone. "I trust all's well," her mother says, taking apart a finicky piece of fish with her fork.

After they have eaten, the doctor appears in the hallway. He is carrying his black case. He puts on his hat and coat. "Are there trains at this hour? I can make it if I walk fast. No—don't trouble about the carriage. I prefer to get some air." He looks harried: he has a morning surgery in the city tomorrow. "Oh, and it's a girl," he says.

The next morning, Ada and her mother enter the bedroom as quietly as possible. Isabella is asleep on her back: Ada's heart flies to her, because she looks so tired and pale, greasy hair spread out over her shoulders. The room smells of antiseptic. Ada's mother holds her hand, and they step over to the bassinet.

The child—the girl—looks raw: prematurely peeled. Her eyes are tight shut and she doesn't move as they bend over her. "Can she hear us?" Ada asks. It seems impossible that this thing is alive in the proper sense. "Oh, yes," Ada's mother says. She checks the bed— Isabella is still asleep—reaches out her little finger, and inserts it into the child's fist. The child opens one eye, then the other: they are smeared with film, like an old person's. After a second's quiet contemplation, the baby sneezes. For a moment, in her expression of surprise, the way the face settles again, it is possible to see the future person in the tiny body. "You see?" Ada's mother says, looking at her finger, tightly curled in the baby's hand. "They hold on for dear life."

Ada goes straight to her bedroom, sits at the tiny desk, and composes a letter to Rolf.

She arrived today. We said three weeks. Let us fix it for the sixth of January.

Her hands shake as she slips the note into the envelope, which now seems to her childish: pale pink and lavender scented.

Whorls of cloud sit on the horizon. There is a shrinking of the orange sun into a speck, then a line, then a haze. On the Neusied-lersee, it is possible to hear the shouts of the fishermen, standing in their rowing boats, hauling up the nets. But it is cold, so cold: they're muffled, their heads are indistinct, their movements jerky.

Five o'clock, and Ada is standing at the living-room window. The fire is eating itself in the grate. Outside, the lawn is grayish-white under its blanket of snow; the trees lining the drive are tall sentinels, and beyond that, the fringe of conifers separating the bottom of the garden from the road is a dark lacework mass.

She puts down her book, walks upstairs, and stands on the landing to listen to the house: the tap of the housemaid's steps on the tiles of the back corridor; the faint sounds of laughter from the kitchen. And from this floor, her parents' and the guest quarters, nothing—nothing—then the rising siren of the baby waking and starting to cry.

She is three weeks old and fretful. Isabella is in the big guest room, resting up most of the day. The baby is in the small maid's room, so it can be checked on easily, and so Isabella can hear it, even if she isn't well enough to get up. Herr Kellner spends most of his time out on business visits with Ada's father, or reading in one of the downstairs rooms.

Ada goes to the child's room and slips inside.

The baby is in the crib. The room is in shadow because the maid has not yet come around upstairs and so its mewling face isn't clear straightaway; Ada lifts her and studies her in the snowy light from the window. She is composed of separate parts, waving fists and capped head and bump-nose, and her eyes appear sealed, like the eyes of baby mice or cats. But her mouth is stretched into a long shape and she is whimpering, the build-up to a real cry.

Ada shushes her, knowing that it's no good, it will wake Isabella; and the door opens, and there she is, thin in her white nightshirt, reaching out for the baby.

Ada puts the baby in her arms. Isabella's face is pale and unmade-up and hovering with anxiety until she receives her child, and then she starts to lull and soften at the edges. "Thank you for looking after her."

Ada nods.

"She wants a feed," Isabella says, and lifts her breast out of the collar of her nightshirt.

Ada looks away. It would be so easy to warn her: *I have done a terrible thing.* Since the birth, Isabella is different: tired and resigned; but when she looks at her child, there's a kind of radiance to her face that has never been there before.

Downstairs, the front door opens and Emil and Ada's father come in, stamping the snow from their boots and clasping their gloved hands close, unfurling scarves, hanging up overcoats. "Ada," says her father, "there you are!"

She steps off the foot of the stairs and he reaches out and twirls her around by the waist. His mustaches tickle her ear. "There," he says, setting her down again. "Isn't she a great fine girl?"

"She is," Emil says. As always, his grin is too bright, disguising extreme pain. Ada's father turns into the salon. They follow.

Ada's mother is sitting by the fire, a magazine in her listless hands. "Oh! You're early!" she says, and the magazine falls to the floor. Ada walks across to pick it up and replace it on her lap. Her father is by the drinks cart, serving himself a brandy—he lifts the decanter and shakes it inquiringly, and Emil nods yes. "Ada?" her father asks, and she shakes her head. It is new, this thing of his, of treating her like an adult. Emil takes his tumbler and swills it, then knocks it back in one mouthful.

"Is she coming down?" Herr Bauer asks, and Emil shrugs like a schoolboy, and then remembers to whom he is speaking. "Not sure," he mutters, more cordially.

"It's always distracting when the baby first arrives," Ada's mother says. Her knitting needles are clacking at speed.

Ada thinks: *Freeze time.* Look at how they are. Father, like some sort of giant restless hound; Emil, worry written all over him, and burning resentment quivering from his ankles to the nape of his neck. Her mother, immobile but for the blur of her hands; eyes fixed on the fire, the books; the brandy; the logs in the basket. The long green velvet curtains, and beyond that, waiting, perhaps already in the garden but more probably in the woods or the beach, is Rolf.

It occurs to her that she could simply run into the woods and shout until she finds him. It would be possible to talk him out of the plan. It has all been a mistake. It must stop. But that isn't how this is going to happen. She wants the plan; "wants" is the wrong word. It is necessary.

Her father is telling an anecdote about a lazy foreman who catches his foot in a machine; the foot has to be amputated. It isn't clear whether anyone should laugh, until her mother says, staring at the knitting: "I think that sounds horrible."

Isabella enters the room; in the confusion nobody has heard her footsteps. She is wearing a plum-colored dress with lace around the low neckline. "You look beautiful, Isabella!" says Ada's mother, and Emil's lips move into something that wants to be a smile. Isabella does a mock-curtsey, her eyes moving over the liquor tray. Ada's father rushes to assist, and Isabella's eyes follow the movement of his hands.

"What's good for mother is good for baby!" she exclaims, lifting the small crystal glass to her lips. Ada's father locks his hands behind his back and rocks on his heels, and Ada moves to the window. There is nothing to be seen, but she feels him out there, waiting.

Over supper the talk is all of the new factory Father is building, and Ada, who has no appetite, pushes her food around her plate and half-listens, half-watches Isabella.

She drinks glass after glass. A drop falls onto the lacework of her collar and she brushes it away with a giggle. Her eyes are sunk deep with sleeplessness. Emil shifts in his seat, and Ada's father speaks more loudly as he senses that the attention in the room has shifted away. The butler stands impassive next to the sideboard.

"When will you go back to your own apartment?" Ada's mother asks, serving herself potatoes.

"We haven't discussed it," Isabella says. Emil's eyes flicker over the tabletop and find the black oblong of the window behind. Isabella puts a spoon to her mouth; pauses. "You'll be glad to see the back of us, I shouldn't wonder!"

"Not at all!" Ada's father spreads his hands. "You know you're welcome here."

"You're very kind," Isabella says. Ada doesn't believe a word of her contrition, but she does believe in the self-pity. Tears fall into Isabella's soup, and nobody knows where to look. "I'm silly," Isabella says, "it's the tiredness," and Ada's mother makes soothing noises.

Strange, Ada thinks. A month ago she would have killed to have just one of those tears on the tip of her finger.

The meal ends; the windows are dark; the candles low. Ada's father takes Ada's mother's tiny hand and leads her to the door. Emil copies him, taking Isabella's forearm in his grip. He makes a movement as if he'll stretch out the other hand to Ada, in a ghastly joke, but then remembers himself, and they too float out of the room.

They are ever so modern, ladies and gentlemen withdrawing together: but, as Ada's father would say, they are a family. He pours more drinks; a cigarette for him, and another for Emil; Isabella, white faced and nauseous-looking, declines.

No one says anything for a while. Father shakes out the newspaper and grunts at the news of the Siege of Adrianople. Emil twists his tumbler of brandy in his hand.

The clock strikes nine o'clock. What tired mice they are! Ada's father stretches and yawns and gets up to go first, delivering a round of kisses-on-cheeks. Then Ada's mother, as befits the senior woman of the household, her small feet swishing under her dark dress.

At last Emil gets to his feet, drops a kiss on the crown of Isabella's head and leaves the room without a word, and it is just Ada and Isabella.

"Shall we go up?" Isabella asks, with a smile. Ada nods, and the two of them leave the room together.

In the upper hallway they separate. Isabella trails her hand through Ada's and it gives her a shock, a tingle of lust; the sight of her wide smile as she drifts in through the open door of her room. Ada stands for a moment. Her room is on the opposite side of the corridor, with the baby's room in between. The nursemaid has turned the lamps down low.

She goes into her room and draws the curtains. Someone has turned down her bed, and her books on the nightstand have been straightened; her nightgown is on the bedpan to warm.

She changes, slowly, reflectively, picking up her feet to unthread her underthings, and pushes her arms into the holes in the nightgown. Her toes stub against the haversack with her things in it for tomorrow—the diapers and blankets, the fifty Kronen taken from Herr K.'s wallet. The key, and the rock hammer with which she will break the glass in the dining-room windows from the outside, to make it look as though someone has broken in.

Midnight: the least light in the sky before the slow crawl to dawn, and the most amount of time left for Rolf to make his way back to the city under darkness. Ada sets down her book and gets out of bed. In the red glow of the lamp, she walks quietly to the door and counts under her breath as she jumps across the floorboard that squeaks. It amazes her, sometimes, how heavy her body has become, compared to the light-bonedness of when she was a girl.

She listens. The creak of the oak tree's branches—there must be a wind rising, though the windowpanes for the moment are still—and from inside the house, someone, somewhere, is snoring.

She opens the door enough to see that there is nobody in the corridor, and then steps out. Her bare feet make felty sounds on the runner.

The door to the baby's room is ajar and she only has to put her palm to it to push it further open and slip inside. The air is hot, and sweet-smelling; there's the sound of a small mouth breathing heavily, and a suggestion of wriggling movement from the crib.

Now is the time to hold back, to stop it all, and now is the time she lets the impulse pass. She moves to the crib, and the thought strikes her that she is like the fairy godmother, the good one, but everyone who suspects her will think she's evil. She lowers her arms and picks up the baby at hip and head, and cradles it. It opens its eyes and stares myopically at her, but doesn't make any sound.

She turns to go, and the door opens and Isabella is there, shivering, arms crossed over her body.

"Ada?" she says.

Perhaps she's only come to say hello, or perhaps she can't sleep.

Isabella simply stands there, and Ada lays the baby carefully down again in its crib. The movement disturbs it and it begins to warm up to a howl. Ada's skin is prickling, she feels a howl starting herself. If it can't be tonight, she cannot go through the process of planning everything again.

They wait together, to see if the baby will cry, and when it doesn't Isabella rubs her hands over her face, as if she'd peel back the top layer of her skin. "Thank God," she says. "Thank God. I couldn't bear it for another moment."

When she lowers her hands she looks entirely different to Ada; a new person.

"Come to bed?" she says.

"What?"

"I want you to come to my room with me."

"Why?"

"Because." She looks tired, in the way that resisting something is tiring. "Come on."

Isabella's room is dark and smells of her perfume and a bed that someone has slept in for too long. The furniture is vague dark shapes—the armoire, the chest of drawers, the white ghost of the fireplace, and Isabella is a pale figure moving ahead of her, going to the big double bed and lifting aside the covers and climbing in.

She lies down and lifts her hair to spread it out on the pillow.

"Are you coming?" she says. Her voice is thick, and odd.

Ada thinks about Rolf, waiting in the woods. If she lies down with Isabella, she may be able to creep out of the room later, and sneak back in again without Isabella realizing she has gone. If she says no, and goes back to her own room and takes the baby to Rolf, Isabella will know that it was her, when the theft is discovered.

Ada goes to the bed, lifts the covers on the other side from Isabella, and climbs in, with a little hop, as it's so high from the ground. The springs squeak, and the mattress is soft. She pulls the blankets up to cover her chest. The warmth from Isabella—she has been, since the baby, in what seems a permanent fever—reaches her across the bed, though they aren't touching. Ada hears the sound of Isabella's hair shushing as she moves her head, and then nothing.

A scream moves over the night sky—shapes blotting out the individual stars, geese flying in formation and calling as they go. Ada and Isabella lie in the bed together, not touching, barely breathing. The clock downstairs chimes half past twelve. She wishes Isabella would sleep, but also hopes she won't. She is driven, by whatever this dark thing between them is, to stay.

Isabella sighs—as though at some tiresome, argumentative comment Ada has made, that she is just now remembering.

"Your father told me what you told the doctor," she says. "What you said. About what Emil did to you. The—caresses. He told me that day we went to walk in the forest, and I showed you the little graves."

Ada doesn't dare speak. Isabella says: "Your father didn't believe you but I believed it, though I told him I didn't. He does have that side to him, Emil, that cruelty, that . . . odd nature. I've known it since we met. I am so tired of pretending. I am so sorry that you were not believed."

She turns on her side to face Ada. "He makes me lie on my front. That's the only way he can be with me. If he doesn't look at my face. I think he had someone else, some woman in the city, for a while. He looks so guilty. Can you see how guilty he looks?"

Ada nods.

"It's just part of who he is," Isabella says. "It's just who he is. And now I am trapped."

Ada lies very still.

Isabella says: "I never wanted him to hurt you. I am sorry that I didn't protect you. I couldn't face it, what it meant."

Ada can feel the rake of Isabella's eyes on her, looking at the gap between nightshirt and collarbone. "You made me feel so lonely," she says.

A click as Isabella swallows. "I'm sorry. I do love him. Did. Do."

"You didn't tell my father you believed me. You let him think I was a hysterical girl."

A flash of the old Isabella, as she says, mutinous: "I've told you I'm sorry."

Ada turns over in bed to stare at her. Isabella's face: a shallow-breathing, pale oval.

This is the decision: she cannot be the one to take the baby out to Rolf. At least there is a failsafe, someone who can take her place. Now it's time for Ada to take what she deserves. Even if she knows this is a temporary madness of Isabella's; even though it can only be for tonight.

She sighs and shifts closer to Isabella; slips her hand into the neck of Isabella's nightshirt and feels her nipple, chafed raw and stiff, under her palm. Isabella groans: it must be painful.

"Don't stop," she says. *Hurt me.* Ada complies.

Frau B.

ALEKSANDRA SIMONOWSKA crossed the foothills of the Carpathians with her family in the hot summer of 1857. One brother died as they made the journey; a cousin and an uncle disappeared one night as they camped on a rocky trail.

What she remembers of the arrival in the city is her father's face, peering at the scrap of paper with his cousin's address. She remembers the way the citizens of the strange new place—ladies in their long velvet cloaks and bonnets and gentlemen in top hats—swirled around without seeming to see them. The evening of arrival day, she turned in the crowd to find her mother and father nowhere in sight. In nightmares, she still feels that corkscrewing terror; even when, in the dream, her mother snatches her up and presses her to her thin chest, as really happened, the nightmare lingers, and every time she has it, she feels a little worse.

The next thing she remembers, looking at her fingers—which still bear the imprint of the pinpricks—is the hats. Her mother and three sisters made them all day and much of the night, in the derelict attic where the family lodged. The only day off was Temple, when she was scrubbed from top to toe and allowed to play outside with the other Leopoldstadt children.

When she was twelve she was courted by a man in his early thirties. He started to appear in the Temple square, and nobody but she thought it unusual that he brought her flowers and chocolates, and nobody but she thought it odd that he asked to speak to her father on her sixteenth birthday. Soon afterward, they were married.

At first all she wanted to do was run from him and what they did in the dark. But then, everyone said it was a pleasurable thing, and in time, it grew less unpleasant. By dint of having nobody to ask and nobody to rescue her, she trapped herself into contentment. Herr Berndt had a pastry business—he sold tortes and croissants and speckled things with raisins. The Sugared Jew, they called him, but they liked his prices and the way the corners of his cakes stayed crisp. Berndt was not his real name; nor was Thomas his first name; he'd changed them to sound more Austrian. In bed, they'd talk about it; he would hold her close and make up stories. "We are leaving our old lives behind." he said. "We are gathering intelligence on this strange new place, and in that way we are like spies, and spies get to assume new identities. I shall have to write love letters to you in code." He chose her something new, too: "Ute, I shall call you," he said. "You will be my Ute." Making it seem like a game took the sting out of it. "It means fortune. God knows we could use some of that."

When the children came—three boys—they were too busy to spend much time with them, Ute helping with the store—"*Mein Herr*," she would say to a hesitant customer, "I have just the thing for you, your wife will thank you, just look at this pretty, dainty cake!" And she would seal the paper bag with a twist and hold out her hand for the money. Thomas Berndt concealed the pain in his hip. The Emperor died (long live the Emperor). The oldest son wanted a commission, which they could not afford; he took a job as a traveling salesman, visited rarely, and wrote even less. Their youngest was seen in opium clubs across the city, and denied everything. Their middle son, twenty-six, threw himself into the Danube over an unhappy love affair, which Ute knew to be with another boy, but Thomas didn't; when they sat shiva, Thomas made speeches about this cruel unknown lover as if she were female. Ute decided for the first time to keep a secret from her husband.

Karl Lueger ascended to mayor. Ute and Thomas had just bought their first really fine suit of clothes each, because everything else went to the boys. Lueger promised much to everyone and nothing to the Jews. A brick found its way through the bakery window, and another, and another. One morning they received news: the factory was burned to the ground. The first thing that came to Ute's mind was that there was no true safety anywhere in the world. Thomas cried and cried and would not leave the bed.

In a few months new growths had popped up all over his body: behind his ears, on his collarbone, like a necklace; he tried to hide them with a scarf. In his last few days the boys came to visit, tall sober men (he had never been tall) who didn't know what to say. Ute encouraged them to speak of their lives now in optimistic tones, and Thomas's eyes pleaded with them, though he could no longer make any sound, to tell him that it hadn't all been for nothing. He died on a Tuesday night at nine o'clock with a light rain falling outside.

Ute took the insurance money from the bakery and factory and went to visit a real-estate vendor in the Hannovergasse. She explained that she wished to purchase an apartment block of which she would be landlady and concierge, and put the bank drafts on his desk directly, to show him she was serious. By the afternoon, she had seen nine properties—it never occurred to her to look outside Leopoldstadt—the one she wanted instantly was a converted schoolhouse over three stories, with a central courtyard and a small apartment for herself on the ground floor. "It just needs a lick of paint," the agent said, half-closing his eyes, so that she could tell he was lying.

Things will be better now, she told herself, as she stood with her broom in the courtyard on the first day of her ownership. She cleared the rats from the attic, recruited youths from the synagogue to help her paint the leftover furniture, and hired a glazier to repair the windows. She cleaned out the water pump and fixed a new handle and stripped the floorboards and varnished wainscoting and visited markets to haggle over dressers and chairs and tables. This was what people did, wasn't it? They went on.

One by one the tenants came. Young Ephraim was first, a violinist who was too sad to keep up with his traveling troupe. She rented him the first-floor studio free for three months and fed him beef broth to build up his strength and when it looked as though he would break down in gratitude and embarrass them both, she pushed him back up the stairs. Heidi and Gunther came next, wandering into the courtyard one day, both blushing: a touch of respectability, although she was certain that Gunther was recently out of prison. Grete, with her clipped Swedish consonants, out of place, but assured in her belonging everywhere: talking so freely about theater, about music, that Frau Berndt's stomach ached with envy. Rolf was a person who followed her home one night. "Just curious," he'd said, when she rounded on him. His smile was charming and uncertain and she understood that he'd thought he might sleep with her for money. Instead, she invited him in and over crème de menthe she listened to his story. "I am a renegade," he said, "I am an original," which she took to mean, *I think I have failed in ordinary life,* and, *I am afraid to be alone.*

And then Julia and Eve walked under the courtyard arch. By this time there were geraniums in terracotta pots outside every stairwell doorway, and she was allowing herself a short nap in the afternoons. The end of life beckoned, perhaps five years away, perhaps ten, and the prospect held no special pain for her. But there she was, Julia, with her bright inquiring smile—"Frau Berndt? Charmed . . ."—and her pianist's fingers, and Ute had no choice.

She watched Julia closely, Julia and Eve both. She made sure to be sweeping the courtyard whenever Julia left the building, with that enigmatic Swedish smile that increasingly lost its sweetness. She left little gifts of herbal tisanes and the occasional box of cigarettes outside their door but still, after Heidi and Gunther's baby, she felt Julia fading away.

One afternoon, Eve and Rolf knocked at the door of her little apartment. She had just poured herself a tea, having spent the day looking after Young Gunther. They explained the plan very gently. At first, she studied Rolf's face, the heightened way in which he spoke to her; then she looked at Eve for confirmation, who nodded that this was serious. "I am afraid she will die," Eve said, of Julia. "And the father, Emil Kellner, is violent. But mostly, this is for Julia." They wanted her simply to step in if anything were to go awry. They showed her an advertisement for a nursemaid at the lake house. Rolf wrote false letters of reference, bought false papers from his contacts. Her name would be different; there would be no way to link this nursemaid character with the real Ute Berndt. Eve sealed the envelopes.

At the interview she met both Ada's mother and Isabella Kellner. Isabella sat in state, vastly pregnant, propped on cushions, while Ada's mother had the less comfortable chair. That told her everything she needed to know. She spoke of her children, and the gap they had left in her life by growing into adults; she was a respectable widow, a fifth cousin of a minor Habsburg, and now circumstances required her to seek employment, but the care of a baby was not truly work, was it? Isabella looked up at this point; Ute saw her expression change: the quirk of an eyebrow, the sense of possibility dawning. Here was someone whom she could exploit.

Ada appeared at the end of the corridor as she was being shown out; they had not yet met, but Ute wished she could fold the thin figure into her arms. She contented herself with a vague smile and promised herself she would report back to Rolf.

Had it gone well? Was she engaged as the new nanny? It had. She was. The plan was a just one, and likely to work. What was life if you could not risk helping those you love? *My children*, she thought, *all of you are, every single one.*

Half past two comes and in the nursemaid's quarters, Ute lies awake, listening for any sound.

There really is nothing. It was agreed that Ada would tap on her door in passing, on the way out, if all was well. She will have to get up. She hasn't undressed, just in case, so she simply swings her legs over the side of the bed, goes to the door, opens it a crack, and listens.

She takes the back stairs, quickening her pace, sure that she won't meet anybody else at this hour—and she sets her chin—it is, of course, perfectly all right to be checking on the baby, even if she is challenged. She could say she had a nightmare, that she dreamed the child was bathed in blood, its hands were waving—she is so busy thinking that she opens the door to the upper corridor wide, without thinking, and sees someone walking away from her, ahead of her, coming back from the bathroom: Herr Kellner, holding a tall candlestick, his nightdress trailing behind him; the receding pool of light. She has caught her breath and held her bottom lip under her teeth, but he wanders on, unaware, his feet making soft blurry sounds on the parquet, and turns into the doorway of his room. His face, half-turned toward her as he enters, is blank and sleepy.

She waits, and waits a little longer, and when there is no movement she steals along the corridor in the opposite direction, toward the baby's room. There is no sound from Ada's room, and the door to the nursery is half-open.

She cannot understand it. The covers of Ada's bed are tumbled and the haversack has not been taken, but her shoes are gone. The only explanation that makes sense is one that confuses her, when she thinks about the closed bedroom door of Isabella's room opposite. Or has Ada had a change of heart, and gone to warn her father?

She makes a choice, for the child, picks up the bag and crosses back into the nursery; picks up the baby—it emits a sleepy squeak— and wraps it in the crocheted blanket that's ready.

She goes downstairs as fast as she can; the baby chirrups as its head lolls, for a moment, unsupported. The hall is in semi-darkness; as usual, a lamp is turned down low on the hall table. There is nobody about.

Despairing of only having two hands, she places the baby for a moment on the floor outside the dining-room door, and goes into the room, pulling the rock hammer out of the bag; then remembers that this isn't right, she has to punch the glass in from outside, so she crosses back into the hall, eases the great front door open and flinches at the bitter cold, and the ice-white glow of the snow outside.

She pulls the door to and takes the few short steps around the portico. Her hand is shaking from the freezing wind around her thin shoulders; she steps up to the glass of the door and taps it smartly on the pane just above the door handle, expecting the glass to shatter. It doesn't. She covers her eyes with her other hand and taps again. Nothing.

She remembers how it was when Herr Berndt came through to the kitchen and leaning on the door jamb in an oddly casual way, told her their son had fallen into the river; squeezes her eyes shut and swings the hammer. There's a sound like tinkling bells, the crinkling of paper.

She flees for the front door. She thinks she has imagined a sound from behind the walls of the house—a snort of surprise, perhaps, someone sitting bolt upright in bed. When she reaches the door she finds it has closed behind her. Back to the dining-room window; she reaches through the hole in the glass, cutting the palm of her hand, and rattles the door handle until it gives, then pushes the door inward and steps through the gap. Glass crunches and grumbles underfoot. This is better, isn't it? More convincing, to have a trail of broken glass leading into the house?

She steps swiftly into the hallway, reaches for her coat, and sees a light coming down the corridor toward her.

Herr Kellner, in his nightshirt—"I heard a noise." He places the lamp on the hall table and sees his daughter on the floor, waiting for Frau Berndt to pick her up. Impasse. There can be no reason for her to have the child out of bed.

"Where are you taking her? Out for a walk?"

He stares at her. Doubt is starting to cloud those fine brown irises. He opens his mouth to say something further, perhaps to call for help. She picks up the lamp; turns as fast as she can and brings it up to connect with Herr K.'s temple. Snapping his head back, it sends him staggering to the floor. She hears a door creaking open to listen, somewhere downstairs: one of the maids, too timid, for now, to investigate.

With the girl in her arms, she runs from the house. Coming across the white lawn is Rolf, staggering toward her through the snow. He catches her hand and takes the child, flattens it to his breast, and pulls her along.

Once they reach the treeline they pause for breath and to look back. At the door of the house someone is standing; then people are issuing onto the patio, where the doorway is an oblong of flickering orange. Snow is already falling again, obscuring their tracks.

They cut through the woods rather than risk the road. "This way," Rolf says—he has practiced several times, and can find his way, even in the low light. The snow is a foot deep; Frau Berndt struggles, and Rolf reaches a hand back to help her when he can.

They emerge onto the road a half-mile beyond the village. A pony and trap: Gunther's big anxious face; he calls to them, and hands Ute up onto the buggy seat. Rolf passes her the baby—she clutches the child close, relieved by its warmth, its regular breathing. Rolf hops up, clings to the running-board, and they sweep away.

They drive for two hours, to the small town of Podersdorf, where Gunther leaves them; he tips his hat and starts the long drive back to the city. The station is a tiny platform and an overhanging roof. Ute and Rolf struggle over the lip. The station clock shows quarter past six.

It is a deep dark black, and a bitter wind blows, and there is nobody. Ute huddles her coat more closely around her, and leans against Rolf. The baby is slipped inside the folds of his jacket like a parcel. He can feel its soft breath tickling the hair on his chest. If the train is not late, they can be in Vienna in an hour, and home an hour after that.

The trees on either side of the railway halt creak and sway, and Ute thinks, holding on to Rolf's arm, of the way Herr Kellner fell, backward with no attempt to save himself, his arms flying up from the downward momentum. The crack of his head hitting the floor; those long eyelashes fluttering shut, and then the lamp rolling to and fro in semicircles beside him.

A man is rising up onto the platform, coming up the steps one by one. A gentleman, with a monocle, and a knee-length overcoat and a muffler obscuring the lower part of his face. He is holding the hands of two small girls, one on either side. The girls, twins, nod at Rolf and Ute politely, and so does their father, as they go to stand some feet away, against the wall of the shelter. Ute smiles reflexively at the children; one girl smiles back; the other looks away, so Ute looks away too, remembering that she must not do anything that might lead to later being recognized.

Nobody else arrives; they don't talk to each other. The baby hiccups, and wakes, and starts to cry, and Ute rushes to remove her from Rolf's jacket; the gentleman arches his eyebrows and then smiles fondly at the sudden appearance. One of the little girls—the one with spectacles—takes a step forward to peer at them, and her father tugs her back with an apologetic smile.

The train rattles in at six twenty-five—steam billowing upward, white on the black sky. It has just two carriages, and they all get on—"No, I insist, after you"—and one of the little girls tugs her father's hand and whispers something, and he says: "We must see if the lady and gentleman mind, they may wish to sleep," and the little girl says something like, *But there's a baby!* And so they all end up in the same carriage, with Rolf sitting with the child on his lap, and the little girls staring adoringly at it, and the gentleman saying apologetically, "All girls love babies, I suppose."

"Of course," Ute says professionally. "I was just the same." She tries to smile at the man's daughters, and wonders whether she should come up with some story: *This is my son, and this my new granddaughter. He is by the lake for his health.*

"Is this your granddaughter?" the man asks. One of the twins reaches out and touches the baby's fontanelle, then retracts her hand, awestruck. Ute nods. Her gaze is fixed on the station clock. She has an image in her mind of policemen rushing, truncheons raised, onto the platform, swarming onto the train, wrestling with her. Twenty-nine minutes past six. The gentleman opposite is asking how old the baby is. She distractedly tells him a month. She listens for the flurry of footsteps in the snow; is that torchlight dancing from behind the halt? Thirty seconds left. The clock's hand barely moves. Rolf seems fixed and still, staring at the top of the luggage rack over the gentleman's head.

There's a hiss and a clank and the wheels begin to turn. They gather speed.

The gentleman opposite, bemused by their situation, the lack of conversation, leans his head back and closes his eyes. The little girls fix their stare on Ute and do not move their lamp-like gaze from her until Vienna.

They get off the train at the Westbahnhof. It is still very dark, but commuters have started to flood in from the suburbs. Rolf tugs them onward—Ute's short legs can't keep up with him. Nothing on the newspaper billboards—not yet. The baby starts to cry as they exit the station; Rolf jiggles it uselessly, looking around at the passersby. "A taxi," Ute suggests, even though it wasn't in their plan. Rolf shakes his head: too recognizable. So they go on, stumbling through the slushy snow, toward home.

Julia

———

IT STILL HAS THE QUALITY of a bad joke. Julia looks at Eve, who has never done any single little illegal thing. She picks up a book and puts it back on the shelf, then takes it off again, and hefts it.

Eve puts her hand over her eyes. "I let him talk me into it," she says.

"And the child is the baby of Rolf's boyfriend?" Julia asks. She shakes her head. "I can't keep up."

"You were so ill—" Eve says. "I thought only of saving you—"

There is a bang and the outer door opens, then footsteps on the stairs. Julia slots the book back into the shelf and listens. The last few steps ring out on the staircase and Rolf and Frau Berndt are there, clothes stained and dark, and Rolf is holding something inside his coat.

He sits at the table, and peels back the lapel, and there she is. Eyelids shut against the cold.

Julia puts the table between them. She cannot trust herself not to snatch the child, to hold it against her; to say, in spite of everything, *You are mine.* She doesn't want the others to see her hunger. Frau Berndt sits; leans forward and rests her forehead on her arms.

Julia says: "We must call the police. We can say we found her on a street corner."

Frau Berndt groans. Rolf says: "Out of the question," at the same time as Frau Berndt lifts her head and says: "I think I killed him."

She explains that Herr Kellner was not where he was supposed to be. She had no choice. She puts her head on her arms again. Rolf's face is strained and white. "You did what was necessary," he says.

Julia: "We will say we found it abandoned. We can take it to the police station. Did anyone see you come here?"

Rolf says: "You'll have to give your name. They will find that Frau Berndt was in the house."

The motor sounds are just starting below: the hiss and tick of the trams, the sluicing of water from the pump in the courtyard. More footsteps on the stairwell. Julia looks around in a panic. The door opens, and Heidi peers around, before stepping into the room. She is carrying a basket of glass bottles full of milk.

"Is that her?" she asks, and steps forward to pick the sleeping child from Rolf's arms. She holds the baby close, bending to smell its hair. "Little one," she says. She shifts the baby into a more comfortable position. "Nobody will hurt you now."

Julia thinks back to that afternoon in the lodge, when she came home from work early, and found them all there. "You have been planning this for . . . for how long? All of you? Heidi, how could you?"

Heidi is red in the face with her righteousness, conviction. She won't meet Julia's eye, and instead looks down at the baby. "It was explained to us what kind of man her father is," she says.

Eve says: "What about Ada?"

Frau Berndt shrugs. "Changed her mind. I don't know what happened. She wasn't where she was supposed to be. So I had to do it alone."

Julia shivers. "You've done this to hurt Herr K.," she says. Rolf looks at his hands.

"I did it for you," he says, but his tone is uncertain.

They sit, all of them, in silence.

"We have to go," Julia says.

Eve looks up. "Go where?"

Julia is shaking. "What did you think would happen? There is bound to be a reward. Someone will recognize Frau Berndt, or they will come for Rolf. They are rich, these people? Where will they start looking, do you suppose? Doesn't everyone believe Jews eat babies?" She pauses; finds a laugh starting. "We're their worst nightmare."

Eve puts her hands to her face again.

"But you'll come back?" Heidi asks. Her big childlike face creased with alarm. "You won't go for good?"

"I don't know," Julia says. "We don't know."

They wait all day in the apartment. The baby wakes and squints into the sun, then starts to cry. Heidi picks her up and hands her to Julia, with a bottle of milk. Frau Berndt stays immobile at the table, staring out of the window.

In the early evening, Gunther returns, travel-soiled and weary; Julia stares at him, as if she cannot believe it of him, that he would go along with any of this, and makes him go to fetch the newspaper. "Go to the kiosk further away—the one by the Augarten will do—where you're not known," Julia tells him.

He is gone for an hour: every minute stretches out. He brings the news and lays it on the table, hands smoothing the creases.

BABY-SNATCHING OF NEUSIEDLERSEE: *Child, three weeks, stolen from the house of Herr Bauer of Bauer & Compagnie. The child was found to have disappeared during the night and intruders to have entered via a downstairs window. The family immediately notified the Police Commissariat at Neusiedl. This morning the nursemaid hired only weeks before had fled and is suspected in the disappearance. She is a sixty-year-old of stout appearance believed to live in Vienna with a faint accent. The reward stands at 10,000 Kronen.*

Everyone looks at Julia; she is in the middle of the apartment with her hands on her hips looking at Frau Berndt, who has the baby in her arms.

Frau Berndt says: "If they catch me, I will say I was acting alone."

Julia is pushing clothes into her valise. "You won't. I won't let it happen. I won't let you go to jail." She indicates for Eve to go to the money drawer, which she does, hurriedly counting out their savings. "We will go somewhere—somewhere else."

"You will need this," Heidi says, handing her the basket of milk, and the jars of prepared baby formula. "We didn't mean for it to be like this," she says. "We thought you could stay here."

Eve says, pleading: "I'm sorry."

"Maybe you could come back one day," suggests Rolf. He, too, looks ghastly.

Julia says: "We had a life here. We worked hard for it."

Heidi starts to cry, big extravagant sobs.

"Give her to me," Julia says. She takes the baby from Frau Berndt, and moves toward the window, where she looks out at the winter view, and then at the baby. "What's your name?" she asks. "What's your name?"

Morning in the greatest city of the western hemisphere. The light streams over the Bohemian plains and the hills around Vienna. The factory windows catch fire first—stained glass with no one to see. The horses are shaking their tails in the royal stables. A priest yawns and slides back the great bolt on the Stephansdom. On the west side, Herr Doktor Freud—a habitual early riser—is smoking a cigar, looking at the linden tree in the courtyard, and wondering how far its roots go.

Trams fizz past, rattling the windows of the tenements. In the ballet school, thirteen-year-olds are stretching their legs above their heads and feeling the burning-cooling pull of muscles under the skin; without pain, no pleasure, no achievement, no life in the greatest city in the West. A fruit-seller on the Donaubrücke drops a crate of oranges, and swears as they roll down the cobbled bridge away from her.

In Leopoldstadt, Frau Berndt wakes from a dream she can't remember, and notices her hand, which has slipped under the pillow in the night, is already curled into a fist. "Pull yourself together," she says out loud, but there is no denying: her voice is old.

In Berlin, Julia and Eve arrive at a cheap hotel near the railway station. Julia sits for a moment, drooping on the bed, then rises again. She will go to the reception and ask for a telegram to be sent to Grete. She returns ten minutes later, to find Eve lying curled with the child in her arms. Both are asleep. Julia closes the curtains and dreams of her homeland: the cabin outside Gothenburg with the familiar quilt from her childhood. The long drifts of snow into which the family can disappear.

In Neusiedl, Isabella sits by Emil's bedside. He has not moved since they found him two days ago; he lies on his back in a clean white nightshirt, spit drooling from the side of his mouth. His hand twitches in hers and she can see his eyeballs moving under his eyelids, like a metronome. Isabella's mind is ticking, too: she is surprised not to feel too much grief about the baby, or not yet. Once Emil is better, then she will allow herself to feel the anger gathering. It goes without saying that then she will hunt the thief to the very ends of the earth.

In the downstairs study, Ada knocks and enters. Her father is sitting at the desk with his head in his hands. It is a question he has been asking himself, over and over—how could this have happened in his house? He does not want to blame Emil but it seems somehow all his fault. Now the Bauer name, everything they have built, will be only about the kidnap of this child. But he can't think these things, and besides, Ada is now here again and asking for his time. She stands before him, and expresses grief at the loss of the child. Would it be helpful for her to go to the school for young ladies this month, rather than in the spring, and begin her path toward being a medical woman? To be out of the way of the Kellners, respectful of their sadness? He agrees instantly. It is a relief. He tells himself it will be better for her to distance herself; in truth, he suspects her.

In Vienna, it is that fine end of the afternoon: the sun like a cigar-tip, flaring and then dying. Rolf has been standing on the Augartenbrücke for two hours, leaning over the parapet and looking at the changing grays of the water. The light seems lighter, merrier, and the faces moving around him stretched into unnatural and suspicious grins. He has come here without a plan and the plan has come to him. On the footpath near the bridge there are mendicants clustered around an upturned barrel; he will wait until they are asleep, so as not to risk being rescued. His chin juts out against an imaginary argument. The past two days, he has become aware of the thinning of the world around him: he was meant to deliver the baby to Julia, and then—nothing. Emil's face is on his mind constantly. He thinks of him, dead already or dying, of how he used to look in sleep; what comes to the surface now is, *You deserved it.*

He grips the parapet. He is thinking of Emil, but also of schnapps in the lodge with Frau Berndt; of a hat he has seen in a shop in the Kärntnerstrasse. Most of all, his thoughts move ahead to the Opera House, where a new production is premiering tonight. It is a revival of Massenet's *Werther* and he plans to sit in the front row, his finger held aloft as the "Breath of Spring" aria is sung to him and him alone.

1938

—

Julia, Eve

———

JULIA LETS HERSELF INTO THE APARTMENT; shouts a hello. Hears a low moan in response. She hangs her coat and goes in search. Eve is reading a book on carpentry at the kitchen table—this has been her great idea, for when, as seems certain, the outfitter she now runs is forced to close. The clientele they served are leaving, and nobody has any money, it seems, for nice things. The grain of the wood should come naturally; doesn't. Eve longs for more delicate work, and so her head is bowed, buried between two fists, compressing her temples, as she reads.

Julia thinks she looks distinguished when she's caught concentrating. She presses a kiss into the top of her head—where the hair is turning into coarser gray wires at the crown.

Eve looks up. She has composed her face, or so she will think, but she is not good at concealing her worry. "All's calm," Julia says brightly, and turns away to put the few packages, the meager bread and elderly vegetables, on the sideboard.

Elsa arrives before the guests, to bustle as only the young know how. She whisks the book away from Eve—"Go and tidy yourself up"—and takes the knife from Julia—"I'll chop that." ("She makes me feel useless," Eve complains, often but without bitterness. "She makes me feel old." But they are, at least if not old, almost there: Julia will be fifty-five next year, and Eve soon fifty-two.) Even Elsa's chopping is busy, and because busy, noisy and inefficient. Carrots fly around the kitchen, and Elsa gets in a temper, stooping to pick them up. Julia wonders if it's time to intervene. Something stops her: genuine anguish on Elsa's face.

"The Mosers left yesterday," Elsa says. Her voice is conversational—Julia supposes it is now conversation, these sudden departures.

"I know," Julia says. Herr Moser was Elsa's teacher from the age of seven, once walking her home when she had been sick at morning break. Julia remembers her hesitation, not because of his Jewishness, but because he was a strange man holding her child's hand. She has heard that the Mosers were looking at passports for Canada, because they had a cousin in Vancouver.

Elsa presses her lips into a governess-ish line. Julia bends to a cupboard and lifts out a saucepan for the potatoes; hefting, making a play of it. Elsa takes the bait. "Let me do that," she says, taking it from Julia and placing it on the stove.

"Will I do?" Eve, standing in the doorway in a fresh shirt and collar, snapping shut the cufflinks Elsa bought her for her fiftieth. Elsa turns, crosses to Eve, and adjusts the collar, then places her palms on Eve's cheeks. "Virtually human," she says.

The distraction doesn't last long. "Do you have the newspaper?" Elsa asks. Something in her voice, something there again: some restless energy. Since she began her job as a governess for a smart family, she takes care to maintain her general knowledge, but this may not be the real reason for her request. Julia shakes her head. Elsa rolls her eyes and crosses to the sideboard where the stack of old bulletins sits, in the sun, so that the edges are parchmenty and starting to crumble.

Eve tucks her thumbs in her pockets and rocks on her heels and looks at Julia, who looks back. *We can't stop her looking.*

Quietly she picks up the work of cooking where Elsa has left off. Elsa stays absorbed in the papers, turning page after page. The newspaper contains such hatred against the people who surround them; things that can't possibly be true. Julia and Eve sit in tense silence. They are both expecting Elsa to burst into a tearstorm. A choke and a sob, and they will cluster around her and calm will be restored, or at least a kind of quiet. But she stays standing.

Eve returns to her woodcraft book, turns the pages with every appearance of interest. She must have read it twice or three times. Julia and Elsa keep up the pretense.

They have lived in this big plain box of an apartment for ten years. They have this flat, and the studio on the other side of the landing, which Elsa moved into at age twenty, to have some independence. If they were honest, neither could say it is home. It is bigger than their flat at Frau Berndt's, on the third floor in Greiseneckergasse near to the synagogue, and in what's considered to be a better part of Leopoldstadt, by which they simply mean there are fewer obvious lunatics, and the Cabaret of Unearthly Delights is less regularly seen—when it came to it, neither could bear to go to the Innere Stadt.

All their furniture is there, but on its glossy parquet one is liable to turn an ankle; its high ceilings suck all the heat from the rooms. The drawing-room curtains smell sinister in the spring and fungal in the autumn. The room that was Elsa's as a child has a spooky feeling. Often, Julia pauses in the open doorway and looks at the solemn single bed and the books that Elsa says she has no room for, and wonders what kind of place her daughter's living in, which has no space for books. Julia thinks sometimes she will have a word with Eve about the apartment, and the subtle ways it is unfriendly. Just last week the ancient kettle spat its lid off as it boiled, leaving her with a vicious wound that's yet to heal. She will say, *The soul of this place is no good.* Eve will understand. It is like the city itself, nowadays.

At quarter past six Julia puts on her best dress and becomes her formal self, the one who entertains. Elsa used to notice and tease her about it, about the way her spine straightens and a gentle smile hovers on her mouth, but since she moved out the teasing has fallen away. Eve sometimes thinks she sees Elsa copying Julia's manners. *Won't you sit down? Something to drink?* And tonight, she moves in Julia's wake: an unsteady duckling, putting out place mats, smoothing the tablecloth. "So," Julia says, smiling, when the lamps are lit and all is glowing, "I think we're ready."

Elsa rolls her eyes at Julia's nervousness. *Why worry, when they're always late?* She flops into an armchair and picks up one of Julia's novels.

Sure enough, the clock hands move around to half past six, and then to quarter to seven. Julia sees that Elsa is growing tearful, with the strain of the delay and the news about the Mosers; Eve's head is buried in her book, her fingers dancing around imaginary hinges and joists. She will leave the comforting to Julia where possible— and then the door shakes with the force of three sharp knocks.

Eve leaps up, almost knocking her chair backward. She opens the door and stands with her arms open and Rolf walks slowly into them, clasps her, and plants two arch kisses on either cheek. As he does so he takes in the room: "Miss Elsa, I see," he says. Elsa is standing, smoothing down her skirts.

Anders, who is shyer and, at thirty-four, only a few years older than Elsa, hovers at the back—Julia goes to envelop him. One of the advantages of stoutness. *Welcome.* He is tense in her arms, stammers something about her kindness in inviting him. She looks into the lovely bright eyes and gives his shoulders a shake. *Don't be silly.*

Rolf is pulling off his gloves finger by finger, and handing his theater cape to Elsa. He has, finally, attained his lifelong dream of becoming a theater impresario, complete with paunch; he manages a small gang of opera singers and artistes. His beard is waxed into a little silver peak.

"You've made changes," he says accusingly, pointing to the table, which has indeed swapped places with the sofa. "Shall I go through to the parlor?" He is childishly competitive: always pretends to be surprised that they have more than one room. "Love your dress," he says to Elsa, as he brushes past her, putting his fingertips against her sleeve.

Rolf takes the best chair—Julia's—and puts his feet on the footstool, and sighs. Elsa is offering him red wine or a dusty kirsch unearthed in honor of the evening. "Anything, darling," he says.

Anders asks shyly for the kirsch. Elsa pours him some. She is alarmed, Julia knows, by their closeness in age, the disparity between Anders and Rolf. Julia catches Eve's eye—she wants to wink—and then there's the fact that Anders is so slenderly and confusingly handsome, like a young woman. Eve hasn't noticed.

She is pink with the happiness of having captured this one evening with friends.

"Hans Richter," Rolf says as soon as they're all seated, "has gone off to join the army." He clicks his teeth. "Thinks it'll keep him safe. Apparently the police were surprised by his enthusiasm. They must have heard the stories about him. But he's ecstatic. All those boys in uniform!"

Julia doesn't know Hans Richter but she laughs, dutifully shakes her head.

"I said, 'I've got all the boy I want back at home,'" Rolf says. Anders blushes, making himself improbably more beautiful, and stares into his drink. Rolf folds his hands. "So that's us. Oh, Anders did a gorgeous recital. They clapped, but not hard enough." He picks at his waistcoat. "Shame you couldn't come; I must confess, I didn't quite see the reason, darling." This to Elsa: "It seems you were working." He blinks at the tedium of it all, and then moves on to Eve: "Shop all right?" He looks at Julia: "Translation all right?"

Eve looks at Julia quickly, and Rolf catches the glance. "Not all right?" he says.

Not having his own children, apart from Elsa, in whom he has part-shares, Rolf doesn't understand that some things should not be discussed when children are present. Elsa composes her face, as if she has known for some time that the shop is in trouble, and folds her hands with apparent calm.

Julia says: "The Ambassador is busy. There's lots to do. I'm interpreting for some men from Poland next week."

Anders nods, very serious. "And what are your feelings on the current political situation?" he asks. He has a fluent, mellow voice: Julia is not immune. She fixes the beam of her smile on him.

"Complicated," she says. Bored already, Rolf has begun to flap at his face with a napkin. He suffers from a flushing condition, exacerbated by polite conversation where the subject strays too far from himself.

He says: "Oh—the best yet. Georg and Anna are getting married." He sits back in his chair with an expression of enormous satisfaction.

Elsa looks in confusion at Julia, who has clapped her hand to her mouth in shame at her own laughter. Anna, a woman they befriended last year, has three girlfriends; Georg runs an establish-ment for discerning gentlemen in Ottakring.

"It's love, apparently," Rolf says, pleased by her reaction. He lets out a great roar, thumping the arm of the chair.

Anders says, pained: "Sweetheart—" He worries when Rolf gets overexcited. Julia is wiping a tear of joy from the corner of one eye.

"She wants babies," Rolf says, mock-serious. "And he's sick of his mother nagging. What do you think it would be like?" he says, wondering. "I mean, when they . . . ?"

Elsa is cross because she is lost and doesn't know these people, and besides she doesn't quite like the way Anders's hand lingers on Rolf's arm: she is protective of Rolf and also of Anders, and angry with them for having found each other. She gets up and walks to the kitchen. "It isn't a laughing matter," she says. "It's serious. At least they are trying to protect themselves."

When she's gone the four of them, drawn together by their sameness, burst out laughing.

"Can you imagine the children?" Rolf asks. A moment of seri-ous contemplation. "And Anna's girlfriend is devastated, of course. She had herself delivered to Anna's apartment in a coffin the other day."

That feeling of safety is back in the room. It has been like this forever, since they met, she and Rolf and Eve. Being together, it is impossible to believe how the world has changed.

Over supper, Rolf questions Elsa—interrogates her—about her position. He wants to know everything about the family. Is there a marriageable son? What about a cousin? Who stands to inherit? One must think of such things. Don't want to end up like him, pen-niless. (Anders's small smile curves up at the side; it is true he has no money.) Elsa grows sullen at the questions, and then, lured on, she begins to bloom into anecdote after anecdote. She tells them about the maid, who hates her, is perhaps jealous—"Of course," Rolf says gravely, "just look at you . . ."—whom she caught last week with the young master's briefs held to her nose.

"So there is a young master," Rolf says, triumphant.

Anders says: "You don't have to answer him," and to Rolf, "Shush."

Elsa says, "He's only twenty-two, and still at the university," and Rolf makes a moue that says, *So what? You're twenty-five.* Anders leans across the table to slap his hand.

"You're happy," Rolf says, satisfied, moving the stem of his wine-glass around.

Elsa snorts. "I wouldn't say happy. Some of my friends—"

Julia sees that the threatened outbreak has come, and that Elsa is holding it in, with the precise gestures of her knife and fork, the jut of her chin. She reaches for her daughter's hand. Elsa throws it off with a movement of the elbow.

"I don't see how you can possibly understand," she says, and then, seeing their shocked, pitying faces—because of course they know what it is like, to lose people, and she knows they know—she does start to cry, in great shameful gulps. Julia moves across to put her arms around her. She knows that later Elsa will worry about having wept in front of Rolf and Anders.

She murmurs into Elsa's hair. Anders produces a handkerchief from somewhere. Rolf's Adam's apple bobs. He has never been able to bear her sadness. Even when she was small, he was always the first to crack. (That fight—Julia trying to punish Elsa; Rolf offering toffee apples. *You are interfering.* But she'd let him.)

Elsa sobs and sobs, swiping angrily at her eyes with her fingers. It is to be expected. She is too young to have her friends disappear, either without warning or leaving only a postcard behind: *Gone to Britain. Sending love.* Anders quietly starts to move the plates into the kitchen. Eve and Rolf get up, pat their pockets for cigarettes, and leave the room.

The balcony: an uninterrupted pleasure. The green roofs of the old city, and the sky touching the hills and vineyards around Nussdorf. The smell of ginger cake from the bakery on the corner.

Rolf squints and presses his lips around a cigarette. "I don't like the sound of this family."

Eve shrugs, both because there is no choice—Elsa has been lucky to get any job, and one in the Innere Stadt, away from the taint of the Jewish quarter—and because Rolf says the same thing about anything Elsa does: he is in a state of permanent, protective suspicion. Nobody—no friend or acquaintance or position—will ever be good enough for her in his eyes.

A small silence. "How's woodwork?" he asks.

Eve smiles. "Unfathomable." Her hands, clasped, hang over the edge of the railing. Rolf does a *win-some lose-some* shrug. He never asks where they get their money from, in case they tell him it's through their own hard work; he only ever asks for the money, and then takes them out for extravagant dinners with it. Eve suspects they are both thinking of the last time, six months ago, just before the Anschluss. Rolf had snapped his fingers and demanded they go to Frauenhuber. Crossing the bridge, everything seemed normal: spring sunshine. People laughed and strolled and shopped, and at the café, there were no omissions to the menu. Rolf, wild-eyed, had ordered drink upon drink, until it was clear that the manager didn't know what to do. Eve and Anders and Julia had taken him bodily home.

"It's getting worse, isn't it?" she asks. Two weeks ago a young lad, no older than twelve, laughed at her in the street, right there in Leopoldstadt, and imitated her walk: arms swinging like an ape, legs grotesquely apart.

"Is it?" Rolf says, vague. He stares out at the city. To the southeast, farther into Leopoldstadt, a thin column of smoke is rising between buildings. "No wonder she's upset."

He means Elsa. Eve nods. She can't think too much about it all, that's how she feels: that she will sit and do some proper thinking. She will plane the curves of her ideas flat and come to some decision. She and Julia will know what to do, and how to help their brave girl.

"The Roschmanns from next door got the passes for Ireland," Rolf says. His voice sounds conversational merely. "Apart from the grandmother. She won't leave. Says she's too old to make such a move, and anyway, they haven't got the papers for her. So she's staying in the apartment on her own. Anders wants to bring her bread in the mornings. I've told him no." He smooths his fringe out of his eyes. "Enough troubles of our own."

Eve nods slowly. "I hope she'll change her mind," she says.

Rolf presses the stub of his cigarette against his lips. "You know Anders's grandmother was Jewish?" he says.

"Was she?"

"I'm sure I told you before. Technically Jewish. I don't think she ever practiced."

He flicks the cigarette butt over the edge of the balcony and watches it tumble, end over sparking end, with the satisfaction of a child.

"I don't know what to say." Eve is cold all over. He must realize what it is he's told her. Anders's name could be on a list somewhere. "Technically? What does that mean? The laws on who's a Jew change every day. What about his mother? Did she register, in 1935?"

He waves a hand. "They'll never come for her."

"But does she—" Eve wants to say, does she *look* Jewish; would she, to an Aryan eye? They both know it's as much about what the Austrians perceive as an excuse to seize your property.

"It will all work out perfectly well," Rolf says, serene.

Inside, Elsa has composed herself, and is the governess again. Anders has been helping dry up dishes, and when he sees Rolf, his face breaks into a look of such glimmering delight and relief that it's almost embarrassing.

"Coffee?" Julia suggests. She can see from Eve's face that there is something to talk about, but is obliged to offer drinks, out of politeness.

Now Rolf's eyes are roving everywhere, as if seeking out a hole to hide in. "I think we'll go," he says, at his full portly height. Anders, used to not asking questions, quietly puts the dishes back on the side.

Julia is standing, gripping the back of a chair with both hands. She releases the chair, stretches her fingers to relax them, and is brisk—for the sake of Elsa, who won't cope with a scene, and for the sake of Eve, who is radiating distress. She busies herself fetching Rolf's cape and Anders's modest coat. Elsa looks from one to the other, at a loss to follow the undercurrent.

"Thank you," Rolf says, as she reaches up to put the cape on his shoulders.

"Thank you," Julia echoes. She wants to hold him at arm's length and look at him, but finds she cannot. Rolf blinks, perhaps too fast, and shrugs the cape more firmly around him.

Meanwhile, Anders is thanking Elsa, and Elsa is thanking Anders, each caught in the net of the other's good looks. "Come on," Rolf says, rolling his eyes, "before you break another heart." Anders blushes and follows him to the door.

"Goodnight, all," Rolf says with a wave of his ringed hand. It seems as though he may say something else, perhaps to Elsa, but he turns and then he and Anders are gone.

Eve, Julia

———

A MEMORY: FLEEING IN THE DARK with Elsa in Julia's arms. The journey to Berlin; every stranger's glance was a threat, and the train went so slowly. In Julia's nightmares—and Eve's too, probably, if she were ever to dare to ask—the baby is taken from them at the border, carried away across a crowd of upstretched arms and out of sight.

Instead, they found themselves, by some miracle, at Cousin Grete's house outside Gothenburg. *Come in, come in.* Grete had married late, a solemn white-ruffed minister—at forty, her acting mania had been transmuted, overnight and without explanation, into religious fervor—and now he stood in the background, not intruding. The appearance of the baby made Grete's big, symmetrical face crinkle in surprise—"Julia! What have you done?" Typical that, despite having known Julia all her life and having only met Eve for the first time that evening, Grete assumed it was all Julia's fault. "It's better we don't explain. Not yet."

Another memory: this time Eve's. Julia, in the rocking chair on the porch of Grete's house, holding Elsa, who was just beginning to want to stand, on tiptoes in her lap. Julia flinging a napkin over Elsa's head; Elsa freeing herself, with a squeak of delight; Julia feigning relief that her baby hadn't disappeared. Grete bringing soup (rejected) and slices of peeled apple (accepted and smashed, one by one, into Elsa's open mouth). Later that same day, Grete buying imported weeks-old newspapers from the town and leaving them outside their bedroom door. The conversation, with Grete: Grete's solemn nod, barked laughter. "You always were the rebel of the family. We will do what we can, my husband and I. We will take it day by day, week by week."

Their great stroke of luck: the disappearance of little Willi Hanser from Graz in the summer of 1914. Willi vanished during a family picnic by the Schwarzlsee one roasting August day. A gypsy camp had recently set up in the area; it, too, disappeared overnight. Like the Bauers and the Kellners, the Hansers were an industrialist family; educated, urbane, in possession of a summer house. Weeks passed, then months, and with no trace of the boy, it was assumed that the Roma were responsible. A comparison was made in the *Vorarlberger Volksblatt* with the Kellners' missing child. Herr Bauer wrote to the newspapers announcing the reward for information about Baby K. was increased to 50,000 Kronen, but there was no new information. Reading the article, Julia pressed trembling fingers to her temples. "Blame the gypsies, always," she said, looking sick.

Heidi and Gunther wrote, in a sort of code, for a number of years until with one final, cryptic note, they announced they were leaving Vienna, and the letters stopped. Rolf and Frau Berndt wrote every week. *Maria and Ephraim have married. Ephraim has not been called up because of his chest. The boys of Leopoldstadt are fewer and fewer every week. The geraniums are in flower all along the courtyard wall.*

The letters made Julia cry. "They are suffering there." But there was no point discussing it. Better to stay in a neutral country. And also because Elsa, tiny as she was, looked like the portraits of Isabella that had been printed in the newspapers: the same eyes and center-parted hair; the same expression of mutiny and mischief. "Nobody will ever believe she's ours," Julia would sob, in the evenings, winding her own red plait around her fingers. "But she is," Eve said.

Julia finds work: a local eccentric who wants his self-published plays translated into German, and Eve has some hours at a cloth-mill in the next town. Grete and her husband request one thing, which is that they attend the church where he is priest every Sunday. What it is they hope to achieve with this is unclear: Grete just presses her palm on top of Julia's and says, "One day, you may see."

It is a small price to pay, and honestly meant, even if Julia never does come to see.

Between the three of them, a great unanticipated swoop of love. They walk in the meadows outside the town in the height of summer, where it gets hard to tell how late it is because the sun is still up, swinging Elsa between them. In the mornings, Elsa opens the door to their room early, pads in and creeps into the bed from the bottom upward, surfacing triumphantly at pillow level. Sometimes—perhaps more often than other children—she has tantrums that last too long. At these times of incoherent rage, Julia looks at her and thinks that she knows something is missing; as though she is a child who's lost a twin.

Elsa turns six. She is enrolled in a Swedish school in the nearest village, where she causes excitement because of her dark hair, and gossip because of her parentage: Grete has said she is an orphaned great-niece from Austria. Elsa takes to her lessons quickly, but is often withdrawn with the other children. She cries and asks to be taken home. *I know the feeling*, thinks Julia grimly, walking her back early from class one afternoon through the snow.

Messages from Vienna have become sparse, because it is difficult, in the immediate aftermath of the conflict, to afford the little discretionary things like envelopes and postage. One day, a letter comes. Frau Berndt writes cheerfully but is unable to quite disguise her despair, and so her notes are often just a few lines: *We had an informal supper party Friday last and everyone brought something to eat.*

This time: *I am sorry to tell you that Rolf has the flu, very badly.* (The communication has taken a week to reach them.) *The doctors are overstretched and he has little help. We are all hoping for a miracle. I know this news will be hard. We are doing what we can.*

Eve is the first to read the note, standing in the kitchen. The flu has yet to reach Sweden; they say that it takes one in eight. She rushes past Grete and into the study where Julia is working on her translations. Elsa is there, too, sitting in a corner with a book open on her knees.

They leave the next day: train to Stockholm, just two suitcases, a surprised peck on the cheek from Grete for each of them: "Godspeed."

They send a telegram to Frau Berndt from the city—WE ARE COMING—and cross the Baltic Sea on the next possible boat. Across land, through the flat Rhineland and the Black Forest, Elsa sleeping propped up beside them. "Are we doing the right thing?" Eve asks, looking at their daughter. "What if she catches it?" Julia reassures, as much as she can: they will be careful. Children are spared where adults in their prime fall ill. She is strong. The decision has been made.

And so home. It is a Monday about five o'clock when the train pulls into the Hauptbahnhof, already dark, and, from the first moment, achingly recognizable: that stale smell of the city after rain. The faces of the citizens are different: grayer and thinner, and more various in dress and coloring as they move through the orange-lit sleet. The tram to Leopoldstadt and then they walk as fast as they can to the Taborstrasse, slipping in their hurry over the broad paving slabs that have replaced the cobbles. The sign for the Cabaret of Unearthly Delights hangs askew; Mitzi's has closed, but Silbers' has expanded into an emporium of hanging goats' legs and slabbed steak, still open into the evening; Herr Silber lifts a hand to wave to them, his face blank with surprise.

The archway is ahead. A few stones have crumbled from the edges; the winter conifers in pots are spindly and brown. A light is on in the window of Frau Berndt's lodge. Everything looks smaller. Julia hoists Elsa onto her hip, and Eve knocks. The door flies open.

"I hoped it would be you," Frau B. says, and then can't say anything more.

Julia goes in first, maneuvering the sleeping Elsa carefully around the doorframe. The silver that used to stand proudly on the mantelpiece is gone; the stove is barely lit. Everything smells unwashed.

Rolf is sitting in Frau Berndt's armchair, with a blanket over his body to the chin. A bowl of soup is half eaten beside him. He wakes when he hears her. The skin is tight around his skull; his eyes are bright and determined.

"Don't get too close," he says, "not with the child." She wakes Elsa gently and tells her to go outside—"I'm just going to chat with Uncle Rolf"—and moves to sit next to him and hold his hand. Eve has shuffled into the room and stands by the door. After a few minutes he goes to sleep; then wakes briefly. "Don't leave me," he says, and they don't.

•

Elsa, growing: the lankiness of a ten-year-old; devastated, at fourteen, because a boy she liked had asked her best friend to a birthday party. Temper tantrums, always hovering; "I don't know where she gets it from," Julia says, exasperated, worried that she knows very well. It is Eve, in these moments, who knocks at Elsa's door and enters without waiting for a response; who sits on the end of her bed, hands laced between her knees, and listens.

Around them, couples of their acquaintance separate and reform in different configurations. For them, the old passions wane to vanishing point, then burst forth at odd moments; they spend a whole year almost without touching. Eve comes home one day to find Julia shyly naked in their bedroom. At first it is stilted, and then it feels necessary. Afterward, they lie in bed and count their blessings. One: to have friends. Two: to have the outfitter, opening soon, helped by a loan from Frau Berndt. Three: to have Elsa. The sense of their own daring swells in the semi-dark room. Four: Julia's fingers prowl toward Eve's waist.

They take a walking-and-swimming holiday together later that summer, to the Grüner See; their first in many years. On the train journey, Elsa, unprompted, reaches for both of their hands. "I'm lucky," she says, her gaze evasive, squeezing their fingers. When they arrive, she undresses and runs into the lake, without looking back.

Elsa

ELSA LETS HERSELF INTO THE APARTMENT on Renngasse—the family allow her a key of her own—and turns to press her forehead into the cool wood of the door, rolling her temples this way and that. She listens. Nothing. Everyone is at the Prater, their Sunday tradition.

The apartment is long, and light, and lovely. She takes off her shoes then her coat and hat; hangs them on the coat hooks in the hallway. She stretches her toes in her stockings, smooths her dress with her palms, and walks the corridors.

She finds herself, as she always does when she is alone here, in the living room. The shutters are open. The books are clear-cut on the shelves; the family portraits gleam; the grand piano is buttery to the touch. She brushes objects with her fingertips, enumerating the things that are not hers: the vases, the lamps, the waxy surface of the side table.

It has been exhausting, being at home. She thinks of Eve's blank face, this morning, when she recounted her dream: "I dreamed the soldiers came for you." There hadn't been a dream, not really; she'd invented it, trying to find a way to urge her parents to take things more seriously. "Darling," Eve had said, "why would they? Don't tell your mother."

She sits in an easy chair, telling herself it is just for a moment; puts her head back and closes her eyes.

She is thinking of him, and then opens her eyes and sees him standing in the doorway.

He has that greedy, knowing look, the one she hates, the smile thin and tilted up at one side. He's in his weekend suit, the charcoal one, his tie red and neatly knotted. His fingers are spidered on the doorframe over his head, showing off his height. He hangs there, pressing into the room, watching her.

Perhaps they have reached the point of knowing each other where they can be open. She is so tired that it would be a relief.

"I was just resting for a moment." He hitches his head up and arches his eyebrows: *Really.*

She stands. She has to move in order to regain control. "I thought you were at the fair."

He makes an indifferent face. She knows he thinks he is too old for these family outings.

He says, "Marie's been in the kitchen this whole time."

Elsa looks down. A small smile. "How long have you been standing there?" she says, before she can consider that it isn't wise to ask. Marie is the maid who cannot keep from staring at him. For her to catch Elsa napping in the master's chair . . .

"Don't worry. I'd protect you."

He's smirking as he says it, but still, he can be gallant, Elsa thinks, with pain. She imagines him at sixty, respected by all, giving a speech. Sees herself in the front row. In the vision they have both aged, and not aged; the city streets are full, and free.

"Max," she says, before she can help herself, and he freezes. He looks her in the eye, uncertain. He looks as though he may escape, and now she wants very much for him to stay. She wants to tell him about Rolf and Anders, about her parents, and she knows she mustn't. "Should you play me your piece for the concert?"

He nods, smiling and formal and ironic, and they cross to the piano, careful not to touch or get in each other's way. He pushes back his coattails and sits, flexing his fingers.

She takes an instinctive breath in, to brace herself, and, "Let's see how I can murder it today," he says, waggling his eyebrows. She loves him for it. He has no musical talent, none: it's his father's wish that he should study the piano.

He raises his hands over the keys and takes the plunge. He winces and grimaces at each terrible discord, and shakes his head as though he cannot stop it, and carries on regardless.

The pantomime is for her, she knows, to make her feel better. She stands by the piano and tries to be stern. "Make sure the trills are even," she says in a mouse-voice, and neither of them can stop their laughter. The Mozart is abandoned with a theatrical final thump, and he rests his fingers gently on the keys and looks at her.

The laughter and the music have brought Marie. She's standing just outside, in the corridor. Max's face turns dark when he sees her; Marie gazes at him with a gleaming, hopeful expression.

"I heard the piano and wondered if you needed anything," she says. Her whole being is poised and quivering for his response.

"No thank you," Max says. His lips are twitching as if he'll laugh.

Marie is suffused with red. "I'll leave you," she says, with a furious little curtsey.

Max shrugs—*What can I do? I'm irresistible*—but he plays a minor third with two thoughtful fingers.

This must stop, so she turns and leaves the room without speaking. As she walks away he restarts the Mozart, playing carefully and making fewer mistakes, to try to bring her back.

Julia

———

TODAY IS THE DAY of the month that Julia goes to visit Frau Berndt, taking her sprig of white elderflower with her—Frau B.'s favorite. Eve never wants to come. Julia cannot grudge her the current hibernation—glass on the streets of the Othmargasse yesterday, again—but it does mean that Julia goes alone. Makes her coffee alone, eats her bit of bread alone at the table, in absolute quiet, and softly closes the door behind her.

She takes the stairwell steps one at a time: the pressure of oncoming rain makes her left hip ache. The entrance gives directly onto the streets through a fine black-painted door; the road is almost empty, apart from a neighbor walking in the other direction, the teenage daughter of a tobacconist. They cross on the sidewalk, with the polite smile of mistrust they all wear nowadays. The girl has slim ankles, a good sway to her hips, and something in the arch of the eyebrows. Julia resists turning for a second look.

The Donaukanal is swarming with currents: the runoff from the mountains has swollen it into an oily mass. She walks across the Rossauer Brücke and on to Seegasse, toward the entrance to the Jewish cemetery.

As she reaches the entrance—a small tunnel between buildings; it is nothing if not discreet—she sees two policemen standing on the opposite side of the road. Boys, really, rather than men: one of them has a chin full of pimples and the other is kicking at a pebble in an undeniably adolescent way.

She readies the well-formed excuse: *I myself am a Gentile, come to pay my respects to a dear friend*—she has never had to use it yet, and cringes when she plays the words forward and back in her head—and then she thinks about Eve's face. She would applaud the lie: *Keep yourself safe. Come back to me.* The young men lift their heads and stare at her. She has always found that a broad smile will get her out of most situations, *nicht wahr?* She strides toward the entrance, still smiling, and ducks right. One of the boys hefts his rifle on his shoulder, and the other scrubs at a patch of sidewalk with the toe of his right boot. Nothing is said to her.

Now she is in the sudden silent boom of the cemetery. It is surrounded by the walls of the apartment blocks and houses on all sides, and she is the only visitor. Silver birch trees among the gravestones are young and slender, their frothy green leaves just turning crisp.

She will be quick. She walks across to Frau Berndt, and as she picks her way across the uneven grass, she takes out the pebble she has brought from her handbag—a small chip of granite from a path in the Augarten, taken during the last picnic of the summer. She places it on the small pile of stones on top of the headstone. Always that stagey self-consciousness, the sense of being observed by invisible and curious faces.

She stands, and as the years wind back, she does what she always thinks she won't: holds her hands folded in front of her like a schoolgirl, reciting her problems to the ghost of Ute Berndt. Elsa is the start and end of everything and so she begins there. *She is suffering. She is angry. Sometimes I feel so angry with her, for being angry. Her sadness doesn't have a root and consequently I cannot pluck it. And then, she keeps secrets from us.*

The question always spills out, sooner or later. *Is it because we took her?*

The only answer is to persevere, and she knows it. She lifts her face to the sky; pinpricks of rain fall on the tip of her chin. *I worry about Eve. I want someone to worry about me. I am tired of being the one who decides.*

Wind hisses through the dry leaves that have begun to fall into the cemetery. Frau Berndt, taken one night in her eighty-third year, her husband's scarf in her sleeping hands. How had she known it was coming? She had, nevertheless, been prepared.

As she exits, a large wagon is being helped to reverse down the street by one of the policemen, who stands in the middle of the road, giving hand signals to help the maneuvers. It creaks to a halt outside the entrance to the cemetery. Four men with spades, chisels, and mallets jump down from the cab. The second policeman pushes his cap back and starts to direct them. They rush past Julia, their tools over their shoulders, without a word.

"Building work?" she inquires, as polite as she can make it. The pimply young policeman has the grace to look ashamed.

At the apartment, she finds Eve dressed and looking through the newspapers for work. She glances up when Julia enters the room, one forefinger still hovering under an advertisement for a home help.

Julia sits. "They are stripping the cemetery. They are going to take the granite and marble first. Ute's headstone is granite. How will we find her? What about all her pebbles?" She starts to cry.

Eve clambers to her feet and comes around the table. A rapid succession of kisses on Julia's parting. "It will be all right," she says.

"How?"

They sit there for a long time, Eve's arms looped around her neck.

"Any luck?" Julia asks.

"They are looking for a lady's maid in Josefstadt. Younger woman preferred."

Julia chuckles. Eve shakes her shoulders, gently and lovingly. "What would Ute say? She would say, 'Keep going,' wouldn't she? 'In all things it is better to hope than to despair.'" Her anxious face is lowered into Julia's field of vision. "Come on, love," she says. "It will be all right."

Elsa

BY NEGOTIATION, ELSA IS ALLOWED TIME in the afternoon for her own thoughts. She has two hours to write, or sleep, or read.

At half past five, from her bedroom, she hears the main door open, and Max's footsteps, then the clatter of the twins' feet in the corridor, running toward him—"Maxi . . ."—then the delighted giggles as he swings them up into the air. She squeezes her eyes shut, and hears his mother, asking how he's spent the afternoon. She will ruffle his hair and press a kiss to his lips, which he is too old for. Elsa hears his steps pass her door as he goes to his own room. She imagines the look he might give, wonders whether his thoughts turn to her as he walks by.

The sound of the table being laid; Marie's footsteps. Stillness, then one of the twins howling. "Where's Elsa?" ("She's in her room, I expect.") "I want Elsa." A high wail. ("You mustn't disturb her.") And then the thump of the door, the handle being rattled from below, and the two little girls rush in and fall on her. She gathers them up. The smaller one smells particularly like him; something infantile in the golden hair.

"Mother says it's suppertime," lies the more brazen of the two.

Elsa allows herself to be led out of the room and tugged down the corridor, where they pull her not into the dining room but into their room, and down among the wreckage of wooden blocks

214

and cardboard figurines. One of them holds up a new doll for inspection.

"I'm going to call her Elsa," she says. "After you," as if concerned Elsa might not understand. Then, unexpectedly, she puts her arms up, and Elsa lifts her onto her hip.

"You're getting too big," she says.

The child plugs her thumb in and rests her head on Elsa's shoulder. "Tired," she says, and Elsa thinks, *Yes.*

The twins are put to bed before supper, yawning and cross; the mother insists on tucking them in herself, and then comes into the dining room smiling and relieved.

The father, Herr Haas, says grace. Elsa bows her head and reaches in her mind for Max, who is sitting opposite. As they raise their heads again, she tests the temperature. He is sulking: he opens the napkin onto his lap and won't look at her.

"Thank you, Marie, for this excellent supper," Herr Haas says, and Marie bobs and leaves the room. Max stares at his bowl without enthusiasm.

They are going to ask about her weekend. She has been preparing for it.

"Where is it your parents live?" asks Frau Haas, lifting her soup spoon, all delicate wrists.

Elsa has told them before, or told them the same lie. "Leopoldstadt," she says. "On the edges. Closer to Brigittenau."

Herr Haas clears his throat. "And what is it your father does? Did? Before he retired?"

"He had a tailor's shop."

"Oh yes," Herr Haas says, remembering, his face clearing. "Off Petrusgasse, you said. I think I walked past it once or twice."

He breaks bread. Crumbs catch in his mustache. "And they are well?"

Elsa says they are quite well. Max's ironic interest in her is like a physical weight. She imagines him mocking her: *They are well, thank you.*

The danger has passed. Herr Haas is talking about someone, another family, whom Elsa doesn't know. There is some talk of a daughter of Max's age; some discussion of having them to tea. It seems the older brother of that family has joined the army, and is distinguishing himself. He is posted on the Western border, and his letters are full of home and country—he longs for Vienna, and cannot wait to see action, if the long-fabled war ever starts. "Now there's a patriot," says Herr Haas blandly. Max tilts his soup bowl away from him to capture the dregs. His mother's gaze flits between them.

As Marie is bringing the meat course, there is a soft knock at the outer door—so soft that at first they are not sure whether they have heard it. Marie continues placing the plates; they lean back to allow her to work. The knock comes again, a touch more insistent.

Marie puts the final dish in front of Elsa, apologizes, dusting her hands on her apron, and leaves the room. They wait, but in truth it is clear who is coming.

The visitor is a new one, one she hasn't seen before: smart in his khaki and red epaulettes, the black boots polished as twin beetles. He salutes Herr Haas—a sharp arm out, as if pointing, then snapping back to his side. "I apologize for disturbing you," he says.

Herr Haas creaks to his feet, and bends to kiss his wife. She nods. She regrets even his smallest absence. Herr Haas leaves the room and there is the sound of Marie helping him into his coat. When he comes back into the dining room to wave a final goodbye and tell his wife not to wait up, he has the armband on, too.

Herr Haas returns at ten o'clock—Elsa hears him fling his coat at the hook behind the door, cursing when it falls, the squeak of his boots to retrieve it, and she knows with the intimacy given by the household that his temper is foul—and she feels Max's sullenness, through five closed doors. He won't be asleep—he will be lying in bed, alternately reading and brooding, one arm above his head.

She hears Herr Haas squeak along the parquet and wait, his hand hovering on the doorknob, outside Max's room. She hears his thoughts: the shame of not being able to persuade this bright, officer-class boy. The worry—*Am I doing the right thing?*—crowded by the comforting thought: it would only be one tour, and Max is gifted at mathematics; he will be found an office post here in Vienna; the danger will be minimal. The sullen rage of wanting to be able to command Max, as his son.

Elsa feels this course of emotions run through her. But Herr Haas is decisive—that is why they have the large apartment, after all, all the trappings of their life—and he does turn the doorknob, and now she pictures him slipping into his son's room, standing there, and Max's slow blink. Sure enough, there's the curt beginnings of a statement—"I hope you'll reconsider, have reconsidered." Elsa feels part of a web of listening ears—Frau Haas's room is just next door, and she sleeps poorly since the German annexation; Elsa sometimes comes across her on her own nighttime wanderings, a ghost in bare feet and lace nightgown. And the twins, who are doubtless sleeping by now, but will be difficult and restless in their lessons tomorrow.

Max's response isn't audible. He might even have turned over in bed to face the wall, a childish maneuver. But she thinks he will aim to irritate, to cause only discomfort. One cannot study mathematics in the army. (Herr Haas, a man of action, will not understand.) Impasse. Finally they are both disgusted.

How to end it? Herr Haas, hand on the doorknob still, white and angry; Max pale with rage. Herr Haas exits: goes to his wife's room, pacing like a big cat, where he will undress in silence and climb into bed beside her and just be there, staring at the ceiling. His anger will transmute into a heavy drugged sleep.

Elsa lies in the dark and feels for Max's thoughts. All the best work in his field is done before the age of thirty, he says, and he's running out of time. He pities his father, but he has the conviction, the absolute conviction, of being right.

Elsa tries to communicate, through the darkness of the sleeping apartment, that she understands him. Further: she could imagine a life together; she could imagine shouldering the scandal for him, taking him through moments of indecision. She thinks about what it would be like to introduce him to her parents. His great and capacious mind could wrap itself easily around Julia and Eve in the Leopoldstadt apartment; around the extended family of Rolf and Anders. Rolf would flirt with him and Max would flirt back.

She turns over and buries her head in her arms. Tomorrow she will do only what she is supposed to do. She will take the twins to the Augarten, and the milky smell of their hair, and their pure cries of laughter, will expunge everything bad.

Elsa

———

SHE KNOWS IMMEDIATELY she has overslept. Blue autumn sky in the skylight, and the giggling sound of the twins bouncing on beds in the next room.

She has slept in—or been allowed to sleep in—for hours longer than she should. In the hallway, she can hear Frau Haas talking to Marie, giving instructions on the shopping—she will be standing, patting her hair in the hall mirror, pulling on her long gray gloves. Then the tap of Frau Haas's footsteps, the pulling-to of the main hall door (Frau Haas is too well-bred to use any force).

The twins are shrieking, and there's the fat sound of them beating each other with pillows and cushions from their beds. The watch on the nightstand: half past nine. She should have been woken by Marie at seven, and taken breakfast with mother and children, before taking them out for an expedition to the park and starting lessons at nine o'clock sharp.

She has a wild fantasy that she has dreamed this whole three-month employment with the Haases, and is in her old room, at home; or that she has become a ghost in the house overnight. Unless. . . . She has an idea, only a vague idea, but. . . . She gets up, frowning, and dresses, frowning, and cleans her own pale pinched face with the water from last night. Her reflection, which usually brings some measure of comfort for its regular, thoughtful lines, does nothing today. She looks ill, which of course she was, last night, a headache growing behind her eyes at eight o'clock and sending her to bed early: embarrassingly like a caricature, the back of one hand pressed to her forehead.

She fiddles with her cuffs, pushing her hair into smoothness, and walks to the door. She has her hand on the handle, takes a breath, then goes into the corridor. As she passes the children's room, the door opens and the twins bundle out and grab her skirts. They escort her, a laughing mass of hands and feet and blonde hair. By the time they reach the salon, she's laughing too. They don't wait for her to stop being nervous: the door is pushed open.

Max is reading the paper at the long mahogany table—legs stretched out, head bent, frowning. The sun in the room catches on his gold hair and eyebrows. Elsa feels the breath expand in her throat; he is very like his father and of course she can never tell him, without creating great upset.

He looks up and says hello. She stands helpless, the twins hanging off her arms.

"I arranged to let you sleep in," he says, and makes a swift nervous movement to indicate her head, and headache; it looks like a salute. "I'll take the pirates to the Augarten."

Hearing their nickname, the twins scream with joy again, detach, and run to Max. He reaches out tickling hands. "Elsa, Elsa," they chant.

"No, no," he says. "She's not well."

The twins look solemn, then cunning, hoisted on his lap. "Fresh air!" they begin to shout, jumping off and running back to Elsa. They tug on her hands, small insistent animals, and the smile that has begun at the level of her stomach and swept upward is now giddy for everyone to see.

"I can come. Only if your brother says yes."

Max looks suddenly free: happiness spreads across his face, a wave. "He says yes." The twins watch, aware perhaps of the small stunned moment in the room. Then they turn and clatter away down the hall.

The Augarten is still and clear and hot, its long gravel alleys soaking up and reflecting the day. The maids rolling their perambulators greet each other with wide smiles; in the distance, a young man walking his paramour around the fountain shouts with laughter.

Max walks with his hands behind his back, smiling. "The weather is very fine, is it not?" he says, sententious, and they laugh. A young couple passes by them, and the boy nods to Max; Max says a big bold hello, and clutches Elsa's elbow, and then doesn't disengage.

His presence is overwhelming; taking over all thoughts of future or past. *Where could we go?* she thinks. She pictures the head gardener's shed, in the middle of the maze. The hot taste of his skin, the smoothness of it. But there is nowhere that would be out of sight enough.

The twins are running ahead, and now they turn and giggle; sly. "Max and Elsa," they chant, and then sprint off down toward the end of the vista.

After fifteen minutes, the twins start to complain of thirst. Max points to a small patch of lawn in the English garden. The twins are first doubtful—Mama may tell them off for getting grass stains—and then ecstatic. They flounce their tiny skirts out and sit; then roll, giggling. Elsa takes the biscuits from her bag, the water for the girls and the flask of coffee, and pours for her and Max; aware of the heat on her cheeks and the backs of her hands, the tingling of her lips. The twins settle down and chatter to each other, spilling crumbs and laughing at their own private jokes.

Max sits back on his elbows and stretches his long legs out in front of him, and blinks slowly against the sun. Elsa floats in it, tilting her head back, eyes closed. She imagines his look traveling over her—the freckles of her now-warm forearms, the arch of her throat. She swallows.

She hears the twins get up and move away, chasing each other. Her blood swells in her veins at the thought that he could take her hand; trail his fingers up her neck. She flies in her mind, with him, to the shed. Everything is light and dark at the same time; she thinks she hears him shift on the grass and her eyes open suddenly, and she sees he hasn't moved, but is watching her with a look of startling, helpless cupidity.

She has truly heard something. A voice, a figure striding toward them across the lawn, hand raised eagerly. Smart twill suit, salt-and-pepper hair; neatly folded pocket square. Elsa looks away, but it's too late, she really has been recognized.

Eve reaches them and stands puffing a few feet away, hands on hips. Elsa sees now that she is realizing her short-sighted mistake—she wears her spectacles on a little cord around her neck but rarely calls on them—she will have thought Elsa was alone with the twins, and now she sees there is a stranger, too, unpeeling himself from the grass.

Max is swiping his palms on his trousers, and extending his hand to Eve. They shake and he says his name, his full name, and stands, hands on hips like her, with a quizzical challenging grin.

"Eve Perret," says Eve, and nothing more. Elsa is straight-backed with the pain of the meeting. This is the wrong parent: Julia would know how to make it all right.

"A pleasure," Max says, and then—she could kiss him: "I haven't met any of Elsa's friends yet."

Eve blinks. "Well, nowadays we barely see her," she says, good-humored, registering the *friends*, registering the *yet*.

"We don't let her out often, it's true," Max says. Fake regret.

Eve is bright and glazed. She brushes down her jacket and looks at the twins, who are playing happily twenty feet away. They, too, are new, only described by Elsa; Elsa sees Eve thinking how different they may be from Elsa's tales, how much more richly dressed, how blonde. Exactly what the Führer recommends.

"Are you having a picnic?" Eve asks.

Max jumps in. "We are. Elsa was so good as to agree to come with us. My sisters adore her." The unspoken corollary: *We all do.*

"Yes," Eve says. She is waiting for Elsa to acknowledge who she is, and now she must see it isn't coming. "We may see you this Friday?" she suggests to Elsa, and then, hearty: "Perhaps you will bring your young friend!"

The twins have paused in their play and are watching the exchange. Eve waves a cheery goodbye at them, and says goodbye to Max too, and walks away. She stumbles a little on the short grass of the lawn.

"Goodbye," Max says. Elsa thinks there is a little wistful turn to the word.

The walk back to the apartment is without speaking. The twins have been made sullen now by the unseasonal heat rising from the sidewalks. They claim to be sleepy and when it comes to lessons, will be unengaged and, later, tearful.

Walking, Elsa sneaks glances at the small zone of Max's face: the point of his nose, the ears that are slightly too large, the full lower lip. If she focuses on these things alone, she will be able to communicate what she wants to tell him, which is everything about her family.

She would like to tell him about the time she was eleven, and a boy in the playground called her unnatural, *a pervert like her mother*. She'd punched him in the nose; she remembers Eve's sorrowful face, later, saying, "You must never do that again, even if what they say is very wrong"; how confused she'd felt, because she'd punched him to defend Eve. She'd say that she has spent her childhood aware of things that her friends weren't, able to see the little undercurrents only adults could; that she has turned herself away from many of her comrades, because of things they've said about sexual deviants, about Jews, and that this is tiring, and only sometimes a gift. She has longed to be normal, in the secret hours before dawn. She would like to say that she goes to Eve for comfort, and to Julia when she has something to show off; that she longs to hear Julia say, *Darling, I'm proud of you*, and rarely does, although she doesn't think this is on purpose. That it is difficult, sometimes, to be the daughter of a woman who is so accomplished, and who is so adored by the other parent. That sometimes she sees Julia roaming the apartment, as if looking for objects that aren't there; she sees the strain and worry over finances. She would like to speak about the strangeness and wonder of being the only child of not just two adults, but sometimes four. She would like to tell about the way Anders unfolds his handkerchief and lifts it delicately to his nose before he blows it; she would like to say that Rolf's fairy stories, when he read them to her, always ended with the prince marrying another prince, garlands and garlands of roses, doves streaming from the castle turrets. That he was the one who told her where she'd come from: "We found you on the steps of the cathedral, darling; we took you in, like in *Snow White*." That however much she might secretly wish to know who her real parents were, it is unconscionable to ask them for any clues. She would tell him, if she could, how she fears for them; how she would defend them, tooth and nail; how much this love makes her angry and afraid.

They reach the apartment block. Liesl starts to cry and is hoisted onto Max's hip while he fiddles with the key to the outer door; Hanna jams her thumb in her mouth and watches.

The hallway seems dark after the bright of the day, the green of the park: or perhaps it's just that she is fighting to control herself, to make herself walk slowly up the steps. There is the whole day to get through before she can be alone. The hours of lessons with the twins; his presence, roving around the apartment.

Marie is waiting as they go into the hallway—the twins scattering hats and coats into her arms. Elsa wants to smack that syrupy smile from her face. Max's mouth is a thin line. "Thank you, Marie," he says—master of the house, dismissing her. He drops his jacket into her arms. She hangs it on the hook as if handling a holy relic.

They go together, she and Max, into the salon. From the street below you can hear people talking, passing by, muffled through the thick panes of glass; laughter oddly magnified. The room's stuffed chairs and footstools, the faded spines of Frau Haas's novella collection, are a comfort. He is dizzying, the nearness of him.

His lips are moving, making silent shapes, one hand hovering over the piano keyboard.

"I liked your friend; your Eve," he says. "I liked her pocket square." A big smile. "It was chic."

She crosses the room, takes his face in her hands, and pushes her mouth into his. She grips the back of his head, strokes the baby hairs at the nape of his neck. She pulls him into her, all the long length and height of him; feels the rising and falling of his chest.

She takes his hand and leads him to her room. They get undressed and she lies on the bed.

She is embarrassed to admit that she has no idea what to expect. She has fantasized about various men, had baroque passions for them, but never the ones who returned her feelings. There have been opportunities with others, less cared-for, but she has never wanted to go further than a kiss. In her darker moments she thinks it's because of being raised by women: Herr Doktor Freud would say she lacks understanding of men. Max, she is sure, has had several romances. There is a friend of Frau Haas who looks him up and down when she visits, in a way that suggests she knows perfectly well what's underneath his suit. She has been tormented by daydreams of Max and other women, together; the sleepy look in his eyes. She imagines that he holds something back, and so gains control over them. That is why Marie, for example, is so driven to distraction.

He looks frightened as he bears down on her. She opens her legs to make it easy. Everything is over, it seems, in a matter of seconds, in a flurry of cries and digging fingernails and flesh fusing and then retreating.

They lie flat on their backs on the small bed, staring at the sky-light. He tries to laugh, but it's too serious for that. The first questions start, silently: *What have we done? What will we do?* He cups her face in his hands.

Anders

———

ANDERS WEBER, YOUNGEST FIRST CELLIST of the Staatsorchester in a generation, carries a pot of petunias all the way to his mother's apartment in Währing. His wrists ache in the first five minutes, but he is too worried about everything to take a tram, and be hemmed in with others, and risk crushing the pot. He worries he will spill soil on an unsuspecting person, and he, Anders, will have to stoop and apologize. Grubbing about on the floor of the tram, he will feel ridiculous.

Frau Weber still lives in the apartment he grew up in: a handsome five-story block on a corner, with views down to a park on two sides. The philosophers' café where he first shyly showed his face, aged fourteen, is still open opposite, the inevitable smell of clove cigarettes hanging in the air outside.

He lets himself into the apartment—cannot suppress a shiver at the sensation of homecoming—and calls for her. Nothing. She is only fifty-six and in good health, but another of Anders's fears is that she may die one day, for no reason. He stands in the corridor, waiting, trying not to think the worst. *Have I always jumped at my own shadow?* he thinks, as the outer door clunks shut downstairs and her face appears, peering up the spiral stairwell at him. *Probably I have.*

She is plump, which is a comfort, and although she puffs at the stairs, her face is ruddy with enthusiasm for the task of shopping.

"Late tomatoes!" she says, brandishing her bag at him. "And real endive!" She looks at the pot that Anders is holding. "Lovely!" she says. Her eyes flash with good humor as she pushes past him, wielding her bags. "Gorgeous boy! Come in!"

"Coffee," she says, shuffling to the kitchen, and lighting the gas with a flick of the match. She puts the shopping bags down on the tiled floor. She hasn't kept a domestic servant since his father died two years ago. *I prefer to look out for myself.*

Anders sits, gingerly, in an armchair. She comes to the doorway of the kitchen and looks at him with satisfaction. "Still too thin," she says with a smile. And then, "I'm sorry I didn't come to your recital. I had a headache."

This is untrue. She will make short trips into the neighborhood but will not venture far. Two weeks ago, some youths had ordered her off a public bench, believing her to be Jewish because of her dark complexion. She had tried to explain the situation; "I am like you," she'd said, "a Gentile." They had not cared.

"How is your man?" she says. "Is he exercising? The calisthenics book I gave him?" The kettle whistles. She shakes her head as she pours the coffee into two enamel mugs, smiling. "And the dog?"

Anders came with a whippet, whom Rolf affects to despise. "She's well," Anders says. He pauses, and cannot resist an anecdote. "We took her for a long walk yesterday and she stole a poodle's ball." His voice is full of pride. The way she lopes across the grass, making it look easy; when she looks at him, eyes like liquid chocolate, he feels whole.

"And Julia and Eve?" She has not met them, but Anders has spoken of them in such warm terms that she always asks after them. She brings the coffee on a tray and sets it down on the table; pulls out a chair and sits. "But you have really come to ask me about the visas."

Anders nods. "Eve and Julia are well, and entertained us to supper last week. As for—"

"Too expensive," she begins. "And anyway, nothing will happen. I'm just an old woman. The incident with the bench"—the way she purses her lips as she says "incident" suggests it was the work of silly boys—"was exceptional and I, too, could have been more careful to avoid trouble. I know things have changed."

Relieved, Anders says: "How do you know they haven't got Oma's name on a list somewhere? Did you know they're taking the stones from the Jewish cemetery?"

"But we are not Jews, Anders," she says; gentle, surprised. "We haven't lived with a faith, ever, have we? We don't keep kosher. I don't agree with it, of course, it is monstrous, but we are not in danger."

He lifts his coffee cup. The gentle rattle of porcelain.

"Oh, Anders," she says, as if he were a little boy again. The coffee has spilled.

"You don't know what it's like. You have to at least try to be safe."

She is about to remind him of the great gap in their years, he knows it, of how she has done well since his father died, shopping and inviting her friends to play cards, ever the merry widow. *Things are better than ever*, she will say, and it's true: without that ogre between them, dominating, they are both closer to each other and less dependent on each other. Then she will say that, perhaps like their relationship, everything revolves back into shape if you wait long enough. She will say: *Vienna welcomes all. It always has.*

He closes his eyes tight and before she can begin to speak he utters a silent prayer that he won't make her cry and says: "We want you to come and live with us. Me and Rolf. You can have our room and we will make do in the sitting room."

She smiles. *She is remarkable*, he thinks, *a remarkable person*. Forty years of marriage to his father, with his simmering rages, and she is intact. "But then you will have no privacy."

"I never want to contradict you," he says. It sounds like a plea. "I want to think you're always right."

She nods, acknowledging the truth. It is a failing, of being so close to each other.

"Well, it is a logic puzzle," she says, smiling and shrugging. "Either you are right or I am right, and we don't know which."

He wipes his nose on his sleeve, appreciating the concession. He has cried, but only a little bit. "Come and stay for a while," he says. "Until things feel more settled."

"I would bring attention. Unwelcome attention. We must be practical."

"Rolf will be so angry with me," Anders says, "if you don't come." This is a lie: he hasn't discussed the plan with Rolf. It has been a design of his own, and an impulse to offer it to her today, like this.

She folds her arms and leans on them. "Tell Rolf he will have me to deal with, if he says any more about it. Now. Your music. Where are you playing next?"

At midday, drinks finished, conversation exhausted, he gets up from the table. "I'm just going to see my old room before I go," he says, and she nods.

He creaks over the parquet—somehow the sound is an imposition in the dusty silence of the apartment—and pushes open the door. His childhood bedroom is long and narrow; a bright window, white-shuttered, a spartan single bed. A tiny desk and a space cleared near the window for a music stand, and a stack of sheet music, edges crisped by the sun. Two cellos in the corner, his three-quarter size and the old scratched chestnut Voigt; now he has a Geissenhof, on loan from the orchestra, worth more than his apartment. On a shelf over the head of the bed, a few adventure stories. He remembers leafing through the pages to get to the illustration of the Moor and the Crusader Knight bathing naked together in the Promised Land.

He takes out the Voigt, tightens the bow, and plucks the strings experimentally. The room smells of how he felt as a child: of loneliness. He plays the sawing opening bars of Bruch's *Kol Nidrei*. His mother won't know it, but he hopes the music will communicate to her this naked plea: *Come with us.* He hears her footsteps, in the kitchen, pause.

Elsa, Julia

"DO IT AGAIN, more slowly."

He hovers his hands, smiling. She smiles back, reaches up to reset the metronome on the top of the piano. "Again," she says. She sits back on her chair next to the piano stool, folds her arms, and waits.

He *tsks* and shakes his head at her sternness. There is a moment—she wonders whether he will grab her for a kiss, when he will cease for a second to do the mental arithmetic: where in the apartment is Marie, where are the twins? It is a week since they started. When Elsa catches herself, in the dark corridors of the house at midday, when she clutches herself for sheer joy, the thing she most often thinks is: *He plays better now.* It's a small miracle. The piece unfurling with liquid precision.

Instead, he seizes the metronome, and turns off its monotonous click. "We don't need to let this unimaginative creature boss us around," he says. "We don't need to play by their rules."

She returns his smile with interest. Then the mood takes him over: the concentration infusing his face and fingers, and he flips back the pages of the music and starts the piece again.

The last stream of notes dies on the keyboard. It is five o'clock. She tells him that will be all—is aware of her own voice speaking, when all she sees is his face, mocking. He catches her hand and presses a kiss to the palm, very quick, and gets up, brushing past her as he leaves the room.

She goes to her room to wait for supper. In the old days, in fine weather, she might take a walk down the Kärntnerstrasse to look in the shop windows, or read, or walk quickly back to Leopoldstadt to fuss over Julia and Eve, hurrying to the apartment in time for the evening meal. Now she just sits on her bed. She cannot read or sew. If the twins come creeping in, hoping to play, she sits listlessly, and they crawl over her, pulling her hair gently—questing little tugs. She is listening for the sounds of his careful footsteps, his voice asking his mother about something. The apartment is too busy for him to visit her at this time of day, but she still requires the thread of his presence. On the occasions when he calls out cheerfully that he is going to the theater or to meet friends, she folds her arms around her knees and dips her forehead onto them. Frau Haas is embellished in her mind, for having given Max to the world; Herr Haas, too, seems golden, generous, and fine. The twins become miniatures of what she and Max might have at some point in the future; it's easy to believe they would look like each other. She imagines Liesl and Hanna as young aunts: perhaps twelve, perhaps fourteen, cradling her and Max's baby, incredulous.

The dinner bell sounds and she leaps off the bed, crosses to the door. She should try to appear pale and calm: that, after all, is her job. The sound of new voices in the hall; laughter; Marie's inquiry, "May I take your coat?" She had forgotten there would be guests tonight. She breathes out, then in, slowly.

In the dining room, Frau Haas is smoothing her hands across the gleaming mahogany, her heirloom porcelain dinner setting—caught in a moment of childish pleasure. "You know our governess," she says to the couple sitting opposite. "Elsa, you've met Gerhardt and Toissl Wolf. Our oldest friends." They have not, in fact, met, but Elsa is too polite to mention it. The Wolfs say hello as if they know her; one governess, she supposes, is very much like another. They are older than Frau Haas, perhaps in their fifties; she all cream and roses, and his beard trimmed to a point. Murmurs of greeting; the weather, it is observed, is fine. Max comes in just behind Elsa, pausing to place a hand in the small of her back as he edges around to his side of the table. She doesn't have time to react appropriately; wishes the contact were lower, firmer. He says a cheerful hello.

The placement means she is to the left of Frau Haas, and Max to the right. She tucks her skirts behind her knees and looks over his head, at the large windows. "My husband will be delayed," Frau Haas tells the table, "we should start."

Marie ladles soup. Elsa tries to eat; he is a constant, burning presence, and she daren't look in his direction. The Wolfs ask about Herr Haas's work; they make worried sounds, and tilt their bowls away from them to finish. They ask about the twins. They themselves have a boy of Max's age, whom they expect to be called up. Frau Wolf dabs at her mouth and lowers her eyes. Marie clears the plates and serves thin slivers of venison, artfully arranged, and potatoes in gravy. Frau Haas asks Max about his day and he yawns—"Not much, played the piano"—then smirks and apologizes to the Wolfs for the yawn. "Are you going out later?" Frau Haas asks, and Max kicks sulkily at the table leg. "Maybe."

Six days ago, he came in at midnight, stumbling into the hall, calling goodbye to his friends in the street below. After a while, the creak as he opened the door to her room. "How I missed you," he said, as he got into bed beside her. Sorrow in his voice. "Did you have a nice time?" she whispered. "I did," he said, reflective. "I did have a nice time."

"And you, Elsa? What do you do for fun? Cinemas? Dances? Is there," Herr Wolf says, "a young man in the case?" Frau Wolf slaps him on the arm with her napkin. He shrugs and slips a piece of venison between his lips. "I can ask," he says.

"Oh dear," Frau Haas laughs, looking at Elsa.

"Nobody special," she says.

"Probably for the best," Herr Wolf says, pushing a potato around his plate. "Don't leave it too long, though. All the good ones have joined up—apart from our Gottfried, of course—and what's going to be left for the rest?"

Herr Haas enters the room: "Hullo, Wolfs, all." He drops a kiss on his wife's head. "Everyone all right in Leopoldstadt, Elsa? I'd heard there were problems."

She is startled. There are troubles every day, round-ups and stones thrown, but nothing on a grand scale.

"I don't think that there were many fatalities," he says. Marie moves around the table collecting plates. "Just some local people getting up to mischief."

"Your family's in Leopoldstadt?" Herr Wolf leans forward, all ears. "How charming."

Frau Haas says: "Of course you may use the telephone. Or do your parents not have the telephone? In which case, you must go—"

She is rising to her feet, but Marie is there—she is always there—reaching for her supper plate. Their elbows knock and tussle. There is a moment where Elsa could give way, or Marie could, and Elsa thinks: *No.*

"*Girls,*" Frau Haas says. The plate sails toward Herr Wolf, who lurches back in his seat with a gulp of surprise. The plate shatters on the table just short of him, taking a dessert bowl with it; shards like white knives lie on the table.

"*Oh,*" says Frau Haas.

Marie has frozen, tears of alarm in her eyes. "Not my fault," she whispers.

"Yes, it was," Elsa says. "May I be excused?"

Frau Haas nods, all her attention on the broken porcelain. Cold, to Marie: "You had better clear that up. Fetch Herr Wolf a cloth for his suit."

"No harm done," Herr Wolf says, dabbing at himself.

"She has always been clumsy," Frau Haas says.

The dining room recedes behind Elsa. Her feet eat up the meters between herself and the hallway; she reaches for her coat. Dimly behind her, the sound of Marie, apologizing, crying.

Outside, the sky is powder-blue streaked with pink. She hurries past the Mozarthaus, past the crowds of young people heading for the theater. The Marienbrücke flies under her feet; then it's the cobbles and narrow streets. Feeling of home, and not-home: no bakery smells; the shoe shop with its racks of clogs and sandals on the Nickelgasse is boarded up. Glass splinters onto the sidewalk. A gang of young men in police uniform are helping themselves to ladies' underwear from the front of the haberdashery. One of them holds up a ladies' wig and tries it on. She passes a splotch of red, a trailing smear of startling brightness that might be blood.

As she sprints along the long sweep of the Taborstrasse, something catches in her nostrils: the fine scent of brick dust. There is a cloud of it, hanging like mist in the air, at the end of the street.

Julia is standing at the doorway of the apartment block. She spreads her arms out and Elsa runs into them. "Where's Eve," Elsa says, and Julia is saying they are all right; mostly it was down the road that the damage happened and the people were angry. "I couldn't help," she says. "I couldn't help."

"I was so sure I'd lost you," Elsa says, crying, as they walk up the stairs.

Inside, the apartment is exactly as it was. Eve is standing at an upper window. "Gunshots," she says, to nobody in particular.

Elsa sits on the big sofa, in the middle. In the olden days she would sleep in their bed between them, wriggling her toes against their feet.

"You need to leave Vienna," she says.

Julia swipes at the dust on the table with a cloth.

Elsa says: "Don't you have savings?"

Julia moves the rag in vague, expanding circles. "They don't target Gentiles. And there's you."

"Don't stay on my account. I have my job. I have friends."

Julia's pitying look is worse than anything else. Elsa loops her scarf around her neck, then raises her arms in a trembling shrug.

"Won't you stay tonight?"

If she stays there is a risk that she will tell them everything, she will see how pitied and pitiable she is, falling for this boy, and then they will fight. She cannot tell them about Herr Haas's armband and the polished boots in the hall.

"You should leave the city," she says. "I really think you should consider it." When Julia tries to reach out for her, she tugs away.

Elsa's footsteps clatter away down the stairs. Julia breathes through flared nostrils, staring at the ceiling. Who is Elsa to talk about leaving? Living at home until her early twenties, frightened of every thunderstorm. Never able to keep a friend.

Eve is watching her carefully. Julia digs fingernails into the flesh of her palms. She has let Elsa go away from her in a state of fear, and that is surely what it means to be a bad mother. She runs to the door, looks out over the stairwell railing, just in time to see Elsa's dark, neat head disappearing through the front door.

She swears, takes herself off as fast as she can go, pouring her determination into the sprint. She reaches the doorway and looks out into the street and sees only the clouds of cloying dust. Calls out, waits, but there is no response.

She stands poised for a moment in exquisite self-pity. Turning, she sees, with embarrassment, that someone has witnessed this. It's a woman, of about Elsa's age, but shorter and mousier. Wearing a cheap dark coat, detaching from the wall by the door of the apartment.

"Can I help you?" Julia asks.

The young woman shakes her head, makes a gesture like buttoning her lip, and moves away into the empty street.

Rolf

———

ROLF AND ANDERS LIVE OFF the Ungargasse, in a one-bedroom apartment near the Conservatoire. When the invasion happened (they will not call it an annexation) they were very glad to be outside Leopoldstadt; when the Jewish musicians from the orchestra and music school lost their jobs, they felt less safe. Still, it is something, to have an apartment of their own, even if they do have to pretend to be cousins sharing a room to save money.

Rolf only occasionally thinks of Emil Kellner. When he does, it is always at times like these, with the sound of boots on the sidewalk three stories below, and the window open over the street, and the scarce light of late autumn flooding in as he does the washing-up. Emil, in these thoughts, is a thin person, edging into the room, sitting gingerly in a chair. He has a flap of skin hanging over his right eye from the blow that killed him. To think of him is to have scar tissue probed and prodded with a scalpel; but if it is painful, it is mainly because of how painful everything seemed at the time. And pain gives way to pleasure when he thinks of Elsa. And thinking of Elsa brings thoughts of Anders's shy face, his thin eyebrows and the mustache he can never quite achieve.

It has been untrue, what the poets observed: that we only have one great love. For the first few years, even with Anders, this was disturbing. Rolf would wake in the night and look over at the sleeping boy and panic would rise in his chest, that he might be snatched from him. He was afraid, always, when Anders was out of his sight. "I'll never leave you," Anders would murmur into his hair, at night. Rolf has come to an accommodation with his terrors, and they have been assimilated into his person. He no longer panics when Anders is not with him; the fear is there, but it is muted, and more than outweighed by the joy when he returns. And Emil's occasional, spiteful visits quickly fade before the broad grin of the whippet. Even now she's lying in front of the stove, chin on her paw, one eye open in case of a potential walk.

Rolf washes the dishes and counts the minutes. At five past five, the door opens and Anders walks in. The whippet, Klara, gets to her feet and clicks over to him, and stands while he fusses her head and ears. She is patient with them both: their house spirit.

Anders takes off his coat and hangs it neatly over a dining chair. He is fastidious in his habits, where Rolf is expansive. He walks into the kitchen and puts his arms around Rolf, who looks at their reflection in the window: his own bulk, almost obscuring Anders; Anders's long fingers encircling his waist. It is evening again. The lights of the Prater wheel are like a theater backdrop. Anders's forehead is buried in between his shoulder blades.

The forehead butts urgently into Rolf's spine. "Don't be angry with me," he says.

Rolf would have murdered him, this father who hurt Anders, and sometimes Barbara, and told him to practice the cello until he bled. Such a womanly-shaped instrument, such a slender boy: Rolf knows it was so that the other pupils would mock him, struggling to carry the cello case up the stairs of the music school. Rolf knows that Anders's profession is necessary to him: there is no other thing he can do. Yet, every time he runs up and down the scales, there is the memory of his childhood waiting for him.

"I won't be angry, whatever you've done," Rolf says, lifting a plate from the suds and putting it on the side.

"I asked her to live with us."

Rolf stands very upright; he is immediately uncomfortable. The old fear: someone will take Anders away. She will come and they will sit in the parlor together and Anders will talk and laugh in a way that he doesn't with Rolf. Always the terror, of Anders turning and Rolf seeing someone else: someone glittery-eyed and scornful.

He says: "And?"

Anders presses his palms into Rolf's paunch, testing the resistance. "She said no."

Rolf turns and Anders leans against him. The fleck of soapsuds in Rolf's beard transfers to Anders's forehead.

"Can she be persuaded?" Rolf asks. Now that he knows Barbara has refused, he can afford to seem generous.

"I don't know." Anders pushes his face into Rolf's for a kiss. "I'll try again next week."

He disengages. Sometimes he is like a small boy, and sometimes a man far older even than Rolf. Rolf has always put this down to his musicianship. Now he has a wide-eyed, contemplative look: as though he's seeing the apartment and everything in it, but in some future time. He waves a hand vaguely, conjuring an invisible spell—Rolf thinks, dizzily, unhappily, that he's wondering where the fold-out bed will go—and then retreats, without a word, to their bedroom, where Rolf hears him starting to change his shirt. This is a new tic: the need to change clothes on returning home from the streets.

Rolf goes back to the kitchen, slings a dishcloth over his shoulder and attempts a meal. They are no poorer, since Anders has begun filling in for musicians who have been fired, but the guilt has taken the pleasure out of the small things. He makes chicken broth from the bones of the weekend meal, and then adds potatoes and carrots, and rosemary from Julia's window box. Stirs, tastes, and it is possible almost to forget the earlier conversation. Anders is practicing, something modern and not to Rolf's taste, in their bedroom. Rolf catches his own reflection in the window: he looks furtive, with the spoon lifted to his lips.

The food is ready and Anders comes out of the bedroom. He looks tired. He rubs his face with his hands as he slumps into one of the chairs by the table, and Rolf stifles his irritation and tries not to set the bowls down too sharply.

"Music sounded good," he offers, as they begin to eat.

Anders slips some of the soup delicately into his mouth. "It was terrible," he says. The correction is severe but factual: dispassionate perfectionism.

In the stairwell, there is the sound of someone ascending one flight, two flights: they both listen, and then the steps go up to the attic floor above them. A lone man lives there. They joke that he always tries to brush past Anders when they pass in the hall.

Rolf says: "What happened to the boys who spat on her?"

Anders narrows his eyes against the steam rising from his bowl. "What do you want to have happened? Who can she complain to?"

Rolf wants to make a joke about giving the boys a hiding, to say something about men in uniform. "If she came here . . ." he says.

Anders pushes back his bowl carefully.

Rolf says: "We don't know our neighbors. And she looks very . . . she is very dark-haired. She is already being singled out on the street. And even though she doesn't qualify as Jewish now, she might in a week, two weeks . . ."

All those nights, when she must have known Anders's father was tying weights to his son's fingers to lengthen them. Her crying apologies, later: "I'm so sorry, I'm so sorry, I didn't protect you. I'll carry that shame till I die. I thought it was for the best."

"I'm just saying that you don't owe her anything," Rolf says.

Anders's shocked, growing pupils. "Don't I?" he says.

Rolf has always felt he is perhaps more cunning than intelligent. He survived, didn't he, all those years of trade behind the Opera House? He has secretly taken pride in, and cultivated, the ruthlessness he feels is his birthright. He has made a living as a theater producer, out of the ashes and of no education. Anders is a more complex, and a more simple, person. The perfect person, really, and now Rolf has hurt him. He says, "It's too dangerous. For you. You could lose your job. It might encourage scrutiny of us, too."

He gets up, takes the plates from the table, and going into the kitchen, flings them into the sink, where one cracks. Anders, who loves every possession in the apartment, lets out a snort of distress. Rolf comes to the doorway, exasperated, and sees the tears streaming down the side of his nose.

"Georg and Anna aren't answering their telephone. Nobody has seen them in ten days. And they were living as man and wife. You've taken lots of work at the Conservatoire. People must be jealous of you."

"You don't understand," Anders says. "How can you? You don't have family."

The whippet, thinking someone is about to leave the apartment, runs to fetch her leash.

Anders has gone to bed when there is the sound of more footsteps on the stairs. Rolf has been brooding, letting the stove burn down. It is eight o'clock at night and so he assumes, at first, it is one of the neighbors. When the steps stop outside the front door he hesitates.

His first instinct, these days, is to freeze where he is. But there has been something familiar about the cadence of the steps. When she knocks, with that brisk competence, he knows it is Julia.

He gets to his feet—as he's going to the door she knocks again. He opens the door with an impresario's gesture. He is resolved not to let her see he is afraid.

"It's starting again," she says. "My sadness. I can feel it."

He holds the door open and she slips inside.

Julia has spoken to Rolf like this once before. Years after they came home, Julia had become frantic and tearful, and arrived at Rolf's apartment without Eve. "I saw her," she had said, meaning she thought she had seen Isabella Kellner on the street. Julia had shivered in the warm circle of Rolf's arms, both knowing and not-knowing it was a delusion. "I know it was her," she had said, over and over, and then, "I can't tell Eve." Within a few hours, he had been able to persuade her that the vision had not been real, because the newspaper had said that Isabella was in America with her second husband, but the next day she had reappeared, sobbing. "I can't make it not be true by thinking." This time, Rolf had put her to bed, and summoned Eve. Julia had stayed in Rolf's bed for two nights and two days and on the third day, Eve had brought Elsa for a visit, and Julia received her gratefully, and seemed to settle. "I am all right now," she'd said to Rolf, determination on every part of her face, when they left.

He presses her into an armchair. "Is it Elsa?" he asks. Always the secret fear.

"The Silbers' boy, the butcher's child—the paranoiac—they took him away this afternoon and closed the shop, and there is a kommissar there, a big blond mountain lad, lording it over all the employees. There's a Star of David in red on the glass—" She waves her hand. Rolf takes it to mean: *Too much loss.* He takes the hand between his two large ones.

Anders is in the doorway from the bedroom, sleepily standing, watching them.

"Eve says nothing, she just sits there—" Julia says, anguished, and notices Anders. "Hello," she says. A measure of calm returns to her. She thinks of Anders like a son: someone to be sheltered from bad news, if possible. "I don't know what's happening to me."

"It's too much," Rolf says, comforting. Eve's shop failing and Elsa being Elsa and their friends leaving; the gallantry, the hope in their departure—*I shall no doubt be reunited with my son and daughter once we arrive in Vancouver!*—and the night terrors about soldiers in the street. Julia says: "Sometimes I just want to walk and walk."

"We need you," Anders says from the doorway.

"I've been walking all day," Julia says, "and never getting anywhere."

Anders pads into the room and sits on the edge of the sofa, and begins to talk about his mother.

Eve

——

THE APARTMENT DOOR BANGS OPEN, and Julia enters, and Eve, who has been up all night, jerks awake. Relief, like being drunk; then anger, even though Eve has suspected that Julia has been at Rolf's. Sadness, that whatever Julia has to do can only be done with Rolf and Anders.

Julia hangs up her coat and walks into the apartment as though nothing has happened. There are days, oh, months—in one case, an entire year—when Eve has wanted to flee. It is hard to manage Julia's crystalline perfection. Other people seem to hold them up as an example—Rolf has whispered that if he and Anders can make it for that long, he will be happy—but the truth is that there is intense loneliness, at times, and never worse than when Julia strides out into the world as if she doesn't need anyone else.

Julia says: "Rolf and Anders need our help."

"I expect an apology. For you leaving last night."

Julia's gaze becomes evasive: "Yes, but not yet."

"What if there had been a problem? With Elsa? You don't think."

"Things are just black and white to you, aren't they?"

Julia has an expression of caustic pity. Eve wants to smack it from her face. She has never touched Julia in anger. A weasel-voice says: *But she didn't care enough to let me know where she was last night.*

Julia explains the situation with Anders's mother, which goes like this: Rolf and Anders want to offer shelter; to do so would involve huge risk. But if Anders's mother were to come and live with them, Julia and Eve, in Elsa's old apartment opposite their own flat, she would be away from them, separate, and away from her home, which is not safe. They could say she was an elderly relative. Here in the heart of Leopoldstadt, among their own kind, who would ask questions?

Eve says: "If they were somehow implicated"—if anything were to happen. "We should be going away ourselves." Wistfully, because she knows Julia won't agree.

Julia sits.

"Do you want to be the kind of person who helps, or do you want to be . . . ?" Julia asks. Her hand waves again. Eve fills in the blanks. *Ordinary? Yes,* Eve thinks, *that is what I want.* She has wanted to be invisible, and never been allowed, because of how she dresses; she has always been picked out, laughed at, and all the time, she has wished simply to be normal. *I have never wanted anything else.*

There was another woman, once. Five years ago, when they still had the tailor's shop, she'd come in wanting a tie for her brother's birthday. She was in her middle twenties, only a few years older than Elsa (the shame of it)—quick-witted, her face alive because of its lack of symmetry. Eve had fumbled with the paper to wrap the purchase in, and she'd laid a hand on her arm: "Don't trouble." A week later, she came back, and as soon as she stepped through the door—blazing with purpose—Eve knew she was a problem.

"I don't suppose," she said, "I could invite you for lunch." As bald as that. As full-in-the-sway-of-the-hips as that. And Eve, knowing it was wrong, but thinking back to every time Julia had laid a hand on a man's forearm and cast her head back, laughing, at a party, said she could.

The café was full of the lunchtime rush. They ordered three courses. Eve was invited, for once, to talk about herself. The young woman listened, nodded, occasionally said: "That makes sense." Eve was able to explain her life. She did not mention Julia. She felt all of her little nicks and scratches, self-inflicted and not, start to fade in the face of this furious, good-humored concentration. The girl said only her name, and that she worked as a nurse for an old woman with an apartment on the Ringstrasse. At the end of the lunch, it was Eve who suggested they meet again.

Over the next week, Eve was furious with Julia over any little thing. The new blankets were too scratchy; she'd wanted coffee, like every morning, where was the problem? Julia floated around the apartment with a thoughtful air, acceding to Eve's demands. The morning of the fabled second lunch came and Eve stood in front of the mirror, smoothing the crease in her shirt-arms, which Julia had failed to make sharp. It felt like her due, to be allowed this one secret.

The second lunch passed as smoothly as the first. Everything seemed to be swallowed to a series of vanishing points: the bone of the edge of a wrist; the way a coffee cup was lifted and tilted. Toward the end of the dessert the girl leaned over the table and asked: "Do you live with anyone?" And when Eve, blushing, silently nodded yes: "Do you live with another woman?"

"Because I do." She dusted the chocolate powder from around her mouth with her napkin, a gesture as demure as it was flirtatious. "I live with another woman. I told you she was my employer but she is something else, too. It's true, though, that she is very old." She toyed with her dessert fork all the while and looked at Eve. Eve didn't want to say any more about Julia, or tell her about their daughter. She was flooded with alarm and possibility. "You could come to the apartment and see where I live," the girl suggested.

She went the very next day. All the time between was busy with anxious delight. She could barely speak to Julia. At one o'clock she told the shop-boy she was going out for the afternoon, and walked the fifteen minutes to the Ringstrasse.

The woman opened the door a crack, then wider. She was wearing a new dress, or one that Eve had not yet seen; expensive in gray silk, and her hair was washed and neatly combed, a blot of rouge on either cheek. The apartment was vast: glistening parquet, long and light-filled corridors. The woman seemed nervous: she took Eve's hand, and led her into the salon. "Wait there." A high wailing sound came from some other room, and the woman hurried away. Eve heard shushing noises, something like pillows and sheets being rearranged; the soft murmuring conversation of a long-standing couple.

The woman reappeared in the doorway; she hesitated, then came to sit with Eve on the sofa. After another moment's hesitation, she picked up Eve's hand—Eve will remember, later, that her palms were very dry and warm—squeezed it and then dropped it; put one hand on Eve's knee, and then burst into tears. "I'm sorry," she said, "I thought I could but I can't, not with her in the other room like this, or maybe not ever. I don't know. I don't know. I'm so unhappy."

The hand on Eve's knee felt like the warmest kind of promise; it sent electricity up and down her spine. It also felt horribly wrong, as though the knee no longer belonged to her, but to Julia; as though this was outright theft. Sick and heady, she gathered the woman in her arms and shushed her. The woman's parting, she noticed, had a few scattered flakes of dead skin. The woman repeated her apologies. She cried in Eve's arms. "It isn't true she is old. She is just ill. She has been ill for a long time."

Eve muttered that she understood it all, the lonely feelings. The woman was becoming heavy and hot in her arms. Eventually she pulled away, dried her eyes on her dress. Eve realized, with a swooping feeling, that she was even more desirable, because of her pain. The teardrops fluttered with the movement of her eyelashes.

"Maybe you could be a sort of friend to me," the woman said. Eve accepted the proposition. The loneliness, they agreed, was the deadly thing. "And I know you're lonely too," the woman said— something of her old self, that perceptiveness, coming through again.

A cry came from the other room. "That's my call," the woman said, getting to her feet, with a brave smile.

They did meet, as friends, five times, in restaurants and cafés, and once for a walk in the Prater. It became harder each time not to turn to look at each other, to keep the contact formal and polite; each time Eve mentioned Julia, she felt a cascade of guilt that was only just outweighed by the warmth in the woman's eyes. At the last meeting, they barely spoke, just walked. The conversation seemed pointless; their pace became slower and slower. Under the Ferris wheel—*Why did it have to be here?* Eve thought. *Why not any other simple unmarked place?*—the woman stopped. It was late afternoon: cotton candy and burned peanuts. She looked at Eve; put the tip of her forefinger under Eve's chin for a moment. "Goodbye, darling," she said, and turned away. Eve watched her thread her way through the crowd. The *darling*—the first and only term of endearment—caught at her. But there was no right to cry, was there? With Julia at home cooking supper for Elsa; wiping her forehead and up to her arms in soapsuds; Julia, ready to listen and understand.

Anders, Julia

———

THEY MOVE ANDERS'S MOTHER, Frau Weber, into the apartment while it is dark. Julia and Eve wait to meet her on the street corner one night at half past ten. Julia smiles when she sees two figures walking toward them: Anders, stick-thin, with his mother on his arm; and she is plump, and shuffling, but as she moves closer Julia can see the gleam of her teeth. She is carrying a pot of petunias.

"Well," she says, "so, here we are! I have my son to thank for setting the pace."

She catches Julia's eye, mirthful, and puts her hand to her chest, trying to get her breath. "Let's go, while I still have the energy for the stairs."

She walks up one by one; Anders has said she sometimes has palpitations. At the door, she pauses. Eve switches on the light. They have cleaned the studio as best they can; it has Elsa's old student furniture and decoration in it, everything cheap and angular. Frau Weber is charmed by it all. She crosses to the window. "A view to the Augarten!" she says. "And I can see the back of the block where my mother grew up. I cannot thank you enough."

This time the palm on the breast is an earnest gesture. Julia beams.

Frau Weber puts the petunias ceremoniously on the stovetop. "Now I must rest," she says; it is a command, and they are gently shooed out of the door. Anders turns one last time and looks

246

beseechingly at her: the look says, *Be careful*, and Frau Weber waves a lofty hand at him.

Anders walks back over the canal, the three kilometers or so to his home. He doesn't know what he feels; he tries to discern relief, or tension, but is met by a black immovable stone.

He lets himself into the apartment. The stove is out. Klara, long-limbed in her basket, twitches in her sleep. He stands in the cool of the salon for a moment, testing the air, and feels that Rolf is awake. He is correct. When he pushes open the bedroom door, the shape in the darkness stirs and turns over.

Neither of them says anything. This is how it's been: acidly polite. One day, chopping vegetables, Rolf said to him, "If anything happens to them," and Anders had been unable to do anything other than stare past him, and pretend to be somewhere else.

Anders runs his fingers up and down an invisible cello scale, replays the tricky Bruch high notes as he gets undressed.

Rolf is moving in bed, drawing his whole body up to a sitting position against the headboard. The sense of him saying something is imminent; something else may be imminent, too. Anders is still a person who has been beaten, and on dark nights, sometimes, his body gives him away: unable to stop it, he curls up. Rolf, who has raised his hand to comfort, retracts it with a little noise of desolation.

Two days after Frau Weber moved in, Julia is fed up of waiting. She suspects that Frau Weber has been keeping to herself out of tact and a desire not to be a nuisance, but still, they are neighbors now, and Julia is curious.

In the early afternoon, Eve goes out looking for work. Julia goes to the grocer's, the butcher's, and the baker's to buy Schwarzbrot, sausage, cabbage. She crosses the hallway with the basket of food, and at first she simply puts it gently outside the apartment door. She raises her knuckles to knock, hesitates, and then makes her decision. A burst of skin and bone on wood, sounding more intimidating than it is meant to.

Julia fixes her brightest smile to her face, and is met by an answering beam, as the door swings inward. Now, by daylight, she can see that Frau Weber is nothing like her son. She is comically rotund, and utterly unselfconscious: she leans her weight on the door handle and puffs, out of breath, willing to make a joke of it. "I've still not recovered," she says.

Maybe it is the strangeness of the times. "I can't see Anders in you," Julia says, wondering, out loud.

"Oh, he is very like his father," Frau Weber says, beckoning Julia in. Julia holds out the basket of food, and Frau Weber takes it and weighs it in her hands. "Too generous," she says. "Really. All of this. Yes, his father was a skinny person. They used to call us Little and Large."

She purses her lips; Julia knows enough about the disaster that was Anders's father to be discouraged from further questioning. Frau Weber moves to the kitchen area. Julia thinks she must have been a marvelous dancer. "Tomatoes! In October!" She holds one up to the light, tosses it, and catches it; Julia thinks she might take a bite out of the fruit in mid-air. "And your parents, Frau Perret? They are alive? I'm sorry that I can't offer you coffee."

Julia waves it away, and perches on Elsa's threadbare old armchair. Frau Weber has been in the middle of making bread. "Do you mind?" she says. "It will sink." Julia nods, and she resumes the pummeling of flour on the table, thoughtful.

"Call me Julia. My parents are both dead," Julia says. It is restful, to say it out loud. Restful to sit in this room with an older woman baking, and the yeast smells, in the sharp October sunshine.

"Call me Barbara, then. Condolences. Long ago?" She looks up with an expression of sincere interest. Her arms are floury to the elbow.

"They lived in Sweden. We weren't close."

Barbara nods. "The state of being an orphan is a freeing one. I sometimes think Anders will only flourish after I've died."

"You've been reading Herr Freud," Julia says, with real pleasure.

"I dislike him intensely and agree with him ninety percent of the time. I found him useful. When it came to my boy."

Anders has said his mother used to work as a typist—using her lunchbreaks to devour the books that would help her understand her son. Herr Freud is liberal on the topic of inverted love.

Propelled by who knows what mischief, Julia says: "Do you know the case study *Dora*?"

Barbara scrunches up her eyes, trying to remember. "The aphonic? Freud thought she was in love with the businessman Herr K., or whatever the pseudonym was. And when she says she's going to leave analysis, he puts it down to transference." She clicks her tongue. "Anyone could see from the case report that the girl was in love with Frau K."

Julia says: "We knew the family, slightly."

"And were they really like that? Vile?"

"He was," Julia says. "Herr K. was. The girl was a fine person."

"I wonder where she ended up," Barbara says.

Her interest has faded, and with it, the sensation of a near escape. She should be more careful. But she cannot resist poking at the scar occasionally, and it has seemed important to her to make as much of a confession as she safely can to Frau Weber. Perhaps then they will be even: she will be in Barbara's power as much as Barbara is in hers.

"How shall we manage it, then?" Julia asks, spreading her hands to mean: *This*. The fact that it would be prudent for Barbara to stay in the apartment as much as possible. It is unlikely she would know anyone on the streets here, but there is always a chance. "Would a food parcel twice a week be enough?"

Barbara nods, and scrapes a shy fingernail along the table, picking at leftover mixture. The dough lies in a flabby lump next to her hand. "I wouldn't presume," she says, "but I think that's best. My son can handle the arrangements."

Julia says quickly: "Oh no, I can do it."

She is never usually so eager to please. And this woman is nothing to her—she's not Frau Berndt, she's not Elsa, she's not Eve. But. She is a new friend, or an almost-friend, and she is someone to discuss Freud with, and she is Anders's mother.

"Settled, then," Julia says, smiling.

"Perfect." Barbara turns to her, shy all of a sudden—and there it is, that owlish quality that makes her look like him for the first time. "I'm grateful. Truly."

Julia says goodbye, leaves the apartment, and opens her own home with a key. Eve is at the table, writing a check for one of their many bills, her hand crabbing across the page. Julia feels a sudden rush of warmth for her. Barbara is a person to rescue. If they can keep her safe, then by superstitious extension of thought, they can keep themselves safe, too.

Elsa, Julia

———

ON EVERY SECOND SUNDAY, before she goes home for supper, Elsa's job is to take Frau Haas and the twins to church for the four o'clock worship. Herr Haas used to be Catholic, but Party membership made it unfashionable. He doesn't forbid his wife and children, however, and even encourages Elsa to accompany them. "Take good care," he'll say, "see you all later," delivering a smacking kiss on his wife's cheek.

Today, Max hovers in the hallway too. The twins squeal. "Is he coming too? Maxi!" And Frau Haas looks around, pleased. "Let's go, then."

Elsa left his bedroom just a few hours earlier—they have become bold—and gives him a broad smile. He looks handsome in his formal green suit and white shirt. He smiles back. One twin watches, perhaps too perceptive, but Max reaches down and fusses with her hair, and the moment passes.

In the street, Frau Haas seizes the hands of the little girls, and strides forward. She loves Sundays, she is humming something under her breath, and leaning down to say something to her daughters, one by one. Max and Elsa fall into step together. She is amused to see how lovingly he looks at the backs of his sisters' heads: their identical plaits, the scrubbed-white napes of their necks.

In the cathedral, she is sitting next to him. She must make do with the brush of the twill of his trousers, rubbing against the velvet of her cape. She can imagine the rest. She is hazy with tiredness from their nights together, and from worry: logic disappears into darkness as soon as she seizes on a thought. She sometimes turns her head toward him, before she remembers that she mustn't.

While Max and his mother go up to receive the sacrament, she waits with the twins. They are in a playful mood, kicking the back of the pew in front—she scolds them, but her mood is too light to mean it, and so they know that she is feeling indulgent. They whisper to each other companionably, and giggle, while she watches Max move up the central aisle of the church.

She is busy adjusting the hem of Liesl's dress when Hanna hops down from the pew and runs toward someone, hurling herself into the woman—the girl's—skirts. "Charlotte!" she screams, and wraps her arms around the person's knees.

The girl puts her hands on the top of Liesl's head, and laughs. She looks, embarrassed, at Elsa.

"I've done my hair like yours," Liesl says, looking up at Charlotte's face.

"So have I," says Hanna, mutinous.

"You both look very nice," Charlotte says. She shakes her head in amusement. "Hello," she says to Elsa, "pleased to meet you."

"And you," Elsa says.

"This is our friend Charlotte," Liesl says, leading her by the hand toward Elsa's.

"Max's friend," Hanna says, always precise.

Charlotte's fingers are very delicate. Elsa holds the hand for a minute, and Charlotte squeezes her fingers and then retracts them. "Both of our grown-up friends together," Liesl says, in satisfaction. Hanna looks worried. She is often frightened by coincidences.

"What are you doing later?" Liesl asks Charlotte. "Do you want to come for tea at our house?"

Charlotte assumes an expression of sorrow. "I can't. I have to go to see my own family."

She beams at Elsa over the top of their heads. Max is coming back up the aisle; Elsa searches his face for a trace of discomfort but he is serene. He bends in to peck Charlotte's cheek. "You've recovered well," he says.

She says: "So have you."

They laugh. Max turns to include Elsa in the joke, embarrassed. "From the Ball," he says. Two nights ago, he'd come back at midnight, lain in Elsa's arms until the morning flight back to his own room—but he'd smelled of wine. Now here is Frau Haas, smug at the sight of them together. She puts her cheek out for a kiss and Charlotte obliges. "Are you coming back for supper?" she asks.

Charlotte shakes her head in regret, and Max says: "Actually, I am going to walk Elsa over the river, to make sure she gets home to her parents safely."

Frau Haas is too distracted to notice anything odd, and the twins have had a sudden loss of energy and enthusiasm, and are struggling with the conversation. "You know it's not always the safest place after dark," Max continues, to nobody.

Outside the church, she and Max take the street northward, and the twins and Frau Haas hurry off to the south. The day is on its last legs, and a fine mist is rolling down from the hills, blending with the fading sunshine; the first drops of rain start to fall.

They fall into step naturally next to each other, although she suspects he has to shorten his stride. She has questions for him, but she doesn't know how to phrase them, and she wants to enjoy this feeling of being next to him, doing an ordinary thing, before she asks.

"Will Eve Perret be there?" Max says. He turns to her with a smile. "I am coming up for dinner, aren't I? That is allowed?"

The haunting feeling that came with Charlotte's smooth passage up the aisle vanishes. It's replaced by a buzzing joy, and also fear. Can she just walk him in? Can she just invite him for supper? Joy again: she will tell them the truth. Rolf and Anders may be there: *Darling*, Rolf will say, eating up Max with his eyes.

"Charlotte is an old family friend," Max says. "I think of her as a sister." She squeezes his hand.

Julia knows she should be going back to her apartment to set the table and change for the family supper; instead, she is playing chess with Barbara Weber. Rain is smearing the window and they are playing on an occasional table by the light of a single candle. It suits Julia's northernness, even though it is for economy's sake—she likes that Frau Weber doesn't feel the need to have light around her all the time, she likes the way Frau Weber bounces off things when she gets up to pour more coffee, in the dark, says "Whoops!" and rebounds affably, all the time her inner gaze fixed on what she's about to do to Julia's queen.

"What time are they coming?" Barbara asks, sitting down smoothly, and studying the board. They don't play with a chess-clock, but the time ticking is on both of their minds, and it seems more honest to be open. Julia arrived at two o'clock with a parcel of wool for a shawl or a scarf and sat down and they have been there ever since.

"Six," Julia says. She can see a line of attack down the right-hand side of the board, but she thinks it's too obvious. "I've made stew."

Barbara is silent. Her eyes sparkle—Julia guesses that she has spotted the impending attack. She moves her pawn forward into the wild space. Julia hisses, and Barbara laughs: full-throated, her head pushed back on the stem of her neck.

"Anders and Rolf," Barbara murmurs. The topic must be introduced gently: she respects how long Julia and Eve have known them, as adults, where she only really knows Anders as her child. Julia's chin is on her hand; she is receptive, but she wants to hear Barbara first. "Rolf doesn't visit. Anders is too thin." Barbara's mouth twists, somewhat spitefully.

"I expect it's nothing," Julia says, aware of the squirm of bad faith in her stomach.

The candles flicker in a sudden access of wind, battering the window panes. "We'll see," Barbara says. "Are you going to move this century?"

Julia stretches. Brings her hand down to touch a chess piece, just brushing it with her fingertips, and then swoops the rook down the board and into the heart of Barbara's defense. Checkmate is perhaps five moves away.

Barbara lets out a long admiring sigh. "Julia Perret, you devil."

A loud "Darling!" from the doorway, and Rolf is standing pulling off his gloves; he looks like a walrus, rugged up in a scarf and hat. Eve is doing the usual dance with Anders, where they are unsure whether or not to hug. She slaps him on the shoulder; both retreat, blushing.

Rolf bends in to kiss Julia's cheeks. "How's the harpy?" he asks, in a breath into her left ear.

"Fine," she says, and thinks that it would be typical if Barbara were to walk in right now. She's resentful, too, of how uncharitable Rolf is, and squeezes his arm in a slightly tighter pinch than necessary. "I beat her at chess, so she's probably sulking."

Rolf grunts. "Elsa?" he says. "Where is our little girl?"

Julia is warm with worry, the worse for the guilt of not having thought of it first. "Late. I don't know," she says. "Do you?" This to Eve, who is showing Anders the view of the red, black, and white flag on the synagogue roof from the window. Eve turns, and shakes her head. Her eyes are full of reproach: *If you spent less time playing chess.*

There is a tinkling sound, and Anders's mother enters the room. She has a shawl with clinking discs of metal at the ends of the fringes, and a burgundy velvet dirndl. Anders's eyes widen. Julia imagines this is a dress of some significance. Anders leans his cheek in for a kiss. Barbara strokes her fingers down his jaw. "Rolf," she says, turning. Rolf nods. He cannot bring himself to touch her; the threat he feels is tangible on the air, in the way his Adam's apple bobs.

Barbara pretends to notice nothing and takes the biggest armchair, the one that is Rolf's, and Julia hears the outer door opening and closing; footsteps coming up the stairs. "Elsa," she says, to everyone and nobody, relieved. Eve moves toward the door as well.

Julia sees her daughter coming up the stairs. Her face, upturned, is full of a happiness that Julia doesn't recognize. It blooms on Julia's own features, before she can stop it, contagious. Then Julia sees that there is someone else behind Elsa. Just a boy—blond, his hair on the long side, in the student style. Not out of breath from the stairs. A face that misses being handsome by the edge of a needle.

Elsa says: "This is Max. I was hoping he could stay to supper." She kisses Julia on both cheeks and loops her arms around Julia's neck, allowing herself to hang there, like when she was a child asking for a favor.

Max stands back. His clothes are ironed so crisply! He looks so much like the typical Austrian youth: rebellious hair but conventional underneath. He steps forward and lifts Julia's hand to his mouth. "Enchanté," he says, and she sees that he means it as a joke but is also deadly serious, and is able to balance these two things in a smile that he aims at her. She feels a long-forgotten flutter of envy, lust, in her stomach. Elsa is trying to keep her composure, but she is clearly very proud of him.

Eve strides forward, hand held out. "Good to see you again," Max says, and Eve shakes his hand in both of hers.

"I'm Rolf," Rolf calls out, arch, from the salon. Max steps into the room, and there is another hurried round of handshakes. Max kisses Barbara's hand, too, and Barbara's eyes meet Julia's, amused, over his head.

"Are you the son of the family?" Rolf says at last.

Max nods, and smiles more broadly. "I see," Rolf says. "Or, no, I don't see."

Elsa says: "It's all right—" and Barbara says, warning: "Rolf—"

Max says: "In your place, I would have questions too." He sounds, Julia thinks, like he is copying someone in authority. Who must his father be? What has Elsa told them about the Haases? She tries to remember, but cannot get past some idea that they are old money.

Elsa says: "Rolf, please," and Rolf subsides.

He smiles at Max. "I am protective, I know," he says. "I am resisting saying, does your mother know you're here, because I assume she does not."

"She knows I walked Elsa to Leopoldstadt, to see her home safely," Max offers. Like a poker player, he stays smiling blandly at Rolf, until Rolf, impressed, sighs.

"Welcome," he says, lifting his glass.

They sit down to supper, and by halfway through the meal, there is a real warmth of feeling in the room. Max has asked careful, tactful questions, has admired the cut of Eve's suit. Barbara has winked at Julia over the pouring of wine and Rolf has laughed at one of Max's jokes. He is surprisingly, genuinely funny, far funnier than he has any right to be in his early twenties. Elsa, for her part, has been so dazzled and joyful that she has dropped her cutlery no fewer than three times. Each time, Rolf has roared with laughter, and Anders has made an inarticulate little sound of desolation on her behalf.

Rolf is asking about Max's studies in mathematics. What does he think about the sacking of the Jewish professors? "Regrettable," Max says, swilling his glass. "Utterly regrettable. Altmann was one of the best."

His sangfroid is impeccable. Rolf catches Julia's eye and they share a smile. This boy could, despite his blondness, become part of the family. Then Anders says: "And what is it your father does in life?"

At first there is protest: we never ask such questions; not these days. Barbara is shaking her head fondly at her son; Julia rolls her eyes, until she looks at Elsa and sees her face. Anders's eyes—he is usually the first to lower his gaze—are bright and open very wide. His hands are breaking bread and rolling the crumbs back into dough.

"He is an Army captain," Max says.

Barbara recovers first. She leans forward, settling herself, elbows on the tabletop. "It must have been very difficult for him recently."

Max looks, for the first time, like a boy. "My father and I don't share the same views." He is very level. Julia supposes it is even brave of him to tell them the truth in this way. "He has a certain optic on the world, to do with natural rank, which I myself find barbaric."

"Elsa," Julia says, "help me clear away."

From the salon, you can hear the sound of Rolf gamely telling a story. Max is laughing—somewhat strained—and Barbara laughs too, keeping him company.

Julia puts the pile of plates in the sink and turns on the tap. She rounds on Elsa. She has switched to Swedish out of stress. All she can think of to say: "You stupid girl."

Elsa's lips are quivering with the unfairness of it, and, Julia suspects, the defiant, growing awareness of what she has done.

"You said they were aristocrats. Why didn't you tell us?"

"You would never have allowed it. And I needed—" Elsa is not so far gone yet that she will allow herself to say the hurtful thing: *I needed to get away from you.* It isn't easy, being Julia's daughter. There are unspoken demands about talent, about beauty, quick-wittedness—Eve, solid but hopeless, is not able to protect her. "He won't tell them. He would never put us in danger."

"How do you know?" Julia puts the coffeepot on the stove; takes cups from the dresser. "He knows, now—about Rolf and Anders, about us. About Barbara. You brought him here, knowing that she was here—"

Elsa says, "You don't understand. He's like family."

She has wilted so thoroughly that Julia almost feels pity. "You want him to be," she says to Elsa. "You hope he is."

"When you and Eve—" Julia puts a palm up between them. "But what if it is like that?" Elsa says. "What if I want it to be?"

"He's still studying," Julia says. "And then what? The army? Don't tell me there's not pressure to join up."

Elsa says nothing.

"You'd better keep him close, then, your Nazi."

"He's not—" Elsa says. She has started to cry. Julia is plastering her smile to her face, ready to see the guests again, and taking the coffeepot off the stovetop. "Stop," Elsa says. She makes a grab for the coffeepot handle at the same time as Julia and they stand, struggling. Julia wins, and Elsa hisses in pain: her finger is burned.

She cries openly now: like a baby, from sheer frustration. The words spill heedlessly out around her sucked finger. "He's going to be family and you're not. You're not, anyway, my real mother . . ."

It is astonishing, this display, in a woman of twenty-five. How the years roll away. At the same time, a part of Julia thinks, it is a conversation she's rehearsed so many times in her head it has felt inevitable.

"I've never hidden it from you."

"Why can't I have what I want? You have always gotten what you wanted."

"Rolf said Georg and Anna have disappeared. The old bar for . . . for people like us burned down last week. Suicides every day. People losing everything. What if it's Rolf and Anders next?"

"We'll have a family of our own, Max and I. My real parents would understand—"

The brutal fact is that Emil and Isabella would, certainly, have understood. She looks so spoiled, so like Isabella, that Julia says: "Your father's dead."

The words bring Elsa to a stop. She blinks. Then says quickly: "You're a liar. What about my mother? My real mother?"

Julia remembers all the times Elsa has needled her, has said any little spiteful thing. All the sighs of shame and rage when Eve dressed in men's clothing. And she thinks of how things are: the dreadful state of the world. "You want to know? I will tell you."

Elsa's eyes widen. Julia dives past her and out of the room. The guests have moved to the salon and closed the door. She can hear laughter—Barbara telling a long story, doing impressions—and the clink of the decanter. She goes to the desk in the corner of the dining room and takes a scrapbook from the bottom drawer, where it lies hidden under layers of other albums.

In the kitchen, Elsa is hunched up against the countertop, her fingers to her mouth. Julia throws the scrapbook down next to her and turns to the first page. *KINDESENTFÜHRUNG IN NEUSIEDL.* The lithotypes of the Kellners: Isabella's heart-shaped face. *Reward 10,000 Kronen. Still no information. Reward 50,000 Kronen.* The dates go up; the word count goes down. The missing Infant K., believed taken by gypsies. Herr Kellner, dead of sequelae to a head wound, June 1913, at home. There is an article about the death of Herr Bauer, five years later, of a stroke. *Reward 3,000 Kronen.* Isabella, in the *New York Times*, with her new husband, the Texan. A short story in a ladies' magazine, clearly based on the case, which got every detail wrong but which Julia felt compelled, superstitiously, to keep.

Elsa says: "It is a fantasy. You have kept these clippings for some spiteful interest—"

Julia turns to the page with Isabella's portrait, and traces the arch of the eyebrows, the point of the chin. Then she flips back, to the page with the sketch of Frau Berndt. "Ute helped us. She was suspected of the kidnapping, and we had to hide you, to get away. She lived indoors for many months. We took you to Sweden."

Elsa is quiet. She taps Ute's printed forehead. It's a good enough likeness. "No," she says.

"Herr Kellner hurt another child, in the same household. He hurt her for years. Do you understand what I mean? He ruined her, or tried to. It was a rescue. So you could have a life." She knows, as she says it, that the explanation will never sound right; perhaps it has never been quite true enough.

"Did Rolf know?"

Julia laughs. "It was his idea. I didn't know until they brought you home. Then I had to choose. We could have taken you to the police. I chose Frau Berndt, and I chose you."

Elsa turns the pages. The thumb of one hand strokes her own cheek; she studies Isabella's face, half-turned, looking back over one shoulder at the Astor Ball. She doesn't look up until she has finished the final article. The salon door opens and closes; Rolf and Anders's voices in the hall, lifted and regretful at not seeing Elsa as they leave. "Tell her goodbye from us."

"Then I could be rich. Could have been." She rounds on Julia. "I could have been normal."

She puts the scrapbook on the table, and reaches out. Until the blow lands on Julia's cheek, Julia thinks it will be a caress, designed to reassure. The sting of palm on cheekbone, the hard crack of connecting bone. Elsa stalks from the kitchen. Her voice, and Max's: "So sorry, no, we're leaving"; Eve, bereft, and Max's surprised, polite goodbyes.

When the apartment is empty of guests, Julia allows herself to be gathered into Eve's lap. She confesses: the secret is no longer a secret. "I can't think what I was thinking of," she sobs. "We've lost her; everything's falling apart," wiping her eyes—it does no good, because they are instantly wet again. Eve strokes her hair, runs a finger down the white line of her parting.

"Maybe we should go away," she suggests again. But Julia's whole body stiffens: "That would mean abandoning her." Later, they will realize that this is the point when they decided not to decide, and therefore made the decision.

Elsa

THE NEXT MORNING, ELSA WAKES to find Max sprawled in her arms. It is light in the room, which means it must be past nine o'clock. She is instantly covered in guilty sweat; he wakes up as if she's spoken, and notices where he is.

They listen. There isn't a sound in the apartment, which signals that breakfast is over. The Haases sometimes let Elsa sleep in on a Monday, in recognition of the fact she travels home late from seeing her family; Frau Haas sometimes takes the girls to the park on her own, and this must be one of these days.

Walking home last night, he'd pouted. "I thought it went well, no?" Made clown-faces to cheer her up. His face in a pool of lamplight, growing worried. "Was it me?" She'd held his arm. There is no way to tell him any of this.

Now he slips out of bed and hops into his trousers; shrugs on his shirt, straightening the collar fastidiously. He goes to the door to listen; opens it a crack, peers out like a spy. He still can't believe the danger they are in, she realizes. He looks back: "All right? See you later." She opens her mouth to say, *I am not who I thought I was*, then closes it again. He picks up his shoes and then, with a last flash of his smile, is gone. It is a physical pain, a sickness, to no longer have him in the room with her.

◆

At eleven o'clock, Frau Haas brings the twins back and Elsa is smiling in the hallway to greet them. She gives them their mathematics and writing lessons and then starts them on French grammar, and all the time she is listening for him, but there is only the sound of Marie humming as she twirls a duster around the salon. Over lunch, her hands start to shake and she has to put down her knife and fork. She thinks of Sweden. She was the only dark-haired child at her school. One day, she'd hit another little girl, who'd said: "Your mama is a man." Julia, coming to collect her early—"You must never do it again"—but surprised, not-so-secretly pleased. The warmth of her approval; the warmth of Eve, later, plaiting her hair in front of the fire.

The twins have their nap and Frau Haas asks Elsa for a piano lesson. Elsa obliges, although she cannot offer any instruction; she sits turning the pages and Frau Haas's phrasing flows out, steadily enough. She takes a pleasure in her music that Max doesn't, but the physical similarity—the same full lower lip, the same little eager forward-leaning nod at the end of a page—makes Elsa's chest hurt. All the time, she is listening for the click of the front door.

When it finally comes, at five o'clock that evening, it is Herr Haas. He comes to stand in the doorway. Elsa and Frau Haas are playing a duet that's beyond their skill as a pair, laughing over the wrong notes. He smiles at them but they feel his consternation, and turn, allowing the music to falter.

His fists are on his hips. "Max here?" he says.

Frau Haas shakes her head. Her pretty brow furrows. She rests a finger on a high A flat and lets the note sound gently. "University, and then he's going to the philosophy café," she says. Elsa looks down at her feet, so she only hears Herr Haas thump the doorframe as he turns away.

Over supper, it feels to Elsa as though they are all waiting for him. Herr Haas carves the joint of meat with a frown; catches the knife on his thumb and curses, putting the cut to his mouth.

When they are sitting, he says: "They're stepping up the measures."

Frau Haas makes a little neutral sound. He says: "It would be advisable for Max to stop his classes and do more for us."

By "us" he means the Party. Herr Haas—the man who took Elsa's two suitcases up the stairs, smiling, the first time they met; the man who asked so solicitously about the bombing in Leopoldstadt—nevertheless thinks his only son should be putting on a brown shirt and being of assistance.

Marie offers more to drink for each of them. She is a smiling mandarin, full of some secret source of satisfaction that Elsa can't fathom. Frau Haas says: "But his studies—"

Herr Haas mops his hands with a napkin. "It's time for him to stand up for the country."

Frau Haas nods to show that she has understood his position. She opens her mouth to say something and closes it again. Her gaze hovers thoughtfully over Elsa.

It is half past eleven when the door opens and she hears his footsteps on the parquet; the shushing sound of his overcoat being hung up, and then the silence as he waits to see if it's safe to come to her. She knows, though, that he sees the crack of light from his father's study door, which is ajar; then there's the sound of Herr Haas calling his name.

He doesn't dare to come to her room that night. She senses him, awake on his back, staring at the ceiling, into the early hours.

The next morning they confront each other, each pale and tired, over the breakfast table. He avoids her eyes. She manages to capture him, finally, dragging him into her room for a half-minute while Frau Haas is scolding the twins for some small misdemeanor.

"You can't tell anyone about Julia and Eve," she says.

"I know." He hesitates—he is thinking whether or not to tell her he is being conscripted into the Party, she knows. Then: "Never mind," he says, and he's gone again.

She returns to the table, lingering over the remains of the food. Marie brings a letter: she knows it is from Julia immediately. It contains pleas, but no apology. *We think you should come home.* Julia talks of being stopped on the way home from the cemetery and forced to eat grass. Elsa tears it up, across and over again. It is not her fault, any of it. Then hears a sound. Marie is still hovering in the doorway: a purse-lipped, resentful shadow. "For God's sake," Elsa says, "who d'you take yourself for?" She picks up the torn quarters of the letter, shoves her empty plate away. "It's rude to spy."

She barges Marie with her shoulder as she leaves the room, and Marie lets herself be turned, pushed, as if she is weightless.

Julia

———

JULIA LEAVES THE APARTMENT at nine o'clock in the morning. She and Eve have slept poorly since the Sunday supper of the week before. They have discussed whether or not to just arrive unannounced at the Haases' address—but it seems unwise and, in the light of day, premature; or perhaps it is that they are too afraid. "She will come back when she's calmer," Julia says. "I'm sure of it."

Julia has bought the elderflower bouquet the day before, so she walks straight toward the river, brisk and firm. It is as coldly beautiful a day as could be hoped; thin trails of mist hover over the canal. She imagines Barbara—Frau Weber—sunning herself in the attic window of her apartment, unable to go anywhere. *Then I will appreciate our fair city for us both.* Her feet move over cobbles and then concrete and the slabbed sidewalks of the Seegasse.

Half the stones in the cemetery are now gone; some have been broken and left snaggle-toothed, pointing out of the ground; some are just blank spaces of lumpy green lawn. Frau Berndt has been spared for now. There is a family, defiant, picnicking in one corner; a grim venue but the only open space still permitted to Jews. Julia clears some lichen from the lettering of Frau B.'s name. Just once, she thinks, she would like to see another person mourning. She imagines they could exchange sad smiles and although they wouldn't speak of the dead, they would know what it's like to feel so much for a person below the ground. How futile, how necessary, how enlivening. *I have been enjoying Frau Weber, Anders's mother*, she tells the pebbles above Frau Berndt's grave, and then she cannot pursue the thought, so she changes the subject. *Elsa is . . . Elsa is—*

She pictures Frau Berndt listening, tries to hear the raspy sound of her voice, but it won't come. She drops a pebble onto the pile and turns and leaves the cemetery.

Walking home, she is aware of a couple of brownshirts on the other side of the road ahead. One is cupping a hand around the flame of a match, lighting a cigarette for his comrade.

Then there are somehow more of them, and they are on her piece of sidewalk, up ahead. She tries to step around them, smiles her most urbane smile. The one with the most epaulettes has a bullied, weaselly face. She feels pity for him—he must have been scrawny and useless as a child, always the back of the pack—and her smile turns.

"Jewish?" he says, stepping forward. One of the others stifles a laugh.

"No," she says, but he steps in front of her anyway.

"Why are you here, then?" He means in Leopoldstadt.

She tries to keep her tone light: "Don't we all have to live somewhere?"

She already suspects there is no right thing to say. "Among the sewer-rats and the larvae," he says. His sneer makes him look even younger. "Are you a sewer-rat or a larva? A degenerate? *Lesbisch*? A freak?"

"I am not," she says, and he seizes her by the nape of the neck.

"Get down onto the grass," he says.

Herr Rosenstein from two doors down was forced to do it, a few weeks ago, and he returned weeping. The next day, when they'd asked him, he'd shrugged. It wasn't so bad. It tasted of home.

She tries for a joke. "This may take some time." She levers, and lowers herself to her knees on the curb. Nobody laughs. He points to the grassy patch by the gutter, where the road, ill-maintained, has started to spring to life through the cracks. "Eat," he commands.

The others set up a gleeful chant—"Eat! Eat! Eat!" On the other side of the road, Frau Herzl scurries past with her shopping basket, head down so as not to see anything.

Julia bends onto all fours and plucks a blade of grass between her lips.

"Oh, my darling." Julia stands in the doorway of the apartment, helpless, and the old words come tumbling from Eve's mouth, like an incantation; the way they spoke to each other when they first met.

"It isn't anything," Julia tries to say, bright and practical. "It's nothing at all."

Eve takes her to the bathroom and unpeels her dress from her; pores over the bruises on her elbows and knees. When Julia is shivering in the warm water, Eve lowers her forehead to the cold porcelain side of the bath. "I'll find them and kill them." She takes Julia's hand, kisses the palm. "We must do something. I have not always told you how much I— There are times when I could have been more—"

"Tell me now," Julia says. She tries to smile. Her knees are drawn up under her chin. Eve takes off her clothes, hangs them on the back of the door, and steps into the water.

Elsa and Max are walking in the fairground of the Prater. There are people everywhere, laughing and talking. It is going on three o'clock and the crowds licking candyfloss are dispersing, holding hands, flooding toward the exits of the park. High above, red, white, and black flags flutter next to the great wheel in the sky.

After a quick, stagey glance around, Max takes her hand and squeezes it in his, then deposits it in the pocket of his jacket. The new uniform doesn't suit him—doesn't suit anybody—and the cheap felt on the inside of the pocket scratches her fingers. She makes a face and withdraws her hand and he doesn't resist.

Last night they tried something new. He made her turn over. All the time she encouraged him—"Faster, more." She thought someone might hear them, this time, the slapping of his skin on hers; perhaps it would have been a relief to see Marie's pointed face peering around the door, so that they would not have to pretend any longer.

He looks tired, she thinks. After he has been to see her after dark, he retreats to his room and tries to keep up with his mathematical studies. She hears him pacing. The brownshirt stuff for him isn't ideological; he tells her, in her arms late at night, that he is desperate not to do it. But it is impossible, because of how his father is. "Does it make me bad?" he sobs.

Last night, she felt he was on the edge of asking something, but he peeled away from her and left the room. She lay awake thinking about the question he might have asked, but didn't, and now the late, cold afternoon has the hazy feeling of a hangover.

Ahead of them, a ring of people is forming; shocked faces looking in, and down. "Give him room," someone cries, "more space." The outstretched limbs of a man in middle age; his toes pointed as if dancing; blue face and lolling tongue. A child stands next to him, wiping its eyes, a stick of candyfloss in one hand. Max frowns, and shoulders both of them into the circle of onlookers. He is taking off his jacket, for some unknown heroic purpose.

They are met by a hurrying reflection. A pair of women move toward the casualty; both in their forties, their strides matched, their pace increasing in tandem. One, with fine silver hair, pushes forward, while the other hangs back; says, "Ada, be careful—" The men in the crowd don't want to let her pass. "He needs a doctor." Her blank stare. "*I am* a doctor." She bends onto one knee, then the other; lifts the eyelids of the insensible man, wipes froth from the corner of his mouth. Her mouth purses tenderly. "Water," she says, reaching back, and her companion runs to a stall, then hands her a paper cup. She lifts his head, pours a little in at the corner of his mouth, watches as it dribbles out again.

Max has sprung forward. "What can I do?"

Elsa hovers beside him. The man is in full khaki, with armband.

The doctor looks up at them. "Nothing," she says. "There is nothing you can do."

She fixes her wide, light gaze on Elsa for a moment; the gaze wavers away, as if she's shy, then back. "Just one of those things," she says, and lets the man's head loll back onto the concrete. She looks at Elsa for a moment longer, then gets to her feet, dusts her hands on her skirt, and goes to find the dead man's child.

They walk on. Max's mouth is flat. "You couldn't have helped," she says.

He isn't a cowardly person. But he is young, and uncertain despite the bravado, and a person so precious shouldn't leave the safety of their family—in other words, he and Elsa should not run away together. She feels him, now, trying to fit his mind around the question, and failing time and time again; she feels his frustration growing, and becoming that bitter, ironic smile he is turning on her. It is the last fine day—high, thin screams from the Ferris wheel on the rapidly cooling air.

"No," she says. "It doesn't make you bad."

Marie

——

MARIE HAS BEEN HUGGING the secret of Elsa's parentage close to herself. She has taken to visiting the Leopoldstadt apartment to look, unobserved, at Elsa's family a couple of times a week, and in her diary she has written up her visits in the manner of a zoologist: *Mannish one (cravat!) left at 21h00. A kiss from the wifely one at the doorway!* At night in her bed—barely the width of two planks—she has lain awake and rotated the knowledge at all angles, to see it to its best advantage.

The first time he came to her room, the summer before last, she had been surprised. She has never been anyone's first choice of face. She'd seen him talking to his friend Charlotte on the street below the apartment that afternoon; seen him catch the young woman's elbow, and tug at it; seen him be rejected. But she never thought that would translate into a shy knock at her door past midnight. He was drunk, it was true, reeling drunk, and she'd had to undo his belt for him. It was her first time; her first time saying yes to someone, that is. He did what he'd come to do and collapsed on top of her. It was uncomfortable, but then he fell asleep in her arms, and she felt something new. All the long dark hours, then tinged with dawn, she had him to herself. She ran experimental fingertips through his white-blond hair.

The next night, he came again; and the next. She got on all fours and swayed and listened to the helpless noises he made. She knew he would marry some girl with half her savoir faire, and have a race of idiotic blond moppets. It was a pity, because she could be good for him: defend him against his father (she didn't give a shit what his father thought), advise him on business matters. They could move in elevated circles. Nobody could take things from her if she were Frau Max Haas.

The first time she saw Elsa was the day of her interview with Frau Haas and the twins. Elsa had given her a frank look. Stood there in the hall tugging on the fingers of her gloves, in a dress that Marie recognized as hemmed and rehemmed, looking at Marie. *Some finesse,* Marie had thought, *please.* And then Frau Haas had swept forward to greet Elsa. Elsa, satisfied that she was better-looking and of higher station than Marie, had smiled and stepped into the hall, holding out her coat as though it was already Marie's job to take it.

Interesting, Marie had thought when the Haases talked over supper, discussing the new girl, and whether she might do; Marie had learned that Elsa was an accomplished pianist and might teach Max a thing or two, in addition to giving the twins lessons. *Interesting.* For Marie's part, it was plain to see that Elsa was no great intellect, and the pettish twist to her mouth meant she was not the steady pair of hands Frau Haas thought. *Even more interesting,* Marie thought, when Elsa moved in the following weekend: when Max and Elsa did a polite do-si-do in the hallway, stepping past each other, each flushing pink.

Marie sat up waiting for Max for two nights and then, when she knew he'd stopped coming, did what she always does: fade into the background. Because Marie is such a farsighted person, it isn't a surprise to find Elsa's piano hour with Max swelling to two and even three hours, particularly when Frau Haas is out of the apartment, the two of them sitting close together on the piano stool. Marie cannot resist letting them know she knows, by offering them a tea tray at inopportune moments, and enjoys seeing Max's mouth become a thin line: *That will be all, Marie.* Poor Maxi. She knows him. She knows how he smells—it is she who launders his clothes—she knows what he sounds like when he locks himself in the lavatory and touches himself. She knows the noises he makes when he is unobserved: the way he cracks his shoulders behind his head, the girlish sigh he gives when he is stuck on a mathematical problem.

Yesterday evening, she followed Elsa and Max to the Prater, keeping a careful distance. She blended in very well with the other servants in their dark dresses and Sunday hats. She saw the way that Max took Elsa's arm and gripped it at the elbow, steering her—*So courteous!* She drank in the scenery and the way that Max turned to Elsa to look at her in between almost every step. She saw a single tear make its way down Elsa's cheek, angrily dashed away, when he left her for a moment to buy candyfloss. The hopeful look he turned on her again, the agonized grin, standing in the queue. Such pathos. Such bravery. Better than a movie. Do they perhaps consider themselves unlucky, to have what they have, their doomed romance?

She will let Frau Haas know tomorrow. She will go into the salon—Frau Haas has no engagements, and if the weather is fine, she will sit in her armchair and flip through a social magazine all morning—and she, Marie, will be the very picture of contrition. *Not sure whether to bring this to Madame's attention. Whether relevant. In light of Herr Haas's situation. Happened to find myself in Leopoldstadt in search of*—some excuse here—*and glimpsed Elsa with two individuals, one of whom*— And—deep breath here—as if deciding whether or not to reveal the final confidence—*sorry to relate, but Max was with them.*

Marie imagines Frau Haas's face: turning to a cold mask, as she sees how she has been betrayed. How easy it is to be led astray by a little bright plumage! Marie will turn away quickly—*I've said too much*—and go to the kitchen, the better to overhear what happens next. She loves the idea of hefting one of the brass pans in her clenched fist, feeling its weight, and hearing Frau Haas call for Max and Elsa to join her in the salon. Elsa and Max will know who has betrayed them, but they'll be forced to admit that they never once spotted her. Never saw any of this coming.

At six o'clock she gets out of bed as usual. It will be important to look vaguely harried, and as though she has passed a sleepless night, so as to preserve the impression of a difficult conscience. Later in the week, Frau Haas will probably turn to her and say, *Don't think we don't appreciate everything you do for us, Marie,* and maybe even squeeze her hand.

She leaves a few strands of hair hanging about the face, slips into her uniform and puts her feet into the buckled traditional shoes the Haases like her to wear. Then she goes to the kitchen to prepare the family's breakfast. The twins call sleepily to each other from their room. Marie used to wish she was a twin—the secret language they share sounded appealing—until she realized she was better on her own.

Over breakfast, the family assembles as usual. How pale Max is. She touches his shoulder as she passes behind him, brushing the fabric of his suit. He doesn't feel it, but she knows she's done it, and that is enough. Herr Haas reads the morning paper and gets bits of food caught in his mustache; Frau Haas leans in and lovingly removes them with her napkin, and Marie thinks it's the last time they will be able to pay attention to small details like this for a while.

She takes their plates—everyone thanks her politely, as usual, but without any feeling—to the kitchen and starts the washing-up. Each bit of crockery has a film of grease that she removes with hot water and cold soap. She listens as she works. The clatter of shoes on the hall parquet. Max calls out that he'll be back later. There is a suspicious absence of sound where she suspects he and Elsa are sharing a kiss. Then Elsa's voice, in the special tones she uses for the twins, and the putting-on of coats and the leaving for a walk. Herr Haas saying something to his wife; then he, too, leaves the apartment, and there is a collective exhalation from the furniture, the room, from Frau Haas, who is relieved to be alone.

Marie puts the last plate on the drying rack and slips into the salon. Frau Haas is very elegant, really, posed in her armchair, with her hair up in the old Imperial style and her magazine at arm's length to study the cover. She looks up at Marie. Always so pleasant: but not wanting to have her quiet morning disturbed, not really.

The doorbell rings. Frau Haas's face tightens. "Are we expecting someone?"

Marie shakes her head, and hesitates, and Frau Haas says, impatient: "Would you answer it, please?"

Marie goes down the corridor to the front door and opens it, and Elsa's—she supposes the word is *mother*—is standing in the marble stairwell.

"The Haas residence?" she asks. Marie nods, and the woman says: "My name is Julia Perret. Would you be so good as to fetch

Frau Haas?" Marie stares and cannot speak—and the woman doesn't wait: simply pushes her aside and steps into the apartment. She stands at the end of the hall corridor, swivels on her heels, and catches sight of Frau Haas through the salon doorway.

Frau Haas looks up and sees her. "Marie—" she says. Politeness tempered by fear.

Marie says: "I tried to stop—the person."

"Frau Haas?" the woman is saying. "I'm Elsa's guardian."

Frau Haas's mouth is pursed, she is frowning in shock, and then she seems to put something together in her mind. "Marie, leave us," she says. She gestures the woman to a chair and closes the salon door, leaving Marie alone.

Marie presses her ear to the outside of the door, and stays very still.

At first all she can hear is the tone of the conversation, and occasional words. Frau Haas isn't talking very much. It is all the woman. She says something about an attack on Leopoldstadt and an involvement. Frau Haas is silent, then objects, and Marie hears the woman say: "Nevertheless . . . formed an attachment." Then there is another phrase: "I felt it was my duty. We want her at home with us . . ." The words are clearer. "I can't imagine your husband would be content."

More silence. Frau Haas is feeling her way. She begins to speak, soothingly: "Of course . . . not ideal." More quietly. "If you wish it . . . we can release her from her duties . . ."

"I do wish it," Julia says. "It would be better for you, and your husband." In a frank tone: "Although they will suffer. He and Elsa. At first."

A thoughtful silence. "Elsa is a fine person," Frau Haas says—and here tears spring into Marie's eyes, as she sees how thoroughly Elsa has convinced everyone of her goodness. And then the final blow: "If circumstances had been different, I might have given them my blessing."

Sharp footsteps coming toward her. Marie springs back, into the kitchen doorway. The salon door opens. "Do I understand we have an agreement?" Julia marches past Marie, not seeing her, and leaves the apartment.

Frau Haas calls for Marie. "Unfortunately, Elsa's mother needs her at home. Pack her things, and have them ready for when she gets back. And then look in the newspaper to see about a new governess. Someone older, I think, this time. But, Marie—whatever's wrong?"

Marie was supposed to be the one to tell her. There were supposed to be consequences, not this meek dismissal. She goes to the kitchen to retrieve a pair of scissors, then walks to Elsa's room. She lifts Elsa's dresses one by one from the wardrobe, and cuts them into long strips, before folding the pieces neatly into her valise.

Elsa

—

EVE OPENS THE DOOR with an expression carefully attuned to pity. Elsa moves past her without a word; sits at the kitchen table with her fists pressed into her eyes. "I'm only here because there's nowhere to go," she says. "So don't talk to me. I don't want to hear your voice."

"Your mother and I—"

Elsa hears her own laugh. "Why should I listen to a word?"

She goes to her old childhood room and closes the door.

She is alone with all her things, the ones she left behind when she moved across the hallway into the studio, and again when she left for the Haases: the plush Steiff teddy Rolf gave her for her tenth birthday, which she'd thought was too young for her, even then. Her crocheted coverlet from Aunt Grete. She thinks about Max; what is sure to be his rage, tonight, when he finds she's gone.

Julia comes knocking. She opens the door without being asked. It has been a long time since Elsa has seen her look uncertain. "You're back," she says. She drops Elsa's suitcase just inside the door. Something else is waiting to be said.

"The other day—when the brownshirts caught me—" Julia advances, and sits on the end of the bed. She reaches for the teddy,

275

running her fingertips over its woolly ears. This was in the letter, too: the green soapy taste of the grass between the lips, the laughter of the young men. *I've never been so frightened. Your Max could have been one of them.* The unspoken continuation: *Do you want that, for your mother? For it to happen again? Do you want to be a part of any of it?*

Julia sits hunched. "One day you'll see that we were right."

"It has all been for a good purpose, hasn't it?" Elsa says sweetly. For a moment, she sees, Julia mistakes the tone: thinks she's been forgiven, and her face clears. Then she looks blank, agonized.

"I know it will take time," she says. "You will see, though, that we were only thinking of you."

Elsa wonders how she could have missed it: there is no resemblance, none at all. She turns away.

The business of the apartment goes on around her silent room: the loud greetings of Barbara Weber; low conversation, perhaps the sound of Julia confiding. She is hungry but the sensation feels remote.

It gets dark. She lowers her suitcase onto the floor and clicks it open; lifts out her dresses-in-pieces. It isn't as though there were many to begin with. She hopes it gave Marie some pleasure. There are old things in her wardrobe here she can still fit into.

She drops a pebble into her own dark well, to try to see what should happen next. Max is young, but not so very young; not to her. Together they could have something different from what is here: a good life. Above all things, she won't be made to eat grass at fifty-four.

The next morning, she wakes late but helps to clear away the breakfast things. It is too early to try to speak to Julia, but it is enough. She feels Julia's confusion, gladness, at the change in the weather. Elsa is contrite; like a patient on the other side of the fever dream. Eve is still abrupt and sorrowful, but that can be smoothed over later.

Julia goes out to her interpreting job, and Eve to visit Rolf, leaving her alone in the apartment. She takes pen, ink, and paper and sits down at Julia's desk to write a letter.

The trick will be for it to appear like a philosophical tract. Raw emotion won't be enough. She needs him to understand she is his equal. She writes about their sex: how he was her first, how it had hurt, but she had never once questioned it. She wants to prove her devotion to him; to show him that she is capable of surviving things that are difficult. There are sure to be difficult years in their future.

At eleven o'clock she is satisfied. She has opened a vein and then edited: the phrases attenuated with luminous cunning. There is a logic there, crystalline and perfect, that he will recognize.

She slips out of the apartment block and takes the letter to the post office. She won't meet the eyes of the postmaster, even though she has known him since she was fifteen.

"Young lady like you, this can only be a love note," he says wistfully, as he gives her the stamps.

Meanwhile, in the second-greatest city in the world—Paris—a young man is buying a revolver from a hunting goods store. He is Herschel Grynszpan: elfin, handsome, Jewish, seventeen, prone to melancholy. His family have written him a postcard of farewell. They have been sent away on a train from Hanover, where they are liked and respected. *No one told us what was up, but we realized this was going to be the end.* He has been spared because he is living with an uncle in the city of light. He is a good boy; he loves his family. He may or may not be in love with a German diplomat, Ernst vom Rath, who may or may not have broken certain promises to him regarding a residency permit. Quivering, he says to the shopkeeper he will have a box of bullets to go with the gun, *pourquoi pas?* He walks to the German Embassy, is shown to the office of vom Rath, Third Secretary to the Ambassador, and shoots him five times. Two bullets lodge in vom Rath's abdomen; one pierces the lining of his stomach. As any doctor will tell you, this is a poor prognostic sign.

There are crowds queuing at the station, as there always are these days; long lines of men in dark overcoats with small suitcases and hopeful eyes. Long arguments, too, at the ticket office—*No, I need three, for Prague,* or whichever other place they have relatives. At the ticket window, filled with unholy excitement, she takes out her purse and asks for two passes to Salzburg, for the three o'clock train, the following day. They are not too expensive; plenty left from her wages to afford a month or two of cheap rent; most people here today want to go outside the country. From there, perhaps, America. "Single," she says, "not return," and the ticket clerk nods. *Obviously.*

She returns to the apartment to wait. She does not anticipate a reply until the evening, if not the following morning, but still, it's hard to settle to anything useful.

She looks at Julia and Eve's things scattered around the apartment. The mannish umbrella Julia insists on carrying, even when rain is only a remote possibility. Eve's boots lined up in the hallway.

At three o'clock she hears the outer door clang shut, and Julia's footsteps. She closes the book she was pretending to read and arranges herself into a chastened pose. The footsteps come up the stairs, hesitate, and then Elsa hears a knock at the door on the landing opposite, and the door softly opening. Frau Weber—Barbara— calling out a hello. "I'm in the back," as though this were such a common occurrence, this popping in and out of each other's apartments, that no formality was even needed anymore.

Elsa swallows; listens to the hissing of the pipes in the cold apartment. Proof, if proof were needed, that Julia has never really had Elsa's best interests at heart. She prefers to play chess with an old woman opposite whom she hardly knows. They have always been strangers to each other. Elsa turns her attention back to her book.

Julia

———

ATMOSPHERIC CONDITIONS ARE STEADY: the temperature will rise to as much as forty-six degrees in the center of Vienna, with no wind. Sleet is forecast for the early afternoon, but for now, a pale sun filters between patchy cloud. Outside the city, the Vernagt-ferner glacier, which has been gently retreating since the last Little Ice Age advance, loses another five cubic meters of ice, as it has every day for several thousand years.

Seven o'clock in the morning; at the offices of the *Allgemeine*, the editor-in-chief is picking up the telephone. He has been waiting for this call all night. Vom Rath, the diplomat in Paris, has died. He listens to the French correspondent's rapid speech; puts his hand to his forehead, scribbles, reads, and rereads the notes he's made. All across the new Empire, countermeasures are recommended in the strongest terms.

By the end of the day, the number of synagogues in Vienna will be three. The other ninety-seven will have been burned by police, soldiers, and like-minded civilians. Most Jewish shops, libraries, gathering places, banks, and civic institutions will have been ransacked or burned. The sky, it's said, turned red from the fires. Four thousand Viennese Jewish people, homosexuals, political undesirables will be rounded up in the course of twenty-four hours and sent to prison camps, to Dachau or Buchenwald. Kristallnacht, the

Night of the Broken Glass—so named because of the glint of the shattered shop windows everywhere—is one of the prettier words for murder.

At eleven thirty in the morning, Julia is on her way home from an optometrist's appointment in the Innere Stadt. She sees three police vans, grinding slowly along the streets. A team of brownshirts moves along the middle of the road. They push past her, but she doesn't seem to attract their attention. As she reaches Leopoldstadt, she sees the broken glass of the Herzls' storefront. Someone—just a shadow from here—the belladonna in her eyes makes things blurry—is moving around inside, and she doesn't dare to ask who it is. The thought comes to her that maybe it's the soldiers themselves.

She enters the apartment, drops her string bag. Elsa is at the table, reading.

"What did the optician say?" she asks, putting the book down. Julia ignores the question; crosses to the windows to look out.

"Any news from anyone?" she asks, staring down into the street below. "You haven't heard anything?"

People seem to be hurrying a little more, that's all, and one man they vaguely know is carrying a suitcase.

"No," says Elsa, with a shrug.

"It's probably nothing," Julia says. "Just more of the same." She considers lifting the sash and shouting out to the man but all she can see is the top of his hat, and then he's gone.

Marie walks fast by her very nature, but today her feet are a flurry.

In the early hours of the morning, the telephone rang: she heard Herr Haas go to answer, and stood in the shadows of the hall to hear what was said. Something about an assassination; then the kind of grim silence that means big change. Logistics; numbers of trucks. She heard Herr Haas return to his room, put on his clothes, and vanish from the flat.

Marie gets up, prepares the breakfast, and watches them eat. As usual, she is hungry, and stares at the scraps of food they leave behind. As usual, the twins push their eggs into the corners of their plates. Poor Maxi, with his pale face, missing his girlfriend. She wonders whether he'll try her room again tonight. The mother looks at the newspaper and says: "Children, you'll have your lessons at home with me today."

So it is very easy, to suggest, with a serious face, that perhaps it would be wise to buy certain food and household essentials...? Frau Haas's gratitude is immeasurable. Marie can see her sizing up the situation: *If Marie should come to harm*—but then, better her than one of the children. Marie can look out for herself. And it is easier still to leave the apartment, and hurry down the street toward the police station.

There is a young man waiting outside the door, his face shining with fatuous self-importance. He asks her what her business is, and she asks to be shown to the office of the Chief of Police.

"What's it regarding?" he asks. His tone implies that she will be at the back of a long queue.

"I have a message for him, from Herr Oberleiter Haas." That will show him. His face changes; he clicks his heels and shows her in.

She is led down a corridor lined with people—some of them already with handcuffs and downcast eyes—and into a large office, where a man sits behind a desk.

He asks her what her business is. She explains that she has been concerned by the association, no doubt not deliberate—she would never suggest that Herr Haas would do anything untoward—of her employer with some undesirable types. She suspects the undesirables, the parents of a recently disgraced employee. She has had occasion to see them moving in, under cover of darkness, an elderly person of Semitic appearance. Of course, she doesn't wish to alarm Herr Oberleiter Haas by raising it with him directly—these things are best dealt with in a way that's least likely to embarrass him. Her only concern is for the family. She is sure he understands.

She walks away from the police station, and, briefly, is at a loss. She cannot go back to the Haases. She shoulders her satchel, looks up and down the street, and chooses a direction.

At one o'clock, with the belladonna dissipating, Julia goes to the window again. There is the sound of running feet and a thick, dull smack. She can smell smoke, seeping in through the cracks in the frame.

She squints at the street below: two brownshirts have got the newspaperman's boy spreadeagled on the ground—a truncheon has connected with the back of his skull, and blood is glistening in his hair. He is kicking and shouting for help and the brownshirts are pulling him bodily along the cobbles. The expression on their faces is pure seething irritation. Frozen on the sidewalk opposite are two people, a man and a woman, with shopping bags, whom Julia doesn't know. The brownshirts pull the boy to his feet and man-handle him toward a van that's idling at the corner of the street.

"How horrible," Julia says to the room behind her. "How vile." It is almost time for the lunch things to be set out, a job that has fallen to Elsa since she came home two days ago. "They're taking that boy, from the newspaper kiosk," Julia says.

She wants to close the shutters and turn out the lights. Eve gets to her feet and moves to the window to stand beside her, but the van is already pulling away. "He can't be involved in anything bad, can he?" she says.

Julia stares at her. Surely the laws cannot have been extended? "They smashed up the Herzls' shop," she says. "Someone did. The police weren't there."

There is a knock at the door, soft and self-excusing: Barbara Weber. "Come in," Julia says, and as she does so the door opens and Barbara is saying: "I heard glass, and I looked, and there was a poor young man."

Her eyes are wide, and she is gathering her shawl around her shoulders, as though it is a personal affront. "I think perhaps I should try to telephone Anders. He was planning to visit tonight and I don't want him caught up in it. In whatever this is."

Julia clicks her jaw back and forth, thinking. "You should stay here," she says. Barbara is dark-haired. "I'll go." They will need to use the telephone at the post office.

Eve gets to her feet, too. She'd never let Julia out alone. Julia looks at the clock. "It's ten past one now. What time was Anders coming?"

Barbara: "Five." Her fingers, heavy with rings, are running through the fringe of her shawl.

"Don't go," Elsa says.

"We can't let Anders walk into this. And then we'll make a plan."

Elsa says: "Then be careful."

They have barely spoken: Elsa is red from effort, from anger. This is the limit of what she can presently bear to give away. Julia turns, softens; presses her lips to Elsa's cheek: vanilla talcum powder.

The post office is closed, but the owner beckons to them through an upstairs window. They telephone on his personal line: once to Anders and Rolf's apartment, where there is no answer, but Julia imagines she can hear the faint scrabbling of the whippet's feet, disturbed by the ringing. Julia fishes out the scribbled number of the music school, and reaches a secretary. Herr Weber is giving a lesson and cannot be disturbed. Fine. A message, then. His mother is unwell and won't receive him this evening. Julia puts the receiver back in its cradle and smiles her most grateful smile at the post-office owner.

"Saw your girl the other day," he says. "She's looking well. Blooming. I said to her, what's that you've got? Love letter?" He winks. It is an attempt at levity. His wife moves about in the next room, clearing her throat nervously; when they were welcomed in, she had burst into tears, and hidden her face in her apron.

When they get back to the apartment, Barbara rises from an armchair to greet them. "Elsa's just gone to find you," she says. "Did you reach Anders?"

Julia unwinds her scarf from her neck—not suspecting anything, not yet—and tells her about the missed phone call. The message will surely reach him. The secretary seemed efficient. "Thank you," Barbara says.

"Outside—" Julia begins, then slumps. The bricks in the street, shattered glass crunching underfoot. "All in broad daylight."

Barbara says: "I should leave you," with a little calming motion of the hands, and Julia says, "No. Stay. It's safer. What time did Elsa go out?"

"Not five minutes ago. She said she would go as far as the end of the road and then come back. She said she would drop some things off with the neighbors."

Julia looks up. "What things?"

"She had a small case with her." Barbara's face opens into worry. "Have I done something wrong?"

Eve starts toward Elsa's bedroom. Julia tries to smile, to reassure. It isn't Barbara's fault, of course—why didn't they imagine this was coming? Eve is back, with an envelope. She hands it to Julia, who rips it open, scans the letter.

By the time you read this I—we—will be far away—

Elsa

———

ELSA WALKS OUT OF THE APARTMENT. In future, she will say to her children: "I was a survivor." There are slogans painted everywhere; a man hurries past her, with four tweed jackets under one arm and two pairs of shoes held in his hand. "Look out," he says, as he passes, "patrol ahead."

Her papers are all in order and, besides, she has a plan, which is to say that she works for Herr Oberleiter Haas and could they escort her to the station, where she is meeting his son? She imagines them handing her into Max's arms on the platform, how graciously she'll thank them. She even has the money ready for a tip or a bribe, ten Kronen, in her hand. There is no cause for alarm.

She sees the patrol in the distance, and crosses the street to avoid them: they have stopped a man with black suit and sidelocks, and he is saying his name over and over again, very loud: "Wilhelm Isaac! I am on my way to the Embassy now to collect our visas! Wilhelm Isaac!" He is pulled toward the back of a van.

A memory: when she was small, and they still lived with Aunt Grete, she'd come into Julia and Eve's bedroom and seen Eve and Julia together. Eve was sitting in an armchair, and Julia was in her lap, astride her. It had been embarrassing—worse because they noticed her, and because of their half-laughing, half-surprised expressions, and how they rushed to her and held her. She's thought of the incident a half-dozen times since she was an adult. And now what she thinks is: *Those people are nothing to me, and soon I will have that moment for myself; my own house; my own person. Max's face, flushed and upturned, as he sits on the chair: the way his hair springs up from his forehead.* She pictures herself laying a finger along the straightness of his nose.

By the time she reaches the station she is tired. Her feet slow by themselves; the clock on the outside says ten minutes to three, and she can feel that her underarms are wet with sweat. She swings her aching arm and the suitcase, and plunges into the crowd on the concourse.

She has never been in such a desperate group of people—the ebb and flow of bodies is new, and so are the whites of the eyes of the men and women around her. A woman seizes her arm and asks: "Have you seen my girl?" Elsa says she hasn't. "Can you see which platform for the Salzburg train?" she says into the ear of a tall gentleman. He is distracted and does not answer. The press of bodies is such that Elsa is lifted off her feet and deposited two feet away.

She finds she is close to the platform entrance, where a line of soldiers is arm-linked, blocking. She holds out her tickets and her identification papers. Next to her, a man and his family are arguing. The soldier, distracted, glances at her, at the papers, and lets her through.

The train is already waiting, hissing, on the platform. Rain falls on the glass ceiling overhead. She looks around, searching for him. There is a businessman, ushering his blonde wife up into one of the carriages; a governess with two small children, waiting next to a pile of suitcases. A group of ten people is let through by the soldiers, and then another ten in quick succession—she looks, but he isn't among them.

"Madam, are you getting on the train?" A conductor, whistle poised in hand, is working his way toward her.

"I'm waiting for someone," she says. He nods and moves past. "Train won't wait," he says, and she wants to round on him, to spit: *I know that.*

Perhaps there has been some error. He may have been delayed. The tickets, squares of card, cut into her pocket. She squeezes them for luck, turns back to look at the barriers, and thinks she sees someone who looks like him, standing talking to the guard. The young man turns and isn't him; it's the wrong face on the right back, the right uniform.

The train sounds the first whistle. Passengers are being handed onto the train. "Last call for Salzburg," the conductor bellows; puts the whistle to his lips and blows. Thin, shrill sound, and everywhere faces gaping in panic, hurrying to board. There's a slamming of doors, an argument over a packing-case. The conductor leaps onto the footboard and presses his hand to his head to keep his cap on. He blows the whistle a second time, and the pistons begin to turn: shriek of gears, a hissing sound. She should run to catch it. There would still be time.

There is a tap on her shoulder and she turns around and reaches out her arms, and collides with his friend Charlotte. Charlotte is wearing a thick overcoat, done up for traveling, and carrying a small bag. She has been running: the wisps of blonde hair at her temples are oily with sweat.

Is it a bad joke? Has Charlotte harbored some secret passion, like a disease, for Elsa, not Max? That time when Charlotte pressed her hand in the cathedral, gripping the angular bones of the wrist . . .

"Is he coming?" Elsa asks.

"I'm sorry. He sent me to say he can't. And to give you this."

Elsa opens the bag. Charlotte hovers, pale and swallowing, as if determined to see some painful operation through. Inside is an object wrapped in tissue paper; Elsa takes the paper away and drops it and there is the glossy chestnut of the metronome from the Haases' apartment, the one that used to sit on top of the piano.

"Why?" she says. "Why this?"

She hefts the metronome. If you move it one way or the other, it ticks to itself, chittering like a frantic insect. The pendulum jumps at an angle; it looks like the goose-stepping of a soldier.

Charlotte says: "I don't know. I'm so sorry," and flinches as Elsa lifts the metronome unthinkingly in her palm.

"Wait," Elsa says, but Charlotte is already running away from her, down the platform, back toward the main hall.

Marie must have confiscated the note. But if that were so, Charlotte would not have known to come. Perhaps Max's father found the note, and has him locked up somewhere. But then, Charlotte would have said: *He is coming, just not yet.*

She hears someone calling her name, and turns to see Julia and Eve, being held back by the soldiers. Julia's arms are reaching out to her.

Elsa turns away; hesitates. She can walk the length of the platform, at least, away from them. A shout, and running feet; Julia has broken through. Her hands land on Elsa's arms. "I must have missed him," Elsa says. "I expect he has gone on without me." A new plan: she will find a soldier and demand to be taken to the Party headquarters, where she will explain herself to Herr Haas. "Let go. I can move on my own."

Julia hauls her back under the linked arms of the soldiers. Elsa lets herself be taken, but holds herself very upright. Relief flooding Eve's face. "I think you should both go home," Elsa says, "there is no need to bother. I'll wait a little longer out here, in case he has been delayed."

She pulls her arm free of Julia's; Eve catches the arm with her hand. "You want me to be unhappy," she says, delighted with her own intuition. She feels this insight will be rewarded by the world: that it is the fairy-tale key, which, when turned, will bring Max running toward her. "Maybe you want me to turn out like you?"

She pulls her arm away, without any real hope of freedom: just to inflict pain. Her elbow flies out and hits Eve's cheek, just above the line of the lip; the blood rushes to the point of contact. Julia's eyes darken with shock, and then—this is worse—sympathy. "You can wait for him at home," she suggests. She looks this way and that, like someone about to cross the road. "That way he'll know where to find you." Eve has pressed her hand to her cheekbone, but she nods, too.

They walk home. The streetlights are coming on, one by one, around them, beads on a chain. Julia and Eve hold Elsa between linked arms. They keep their heads down, and stay quiet. A man catches at Julia's arm, mutters something at them; his face looms close and she shakes him off.

Outside the Stephansdom, there is a crowd of people, palms together, swaying in prayer. They push on, over the canal and into

Leopoldstadt. Eve grunts at the sight: all the shop windows in the Taborstrasse are broken. There is nobody about, but the front doors of the apartment blocks are either pushed inward or kicked in. A woman in a lopsided wig is wandering down the street toward them. "My husband," she says.

The front door of their apartment block is open. Julia pushes it open with the toe of her boot, but there is nobody behind it; they enter the stairwell.

On the second landing, Herr Silbermann's door is shoved in. Julia knocks at the opposite apartment, but there is no answer there.

The third floor: their door is untouched. Julia presses a hand, in relief, to her breastbone; then resists the urge to cover Elsa's eyes. Barbara's door has a hole where the lock is. It is splintered and half-open.

They go into Barbara's apartment. They call out and nobody answers. Julia finds the candle on the mantelpiece, and lights a match. The ingredients for goulash lie neatly chopped on the table, the knife placed beside them; a paperback detective novel is sprawled open on the countertop. The only thing different is that Barbara's usual chair is turned over. So, looking at the chessboard, is the black queen: tipped on its side, in a formal gesture of surrender.

Anders

THE MUSIC SCHOOL, EARLIER THAT DAY. Anders, fingers to chin in enraptured concentration, shakes his head at the secretary who's popping her head around the door, mouthing: *Telephone.* The boy who's playing, you see, is a marvel—it isn't too early to use that word. It is one of the new pieces, all sliding terrors of imminent doom, and the ten-year-old handles it beautifully, and really, whatever it is, on the other end of the electric line, can wait. And they say he also composes! For now, mere doodles, but there has never been a day when this student has hit a block, or gone backward, or failed in his practice. The secretary must see it's useless: she ducks her head out and closes the door.

The boy finishes the piece with a flourish that Anders must tame out of him. "You're not a maestro." Not yet. The boy, who can be vulgar, stops just short of sticking his tongue out.

Oh, Anders knows what Rolf would say: he is interested in this child because of his own father. It is a chance for the recoiled parts of Anders to uncoil. Something he has never been able to fully explain to Rolf: it really is all about the music.

"You aren't a maestro," he repeats. "Do it again." The boy picks up the bow. A suspicion of flirtatiousness in the way he settles his fingers on the strings at the instrument's neck—Anders wonders about the child's proclivities—is ten too young to know your own mind? But then all trace of the person vanishes. The phrasing is immaculate. The boy, himself, is absorbed: his eyes trained on the sheet music, but far beyond that, too.

Halfway through, the bell rings—that signal for the great up-heaval of people from one corridor to the next, and a break in teaching for him. Anders and the boy both sigh; there is the maneu-vering of the cello into the cello case; the flourishing of the key-set in Anders's hand; the sound from across the school of chords sud-denly interrupted.

Anders heads for the colonnade that is the building's heart. There is a garden in the center, in the Arabic style: squares of faded grass, hexagonal tiles, linden trees with their branches stripped of green. He chooses a bench in a patch of sunlight to eat his bread and cheese.

He is thinking of nothing—but really nothing, a blank space where thought should go. A bird, unidentifiable and high-pitched, sings in the uppermost parts of the tree. He remembers the secretary—whatever she can have wanted—and through the haze, it comes to him that she must have had important knowledge, even to consider interrupting his lesson. His thoughts fly to Rolf, a clutching at the heart, and to Klara. Such nightmares they have of the dog being run over: blood on the street, her long hopeful snout, the eyes glazed and unrecognizing.

He meets the secretary halfway—she is making a second attempt at finding him—in the colonnade. "Herr Weber, news regarding your mother, she is unwell, and asks you not to visit." The phras-ing doesn't sound like Barbara, and there is no disease that could prevent her from seeking him out; he immediately recognizes it as some kind of code. To what purpose? Why doesn't she want him to come? His mind flies up the arpeggios of potential solutions. *I wish Rolf were here.*

Some instinct propels him to ask: what is the state of the city today? Is there anything unusual? He isn't sure of the secretary: she knits, and speaks of a husband and three children, and is three gen-erations Austrian.

"Sir, I hear they are burning the synagogues," she says, with a blush that very prettily says: *Not that the burning of synagogues should concern you.* So that's it: the vague smell of smoke he's been ignoring all morning.

"Terrible," he says, "dreadful," forgetting himself, and she says: "Yes," though she sounds unsure. "But it's reprisals. For the diplomat who was murdered."

She is pink-faced and rebellious, blonde, *echt österreichisch*; he outranks her, but in this one instance she will stand her ground. He has known her for ten years and thinks this will be the last time they can have an honest conversation. Have they ever had an honest conversation, or were the battle lines drawn years back, and he never knew? "Thank you," he says.

Trying to reach his mother on the telephone will be useless, as there isn't one installed in Eve and Julia's apartment block. He will have to visit this evening. Except that she has forbidden it. His thoughts chase themselves. The bell sounds. Is the music school a target for the vandals? Rolf has a half-day at the theater and will be safely home by now. Now he is in his next lesson; he isn't listening to the small girl playing him some Bach. She is fragile, aware of her deficit of natural talent, and turns pale eyes full of tears to him. "Very good," he says. "No, really. You've made great strides." She will not be a professional, not even close; but she smiles and, without being asked, looks at her music stand and thoughtfully turns the pages back to the beginning of the piece with the tip of her bow.

She is standing waiting for instruction. "Play it again," he says, but fear runs through him. He wants to scoop her up and carry her to safety. The image comes of war—everyone says it will end that way and maybe it has already begun—a building on fire, masonry falling on her. He thinks of Klara whimpering and this decides him. "I have to go," he says. "We'll leave it there."

She freezes for a moment; then falteringly she continues to play. "No, I mean it. We'll finish now. You may go to sit in the library until your father comes."

He is collecting up his scores and his cello case. She places her bow carefully on the table. He knows, from the same inner place that knew when he met Rolf he would never have anyone else, that he won't see her again. "Good luck," he says. She nods politely. "You too."

Rolf

FIVE YEARS EARLIER. The last of what Julia, Eve, and Rolf would call the fizzy days, when champagne was cheap as beer. They were all mourning Frau Berndt. The consolation for having to put their old friend into the ground was a concert, the tickets bought by Rolf. *We will go and hear her favorites. It will be like she is listening.* Eve and Julia are dubious of this blatant sentimentalism but perhaps the music will help; something has to. Rolf has come by the tickets by some nefarious contact or has stolen them from the box office, but there is no reason to snub him when he's feeling generous.

The last gleam of daylight, deep summer: the three of them arm in arm, walking into the Innere Stadt. The champagne has begun early; they have sat in the courtyard on Frau Berndt's wrought-iron chairs since lunchtime—the ones her sons haven't taken—Julia has spent the afternoon frankly weeping over her lost friend; Eve, embarrassed by her open affection, has patted her arm in comfort and looked with panicky eyes at Rolf. "It's just that I can't believe she's not here," Julia has found herself saying, and all the other clichés—"It doesn't seem real," and "Don't you imagine she will just come walking in any minute?" So the only way through has been for Rolf to send another cork fizzing skyward, and pour for the four—no, three—of them. *Absent friends.* He, belching, raising his glass in a toast: "May her gossip in the Hereafter ever turn out to be true. May her geraniums never wilt." The unspoken thing is how much they owe Frau Berndt. The question hovers: did she expect more from them? Did they do enough, at the end?

So the three of them find themselves giggling and staggering over the ever-flowing river. "You," Rolf tells Julia, finger raised, "are the prettiest thing this side of the Elbe. Yes, yes you are," as she protests. "If it ever came to it I'd marry you." They laugh; Eve, uneasy, swiping at her blurry eyes. He could drag Julia into a church and demand the service, there and then. "And you," Rolf is saying, turning to Eve—he is flanked by them, he always walks in-between the two—"are a gold-clad Narcissus. Wed you like a shot."

Drunkenness brings clarity and the clarity is that sometime, somewhere in the world, such a union might be possible. Eve hiccups. The thing is that none of them is young anymore. Frau Berndt's loss has made her think of that, all of a sudden. The big decisions, surely, are in the past.

She wants to try to say some of this, but Julia stumbles over nothing, and brings them all down, giggling, into a heap on the cobbles. "We shouldn't make a scene," Julia says, allowing herself to be helped up and dusted off. Eve squints into the bright late sunlight, and feels sick. It is always such beautiful weather the day after someone dies.

They are late for the performance, which is something discordant for a string trio—an in-demand ticket, but they are already so giddy that they slump and sulk in their front-row seats, and complain to each other in whispers about the music. Unspoken between them is that Frau Berndt, who was modern in her tastes, and who treated them to such concerts blaring on her new radiogram, only pretended to like the new things. When nobody else was listening, they all suspected, she loved a waltz. The thought of her waltzing alone in her lodge is too much for any of them to bear.

Rolf, out of sheer self-protectiveness, has made himself notice one of the violinists: the shape of his waist to his shoulders a perfect triangle. His bowing hand is vigorous. He frowns with concentration that excludes all else and Rolf thinks: *I would like to take your clothes off.* He imagines the pleading look in the man's eyes, if Rolf were to take him to bed, if he were to pin him down. Not unusual, for Rolf to feel like this, to want to dominate—since Emil, he has never allowed anyone else to top him—but so soon after a grief? Perhaps it *is* the grief. Rolf decides he'll have this person: he will take the man home tonight. So he clutches Eve's hand on one side and Julia's on the other and watches the man's every movement for the entirety of the first half.

At the interval, he whispers to Julia and Eve that he'll be back and he walks upstairs to the second-floor gentlemen's toilets. If the violinist is one of his kind, that's where he'll be, along with the other hopeful queers. The alcohol has dissipated, leaving just a thin headache and a vague paranoia; he pushes the door open anyway.

The usual crowd, standing waiting for a cubicle, or lounging with a glass of something, chatting in the shadows. All eyes fall on him; some linger; some discard him quickly—it still stings, not to be as handsome as he was—and a voice from the end of the stalls says, "Well, if it isn't."

Billy is leaning against the wall, taking a long drink from a tall glass, watchful. He holds out his hand for Rolf to kiss it. The years haven't been entirely kind: he is long-legged, still, but the charm has become insect-like and predatory. "You're no oil painting, your-self," Billy says, reading Rolf's face, pushing back what's left of his fringe. "Who are you here for? Let me guess: Thor, the violinist."

Rolf nods slowly, and Billy coos with laughter. "Join the queue," he says. At the noise, the mention of the name, several of the men in the room have started, and looked at the door, guilty.

Rolf is caught out; angry. He and Billy no longer know each other. "I've lost someone," he says.

Billy makes a sympathetic face. "Sorry to hear. But be realistic, darling." With a final slurp of his drink he's gone. One of the young men standing at the urinal looks at Rolf. Rolf crosses to stand beside him; pretends to need to urinate; can only manage a few humiliat-ing drops, shakes himself, and then walks back downstairs, raging.

The performance ends with an ovation. Eve is on her feet. The music has spoken to her of the uncertainty of being a person. She has understood something about Frau Berndt that is new and unexpected. She will seek out this composer, and go to every concert; she will make them her special pilgrimage, to keep her friend safe inside her mind.

Rolf slips past them both, saying he will see them in the foyer; he has no intention of meeting them again tonight, but they will eventually give up waiting, they are used to fending for themselves; he cannot bear questions just now.

He walks out of the building and around to the stage door. A group of autograph-hunters—mostly students and young women, but a few men—is already waiting for the star violinist. The evening has finished in summer rain, hot and close, which is typical, he thinks sourly, turning up his collar.

Not long to wait: the violinist must be keen to get home. He smiles at the crowd, and reaches for a few autograph books; at the end, all that is left are the other men, and Rolf, who has purposefully hung back. The violinist falls in with them, laughing and telling jokes, and his eyes—does Rolf imagine it—flicker over to where Rolf is standing.

He moves closer, into the circle of speech, and sizes up the competition. Billy isn't there but the others are notorious queens from the circuit, in dinner jackets at least ten years old. One of them is tapping the violinist on the chest, to emphasize some flirtatious point; the violinist tolerates it. Then his eyes settle on Rolf, and he extends a hand, and just like that, the selection is made.

"Thor," the violinist says.

Rolf smiles. The other men melt backward, already turning to see who else is around.

He is easy company, this boy, walking with his hands in his pockets through the night streets. Rolf thinks, inescapably, of Emil: there are contrasts and similarities. This one is full of the confidence of good looks. None too bright, maybe, but Rolf isn't interested in his intellect. "I saw you staring at me," Thor says, "in the first half. I looked for you in the bathroom during the interval.

"I prefer to go on top," the boy tells him, with pride, and Rolf winces. This is new, in the last ten years. It's possible to speak openly; to discuss, with a modern frankness, the sexual arrangements that can be made—but it always feels vaguely improper, cheaper, to Rolf, far more transgressive than the act itself. He says in a calm voice, "Fine," thinking to himself that he can change this young thing's mind later.

"We're here," the boy says, jangling the keys to an expensive apartment block in the Milchgasse. Rolf looks up at the frontage. He wants to have the boy here in the gutter; he wants to take him and push that perfect profile into the stone of the archway. Does the boy think he, Rolf, should be grateful?

Thor runs up the stairs, whistling under his breath; Rolf follows. It needn't take long; just enough time to have Thor say Rolf's name. Then the keys are in the door and Thor enters, Rolf after him, their shoes squeaking on parquet.

A light is turned on, and Rolf sees expensive furniture and music sheets and books everywhere. Then two things happen: first a pale face floats out of the darkness, and then there's a skittering sound—a whippet, not quite fully grown, runs toward Thor and shoves its nose into his hand. Great dark eyes look dubiously up at Rolf, who is instantly chastened. Of course nothing rough can happen with a nervous animal nearby. The first face comes out toward them and is a small, dark young man, with spectacles.

Rolf rolls his eyes and turns to go. He isn't in the mood for complications. Thor grips his arm. "No, stay," he says. Then, to the boyfriend: "You said you'd be out."

The other man is trembling but holding his ground. Thor steps forward, takes him by the shoulder, and moves him roughly into the next room.

Rolf should go home. The dog pushes its nose into his palm, retreats, and barks once. The door between the rooms slams, and there is a second slamming sound, of a body being pushed up against the door. Someone yelps, and there's crying, and the sharp crack of a slap. Rolf really should go home. *Not my circus, not my monkeys.*

The dog starts to bark at the closed door. It's dancing, lifting all of its four paws in succession, it whines and growls; then looks back at Rolf.

Rolf sighs. He crosses the floor and pushes at the door, which is shut. The dog yelps, approving. Rolf takes two steps back, three, because he has only ever seen this happen on stage, and then aims a kick at the door handle, which cracks. His bulk is another blessing, because his weight and the force of the kick are such that the door flies inward and sends the two men inside tumbling to the ground. Rolf notices the orange candlewick, neatly made, someone's heirloom; the matching lamps on the bedside tables. Thor is fumbling with his open fly, half-sitting on the floorboards. The other man is crouched against the inside of the doorpost, flinching away from being hit.

"You," Thor says. He sounds as though in all his twenty-five or so years, nobody has said *no* to him. He waves, imperious, at Rolf. "Stay out of it."

Rolf's palm lands on his forehead, pushing him back to the ground. "Cur," he says. Thor stares up at him, and his expression softens into mockery. Rolf always sees Isabella Kellner in any unwelcome person's features, just as he sees Emil in any future beloved. He reaches down, tender as a lover, and punches Thor hard in the face.

Julia and Eve are sitting in the courtyard. They will move out next week; their furniture already boxed up. It's warm enough, though past midnight; the moon hangs low, a meteor sent to destroy. Empty champagne bottles stand neatly on the ground around their chairs. Julia is lifting the last dregs in her glass to the sky, about to say how you never see the stars anymore, when Rolf and someone else—and a dog—walk in under the archway.

Rolf is pulling the young person by the hand, and the young person, who has a superlative black eye, is allowing himself to be led. He looks, if anyone can look like any emotion or behavior, like he will turn out to be shy. The whippet looks up at him, grinning and expectant.

"This is Anders, who's coming to stay for a while," Rolf says. "And this is—"

"Klara," says the young man, Anders. He pulls a pair of spectacles from his pocket. One of the lenses is smashed and he polishes it apologetically, anyway. The dog dances at its name.

Anders

——

HE WALKS FAST, HEAD DOWN, cello case strapped to his back, willing nobody to look at him, toward their flat. Ten past three: Rolf should be at home, humming and brewing tea, with Klara stretched and yawning on the carpet. It is unconscionable that anything could go wrong. In music, beautiful things have their own repetitive motif, and never really end. Anders has always thought (hoped) it won't be Rolf who dies first; when Anders goes, of some improbably operatic wasting illness, Rolf will be the last thing he sees.

Some people are walking fast with suitcases. In the distance one can hear the slamming of doors and perhaps gunshots. He suspects the sound is wafting over the canal from Leopoldstadt. He passes a neighbor who does not greet him. He starts to run when he is two hundred meters from the apartment. The cello case bangs against the back of his calves: he remembers running the long-distance mountain race at school, shivering in the cold. *Despite it all we must find a way to live,* he says to himself. He doesn't know what the words are a rehearsal for.

Their avenue is empty of cars and people. The front door of the apartment block is intact; he allows himself a deep shuddering breath, and hears his mother's voice: *What must you look like?* Always panicking—so he slows and stops and climbs the steps with an apparent cheerfulness, even though his collar is wet with sweat.

The door to their apartment is ajar. He pushes it and immediately sees that there is no Klara. The apartment is silent and she isn't resting on the bed, either, because she would get up and come skittering over to him. He calls Rolf's name and goes to the bedroom and the tiny water closet and the kitchen, but he already knows that he won't find him. There is no sign of anyone resisting anything: only that Rolf's briefcase is by the door but knocked onto its side. The wardrobe door is open and a coat has been pulled out, their holiday bag and some of their clothes. The washing-up is drying in the rack, still wet with soap. These are facts that he must try to tell himself the correct sequence and story of.

The fact is that Rolf is not there. Anders moans out loud. Klara has delicate paws. She cannot walk very far and hates being out of sight of the apartment. The cello case, its straps, chafing; he tears it off, throws it across the room—it bumps against the wall, and rebounds onto the parquet. He stares at it. Disasters have happened elsewhere, while he was looking at the wrong things; perhaps all his life. He crosses the room, opens the case, picks the instrument from its velvet nest, and, holding it by the neck, with both arms, beats it against the floor. It takes a couple of blows, and the body breaks, the strings snap, and the bridge splinters. He lifts a foot and stamps on the heart of it.

He has no idea what he should do. He thinks perhaps if he goes to the police station he can find them, he has heard of such things happening. There can sometimes be a plea or a bribe or sometimes one is told at least a prison camp name. He runs to the bedroom, pulls the strongbox from under the bed, and opens it with the key he keeps around his neck. It is empty. It shouldn't be empty. Rolf must have taken the money when he left; he must have pleaded with the soldiers. He doesn't know how much these things cost. Maybe he will be lucky. Maybe he can influence something if he gets there quickly.

Stairs two at a time, out into the deserted street. A car drives slowly from the west end toward him but he won't slow down, not even if it's the police. The van passes and he hears, somewhere far away, a yipping, then a whimper. From the van? He would know her sounds anywhere; he chose her from the litter. He wonders whether to run after the van, and the bark comes again, louder, and as the van sound dies away he sees them at the far end of the street. They are walking away from him but now they are turning back toward him: Rolf is bending to unclip Klara's lead.

Klara barks frantically loud and comes racing to him. He bends into the smooth patch of forehead between her ears. Rolf is running too, puffing toward them, holding the holiday bag over one shoulder.

He stares at Anders, putting it together. "You heard? They're rounding people up. I was coming to the music school to get you."

Anders stares at him. There is never usually a tear on Rolf's serene, mocking, generous face. "Don't flatter yourself," Rolf says. "I wasn't frightened. Where's your cello?"

Anders does the gestures, including the death-blow of the stamped foot. He is sorry, now, for it, about it. Rolf gapes. "But you loved it," he says. They laugh, at how things are, staring wide-eyed at each other, and start the long walk to Leopoldstadt.

1946

—

Julia, Eve

————

THEY TURN INTO THE STREET where they used to live at half past four on a rainy Friday in April. The lindens are in blossom, the air laden with sap, pollen sticking to Julia's skirts and making her eyes water.

Someone has boarded up the main door. Nobody is around to see, or nobody in authority, so Eve pulls the rotting wood from the frame and they climb through, Eve hitching her trousers to avoid catching the hems. "Help me," Julia says, holding out a hand.

Broken glass still glints on the hallway floor. The air is clogged with dust; the windows in the stairwell are streaked with bright-green moss.

On the third-floor hallway, the splintered hole in Barbara's door is just as it was. Paint peels in long hangnails from the walls. Julia kicks the door of their apartment, and it gives straightaway. Blinking against the clouds of dust, they step over the broken lower half.

Everything movable has been removed, everything fixed has been crushed: the big chestnut dresser has been tipped onto its side, its glass front shattered, crunching underfoot. It is what they expected. Eve pokes the remains of a small oil still-life with her foot, a dash of yellow—the canvas slashed through the globe of a lemon.

"How long?" she asks, meaning *how long can we spend here*. They have agreed they will not admit to visiting the apartment, and they

305

won't meet the train; they'll go directly to the restaurant, which they have been saving all their tokens for.

Julia tells her the time: quarter to five. They can stay a little longer. She prowls the length of what was the dining room, picking over the dust and grit under her feet; tiny fragments like sand.

Eve watches Julia move around; watches as she stoops, peers, and picks up a rectangular wooden object. "Oh—" she says, in surprise—not welcome surprise. "Look. I'd forgotten, entirely—"

When she tips it, frowning, the metronome ticks; Julia would know if *lento* or *allegro*. She passes it to her other hand; picks at a spot of decay on the brass casing. "Will Elsa want this?"

Eve shakes her head; Julia nods her agreement. She crouches, puts it down where she found it—the disc of dustless floor is once again covered—and moves on.

Eve suspects they are both thinking of that day: of Rolf and Anders arriving, sweating, in Leopoldstadt, just as they returned from the station with Elsa hanging between them. Of Anders's small cry of desolation, seeing Barbara gone. Their hurried departure, to the nearest police station, to see if a deal could be struck, some negotiation for Barbara's release; leaving Julia, Eve, and Elsa together.

When it had come down to it, the decision was made in the blink of an eye. "Elsa, you were going to Salzburg, no? Why not? Why not try?" Julia, pressing her fingertips to her eyes, distressed; then collecting herself, gathering a suitcase together. Elsa, refusing to move. "We don't know anybody there," Eve had said, uncertain. And Julia'd said, clear-eyed, full of rage at the world: "That's never stopped us before."

After a moment of struggle, the catch gives way, the window opens without a fuss, and Julia places her elbows on the sill and leans her face out. An unexpected summer breeze, whistling straight from the Caucasus, makes her squint. She takes off her spectacles to polish them, replaces them on her nose. Eve crosses to join her.

From up here you can see it all. The green-and-white expanse of the Zentralfriedhof; over to the Looshaus, or what's left of it;

the gray gleam of the Stephansdom. The blank spaces where parts of the city fell, like gaps in a row of teeth. You could imagine you can see the places where the city has been partitioned into occupied zones: American, British, French, Russian. Grinzing, Unter-Sievering, the villages in the foothills. If you almost close your eyes, you can imagine the Alps, and away to Budapest, melting into the horizon. You can almost hear things, too: the rattle of a train coming into the station; a bell attached to a headstone, singing in the wind.

"It's time," Eve says.

They leave as they came: on foot. The restaurant is just a place that has kept open, like a small miracle, in the Mahlerstrasse. Julia and Eve have been on one or two occasions, alone, since their return to the city a month ago, and have suggested it because it is in a familiar spot; perhaps they think it will be non-threatening, neutral territory. On Fridays it is always full of people, eating slowly, carefully, dressed in their finest, wide-eyed and looking at each other; the frank stares of escapees and chancers.

Anders is sitting at an outside table, and they see him before he sees them. His head is bowed in study of the menu: a single battered piece of card. His spectacles are the same, surely, as the ones he left with: the gold wire hooking over his ears, and he reads in that patient, cautious way, giving every word its due. He turns the menu over to see if there are any more dishes on the obverse, and puts it down, with the same patience, and no sign of disappointment, when he sees there aren't.

At the sight of him, Julia almost cries where she stands. Inconceivable, that someone could still be the same person, after everything that's happened; that he's finally here. Eve dances forward, taps him on the shoulder—feels Julia's disapproval, because Anders was never someone to creep up on, even before—and he turns. He looks dazed. "Oh, hello." He rises to kiss them on both cheeks.

There is a dance, now awkward, but which never used to be, in which he grips their shoulders, seems to move toward an embrace; they stand frozen, holding each other at arm's length, and this makes Julia want to cry even more. "Yes," Anders says, "well," and lets her go. The worst of it, she thinks, is that he is so easily embarrassed; he may worry about this little social failure. Or at least, that's how he used to be.

From under the table, a snout. Klara's nose, now graying, protrudes; amber, anxious eyes. She sniffs the palm of Julia's hand. She is thin, but aren't they all? Eve pats her pocket and retrieves a biscuit. Klara takes it, and retreats beneath the table.

"So kind," Anders said, "always so thoughtful—"

They slide into their seats. "I am afraid the options are potato or potato," Anders says, waving the card.

"It will be a feast," Julia says.

They sit blinking in the sunshine. "How is Elsa?" Anders draws a little line in some leftover sugar on the tabletop.

"She is well. She writes good things of her new situation." Elsa could not come back to Vienna. She has taken on the whole lease of their old apartment in Salzburg; she has found a job in a primary school. She goes out rarely and has few friends, and it suits her. It is, she says, a life; little, but manageable. She walks in the mountains regularly, and thinks her thoughts in the peace of their shadow, and likes their blank refusal to judge.

It seems impossible to ask Anders how he is. The letters they have exchanged during the long separation have kept them up to date on the specifics: he teaches the cello privately, to the same old Innere Stadt families who can afford to educate their children, who have seemingly never stopped having money.

"We went to the old apartment," Eve blurts.

"Did you?" Anders blinks. "Really? What for?"

They look at each other. It occurs to Julia that she has no answer. "Well," she says, "to see."

Eve says: "It was the same."

Anders looks at the menu again. No sentiment. Eve thinks, once, he would have leaned forward: asked, *What do you mean, the same?*

Julia has hailed the waiter; she is leaning back, indicating their choices; his careful nod. Klara's face peers out, hopeful. Anders reaches down and scratches behind her ear.

Wine arrives in the waiter's arms; sparkling white from the Weststeiermark. Other diners look enviously at their table. "Just a little something," Anders murmurs.

"You shouldn't have," Julia says, and Anders shrugs. "You're only sixty-two once," he says. "And we were so sorry to have missed your sixtieth." A flash of a smile. "Events intervened."

Tears are stifled by Julia's lashes. She lifts a hand to her nose and looks away, her throat working; leaps to her feet, because Rolf is here. Her arms go up and around his neck as he arrives at their table; she hangs from him.

"Sorry I'm late. I went to the Kärntnerstrasse to get your present—not that there's much choice," he says, dazzled, hefting a package wrapped in brown paper. "Hello," he says. He plants a kiss on her forehead.

Eve jumps up, hovering—tries to shake his hand, and is drawn into his embrace. "What is this?" he says. "Are we crying today? I think not!"

He puts the parcel down next to Julia, pats it, and sits beside her. Now he flexes his fingers, reaches for the wine, pours himself a glass. Anders *tsks*, but he lifts and drains it, then reaches for more. "What? Isn't it a celebration?" The only sign, they think, is the way he moves: arthritis from breaking the stones.

For months after they'd arrived in Salzburg, they'd written to each other. Rolf and Anders were back in their apartment. The situation remained volatile. *Of my mother, no report. She is lost. Rolf was almost taken the day we went to look for her at the police station. He kicked up such a fuss.* They told Eve and Julia how much they were missed.

A year passed, and Rolf and Anders stopped writing. Julia forwarded their new address to the old apartment; telephoned the Conservatoire asking for news. A few more months, and the note came. *I must be brief*, Anders wrote. *It was very quick and sudden. He was simply in the wrong place at the wrong time.*

After some months, Anders had found the prison camp to which Rolf had been sent; had applied there without success. He visited, standing outside the gates in the rain, until the guards began to laugh, and threaten. So he returned to the city. There were no lawyers to hire, even if he had the money; nobody to help. He sent food parcels when he could, and wrote letters; sold everything he had; stayed alive. When he will describe it to them, later, he will say it was like being dead already. He will say he cannot remember most of it; he was just a fox in some hole, hiding from the hounds.

Rolf, arriving, back at the Westbahnhof, a bright summer's day two years ago. "Can't keep a good man down, darling." There had been just twenty-four hours' notice, Anders said later. He'd flown to the station; seen the rows and rows of men and women returning; picked out Rolf, walking very straight among the bowed heads; "So you'd see me right away," he'd said later.

Their letters had dwindled, after his return. Julia and Eve thought they should visit, but the months turned into a year. Christmas cards were exchanged, full of pleasantries, but only superficial news: Anders has a new pupil, a real little monster, the son of some collaborator; Rolf strides out in the Augarten every morning now; it is as though nothing has happened. Julia, standing by the window, looking out at the green hillside, could not understand her own reticence. They knew they should go; they should send money, food; they should provide the comfort of their presence. And yet, day after day, week after week, she and Eve promised themselves a trip to see their friends that never came.

Anders reaches down to massage Klara's forehead; she closes her eyes. Rolf talks about the shops this afternoon—*the queues!* Then he says, "Oh, hell," and stares at the tabletop, blinking.

They all begin to talk. It is impossible to speak fast enough to say what one means. Julia says: "We should have come, when you were first released. I can't think why we didn't try. We should have been in touch more," and Rolf waves it away, pretending it is he who should have visited them. Train tickets were too dear. Salzburg was too far and—Rolf rolls his eyes—too boring. And they have only been back five minutes, haven't they? There have been food shortages. Responsibilities. The bloody Russians. Always someone to comfort. They have all had their own lives to contend with. "Anyway," he says, "you're here now."

"Nevertheless." Julia blows her nose. *Perhaps*, she thinks, *it was all simply too hard.*

There is a lot to say, then periods of not speaking. Julia thinks that Anders may be the one who will find it harder to forgive; his hands break bread, sprinkling crumbs. Rolf taps the edge of the table and cranes his neck back to watch the waiter. Food is brought; is toyed with, frowned at, salted. It is not like the old days, is it? But then, were the old days always so perfect? Klara dozes in the last of the afternoon sun. There is some thought of a walk in the Prater later, a spin on the Ferris wheel to see the city lights from above; perhaps a film—though Rolf says, approvingly, that the cinemas are full of perverts.

Eve watches Julia; how her mouth opens wide as she smiles. How she leans forward, tilting her chair in at a childish angle; laughing at Rolf; a little pout as she catches Eve's eye; the barest flicker of a wink. She reaches for Julia's hand under the table. The waiter clears the main course and passes her the menu. Julia looks down, lips parting as she reads. Then she looks up: bright, interested. "What next?"

Acknowledgments

———

I would like to acknowledge the financial support of the AHRC, the South-West and Wales Doctoral Training Partnership, Bath Spa University, and the Being Human Research Centre at the University of Gloucestershire.

Thanks to Professor Tracy Brain and Dr. Tasha Alden, for their wisdom, kindness, and patience, and to my life-colleagues Senja Andrejevic, Mike Johnstone, Angela France, Lania Knight, Nigel McLoughlin, Duncan Dicks, and the inimitable Martin Randall.

I'm enormously grateful to Laura Macdougall, Olivia Davies, Rebecca Gray, Lottie Fyfe, Alison Tulett, and most especially to Leonora Craig Cohen for steering the book to safety.

Above all, this is a book about family—genetic and accidental, found and lost—and so it is for Vin, Bruce, and Rose Bondah-Davidson; the FLOGs; Jen Risk; Vernon Sear; Em Geen; Anna Rutherford; Alison Bown and Fiona Place; Sophie Lewis; Katie Ward; Kim Renfrew; Claire Cavanagh; Laura Harley; Alex Clark; Layla Barron; Trish, Chris, Lawrence, and Julie Webb; Dominic and Milù Murch; Churnjeet Mahn; Jo Hennessey; Tim and Ed Woodman-Evans, and Lucy Davidson; John Hodson; Ellie, Wayde, and Olivia Edwards; for my parents, Jay and Richard Hitchman; for Trish Hodson; and for my late, dear mother-in-law, Lesley Hodson, whose memory is a blessing.